PSYCHOSIS DIAGNOSIS

WELCOME TO THE CHURCH OF SALVATION, WHERE YOUR SOUL CHECKS IN BUT NEVER CHECKS OUT...

CHAPTER I
MAY IITH, 1997
CORAKI, AUSTRALIA
∞ MONROE ∞

Flies swarm above the cereal bowl, which has been sitting on the windowsill since this morning, buzzing to their hearts' content. It's evening now, and the remaining milk has begun to curdle with the day's heat. A fierce gush of wind rips through the shack, causing the blinds to flap and the doors to rattle. Ma's precious tinfoil of ice flies off the coffee table in front of me, scattering the remaining crystals across the carpet.

She races over and drops to her knees, plucking through the carpet fibres in a frenzy. "For fuck's sake."

Black speckles of yesterday's mascara encircle her bloodshot eyes, and her bleach-blonde hair sits atop her head like a wild bird's nest.

My half-sister, Jackie, says she was beautiful once, but looking at her now, I find that hard to believe. She's as thin as a rake with more wrinkles than a dried-up prune.

The living room lamp flickers, along with every other light in this rundown shack.

"To hell with this goddamn place." She pummels the carpet with her fists.

My insides bunch as I brace myself for another one of her colossal meltdowns.

Whenever a storm hits, this dump gives the full strobe light effect, and as luck would have it, it's stormed almost every night since we moved in. This is our tenth home in four years, and the houses get more dilapidated with each move. This disgusting shanty is barely fit for possums to live in, let alone humans.

Ma glares at me, frothing from the mouth.

"It's your fault," she wails on repeat. "Your fault, your fault."

Resentment burns within me. She blames me for picking this dump, but I'd never even laid eyes on it until we moved in.

"This is the last place I'd want to move to," I argue. "There's nothing in this backwater town. Besides, you're the one who signed the rental agreement sight unseen."

"Only because you forced me to."

She plucks out a cigarette and places it between her twisted lips. Her accusation is groundless, and we both know it.

My jaw clenches, holding back the argument sitting at the tip of my tongue.

It's my eighteenth birthday in a months' time and my half-sister Jackie is letting me move in with her under the condition, I straighten myself out.

"*No drinking, no drugs, no parties, no fights,*" she made me promise.

She says I can stay with her until I can afford to stand on my own two feet. Her husband, Raj, owns a pub in Coffs Harbour, and they're willing to pay for my Responsible Service of Alcohol course and put me on as one of their bartenders.

I can't wait to get out of this hovel and never look back. Ma and her new boyfriend Freddy, or Freddy Krueger, as I've nicknamed him, blame me for our dire situation. Meanwhile, they're the ones who have been digging *heavily* into the supplies. We're currently in a world of debt. It's the reason we left our last rental. Ma knew it was only a matter of time before the drug lords sent their thugs to bash down our door and demand payment, and it wouldn't be the first time this has happened, either.

"Where's me damn lighter, Monroe?" The accusations keep coming.

I hmpf. "Don't look at me, I don't have it."

"Don't start with me. I saw you swipe it off the bench this morning before you left."

"I don't smoke anymore," I retort. "And I haven't left the house today. My bet is Freddy Krueger took it." I glance at Freddy who's sitting on the armchair adjacent to me.

He snarls, flashing a rotten set of teeth in my direction. "I've got me own lighter, Boy."

"Don't tell me you're suffering with those damn blackouts again," Ma spits at me for the umpteenth time in a matter of weeks. She flicks the unlit cigarette at me. "I should have let them lock you up in that institution—for good—when you was a kid. I lost the wrong twin, you hear me, the wrong one. You've been nothing but trouble since the day you was born."

I absorbed my identical twin brother, Elias, in the womb, as my mother constantly likes to remind me. Vanishing twin syndrome, the friendly-faced psychologist had called it. As a child, I used to have terrible nightmares about my brother being torn away from me at birth. By the age of ten, my mental stability had become so unbalanced I attempted to jump off the Leycester Creek Railway Bridge. Thankfully, a middle-aged man cottoned on to my intentions and came across to talk me down. The free therapy I've received through Health Care and my quick stay at Lismore Hospital's Mental Health Unit have since helped me to overcome the nightmares. Still, I wish Elias had survived and that we'd grown up close. I could have really used his companionship over the years. Ma doesn't have a maternal bone in her body. She's never been the type to give me warm hugs and kisses or tuck me into bed of a night.

"Any blackouts I've had have been drug-induced," I retaliate with venom. "And you only have yourself to blame for that."

Most mothers leave fruit bowls or cookie jars on their kitchen countertops, but my mother has always left weed, bongs, ice, and crack pipes.

I've managed to steer clear of ice–too afraid I'd turn into a weathered husk like Ma–and I've recently weaned myself off the weed with the incentive that Jackie will only take me in if I'm clean.

Ignoring my jab, Ma stumbles to the fridge, grabs out a beer, and then slumps onto one of our unpacked boxes in defeat.

We've been living in this sorry shack a full week, yet not a single box has been opened. We don't bother with unpacking anymore. I don't even know why we keep any of our stuff. Clearly, we don't need it.

There's another loud thunderclap and the power completely shuts off.

"You bloody bastard!" Freddy Krueger shouts, and I hear the clank of the TV remote being thrown at the blank screen.

I roll my eyes, knowing he can't see me in the dark. God forbid he misses any of the football.

When I slip my hand into my pocket to grab out my flashlight, my fingers brush over the smooth guard of a lighter's spark wheel. Surprised, I slide my hand in further and feel the rectangular casing that holds the butane.

Ma's lighter.

My legs bounce on the spot as worry worms its way through me.

She's right about the blackouts. I've found myself in the strangest of places these past few months, without any recollection of getting there. I thought with the weed out of my system, the blackouts would stop, but perhaps it's too soon. My body needs more time to reboot. Not wanting to admit fault, I toss the fluid-filled piece of plastic across the room–the darkness covering my furtive movement–and then dig back in for my flashlight.

I've barely even flicked the switch when Freddy Krueger pegs his empty beer bottle at me, sconing me dead on the cheekbone.

"Hurry up and fix the power, you useless sponge."

The force from the impact has my teeth rattling painfully inside my skull.

Blood boiling, I leap up from the couch and launch myself at him, ramming him back-first into the TV unit. The cheap laminate-chipboard buckles under his weight, and the second-hand TV Ma picked up from the side of the road smashes through the front window with a resounding crash. The hunk of junk had an old coat hanger for an antenna, and the picture was always snowy, so unlike Freddy Krueger, I won't miss it.

Ma bolts to her feet and steps up in my grill, cursing and squawking like a caged galah. Her voice is shrill and grates on my nerves. It hurts, but it's no surprise she's siding with her boyfriend over me. It happens every time.

As soon as she gets to the, "You're a disgrace, just like your father" and "You should've been the one to vanish" spiel, I'm out. We both know the only reason she's kept me all these years is because she needs my help moving the drugs. She sends me out to do all the work while she lazes around getting high all day, yet she's the one taking all the dough.

Go figure.

Freddy Krueger's thudding footsteps sound behind me as I make my way to the front door. I spin to face him—not realising how close he is—and I'm met with a set of hard knuckles to the face. I stumble backwards, cupping my stinging lip.

He's busted it, *the bastard!*

I can taste the metallic tang of blood seeping onto my tongue.

"You'd better find a way to pay for the damage you've done, Boy, or don't even think about coming back."

Freddy Krueger's breath is as foul as I imagine the fictional character's to be, and his poxy skin and bloodshot eyes certainly help to complete the picture.

Instead of retaliating like usual, I do the smart thing and take off, honouring my promise to Jackie.

Jackie's conditions replay in my mind. *No drinking, no drugs, no parties, no fights.*

I've managed to obey three out of the four rules so far, which is progress from last week.

"Good riddance," I say, slamming the front door behind me.

Within seconds of stepping off the porch, my clothes are drenched. The rain is torrential, coming down in heavy sheets. Most of the houses in town are single-story and elevated on stilts. When heavy rain sets in, the Richmond River floods, and Coraki goes under. Our shack faces the river, which is the one and only positive amidst the negatives. It's been raining a hell of a lot, and the water's surface appears higher than it did a few days ago. I sure hope it doesn't end up flooding, or Ma will be straight on my case.

"It's your fault, your fault," she'll tell me.

Everything is my fault. Even down to the lousy weather.

Not wanting to stick around, I flip my hoodie over my head and duck around the side of the house to grab my bike. I'm unchaining the back wheel when a nearby squelching sound makes me whip around with caution.

"Who's there?" I squat and grab a fallen tree branch before bouncing to my feet again and pointing the jagged end out threateningly. "Show yourself."

The tension in my shoulders eases when a tall, willowy young woman with dripping ginger hair steps out from the shadows. A wet, long-sleeved white dress clings to her frame, accentuating her slenderness, and her pasty skin glows in stark contrast to the gloomy night sky.

"Sorry." I drop the branch, not wanting to alarm her. "You can never be too careful."

With a sharp intake of breath, she rushes towards me and–to my astonishment–flings her arms around my waist. "Enzo."

My surroundings ripple around me, and my knees threaten to buckle where I stand.

"I'm sorry, Darlin'." I blink like rapid-fire, attempting to right my vision. "But I think you're mistaken. My name's Monroe."

The young woman skims my face, her ice-blue eyes searching intently for some type of recognition, and then, with a look of disappointment, her arms drop, and she releases me.

"I'm sorry, I can see that now."

As I examine the young woman in return, I'm surprised to find dirt—or is that dried blood—smeared across her cheeks. The heavy rain has diluted the marks, making it hard to decipher. Concerned, I step back and glance her up and down. Her dress is marred, too, as though she's been in a scuffle.

"What were you doing hiding in the shadows?" I ask, craning my neck to scan beyond her. "Is everything okay? Ain't nobody's trying to hurt you, are they?"

"I heard some yelling," she says, her *strine* accent thick like mine. "And a loud crash, so I climbed out my window to investigate." She tilts her head, gesturing to an open window next door.

Did she fall out her window?

"It sounded like someone here was getting hurt."

I scratch my hairline, my cheeks heating with embarrassment. "There was just an incident with the idiot box. No big deal."

Her gaze drops to my busted lip in question, and she takes a step closer, running an icy finger along it. "Was it your father who did this?"

I draw away with a wince.

"That dead-beat inside isn't my father," I say in spite.

I'm not about to admit I don't know who my birthfather is—that my mother has spent the majority of her life jumping from one bloke's bed to another's. My sperm donor didn't even last long enough to make it onto my birth certificate, which means I have no way of ever finding him. I've assured myself it's for the best. He'd only be another low-life scumbag like the rest of the losers she's brought home. I'm better off without him in my life.

I copped countless "Your Mama" slut-shaming jokes at the

numerous schools I'd attended. At first, I would get into brawls over them, but after a while I quit taking notice. Correction: come year ten, I quit showing up at school. Hence, there were no more jokes to take notice of.

Sensing my discomfort, the young woman backs up a step and lifts the sleeve of her dress to reveal multi-coloured splotches and thin scars. Most of the scars are silvery, but there are a couple of risen pink ones too, which indicate they're fresh.

"You don't need to be embarrassed." She swallows and then adds, "My father beats me too. He says I have the Devil inside me."

"He says, what?" Shocked by the severity of her injuries, I shoot an accusatory glance in the direction of her house. "That ain't right! You need to tell someone."

"My complaints only fall on deaf ears. Jerimiah is the church pastor, and he has everyone in our denomination under his control, my father included. He says that young women like me need to be kept in line, by force, if necessary. Otherwise we'll taint the community. But Enzo says it isn't true. He says it's just Jerimiah's way of controlling us."

"Who's Enzo?" I ask curiously. "It sounds like he knows better."

The young woman glances away, the look in her eyes despondent. "He used to be our clergyman, but our community shunned him because Jerimiah claimed he was doing the Devil's work."

"Devil's work?" I repeat, brows furrowed. I shake my head, unable to fathom how an entire community can be brainwashed with such nonsense.

"What about you?" Indi asks, backtracking to our previous topic. "Have you spoken to anyone about the abuse?"

I shift uncomfortably, aware I should heed my own advice. I've never reported any of the vile things that've happened to me, I haven't even told Jackie, but the abuse isn't ongoing, it comes and goes in waves depending on Ma's boyfriend at the time, and the flow of drugs and money. Moreover, I'm too embarrassed to talk about it. Admitting it aloud makes me feel weak.

"I don't plan on sticking around much longer," I say, blowing off the question. "My sister Jackie says she'll take me in. I just have to wait until I turn eighteen so I can work at her husband's pub."

The young woman's eyes meet mine, sparkling in the dim light.

"You're lucky. I tried running away when I turned eighteen, but my father hunted me down. He said, it's women like me who brought sin into the world, and that I need to be contained until I'm married, otherwise the Devil will rise out of me, and set this whole blasted world aflame."

I frown, appalled. "You don't actually believe that garbage, do you?"

She shrugs. "Folks at my church believe it. All the young women are kept under ball and chain until they're married. It's customary in our denomination."

I stare a moment, mouth agape.

This is some twisted shit.

"I'm not religious," I say, spluttering against the rain. "But I know right from wrong, and what your denomination is doing is just plain wrong."

The young woman nods like she's agreeing with me, but I can tell she's undecided. For someone who has already turned eighteen, she seems much younger than I am. Almost childlike. Chances are she's been sheltered and brainwashed with this garbage her whole life.

"My name's Indiana, by the way, but folks at church call me Indi."

"It's nice to meet you, Indi."

I glance between Indi's sopping-wet figure and my bike, wondering what I should do. The rain is relentless, but to wish her all the best and then ride off on her seems rude, especially when the poor thing is shaking like a leaf.

"Are you planning on sticking around?" I ask curiously. "If so, our back patio has some shelter."

Her eyes flick to the empty driveway outside her home and her trembling intensifies. "I'd sure appreciate it if you don't mind. My father will be home from the pub soon, and when he drinks, he...well..." She swallows.

"Come on." I gesture for Indi to follow me down the side of the house, and around the back, feeling secure that Ma and Freddy never venture out into the yard after dark.

The patio area isn't big, and the fibreglass roof has holes in it, but it's better than being out in the open. I usher her over to the back corner, where it's the lightest and driest. Thankfully the back neighbour has left his spotlight on, giving us plenty of light to see by.

"You should've shut your window," I say, glancing over the fence separating mine and Indi's yards. "Your room's gonna be flooded by the time you get back to it."

"I need to be able to climb back in again before sunrise." She lets out a shaky breath and adds, "Before my father wakes up."

"Won't he notice you're missing when he gets home?" I ask.

"Yes, but he won't remember anything by the morning. Ma says his brain shuts off when he drinks."

The same could be said for Freddy, I think, praying he'll forget about our spat by the morning and will simply wonder what in the world happened to the TV.

I drag a couple of old plastic chairs over for Indi and me to sit on, hoping she'll stay a while. Misery loves company, and it's going to be a long, wet night out of the house.

Indi takes a seat, smiling gratefully. "Thank you. I shouldn't really be here talking to you," she says. "Talking to boys outside of our church group is forbidden. It's a sin that'll lead us straight to the Devil."

"Well, if you're going to Hell anyway, you might as well tell me everything," I say.

"I'm gonna be married soon." She twiddles her fingers as she speaks. "The date's already booked. June 21st, in line with the Winter Solstice."

That's the same date as my birthday, I think to myself.

Ma says the reason I've got such a dark side is because I was born on the darkest day of the year—whatever that's supposed to mean. As far as I'm concerned, I'm a beacon of light in comparison with the scum she likes to surround herself with. The only thing *dark* about me is my skin tone, which I must've inherited from my father.

"I'll release my inner darkness to the darkness," Indi continues as if quoting from a passage, "and then I'll start my new life in the birth of light."

I lift a brow in question. "Forgive me for saying, but aren't you a bit too young to be getting married?"

"My father says Jerimiah is a fine, devout man, and he'll make a respectable woman out of me." Indi swallows and then adds, "But the way Jerimiah looks at me makes my skin crawl. I've tried telling the other young woman at church, but they don't see it. They say Jerimiah's fiercely handsome, and I should be grateful for God's blessing."

"Jerimiah," I repeat in alarm. "As in the church pastor?"

Indi nods with a look of dread, and I find myself worrying about what kind of future she's going to have.

Glancing away shyly, Indi admits, "I had a secret someone who I was hoping would ask for my father's blessing, but he up and left without saying goodbye." Her eyes flick to mine momentarily before continuing. "He's the reason I took off when I did. I wanted to find him, but I barely made it past the bridge on Swan Bay Road when my father found me and hauled me back home. Most of the neighbours are from our church, and the biddies in our community like to tattle-tale. That's what happens when your denomination lives in clusters. Folks talk."

I'd heard rumours of a religious cult overrunning the streets of Coraki and asked the local grocer if he knew anything about it. According to him, the group were a satanic cult that practised dark rituals and human sacrifice.

When I'd shown genuine concern, the bloke behind the counter had laughed and said, "Don't worry, mate, the group has long since moved on. I'm talking way back in the '70s."

After everything Indi's shared with me this evening, I find myself wondering if perhaps the cult never left. It's an unsettling thought.

"If you don't want to marry Jerimiah, then don't marry him," I say. "You can't let your old man force you into it. It's your life, not his."

"You don't know my father." Indi's whole-body quavers. "I don't have a choice. I'm afraid if I don't do as he says, he'll punish me severely."

I bite my lip, trying but failing to come up with an appropriate response.

Indi's ice-blue eyes plead with me for help, but I can't fix this young woman's problems. I've barely got a handle on my own problems.

"You need to tell the cops," I suggest. "The station is only down the road. I could take you there first thing in the morning on my bike."

She shakes her head. "Sergeant Adams is my uncle, and he and his wife are a part of our church group. Besides, they've got their own two daughters they're trying to keep the Devil out of."

"Oh…" A pit opens in my stomach, and acid rises in my throat. "I don't know how to help you," I admit at a loss. "And I'm not the best at giving advice, but I'm happy to keep listening if you need someone to talk to."

A gust of wind blows through the patio, rattling its shoddy framework and she leans against me protecting herself from the wind. Something about the gesture brings out my protective side. I'm not used to being used as someone's shield; I've only ever been someone's punching bag.

She waits a beat before saying, "I'm nervous that once I'm married to Jerimiah, my life will be nothing but misery. I'm to cook, clean, and obey his wants and needs without question, just like the other women of our church do for their husbands. I'm also never to challenge or argue with him, and I'm to bear healthy children who will help to carry on the Lord's work."

"That's some medieval notion right there," I say in disgust. "It's the 20th century. Women have rights. Why don't you and the other young women band together and fight against the men?"

"Because the other young women all idolise Jerimiah and they're happy to fall in line with his beliefs. My mother and I are the only ones who question Jerimiah's word, and that's why we're always getting beaten and locked inside our rooms. Jerimiah says we're being influenced by the Devil."

Not only am I beyond appalled, but I'm also confused.

"If Jerimiah believes that, then why has he chosen *you* for his wife?"

"He told my father he would take my hand in marriage to help lead me back onto the righteous path, but he made it clear he couldn't promise anything after what happened with his first wife, Caitlyn, who vanished without a trace."

The grocer's words, "human sacrifice," immediately replays in my head and my blood runs cold. "What happened to her?"

"Jerimiah told us he tried hard to lead Caitlyn back onto the righteous path, but she was weak-willed and had completely given in to the Devil's persuasion, following him directly to Hell."

For alleged Satanists, these people seem awfully spooked by the Devil. Something doesn't quite add up.

"Do you believe him?" I ask, unconvinced.

Indi shakes her head. "Enzo said never to trust Jerimiah, that he has an evil agenda and a black heart."

"You need to escape from this life before it's too late," I urge, worried for her safety.

"I want to break free, but I don't know how," Indi says helplessly. "I'm afraid I'm trapped here forever, just like Ma. Enzo had promised he would save me, but the last time I saw him, he said, 'It's too late now,' that I'm already bound to Jerimiah."

"But you're not even married yet," I argue, irritated by his nonsensical excuse. "I take it Enzo was your 'secret someone'," I say, piecing it together, and she nods. "I know it's none of my business, but I think you should let him go. Clearly, he's chicken shit, and only looking out for himself. You need to find someone who will put you and your safety first."

"Enzo has given up on me anyway, and I have no one else to turn to." She hesitates a moment before adding, "Could you save me, Monroe?" Her lashes flutter pleadingly, and my insides twist. I'd like to be able to help her, but I can't really afford to be putting my future on the line for someone I've just met.

Come the 21st of next month, I'll be out of here for good, and heaven knows I don't need any added trouble. Besides, I don't have the means to get out of this dump without Jackie's assistance and there's no way I can ask her to take us both in.

But what kind of person would I be if I left Indi here when I know myself what it's like to feel trapped, beaten, and broken?

There's got to be some way that I can help her, I ponder, *even if it means doing things I shouldn't.*

My mind kicks into overdrive trying to formulate a plan.

"I'll do what I can," I say. It's the best answer I can give.

CHAPTER 2
JULY 11TH, 1928
NEW ORLEANS, AMERICA
∞ ENZO ∞

The first time I met Jerimiah, I was a tall, gangly eight-year-old with a classic afro and a fresh set of adult teeth. My mama and I lived in the French Quarter of New Orleans, above a small apothecary shop, which my pa bought and set up for Mama before he died. I spent most of my weekends at the shop helping Mama clean the floors and restock the shelves. Our shop was jam-packed full of herbs, potions, and candles, as well as an array of other occult goods, which we kept at the back, divided by a black velvet curtain.

I overheard gossiping folks calling it "The Wicked Witch's Shop" or "The *Black* Magic Shop", which was a play on Mama's skin colour.

I wished Mama ran a general goods store. Maybe then people wouldn't be scared of us, and I would have someone to play with on the weekends instead of working. Many of the locals feared Mama, drumming up rumours she was a wicked witch. Nobody wanted their kids hanging out with me in case I cast an evil spell on them. Little did they know, my mama never dabbled in dark magic and had warned me never to dabble in it either.

"Only selfish people use dark magic for malevolent purposes," she told me. "The magic we practise is done in the workings of Mother Nature and spiritualism, and the spells we perform don't forcefully manipulate natural energies, and their directions like dark magic does."

I never got away with much while growing up. Mama had a way of seeing and hearing things other people couldn't. It was her gift and my curse. She also used that sixth sense of hers to help people, even those who spoke out against her.

I was resentful of the locals and begged her not to show them any kindness. In fact, I urged her to curse them all, but Mama taught me better, insisting, "There is no peace without forgiveness." My mama was kind-hearted like that.

It was Sunday afternoon, and I was inside sweeping the floors, watching on in envy as some of the local kids played ball outside the shop window. My mama would bring in a pack of cards, knuckles, and board games for us to play when the shop was empty, but when there were kids playing out the front, I couldn't concentrate. Instead, I kept myself busy by the window so I could see exactly what I was missing out on.

When a young boy around my age stepped inside the shop, my heart thudded. He was dressed well, in formal attire, with blond hair poking out from the sides of his white-brimmed hat. I presumed he was eager to give me a piece of his mind like the other kids always did.

They would poke their heads in the door and shout, "You're going to Hell," just for the fun of it.

I'd thrown a candle at the first kid who did it and was quickly reprimanded, so I used my imagination to retaliate after that. I would close my eyes and picture throwing everything but the kitchen sink at the offenders, which helped to make me feel a little better.

When the boy moved closer, I dumped the broom, not wanting to appear like a servant.

"Is this your shop?" he asked.

I side-eyed him warily. "It's my mama's shop."

"Is she really a witch?" His dark eyes grew large with anticipation.

I knew where his question was leading to, so I glanced away and said nothing, pretending to busy myself with some candles on the shelf.

After a beat, the boy surprised me by adding, "I wish my mama were a witch."

He stepped alongside me and picked up a red candle, asking what spells red candles were used for.

When I'd said, "Sex, love, power, and vitality spells," he smirked but appeared genuinely interested, so I continued.

We went through the different coloured candles and discussed their uses, too, before moving onto the herbs and minerals inside the glass jars.

"What's behind the curtain?" he asked.

"That's where we keep the occult goods and where my mama does her spells, readings, and healings."

The boy lifted a brow with interest. "Can you show me?"

He asked a lot of questions about the occult goods we sold, and their purposes, and seemed impressed with my understanding of witchcraft. I gloated inside, proud of myself for having the knowledge to impart sensible answers to his questions. I was also glad to have someone my age to talk to.

"I've heard the rumours about what your mama did to your pa," the boy said directly but without malice. "Are they true?"

I never got the chance to meet my pa. He died in a horrible accident before I was born. Apparently, he was a wealthy Caucasian man who had lived on a plantation on the banks of the bayou. I overheard locals saying his death was no accident—that my mama had cast a spell on him and that he'd died slowly and painfully of a mysterious illness.

When I asked my mama about it, she denied their claims, telling me, "People are always afraid of what they don't understand, and they're not always welcoming of those who are different from themselves."

The topic of Pa's death was a taboo subject and something she refused to discuss. It was clear she must've really loved him, though, because she still kept a small photo of him in her locket.

"It's not true," I answered, avoiding any eye contact. "My mama loved my pa."

The boy nodded, accepting my answer without question, and offered his hand for me to shake.

"I'm Jerimiah," he'd said with the confidence of a full-grown man.

There was an air of sureness about him which had me standing at attention.

"Lorenzo," I said. "But you can call me Enzo."

When Jerimiah finally made his purchase, I was sad to see him go, but to my delight, he stopped by the shop every Sunday for the next several months, buying one or two items from the occult section at a time. He always had questions to ask, so I made it my mission during the weekdays to learn as much as I could about witchcraft and spellcasting, eager to share my growing knowledge. I even offered to help my mama with some of her spellcasting, which made her happy.

On Sunday, December 16th of that same year, Jerimiah came into the shop and handed me a folded note with his address and a map of sorts inside.

"Next Friday, December 21st, is the Winter Solstice," he told me, glancing over at my mama and then back at me.

My mama was too busy with paperwork to pay us any mind.

"I was wondering if you wanted to come to my place in the evening to cast spells?"

A smile stretched across my face, but I turned away, not wanting to appear as eager as I'd felt.

"Sure," is all I said.

"My parents will be away, which means my nanny will be taking care of me, and she's not one to check up on me after bedtime. She has her own secret pastimes she prefers to partake in, so while she's busy doing whatnot, I'll slip out the back." He pointed to an image on the map he'd drawn, which had the words "treehouse" written below. "Meet me here at 9 PM," he said.

Given the nature of the invite, I chose not to tell my mama about it. For reasons I couldn't understand, she wasn't pleased about my newfound friendship with Jerimiah.

"Be careful, Enzo," she would tell me. "I don't entirely trust that boy. He's not the friend you think he is."

I snuck out after Mama retired to bed, hoping her sixth sense would dull down during sleep. It was only a fifteen-minute bike ride from the French Quarter to Esplanade Avenue, so I didn't need an escort. I was old enough to look out for myself. All I needed was a flashlight.

When I arrived at the address Jerimiah had given me, I stopped and stared, jaw slack. The double-story, Queen Anne style home with a peaked roof was a sight for sore eyes. Tall and white in all its magnificence. The apartment I shared with Mama could fit inside the building's structure five times over with ease.

Following the map Jerimiah had drawn for me, I carefully made my way over to the side fence and unlatched the gate. From there, I followed the cobblestone path to the backyard, where I discovered the treehouse. It sat high in a giant oak tree, the windows glowing a faint flickering orange.

A ladder leaned against the thick trunk, leading to an opening, and I used it to climb inside. My eyes grew wide, and I lurched at the sight of a young, blonde-haired girl lying atop a chalk-drawn pentacle with sprinkled minerals and unfamiliar symbols displayed within an outer circle. Black and red candles surrounded the perimeter of the outer circle, burning fiercely in the darkness.

The girl was only young, six at most, with sickly eyes and drool dripping down from her mouth. I wavered by the entry a moment, something inside me protesting. The energy inside the small treehouse had an eerie feel about it, as if there was a sinister presence lurking.

"You're late," Jerimiah said as a way of greeting.

"Sorry." My shoulders sagged. "I had to wait for my mama to go to bed."

"Never mind, I'm only just getting started." He tapped the spot beside him. "Come and join me."

I glanced at the book lying across his legs, and a sense of unease stirred within me. The open page was filled with symbols and incantations I wasn't familiar with.

"What exactly are we doing?" I asked, my eyes shifting anxiously to the girl. "Who is she?"

"*She* is my sister, Bonnie, and *she's* sick," he said matter-of-factly. "Regardless of how much I pray, God's refusing to make her better, so you and I are gonna take matters into our own hands."

I swallowed with uncertainty. "What's she sick with?"

"Polio. I want to heal her before she becomes completely paralysed."

"You know, my mama could probably help her. She has a way of healing people who are sick."

His gaze lifted from the open page to meet mine, dark and defiant.

"We don't need your mama. We've got everything we need right here."

Despite being uneasy, Jerimiah was my only friend, and I wasn't ready to give that up over a nagging feeling that something wasn't quite right.

Jerimiah angled the book so that I could read the script. "Repeat this after me."

I didn't know the meaning of the script because it was written in Latin, like some of the occult books in our store, but I recognised words like *Deus, sacrificium, puella,* and *pax.* I considered asking what the incantation translated to, but I hadn't wanted to look stupid in front of Jerimiah. I wanted to earn his respect, so I followed in sync, concentrating on matching my pronunciation and tone with his.

He chanted the verses softly at first, but as he continued, his voice grew louder and stronger. Electricity crackled in the air around us, and a bolt of lightning flashed out of nowhere, lighting up the treehouse as though it were daytime. The magnitude of it was so great, it felt like the electrical current was running right through me. A rumble of thunder followed, vibrating the structure and making the glass jars rattle and clink. Another lightning bolt struck, hitting a nearby tree branch with an explosive burst of white, followed by sparks of orange and red, which cascaded to the ground as though it was raining fire.

I paused momentarily, but Jerimiah prompted me to keep going.

The storm raged on, intensifying as we continued to chant, which I found terrifying yet invigorating all at once. We were near shouting when books went flying, and the glass jars exploded simultaneously. My hands flew up to protect my face as shards clinked against the walls and floor. Some nicked my skin, and blood trickled, but I didn't feel any pain. Still chanting at the top of my lungs, I peered through my fingers to watch the chaos unfolding. Mineral powder clouded the air like a sandstorm, and potions ran in swirls of colours across the wooden floorboards.

Just as my voice was about to croak out, a gale-force wind blasted through the treehouse with an almighty howl, sending Jerimiah and me flying backwards. The candles blew out, and all went pitch black on the darkest night of the year.

I fell on my back in a blissful daze, momentarily unperturbed by the glass digging into my skin, or the mix of potions that were soaking through my shirt.

It wasn't until the rain started and I felt a small splash come in from the open window that I forced myself to sit up and check on Bonnie.

I plucked the flashlight out of my pocket and flicked the switch, bringing a halo of light to my surroundings. Establishing my bearings, I eased my way over to the young girl, shining my flashlight directly on her face. Her eyes were open and glassy, and her mouth hung slack. Panicked, I swept the light beam over her body, watching for the rise and fall of her chest.

Nothing.

A sick feeling rose in my throat, and my dinner threatened to leave my stomach.

"God's will must've been stronger than our desires," Jerimiah said, startling me. "At least she will find peace in heaven."

My body trembled as I stared at Bonnie's lifeless body in horror. I wondered if it truly had been God's will or something we'd done wrong. Despite the faint pulse of electricity still pulsating from the tips of my fingers down through to my toes, goosebumps bristled my arms. Everything had felt so right, yet so wrong.

Jerimiah slipped a blanket under his sister's side and rolled her over twice, so she was cocooned in it. "Help me to carry her down."

It was a struggle getting Bonnie down from the treehouse by ladder, and at one stage, my wobbly arms nearly dropped her, but somehow, we managed. Once we were safely back on the ground, Jerimiah guided us over towards the back door, and we placed Bonnie's body down under the awning where it was dry.

"I've got it from here," Jerimiah said. "You should leave before my nanny sees you and calls the sheriff."

I nodded vigorously in fear and took off with my flashlight to grab my bike. Not only was I confused by the mix of conflicting emotions circling within me, but I was soaked to the bone and shivering all over.

When I arrived home, my mama was up waiting for me.

"What have you done, Lorenzo?" Her eyes were glossy with tears as she repeated with disappointment, "What have you done?"

It was clear I'd done something terrible. I'd never seen my mama so devastated. It was also clear I was in trouble because she was calling me Lorenzo. I swallowed hard and hung my head low, unable to defend my actions. A part of me knew what Jerimiah and I were doing was sinister, but I was so desperate for a friend that I was willing to risk everything, even my relationship with my mama. I wasn't sure if Jerimiah had actually intended on killing his sister or if we'd done it by accident, but he hadn't seemed at all distraught when I left.

"I'm sorry. I didn't mean to hurt anyone. I was just following Jerimiah's lead."

"There is evilness in Jerimiah. I can sense it, and now a shadow lurks over you, willing you to succumb to the darkness." Mama shook her head in sorrow. "This is exactly how it started with your pa."

My eyes darted up at the mention of Pa.

"Dark magic has a way of warping good people," she continued. "The more you use it, the more it corrupts you and eats at your soul."

Instead of sending me to my room or punishing me, Mama took me in her arms and squeezed me tight.

"My poor foolish boy, if you don't be careful, the darkness will consume you completely, just like it did with him."

When I told Mama exactly what'd happened in the treehouse with Jerimiah and his sister Bonnie, she cried and told me she didn't want me associating with Jerimiah anymore. She also made me promise that I would steer clear of dark magic.

I nodded in agreement, but I couldn't forget the feeling of euphoria and give her a genuine promise.

CHAPTER 3

MAY 18TH, 1997
CORAKI, AUSTRALIA
∞ MONROE ∞

Lightning flashes, and from the corner of my eye, I spot a tall silhouette entering my room. The figure rushes towards my mattress, and I bolt upright, reaching under my pillow and patting around in search of my pocketknife.

"Enzo?"

Forgetting the knife, I flick on my flashlight and shine the light upwards to find Indi crouching above me. Her ice-blue eyes are wild, and her cheeks are wet with tears.

I scramble upright to console her. "Are you okay? What's wrong?"

Despite being alarmed by her distraught appearance, a wave of relief washes over me, knowing she's still in one piece. I hadn't caught so much as a glimpse of her since last Sunday night, and I was beginning to worry that her father had spotted us chatting and punished her for "talking to a boy outside her church group". I'd contemplated sneaking in through her open window to check on her, but had her father sprung me in the act, there was a good chance he would've beaten me to a pulp or called the cops, and I can't afford to have any more charges against my name. I'm trying hard to keep my nose clean.

"Enzo, you have to help me. My father's gone mad." A hysterical cry escapes her. "He went out drinking after church again, and now he's raging and out for blood. Ma tried sweet-talking him to bed, but he silenced her with a backhander, and I knew if I didn't get out right away, I'd be next."

She's mistaken me for Enzo again, which concerns me, but that's far from what's important right now.

"Shhh...shhh..." I jump to my feet and take her trembling hands in mine. They're as cold as blocks of ice, so I blow some warm air on them and give them a rub. "Everything's gonna be okay."

It's not entirely true, but I need her to calm down before Freddy rouses. He can be a violent man when he's been drinking, too, and I'm not equipped for double trouble.

Indi glances at my mattress and swallows. "Can I stay?"

"Of course, you can stay," I reply instinctively, then hesitate, thinking better of it. She seems off–delirious even–and I don't want there to be any confusion on her part. "But you do realise I'm Monroe, right? I'm not Enzo."

"Monroe?" Her gaze lifts to meet mine, and recognition fills her features. "Yes, Monroe," she says with a nod. "I know. Enzo had to leave again."

Her words repeat in my head, and I find myself wondering if Enzo's been back to see her this past week.

Curious, I ask, "Have you spoken to Enzo again recently?"

"He comes and he goes but never stays long. He can't. He's afraid if Jerimiah catches on to his new identity, he'll kill him once and for all."

The thought of Enzo using Indi and feeding her broken promises troubles me. He's preying on her weakness.

Poor girl. She's being played for a fool.

"You should let him go," I say, reiterating the same advice I'd given her last weekend. "If he really cares about you, then he would stand up and fight for you, consequences be damned."

Indi doesn't argue the matter. If anything, I can see the cogs turning behind her pale eyes.

Uncovering the truth about her and Enzo's secret trysts makes me uncomfortable about her staying the night. While I am worried for her safety, I'm not particularly thrilled about being her fill-in protector while her boyfriend is out of town. If I'm going to wander into dangerous territory for Indi, then I'd like to know where I stand. I'm happy to keep helping her—no strings attached—but I've made some unsavoury choices this week with her in mind, and I'm not prepared to risk everything just so she can use the funds I've scraped together to run off with Enzo.

"Is something wrong?" Indi asks. "Do you want me to leave?"

The desperate look on her face brings about my sympathy, and all my concerns melt away. I could never turn her out, not when I know what it's like to be cold and scared with nowhere safe to go.

"No, you can't leave. It's not safe." I head to the corner of my room, where a bunch of my clothes sit in a pile. "Why don't you put this on?" I say, handing her a clean Billabong shirt I'd nabbed from a neighbour's line a few months back. "You're soaked."

I turn my back while she changes into the t-shirt, and then we park ourselves awkwardly beside one another on my small, spring-ridden mattress.

"This isn't exactly The Hilton," I joke in a bid to hide my embarrassment. "Truth is, I picked up this mattress off the side of the road."

A ghost of a smile brightens Indi's face in the dim room. "I've slept in worse places. At least it's warm and dry."

Her words hit home. I've spent many nights laying out in the cold due to Ma's abusive boyfriends chasing me out of the house.

I lay the thin blanket over us, and she snuggles right into me. I consider establishing boundaries then and there, but the feel of her body pressed against mine is heavenly.

"I've spent the past week coming up with a plan to help get you out of here by next month," I say, pushing Indi's fringe back from her face so I can look into her eyes. "I've picked up a secret side hustle doing store break and enters." I search her eyes for any sign of judgment before adding, "I'm not raking in a heap of dough, but I'm hoping to make enough money to be able to pay three months' worth of rent on a small unit at Coffs for you. The only catch is you can't tell Enzo. If you want to ensure your father doesn't find you, then you need to make a clean break. Enzo is a weak link, and in all honesty, you deserve much better."

Instead of showing any kind of enthusiasm, Indi appears nervous. "Does that mean I'll have my own place?"

I nod encouragingly. "That's the idea."

Indi's eyes beseech mine. "Will you be coming with me?"

"I'll be living in Coffs Harbour, but I'll be staying at my sister's place temporarily."

"Why can't I come to your sister's place too?" Indi asks, taking me by surprise.

"If I could bring you to my sister's place, I would," I say, and I mean it. "But I don't want to put that kind of pressure on Jackie when she's already going out of her way to accommodate me."

"I see," Indi says, appearing to accept this, before asking, "Is that how you make your money?" Her expression is curious, not judgmental. "By stealing from stores?"

"Not typically. Store break and enters are difficult, and it's easy to get snagged. I haven't stooped this low since I was caught and cuffed two years back," I admit with burning cheeks, "but I've justified going back to it by telling myself that I'm saving you from a life of abuse."

Indi bites her lower lip, appearing sheepish. "I sure appreciate your help."

"Ma and I would usually make our money by selling drugs and small-time stolen goods to the local trash," I explain. "But since she met Freddy, it's all gone down the gurgler."

"I've never stolen anything. Jerimiah says it's a sin that'll–"

"–Lead you straight to the Devil," I finish for her, and she chuckles softly with a nod.

"Well, my ma, Leonie, is the embodiment of the Devil," I say. "She had me out and hustling by the age of five. I hadn't realised just how wrong it was until I got older, but in a bid to keep the roof over our heads, we needed to keep at it or wither in the gutter along with the rest of the debris. When I turned fifteen, I tried applying for a handful of legal jobs, but nobody wanted to hire a scrawny, sickly-looking kid dressed in tattered clothing. When folks look at me, all they see is trouble."

"What does Freddy do?"

"Absolutely nothing," I spit with resentment. "Freddy has been a lazy bludger from day one and a drinker to boot. I do my bit, as I always have, but there's only so much gear I can move on my own, and our food money has since become Freddy's drinking money, that's why we're broke, and my clothes are swimming on me."

"Why doesn't your ma find a different partner who's a good provider?" Indi asks, with the innocence of a small child.

A dark laugh escapes me.

"My ma's had countless partners over the years," I admit in shame. "Some far worse than Freddy. Weasley–whom I'd nicknamed Weasel–was the worst of them. He taught Ma how to rotate drug lords so that they could take the majority of the meth for themselves. They'd only cut down a portion of the crystals we were given to distribute, and then they would mix them with all kinds of nasties, taking the clean, uncut portions for themselves. Ma had me out on the streets selling stolen goods while they partied. That way, they could get away with their scam for months at a time. The money we made from the swag would help to provide enough crumbs to keep the head honchos off our backs before we could move to another town, where they'd find themselves another drug lord."

I pause a moment, worried that I'm oversharing, but it feels good to finally talk to someone who understands what it's like being brought up in a broken and abusive household.

While my sister Jackie cares about me and always has my best interests at heart, there's no way I could tell her my deepest and darkest secrets. She'd be horrified. We come from completely different worlds. Her dad, Sean, is a decent human being with his head screwed on right, and more importantly, he comes from money. He and Ma were high school sweethearts, who found themselves in a sticky situation when my mother fell pregnant during their senior year.

Much to Sean's parents' disapproval, they'd moved into an apartment together in Sawtell and tried to make their relationship work, but in the end, my mother decided partying, drinking, and taking drugs were far more important to her than her family.

Sean eventually gave up on my mother and moved back into his parents' house with Jackie so they could help raise her.

"What ended up happening with Weasley?" Indi asks, prompting me to continue.

"After two years of scheming and scamming, he and Ma became completely drug dependent and sloppy. Eventually, a group of thugs were sent to ransack our place and beat us all senseless. One of the thugs started laying his filthy mitts into me and beat me to the ground, but the leader of the group pulled him off, saying, 'Take it easy, he's just a kid'. I'd felt sore and sorry for myself, but the incident turned out to be a cloud with a silver lining because the thugs beat Weasel to death."

I glance away before admitting, "It's a sad thing, staring at someone who is bleeding out before you and thinking, hurry up and die, you bastard. Die. I was only fourteen at the time, yet I was filled with such darkness and hatred."

"Don't worry, I understand," Indi says, threading her fingers with mine. "There are days when I wish that someone would kill my father."

CHAPTER 4

1921 - 1941

NEW ORLEANS, AMERICA

∞ ENZO ∞

I struggled with my inner demons for weeks after what Jerimiah and I did to his sister.

A voice inside my head kept insisting, "The depression you feel can only be lifted by practising more dark magic". I hadn't known it was dark magic Jerimiah and I were using, let alone it was dark magic that'd led my pa to an early grave. I wish Mama had been more open with me about Pa's death from the very beginning. Perhaps I would've been more cautious about partaking in spells I knew nothing about.

Mama was fiercely protective and wouldn't let me succumb to the demons. She pointed me in the direction of music and paid a local musician to teach me how to sing in tune and play the trumpet to help soothe my restless soul. Louis Armstrong, AKA Satchmo, was my idol, and I wanted to be just like him. I practised all of Satchmo's songs on repeat to the point where the neighbours started complaining. I couldn't quite match Satchmo's gravelly tone, but it never stopped me from trying.

Jerimiah came to our store the Sunday after the Winter Solstice, and Mama shooed him back out the door with the broom. "You're no longer welcome in this store, Child," she said, holding the bristled end out towards him threateningly. "And I don't want you coming anywhere near my son again, you hear me?"

I'd expected backlash from the locals or his parents after the fact, but the whole thing just blew over, and Jerimiah never returned.

Mama may have been right about Jerimiah being evil, but it still broke my heart to see my only friend being chased out the door.

When I finished school, I got a job working as a bartender at The Rhythm Club on Jackson Avenue, which hosted some of the hottest bands in the country, as well as top local talent. I still lived with Mama, but I needed some sort of independence. An outlet that was uniquely mine. The Rhythm Club was one of the few black dance halls in town that was big enough to host large marquee touring bands, and although it had been a segregated venue, the club's proprietors, the Mancuso brothers, were happy to hold seats in reserve for white customers who were willing to cross the line for a night's worth of entertainment.

I still helped Mama at her shop during my days off. I would clean the floors and restock the shelves so she had more time for her healings and readings.

Bartending grew my self-confidence because it allowed me to converse with folks without the pressure of social condemnation. Admittedly, the regulars who hung around the bar blabbering until close were mostly a ragtag of drunks, but they made me feel somewhat included in society.

It was Saturday, December 13th, 1941, when Jerimiah stepped up to the bar where I was serving, surprising me with his self-assured grin.

"Hello, my friend," he said, and my stomach backflipped. "It's been a long time."

It'd been thirteen years since I last saw him, yet I recognised him immediately. His light hair and dark eyes were a stark contrast and made him stand out like a beacon in a sea of coloured people. Jerimiah still had a confidence about him like no other, and when he spoke, his words seemed to have a mesmerising effect. I felt drawn to him and missed our friendship, even though he'd caused me so much trouble in the past.

The sound of Mama's voice whispered warnings in my ear, telling me not to engage, so I smiled politely and asked, "What can I get you?"

"So that's how it's gonna be now, is it?" he said with a chuckle. "In that case, I'll have a gin and tonic."

When I finished mixing his drink, I placed it in front of him. "Can I get you anything else?"

He handed me a dollar bill, along with a written note and winked. "Keep the change."

My head hammered as a sense of déjà vu overwhelmed me. The last time Jerimiah handed me a written note, nothing good had come of it.

The bar was busy, and the patrons were getting antsy, so I shoved the note in my pocket without a glance and continued to serve.

It hadn't been until the bar closed for the night and the last of patrons dwindled out that I plucked the note back out of my pocket to read.

Come meet up with us on Sunday at 10 am at The Church of Salvation.

According to the map sketched below, the church was located on a private property on St Charles Avenue in the Gardens District. I considered tossing the note in the trash and forgetting all about it, but even as I tried, my fingers couldn't seem to let go of the paper.

The night of the Winter Solstice, when we'd cast the spell on Jerimiah's sister, Bonnie, flashed through my mind, and I remembered the exhilaration I'd felt. It was a rush I'd been chasing ever since through music, recreational drugs, and spells of my own, but I had yet to find anything to compare to the euphoria I had experienced.

I wondered why Jerimiah had gone out of his way to find me after all these years, and why he was so interested in inviting me to church.

I tried to convince myself that perhaps my old friend had turned over a new leaf. We were only kids when we last saw each other, and boys–especially–tend to make terrible mistakes. A lot could've changed in thirteen years. Jerimiah could be attending church in hopes of absolution for our hand in what happened to his sister. Perhaps he wanted me to receive absolution, too.

It was amazing that he'd recognised me. While he looked like an older version of the boy he had been, I'd changed a lot. I was no longer the awkward, gangly kid with big teeth and an afro. I'd grown into myself.

I went home fully intending to abide by my promise to Mama and forget about Jerimiah and the invite he'd handed me, but as much as I tried to convince myself that reconnecting with Jerimiah was a bad idea, a part of me was curious to see what this Church of Salvation was all about.

The next day, after Mama went to the shop, I jumped on my bike and rode out to St Charles Avenue, which was a thirty-minute ride from the French Quarter.

Tall oak trees lined the roads, and streetcars ran down the middle island with tracks for travelling in both directions. A streetcar passed by me as I rode, carrying dozens of passengers, and the young children aboard smiled and waved vigorously from behind the glass windows.

When I arrived at the property, which was located on the map Jerimiah had drawn, I stared down past the long driveway with piqued interest. There were two buildings situated on a large block. The main house itself was a Queen Anne style building, similar to Jerimiah's old family home, with a small church-like building–the size of a streetcar–built at the side. The small building stood gracefully amidst a backdrop of greenery, painted white like the house, with clean lines and a gabled roof. The arched windows which adorned its sides were made of lead light depicting biblical images. In place of the usual cross icon I'd seen at most churches stood a large symbol painted in red with gold trimming.

There were a handful of people, both white and people of colour, congregated around the front of the building chatting, and when they saw me staring, they stopped talking and walked up the driveway to introduce themselves.

"Why don't you come on in," a man with no teeth said with a slur, and he opened the side gate, stepping aside for me to pass.

They were a ragged-looking bunch, but they seemed friendly enough all the same. Nobody knew who I was, or if they did, they didn't seem to care. I was accepted, and I was welcomed without condemnation, which was all that I cared about.

I stood outside a while and exchanged pleasantries before entering the church in search of Jerimiah. As soon as I entered the arched double doors, I was surprised to see Jerimiah at the altar with his back to me, lighting a row of candles. He wore a golden cloak with a large red symbol embroidered on the back. The stitched symbol was a replica of the symbol on display at the front of the church.

When I accepted his invitation to "The Church of Salvation," I had no idea he'd be the one giving the sermon, but given his cloak and preparations, it was blindingly obvious he was in charge.

Was this his property? I wondered. *Was this* his *church?*

When he turned and saw me, he smiled widely.

"Enzo, my friend." His greeting was warm. "I'm so glad you could join us."

A thin, blonde-haired lady with decaying teeth patted the pew next to her, inviting me to take a seat. She was dressed more for a night at the disco rather than church. Bright and sparkly, with caked makeup layered on leathery, dehydrated skin. As I sat next to her, I could see she was, in fact, much younger than I'd originally thought. I quickly picked her as an ex-substance abuser, looking to reconnect with God for guidance, and there were a couple of others whom I met out front that I'd grouped in the same category. I wondered if they joined The Church of Salvation of their own free will or if Jerimiah had recruited them. People who were desperate, depressed, or suffering were particularly vulnerable and often needed a belief system to help give their life purpose.

The sermon lasted two hours, but I was interested in what Jerimiah had to say, so the time flew by. Although Jerimiah had spoken in a biblical sense, nothing that he said was truly biblical. Jerimiah hadn't been asking these people to put their faith in God or The Bible. He'd been asking them to put their faith in him. This made me question his true intentions and had me backpedalling on my earlier thoughts about him turning over a new leaf.

The congregation hung on to his every word as though he were a demigod. In a way, I was envious of him. You were either born with charisma, or you weren't, and the two of us had been a perfect example of that, Yin and Yang. He had it in spades, whereas I was totally lacking.

I was invited to stay for morning tea after the sermon was over, but I politely declined, certain that my visit had been a one-off. However, the following Saturday, Jerimiah came to visit me at the bar again and asked me to join the group on Sunday evening for the Winter Solstice Service. He told me he had a special ceremony planned where they were going to do sacred spells to rejoice in their Lord and Saviour.

The last time I joined him for a sacred spell on the night of the Winter Solstice had been the best and worst night of my life. The sensible part of me knew to say no, but my desire for that same feeling of euphoria was hard to dismiss.

I was certain the "special service" had nothing at all to do with their "Lord and Saviour", but I couldn't bring myself to turn him down and miss out on the opportunity to have the electrical current that had made me feel truly alive, magically coursing through my body again.

I entered the church ten minutes after the service started and went to slip quietly into the back pew when Jerimiah startled me by calling my name and beckoning me to the front.

"I don't know if any of you were told this last week, but my friend Enzo, here, is a very special person who possesses exceptional powers."

My neck shrunk into my shoulders with embarrassment momentarily, until the crowd turned to where I stood, staring at me in awe.

"For that reason," Jerimiah continued, "he will be helping me with this evening's ceremony."

I approached the front, heart thumping, and he draped a golden cloak around my shoulders. It was much like his, the only difference being it was embroidered in black not red.

"Tonight's ceremony is about healing our souls and stripping away our sins," he announced. "We will release our inner darkness to the darkness and start our new lives in the birth of light."

The group stood and clapped, glancing from Jerimiah to me rejoicing.

For the first time *ever*, I had people treating me as though I was someone important. Jerimiah had claimed I was special, and to his followers, his words were gospel.

I spotted a chalk-drawn circle displayed in front of the altar, and I gulped. The circle was decorated with rose petals and outlined by black and red candles. The symbols inside the outer ring weren't the same as I remembered from the last time we'd cast a spell together, and there weren't nearly as many of them, but just the sight of the pentacle alone had my mind quaking and stomach twisting with conflicted emotions.

Regardless of my inner conflict and my mama's voice of warning inside my head, I stayed and partook in the ceremony, helping to "bless" the people inside the circle. We called over three small groups of twelve at a time and asked them to chant along with us. A raging storm came and went, bringing about an electrical energy and a magical euphoria to all. Everyone felt buzzed and uplifted, and more importantly, everyone was still alive.

The whole ride home, I wondered if Jerimiah truly was trying to save his followers from a life of drug addiction by getting them addicted to magic instead. It seemed the lesser of two evils and felt much more invigorating than any other high.

Perhaps Jerimiah's not as bad as Mama first thought, I pondered, but as soon as I entered our small apartment and caught sight of my mama's face, I knew for certain I'd gotten it wrong.

Without saying a word, she slapped me hard across the cheek and then stormed off to her room, where I heard the faint blubbering of her cries for the next few hours.

I should've cut ties with Jerimiah there and then. My mama should've been the most important person to me, but she wasn't.

I stayed on as Jerimiah's right-hand clergyman at The Church of Salvation, knowing all too well it was more of a cult than a church group, and that I was doing more harm than good. I relished the feeling of being wanted and important.

"These people need us," Jerimiah would say. "Without us, they'd have no direction. They give to us, and we give to them."

The more time went on, and the more spells we performed, the more the people worshipped us, and the more they withered. Without their knowledge, we were slowly sucking the life out of them and injecting a small piece of their souls and energy into ourselves. The ex-junkies craved their weekly high, and we delivered it to them at the cost of their youth and health.

My mama was livid with me for being "Weak-willed," as she put it, and warned me, "Stop with the dark magic or leave our apartment."

She was completely broken-hearted when I chose to leave. I moved into one of Jerimiah's guest rooms and paid nominal rent. It'd been a good fit because I never saw much of him. He was attending medical school, studying to become a doctor, and I continued to work nights at The Rhythm Club, where I would persuade the struggling addicts to come and join our church group.

One evening, after I finished work, a middle-aged white woman came over to chat with me, offering me a cigarette.

"Enzo, isn't it?"

I waved off the cigarette and said, "Yes, ma'am."

"I believe you know my nephew, Jerimiah."

I nodded cautiously.

"My name is Roseanne. I was speaking to your mama, and she'd asked if I'd come and see you. She's worried about you. She says you don't seem to realise what you've gotten yourself into."

"Is that so," I'd said dismissively.

"Jerimiah might be my nephew, but it doesn't mean I'm blind to his faults. That boy was born pure evil."

When I didn't reply, she continued.

"Your mama says you were born with a white aura, but my nephew helped to cast a shadow over you. She believes there is still hope for you, and she wants you to come back home."

"If that's so," I said, crossing my arms, "then why doesn't she come down here and tell me this herself?"

"She's scared you'll reject her. There's a hole in her heart where you used to fit."

I snuffed. "How do you know my mama anyhow?"

"She reached out to me. She wanted to know more about my nephew and what'd happened to his immediate family. She heard whispers about Jerimiah's parents passing away in a freak accident and how they left him their entire estate. She wondered if it truly was an accident, or if there was more to the story."

"And?" I'd asked impatiently, although deep down, I was curious. Jerimiah never spoke about his family.

"Ever since his sister, Bonnie, came along, Jerimiah's evil side took front stage. Bonnie was born with cerebral palsy," she said, catching me by surprise, "which meant she took up a lot of their parents' time. Jerimiah resented this with a passion. Instead of loving Bonnie and helping her like any good brother would, he derived pleasure from taunting her and causing her distress. He told his parents he'd wished she was never born."

The smoke from Roseanne's cigarette wafted through the frigid air in wispy tendrils, creating ephemeral patterns.

"My sister, Martha, never trusted Jerimiah; she said he had no regard for consequences and lacked empathy. He was all too consumed with his own selfish desires. She was afraid of him. *Afraid of her own son,*" Roseanne dragged out her words in emphasis. "Martha feared that Jerimiah would do something terrible to Bonnie if ever he had the chance, but her husband, Charles, was more trusting and blind to their son's faults. Jerimiah could be charming and charismatic on the surface, and that's what most people saw, but it was a mask to cover his deeper, darker side which brewed beneath the surface."

I was aware there was truth in what Roseanne was saying, but I couldn't bring myself to badmouth Jerimiah, even after learning he'd lied to me about Bonnie's illness. He'd told me she was sick with polio and that we were casting a spell to make her better, but a part of me knew he wasn't being entirely honest.

Had I known he was planning to kill her, I would've left and saved myself from the years of depression that followed, but what was done was done, and there was no turning back the clock.

"Charles talked my sister into going away with him for a small break," Roseanne's voice cracked. "When they arrived back home, the nanny was beside herself. Bonnie had passed away during the night. All the while Jerimiah was in his element, he had his parents' full attention again." Roseanne turned to face me, her eyes imploring mine. "The point is you can't trust Jerimiah. Things might seem all well and good right now, but as soon as he stops getting his own way, he will turn on you, and I promise you it won't end pretty."

AFTER LEARNING the truth from Roseanne, I considered confronting Jerimiah and telling him I was leaving The Church of Salvation, but after carefully thinking everything over during the ride back, I'd done a complete backflip and reconsidered.

Without Jerimiah or the church, I was nothing–a nobody. My love for music and the church were the only two things that made me feel alive. I'd spent so many years hanging my head in shame, feeling like a parasite in the community. Yet, since I'd joined The Church of Salvation, everything had changed, and I'd been able to hold my head up high with pride. I'd spent my whole life craving acceptance and I finally had it. It seemed idiotic to throw it all away over an incident that took place so many years ago.

All kids lie at the age of eight, I rationalised. *And perhaps Jerimiah hadn't fully understood his sister's condition. Besides, was I really any better than Jerimiah?* It'd never crossed my mind to put a stop to what we were doing to The Church of Salvation followers. As far as I was concerned, it was a fair trade. We helped keep them off the drugs, and in return, they helped to keep us youthful and invigorated. We weren't outright killing them; we were merely stealing their years.

CHAPTER 5

JUNE 15TH, 1997

CORAKI, AUSTRALIA

∞ MONROE ∞

I'm riding home from Casino after another long evening of break-and-enters, feeling relieved I'll be gone in less than a week. I spoke to Jackie on a payphone tonight–reverse charge– so we could nut out the arrangements. I didn't ask if we could give Indi a ride to Coffs Harbour. I figured it'd be easier to spring the question on her last minute. That way, it'll give her less time to consider the idea and say no.

Sweat beads drip from my brow as I ride, stinging my eyes and blurring my vision. It's a two-hour trip from Coraki to Casino by bike, with the return trip being much more challenging because the only light I have to see by is the faint, yellow glow emitting from my torch. Most days, I do it hard, running off little to no sustenance, but today, I was lucky enough to convince a kind woman at the servo to buy me a pie and coke. I told her I'd lost my wallet while riding, and she'd believed me. Out-of-town travellers are always more gullible and trusting than the locals.

I've seen homeless dudes around Casino, scabbing leftover food out of the bins, but there's no way I could stoop that low. Just the thought of it turns my stomach. I'd rather die of starvation than live like a rat.

I could use the cash I've made from the break-and-enters to buy food, but it would mean less rent money for Indi, and with the short time frame I'm working with, every dollar counts. I've been hiding the envelopes in the base of my bedroom drawers, pretending they don't exist.

After arriving home, I chain my bike wheel and tiptoe up the steps to the patio, carefully cracking the front door open so as not to wake anyone. Unfortunately, my luck is out. My mother charges over to me in a flash–getting all up in my face as she does.

"Where the hell you been all night? Huh? Huh?"

She's got a black eye and her teeth that'd once been pearly-white and straight in her younger years, are chipped at the bottoms and rotten around the gums. I can't stand the sight of her. She's an embarrassment.

"Answer me, God damn it. Where've you been?"

I scrunch my nose in protest and glance at my watch. Her foul breath reeks of rot and decay.

It's midnight, I quickly discover, and I'm well past exhausted. I'd imagined Ma would be in bed, but instead, she's all wired up and ready for a fight. She must've found a small stash of ice lying around the house somewhere. Either that, or she's slept with some desperado in town in exchange for a hit. It's what she does when she gets desperate. She sells herself for drugs.

"I was just at a party," I say, shouldering past her.

She follows me down the hall, nipping at my heels like a chihuahua. "Who's party? Huh? Ain't nobody said nothing about a party."

I feel a tug on the zipper of my bag, and I whirl on her.

"You were out selling on the street without me, weren't you? Huh?" She sneers. "I bet that's where the rest of our gear's gone. You've been selling on the sly and filling your own pocket, haven't you?"

Overtired and fed up with her constant accusations, I shove her hard against the hallway wall.

"There's nothing left because you and your scumbag of a boyfriend smoked it all, so don't you dare go accusing me."

My eyes glare into hers with pure and utter rage. It's times like these when I hate her with a passion, and I find myself wishing she'd met the same fate as Weasel. If she'd been killed alongside him, I doubt if I would've even shed a tear. I would've been free.

"Freddy," she screams. "Freddy!"

What kind of mother calls on their abusive boyfriend to beat up her teenage son in the name of drugs? My mother, unfortunately.

I can't afford a beating, especially when I'm only a week off leaving, so I release my grip and back up a step. I have more jobs lined up for Monday, Tuesday, and Thursday evening, and I need my strength to ride the distance.

Doing the smart thing, I make a beeline to my room, wedging my door shut with a set of pine drawers I'd managed to pick up from a garage sale for five dollars.

The runners are stiff and squeaky, but it works. I pull the bottom drawer completely out and place tonight's cash I'd made in the lower hollow section along with the rest of the secret bills I've got stashed.

My gaze shifts to the door when it vibrates against the architrave with several loud thumps.

"Open up, Boy!"

Ma must've gone and woken Freddy.

Bitch!

I ignore him, hoping he'll give up and leave me be. For a moment, I think it's worked until I'm startled by the sound of my bedroom window smashing. My pulse skyrockets as Freddy springs through the broken window and charges straight for me. He's cut his hand on a shard of glass, but he doesn't seem to notice, and I watch as his blood drips across the floor. He takes a swing toward my cheekbone, but I duck, and he hits the wall behind me instead. He growls and then knees me in the guts. While I'm bent over gasping, he clocks me across the temple, and I swear my brain ricochets inside my skull.

"Your mother says you took all of the goods. Now, where'd you put it all?" He picks up my bag and shakes it upside-down, emptying its contents.

"I don't have anything," I splutter. "We're all out."

He reaches for my top drawer and rips it right out, sending me into a state of panic.

"I don't have anything," I repeat, forcefully shoving him.

My reaction gives me away because the look in his eyes screams jackpot.

He lunges forward, knocking me over, and rips out another drawer before whacking me over the head with it.

Stars dance in my vision, and the next thing I know, Indi is crouched above me, shaking my shoulders and crying Enzo's name in concern. I hate that she still confuses me with Enzo sometimes. It's been a month since we first met. Surely, she could get my name right by now.

"I'm Monroe," I snap with a resentful edge, and Indi lets go of me with a jolt.

The hurt in her eyes has me immediately regretting my outburst, and I lever up to console her.

"I'm sorry. It's just..." My disembowelled set of drawers catches my eye, bringing back an alarming flash, and I scramble over to them in a panic. "No." I shake my head as I glimpse inside to find an empty base. "No. No. No."

"What is it?" Indi rushes over. "What's wrong?"

"The money is gone." I glance around my ransacked room, but I'm quickly left in despair. My emptied drawers lay across my floor in a heap, and glass from my broken window glitters across my mattress. It's raining of course—just to make matters worse—and the wind is blowing heavy droplets directly onto my mattress, too, soaking everything from my pillow to my blanket.

My gaze drifts to Indi, and I swallow hard before clarifying, "Freddy's taken your rent money."

Despair flashes across her face, and her eyes well with tears. "Does that mean I'm stuck here now?"

"No." I wrap my arms around her and draw her close. "It just means that I need to come up with another plan."

I still have a few days of "work" left, but I'll barely earn enough to cover a bond, let alone any rent. I don't mention this. Instead, I hold her tight, rummaging through my brain in hopes of coming up with another game plan.

Indi's eyes lift to mine. "Can I stay again?"

She's stayed over every Sunday night for the past month, as well as a few sporadic weeknights here and there. We snuggle each other safely to sleep, and then she slips out in the early hours of the morning before her father wakes up.

I glance towards my mattress and back at her. "Of course, but we won't be able to use my mattress." I release her from my grip and grab hold of the empty drawer frame, tugging it away from my bedroom door. "Wait here a minute," I say, afraid that Freddy might still be lurking, "I'm going to pinch the cushions off the couch."

I step out the door and close it behind me, grateful that Freddy is nowhere to be seen. When I get to the living room, I find Ma out cold on the floor with a busted nose, compliments of Freddy, I'm sure. I doubt if he'll be back now that he's pinched my money. The least he could've done is take my mother with him.

I leave her lying in her own disgrace and nab the cushions from the couch before stealing a pillow and blanket from her bedroom. If Freddy's gone, then I have nothing to fear.

The cushions lined up are much shorter than my mattress, but the nights are much colder in June, so I'm happy to curl up. I flick on my torch and turn out the light before snuggling in next to Indi.

"Are you okay?" she asks, touching my face.

The side of my head feels swollen and painful, but I blow it off and tell her, "I'm fine."

"Just think, in less than a week, we'll be in Coffs Harbour." Her eyes are lit with eagerness. "I've never been there before."

I force a smile, praying I can still get her there like I've promised.

CHAPTER 6
JUNE 20TH, 1997
CORAKI, AUSTRALIA
∞ MONROE ∞

Lightning flashes, illuminating my room in a burst of white, exposing the warzone Freddy left in his wake. I haven't bothered to clean up after him, preferring to just stick to the couch cushions for a matter of a few days. The dampness in the air from my broken window accentuates the mustiness of my water-logged mattress, but I don't have the energy to do anything about it.

Despite my promise to Jackie, I've spent the past few days getting high.

I'll be eighteen tomorrow, and she will be swinging by to pick me up so we can celebrate the start of my new life. I've got my get-out-of-jail-free card perfectly lined up, but sadly, it doesn't come with a plus one.

There's no way I can leave Indi here to become Jerimiah's possession. She deserves to live a normal life, free from brainwashing and continual abuse, but now I don't have any money, compliments of Freddy.

Ma blames me for Freddy leaving, so as a payback, she cut my clothes to shreds and slashed my bike tyres. This meant I couldn't ride to Casino for my last three jobs. I thought of borrowing her car, but I didn't trust her not to call the cops on me and report it stolen, just like she did with her boyfriend, Lance.

A soft tap at my bedroom door catches my attention, and I rush across the room, shoving a bunch of empty beer bottles aside before swinging the door wide open. Freddy fled in a hurry, leaving behind a full case of VB in the fridge, and I took advantage. I'd damn well paid for them a hundred times over with all the cash he took, and I've needed something to dull out my depression and the ranting and raving of my "poor heartbroken mother".

Indi stands on the other side of the door, her hair glued to the sides of her face, limp and dripping from being out in the rain.

I close the door and pull her close to me. Drenched and all, I don't care. I'm so glad to see her, my heart nearly explodes.

"You managed to get out," I say with relief.

Indi rests her chilly face in the crook of my neck, making me shiver. Her skin's always freezing. She doesn't have enough meat on her bones to keep her insulated. "I'm still coming with you, aren't I?"

"I wasn't able to make the money back," I blurt out. "But I'm going to ask Jackie if she'll put you up until I can make a few bucks to rent you an apartment."

This wasn't the path I'd planned to take, but I'm desperate and out of options. Jackie will scold me for taking advantage of her hospitality, and there's even a chance she'll refuse to help altogether, but I can't let that happen. I'll get down on my hands and knees and beg if it comes to it. I'll do anything she asks of me. Now that the money is gone, I need Jackie's assistance to get Indi out of here. It's our only chance.

"I thought you didn't wanna involve your sister?"

"I didn't," I admit. "But we have no other choice. We both know you can't continue living like this. The abuse is never gonna stop. Plus, if you stay, you'll end up being tied to that creep Jerimiah for life."

Her eyes flash white, and her lips distort, scaring the living daylights out of me. I jerk backwards, nearly tripping over the pile of empty beer bottles.

The first night I met Indi, she'd said, *"My father beats me too. He says I have the Devil inside me"*, and for a split second, I believe it.

"What's wrong?" Indi asks, and just like that, her face is back to normal again.

It was always normal, I tell myself, shaking off the prickly sensation at the nape of my neck.

Your alcohol-addled brain is playing tricks on you.

"I thought I saw something," I say, trying to blink away the image. "My head's not right. I haven't slept much." I lean back in and press my lips to her forehead, assuring her everything is okay. "Things will be better soon. Come tomorrow, you and I will finally be free."

CHAPTER 7

JUNE 21ST, 1997

CORAKI, AUSTRALIA

∞ MONROE ∞

I wake up with a jolt to distant screams and an empty side of the bed. Indi was supposed to stay the whole night, but she's no longer here.

Why in the world would she go back?

I bolt out of bed and race outside, following the sounds of her screams.

"Indi!" My voice cracks with hysteria. "Indi!"

My knuckles scrape red raw as I pound on the neighbours' front door to no avail. White paint curls from its exterior, cracked and blistered from decades of the scorching sun.

The sky flashes white, and a crack of thunder reverberates, drowning out Indi's curdling screams. When the rumble finally subsides, the silence is foreboding. My blood turns to ice.

"Indi!"

I hurl my shoulder against the door, throwing the bulk of my weight against it in a desperate attempt to break through. The hinges might be old and rusted, but they're sturdy, and the hardwood is thick and impenetrable.

When it doesn't budge, I revert to pummelling again, this time with more ferocity. Red splatters soon splay on the weathered surface as the skin from my knuckles peels from the bone.

I freeze, but not because of the pain; my hands are numb with adrenaline. *There's got to be an easier way to get in.*

Heart racing, I vault over the porch rail and leap the sagging wooden fence into the Walkers' backyard. Rainwater stings my eyes, and tall thistle weeds scratch at my lower legs as I sprint across the unkept lawn to the backdoor steps.

The bottom steps have rotted with age and groan beneath my weight. I reach for the rusted doorknob and forcibly twist, but my hand—slick with blood and water—slips on the metal. Using the bottom of my shirt for grip, I clasp on tightly and give another solid twist, but all that moves is my wrist. It won't budge. It's locked.

Another ear-piercing scream escapes from inside the house, and my body thrums in fear.

"Indi!"

I glance about frantically, looking for a loose brick or something equally as solid to throw through the back window, when a hopeful thought penetrates my hysteria, and I race around the side of the house.

Indi usually leaves her bedroom window open.

My eyes light up when I round the corner to find the hung sash window ajar. The runners squeak as I force the lower frame up higher, but to my relief, no one comes running into the room to investigate. I climb the splintered latticework and slip through the window's opening, falling to the floor. The old shag-pile carpet squelches beneath me, damp and rank from the rain. My nose curls in protest—and not only due to the smell. I survey the room from wall to wall and across the floor, brows creased in confusion. Indi's bedroom isn't anything at all like I'd imagined it to be. Besides a scattering of mouldy boxes, the room is barren. There's not even so much as a bed. *Where does she sleep?*

Pushing the question aside for now, I lever to my feet and light-footedly creep across the room to the door. Now that I'm inside, I don't want to be caught. I could really use the upper hand.

The doorknob twists with the slightest of squeaks, causing me to wince before stepping out into a hall. I take a moment to scan both directions, ears pricked, but the tap, tap of heavy water droplets pelting on the tin roof is all that can be heard.

At the back end of the hall sits a laundry crammed with outdoor gear. I spot a spear gun hanging by the doorway alongside two fishing rods, and I head straight for it, taking it to use as a weapon.

Pointing the gun firmly out in front of me, I make my way down the hall, poking my head into each of the doorways as I pass.

Four entryways later, I find Mr Walker and his wife huddled in the living room, their frames merged as they peek through a small gap in the window shutters.

I know their last name is Walker because we received their mail by accident once.

Mr Walker leans forward on his cane and rubs his wife's back. "I think he's gone."

I stare at the solid stick in his hand, wondering how many times it's made contact with Indi's skin over the years. Short and crippled with a bulging belly, I bet the force of using it on her gives him a sick sense of power.

Mrs Walker's body trembles violently despite her husband's reassuring touch. "What does he want from us?"

The wooden floor creaks as I step inside, and both heads snap in my direction. When the pair spot the spear gun in my hand, their eyes bulge. Mrs Walker screams and cowers while Mr Walker raises his hands and steps protectively in front of his wife.

"Where is she?" The words leave my lips in a roar. "Where's Indi?"

Mr Walker's leathery skin shimmers with perspiration. "Now, now, Son." His Adam's apple bobbles. "I don't know who this Indi is you're speaking of, but I'd be willing to help you find her if only you'd put your weapon down."

I know the game he's trying to play, and I'm not falling for it.

I raise the spear gun, pointing it directly towards Mr Walker's head. "Don't lie to me. I've heard about the vile things you've done to your daughter and the fact you're marrying her off to that creep, Jerimiah. She's told me everything." My teeth grit. "Now, where the hell is she?"

He flinches but doesn't recoil. "Boy, those darn drugs you take have got you paranoid. We don't have a daughter. We've only got a son."

Indi has never spoken of her brother, but I've seen Mr Walker talking to him in the yard. He's tall and broad-shouldered, unlike Mr Walker, who's short and all stomach.

"You can't lie to me." Apprehension over Indi's safety and where-abouts causes the spear gun to shudder in my hands. "I heard her screaming. You were torturing her."

"Like I said, we've only got a son, James, and he's not here right now."

Indi's screams echo around me, but I can't get a sense of where they're coming from, which has me feeling dizzy and disorientated.

Losing my cool, I jab the pointed end of the spear beneath his chin, nicking the skin.

"Enough," I shout. "I'm not deaf. I can hear her. Tell me where she is right now, or I'll pull the trigger."

Mr Walker squeals, stumbles, and drops his cane. He would've toppled all the way over, too, if it wasn't for the close-by window frame he manages to grab a hold of.

Noticing the blood trickling down his neck, Mrs Walker lets out a shriek and dashes for the door, leaving her trembling husband to fend for himself.

"Please." Mr Walker's tone is pleading. "I don't know who this Indi girl is, but I'm willing to help you find her. I don't want any trouble."

I step aside, keeping the bloodied spear angled toward his throat. "Rubbish. Take me to her."

He glances at his walking stick lying by his feet. "I need my cane to walk."

I shake my head. There's no way I'm retrieving it for him when it could easily be turned on me as a weapon.

Using the walls for support, Mr Walker leads me back down the hall, hobbling with his lame leg. He pauses at each door to scan inside, and my anger ignites as I clue on to his tactic; he's deliberately stalling.

I thrust the spear gun upwards again, this time leaving a nasty gouge at the base of his neck. He stumbles forward, grabbing hold of the doorframe. Blood gushes from the gaping wound, turning the neckline of his wife-beater crimson.

"Quit playing games with me. Take me to her now!"

His body quavers. "Please, I...."

A low creak behind me has my head whipping around, but it's too late. Strong arms seize mine from behind, yanking them downwards.

"Run, Dad. Run." I recognise the voice. It's his son, James.

Mr Walker said he wasn't home.

Lies, lies, lies.

Not willing to let Mr Walker get away scot-free, I pull the trigger, and the spear launches, landing a deep puncture wound to his thigh. It won't kill him, but it makes him drop and squeal like a stuffed pig, at the very least.

"No!" James' arms reef me off balance, and we both stumble backwards, landing in a heap on the floor.

I struggle to break free from his iron grip, but he thrusts me to the side, smashing my head onto the hardwood floor with a thump. A metallic tang fills my mouth, telling me I've bitten my tongue, although I can't feel it. I can't feel anything.

The hit to my head renders my body immobilised, and James

uses this to his advantage. He bolts upright and pins me down with his knee to my chest, landing his solid fist on my face. I'm pounded by blow after blow until green and purple splotches fill my vision.

"Indi," I croak in despair before slipping into blackness.

CHAPTER 8
1960 - 1965
NEW ORLEANS, AMERICA
∞ ENZO ∞

B y 1960, a long list of our followers had come and gone, fading out well before their time. We drained them of all the years they had left, and while they aged prematurely, Jerimiah and I remained young and sprightly. Neither of us looked a day over twenty-one, which had become problematic. It'd gotten to the point where our youthful looks were inconceivable. To look as though we were in our twenties while we were in our thirties was considered lucky and would often be put down to good genes or comfortable living, but come nineteen years on, we were pushing our forties, and the idea of still looking twenty-one was implausible.

After much discussion, Jerimiah put his property on the market, and our plan was to create new identities and move to Texas, where we would start up a new Church of Salvation.

Not only had Jerimiah completed his bachelor's degree and finished his medical training, but he'd also done a four-year residency in psychiatry and had since become certified as a full-fledged psychiatrist.

Meanwhile, I was still practising music and working at The

Rhythm Club on Jackson Avenue. I'd grown a beard to give an illusion of maturity, but it was only going to suffice for so long.

Every year, Jerimiah always did a special ceremony for the Winter Solstice. He mentioned he had an extra special ceremony planned for our last celebration in New Orleans, so imagine my surprise when only a single girl showed up. She was a scrawny teenager with scabs and scratches all over her skin and pupils as large as saucers. Her hair was lanky and oily, and her clothes were tattered and musty smelling. It was clear she hadn't had a wash in a long while.

After giving her a scrutinising once over, I made my way down the aisle of the nave towards the pulpit where Jerimiah stood, curious as to what his plan was.

When I got to the sanctuary, I froze, my breath hitching. A chalk circle had been drawn before the altar, displaying the same symbols, candles, and minerals we'd used to cast the spell on his sister.

"How long will this take?" the girl asked impatiently, twitching and jittering like a frightened rabbit. "I've got somewhere else I need to be."

"These things can take a long while."

I hoped she might pull the pin, but to my dismay, she just groaned and said, "I need a smoke."

While she slipped outside for a cigarette, I made my way over to where Jerimiah was kneeling, lighting the candles of the circle by the altar.

"Where is everyone?"

"It'll only be the three of us tonight."

"Why?" The base of my neck prickled. "What kind of spell are we doing exactly?"

He stood, looked me square in the eyes and said, "She's sick, so you and I are going to heal her."

Resentment bubbled inside me. Jerimiah was supposed to be my friend and partner in all of this, yet here he was, deceiving me once more. He hadn't even batted an eyelash. The lie slipped so easily off his tongue.

Infuriated, I flew at him. "Do you think I came down in the last shower of rain? You're not interested in healing these types of people. You never have been. You're only looking to help yourself."

"Now, now," he said in warning, but I wasn't done.

"I heard what happened to your family, and I know you deliberately killed Bonnie. You've willingly killed your own flesh and blood for self-gain, so don't pretend like we're saving that junkie out there."

My heart was hammering. In all the years I'd known Jerimiah, I'd never confronted him with the truth. I wanted to leave the past behind us, but a case of déjà vu had me seeing red. We weren't eight-year-old kids anymore; we were adults, and he knew better.

"My mama was right about you," I said in spite. "You're pure evil."

Jerimiah grabbed me by the collar and pulled me roughly to him, levelling his face with mine. "You mean *we* killed my sister," he spat in a hushed growl.

His dark, soulless eyes pierced mine, appearing like black holes in space. Places where gravity pulled so hard that even light couldn't escape. At that very moment, I realised how fitting that analogy was for Jerimiah. He truly was a black hole, sucking the light and life out of everyone around him.

"Don't pretend you're innocent," he continued. "You knew something didn't feel quite right that night, yet you didn't argue or say stop. You stayed and helped willingly." He pulled me in closer, putting us nose to nose. "I saw it in your eyes. You enjoyed the surge of power the dark magic gave you. You still do. That's why you're still here. You're not an innocent man, Lorenzo; you have been voluntarily aiding me in stealing the youth from these types of filth–" he pointed to the window, where the young girl was standing outside, taking a long drag of her cigarette "–for years, and you're reaping the benefits. Why should what we're doing tonight be any different?"

"It's not the same as what we've been doing," I said, shaking my head. "This is a whole new level of wrong. It's outright murder, and I refuse to be a part of it."

Jerimiah let go of my collar, but his penetrating eyes drilled into mine with contempt. "If you want to pack up and leave, suit yourself, but know this... That young girl out there is a hopeless drug addict. She leeches off others to score her next hit, and as time goes on and things get desperate, she will rob and potentially even kill others for that high. We are doing the locals a favour, and in return, we will be rewarded. Sacrificing this one girl would be the equivalent of several years' worth of draining many, and it would significantly strengthen our powers. It will be quick, and she won't ever suffer again. Don't you see? This is a mercy killing. We are saving her from herself."

While he tried to rationalise it, I sadly came to realise we were no better than the junkies we were draining. We were addicted to the power, and Jerimiah was willing to outright kill for it.

"I won't help you," I'd said again and took off, leaving him to cast the spell on his own while I went inside the main house to pack up my things.

IT'D BEEN years since I'd seen my mama, yet when I arrived at her place, she wasn't at all surprised to see me. She said she knew I was coming; she'd foreseen it.

She cupped my chin with her hand and pivoted my face side to side, marvelling at my youthful appearance with puckered brows.

"My poor foolish boy, what've you done?"

A sense of déjà vu washed over me for the second time in one evening as my eight-year-old self flashed to mind. I really was a fool. I should've listened to my mama.

Mama looked much the same, only older. She had a few more facial lines and grey wisps of hair, but her figure had remained trim for that of a sixty-year-old woman.

When I told my mama about what Jerimiah and I had been doing over the years, she was disgusted with me.

"And all this time you've been transferring your darkness to those poor, undeserving people. How could you?"

I hadn't realised this was what we'd been doing until she pointed it out, but suddenly it made perfect sense. I hadn't felt any darkness or depression since joining The Church of Salvation.

When I mentioned Jerimiah intended to sacrifice a young girl this evening to increase his powers, she threatened to call the sheriff.

"Stay out of it, Mama," I begged. "Jerimiah isn't a man you want to get on the wrong side of."

"He must be stopped now before his power grows too strong. Otherwise, he'll–" Mama launched up from the sofa, mid-sentence, with alarm. "He's here."

Not a minute later, the front door flung open, revealing Jerimiah and a band of our followers on the other side.

"Now," Jerimiah ordered, and they rushed at us armed with metal poles and old planks of wood. They swung hard and fast, walloping us from all angles until we were beaten to the ground. As Mama and I laid there, they dropped to their knees and pinned us down while Jerimiah began to chant.

He strode over to where my mama was laying, carrying a jar of liquid and a needle and thread.

"No!" I shouted, struggling to break free. "No..."

My mama tried to say something, but Jerimiah paused chanting long enough to tell one of our followers to cover her mouth.

"She's possessed," he declared. "Don't be fooled by what she says. It's the Devil talking."

"Don't listen to him," I shouted. "He's the Devil, and he's got you all fooled. He's stealing your years. He's–"

As I spoke, Jerimiah told one of his followers to shut me up. My words were smothered as a gag was stuffed in my mouth. I never got to finish what I was saying, although I was sure my warning was said in vain.

I heard the splash of liquid being poured, then a sizzling sound. My blood ran cold as a tortured scream escaped through the hands held over Mama's mouth.

A surge of adrenaline raced through me as I tried to break free, but then something hard and metal came crashing down across my cheekbone. The last thing I remember was Jerimiah and his band of followers chanting in Latin before I lost consciousness and slipped into darkness.

When I awoke, I could barely open my left eye, my cheek was so swollen. I gingerly touched my cheekbone and extended my limbs, relieved that nothing appeared to be broken. With tremendous effort, I struggled to my feet, and I spotted my mother sprawled on the floor with her lips sewn shut. At first, I feared she was dead, but when I touched her, she flinched, and her eyes flung open.

I stumbled backwards, in shock, my breath catching in my lungs.

Her eyes, which had been a deep shade of brown, were now milky white, as though they'd been doused in peroxide. My stomach turned when I realised the sizzling sound had been the peroxide being poured onto her eyes.

"I'm so sorry, Mama." I took her hand in mine. Tears filled my eyes, and my voice cracked as I spoke. "I'm gonna call for help."

Before I had the chance to move, her hand tightened to a vice-like grip.

"No," it sounded like she'd said, and she lifted her other hand to show a scissors gesture with her index and middle finger.

When she loosened her grip, I grabbed a pair of scissors before carefully cutting the string sewn through her lips. My mama grimaced but didn't whimper. Strength was her virtue.

"I'll kill him," I said, Jerimiah's face flashing to mind. "I swear to God I will."

"You're not strong enough. My magic has been linked to..." Though she tried, she couldn't finish her sentence. Her lips pulled and tugged, but they couldn't seem to part. It was as if an invisible string had taken the place of the actual string I'd just removed.

"Jerimiah," I said for her, knowing it was his name sitting on the tip of her tongue.

"'Linking' spell," she croaked. "And 'Keep My Secrets Binding'." Nothing more needed to be said. I was able to fill in the blanks.

I stayed and ran my mama's shop for her while she was recovering. She was also cautious of folks being afraid of her appearance and spreading wild rumours.

The following Sunday evening, when I was tallying up the register, Jerimiah strolled in, calm as a cucumber.

"Hello, my friend," he said, as though everything was still peachy between us.

I opened the drawer and took out a pair of scissors, but a powerful force took over my hand, making it shudder violently until I dropped them again.

"I wouldn't try anything if I were you." Jerimiah's expression was smug. "I'm linked with your mama now, so anything you do to me will be done to her."

My lust for revenge burnt through me, but I held it in check, uncertain if he was telling the truth or not. I couldn't risk him hurting my mama.

"You're not my friend. Get out," I commanded.

"I was unable to complete the sacrifice ceremony successfully last Sunday. I need someone with your inner power for the spell to work as I intended. The son of a warlock and a witch."

Jerimiah had said that sacrificing the young girl would significantly enrich our powers, and added power in his hands would only be used for evil. As much as I missed the feeling of dark magic coursing through me, there was no way I would give in to him, especially after what he had done to my mama.

"Forget it." I stood my ground. "I'm done with you."

"If you want your mama to live, then you will help me with the spell. It seems an easy enough trade, the sacrifice of a worthless junkie for your mama's life."

"You won't kill her," I said with sureness. "You're linked."

Jerimiah sneered smugly before clicking the sides of his mouth while he tsked. "You see, that's where you're wrong, my friend." He moved closer, and it felt as though the whole store was closing in on me. "It's a one-way tie. Your mama and her powers are tied to me, but in no way am I tied to your mama."

My shoulders drooped in defeat, and my heart sank. He had me by the balls, and he knew it.

"The sacrifice of a worthless junkie for your mama's life," he repeated. "Do the spell with me, and I will leave you and your mama be."

Against all my principles, I gave in to him and reluctantly participated in the sacrifice, all the while feeling sickened with guilt. At the end of the day, my mama meant more to me than the young girl, and she'd already suffered enough.

It saddened me to see that Jerimiah had her all dolled up for the sacrifice. She looked quite different to the last time I'd seen her. She was washed and dressed in a white gown, which was simple but pretty. She wore makeup that helped cover her scabs and scratches, and her hair was loose and neatly brushed.

Before we started, he injected her with a sedative, bleached her eyes, and sewed her lips—just like he had done with my mama—destroying her lovely makeover. I could barely bring myself to look at her while we chanted.

By the time we finished, and the dark magic was coursing through me, I lost all sense of guilt and disgust and was lost in a state of euphoria. However, once the rush subsided and the evening ebbed out, the guilt and disgust returned twofold, sending me spiralling into a deep depression.

The next day, I spoke to Mama about selling the shop and moving as far away from Jerimiah as possible. Given that Jerimiah had blinded her and destroyed any chance she had of running the shop without scaring the locals with her frightful appearance, she willingly agreed.

If she knew I'd helped to sacrifice the young girl, she didn't mention it, but then again, she was bound to keep Jerimiah's secrets, and as it turned out, his secrets were my secrets also.

It took several months for the store to sell, but by the time the final paperwork went through, we'd sorted through all of Mama's things and come up with a rough plan. As soon as the money was deposited into Mama's account, we immediately bought plane tickets to Sydney, Australia, and flew across to the other side of the world.

It'd been hard taking Mama through customs because she couldn't wear sunglasses to cover her eyes or a scarf to hide her mutilated mouth. Some people stared in horror, while others moved away from us in fear. The holes around Mama's lips where the stitches had been still looked risen and angry, and her unseeing eyes were like milky white marbles and looked ghostly, like she was possessed.

When we first arrived in Australia, we stayed in a hostel for several weeks until I got a job with the railway. The company was government run and sponsored me for Australian citizenship.

Eventually, we bought a property in Springwood, which was situated in the lower Blue Mountains. The area was much more affordable than the inner suburbs of Sydney. Plus, it was a quaint town with old-world charm. The cottage we bought had a lovely rose garden and a log fireplace for the winter months.

Apart from the shadow that lurked over me, haunting my dreams, life was good and peaceful for seven whole years, but come June 1965, we were distraught to find an unwanted visitor at our doorstep when we returned home from shopping. It was through his link to my mama that Jerimiah found us. It'd lead him straight to our door.

Before he even said a word, I knew the reason for his visit. Our timeless appearances were under the clock again, and he wanted me to join him for another sacrificial spell.

Once again, I folded to his will under the threat of what he would do to Mama.

When I returned home, my mama was a mess. She was sitting on the living room floor, surrounded by scissors, knives, and the axe I would use for chopping the firewood, her face wet with tears.

"What've you done?" I asked, frantically checking her over for injuries.

"What've *you* done?" she wallowed in return. "I'd tried doing what ought to be done, what'll put a stop to all of this, but I–" her lips tugged and pulled, unable to peel apart. "You must do it," she said, handing me a knife. "If I'm gone, he'll have no hold over you."

She'd tried taking her own life, I realised, yet she'd been unable to. Jerimiah must've put a protection spell on her, which meant he needed her to stay alive. He never had any intention of killing her. He'd been bluffing to get me to cooperate and deceiving me all along.

I took the knife, placed it down, then wrapped my arms around Mama and squeezed her in a tight bear hug.

"I'm sorry, Mama." My heart was heavy with guilt. "I'm so, so sorry."

CHAPTER 9
JUNE 19TH, 1998
ROZELLE HOSPITAL, LILYFIELD, AUSTRALIA
∞ MONROE ∞

T he freckly-faced councillor flicks her long, auburn hair over her shoulder and looks down her glasses at me.

"It's your turn, Monroe." Her voice oozes with sickly sweetness.

Eight sets of eyes glance in my direction. Two of the newer patients stare wide-eyed with interest while everyone else slumps, bored by the prospect of the same old story. Not to mention, I've become far less interesting since swallowing my meds and falling into line. My heart beats evenly in my chest, keeping my body relaxed and my mind steady. I'm the perfect patient, quiet and zombified, just like they want me.

We're forever told, "Honesty is the best policy," but if I were to say, "My only regret is not killing Mr Walker," it'd only buy me more time in this God-forsaken place. Today's my last day at Rozelle Hospital, and I'm prepared to lie through my teeth if it means freedom.

Indi. Her scarred and beaten body flashes to mind, and I grimace. I've spent the past year worrying if she's been severely punished for my actions. Instead of taking care of her—like I'd said I would—I've left her to fend for herself.

"Monroe," the councillor prompts.

Keeping my expression neutral, I say, "It's been a year since I've touched any alcohol or illicit substances."

Everyone claps as if I've accomplished some amazing feat. Little do they know drugs and alcohol were never my issue. If anything, they've been my saviour. My "drug-induced psychosis diagnosis" is my key to getting out of this joint without any real jail time.

The new girl sitting across from me, with scratched-up skin and bloodshot eyes, twitches distractingly as I share my rehearsed tale of violence and regret. "Oh, how sorry I am for the lives I've affected while drugging," and so on and so forth. Every time I use the word "drugs", those bloodshot eyes widen further, and she lifts her hand from her lap as though she'll be able to pluck the word right out of the air and materialise it for the taking.

This won't be her last visit to this clinic. She's a repeat offender in the making. You can always tell.

Lindsay—my closest friend in this place—glances across the room when Dr Richards enters.

Lindsay reapplies her lip balm and batters her long lashes seductively, giving Dirty Dick a reason to reposition his folder in front of his crotch.

I can see why Dr Richards is so taken by Lindsay. Her long, dark hair and almond eyes—which curl up like a cat's—give her super sex appeal. She's also curvy in all the right places—and she knows it.

Apparently, Dr Richards has blonde hair in *all* places.

Lindsay and my other friend, Becca, have shared far more intimate details about Dirty Dick than I'd prefer to hear, yet somehow, they haven't stumbled across each other. Lindsay calls Becca my imaginary friend, which irks me. I get the feeling she doesn't like sharing, which is exactly why I've never told her about Becca and Dirty Dick's secret affair.

I'd considered reporting the perv for taking advantage of his patients, but Lindsay swore me to secrecy. Besides, Dirty Dick is good friends with Dr Ross, my doctor, so it'd be a conflict of interest. They'd only find a way to turn the accusations back on me.

I'll wait until I've been released before spilling sexual assault accusations, and I'll do it anonymously, save my friends—or anyone else—from knowing it was me.

Noticing me scrutinising him, Dirty Dick's dark eyes flash my way, sharp and penetrating, like a predator in the night. As much as I would love to death-glare him in return, I lower my gaze, not wanting to jeopardise my freedom.

He'll pay eventually... When the time is right.

Becca is sitting on my bed when I return to my room to pack my belongings. She's dressed in her usual 1970s knee-length pink dress, along with a matching headband. She's got this small quirk where she thinks it's the year 1978—the year before I was born. It's now 1998. Two decades have passed, but I've never argued the matter or made an issue of it. Indi used to suffer from reality confusion, too. She was always mistaking me for Enzo. It peeved me originally, but I quit being resentful because she never quite seemed to be in her right mind when saying it. She was always vague and confused.

Dr Ross has said reality confusion of any sort can be a side effect of trauma, adding pointedly that blackouts can also be a side effect of trauma. I'd argued my blackouts were due to drinking and drugging, nothing more, not wanting to admit I still suffer with them from time to time.

"You're leaving," Becca says, her green eyes glistening with tears.

I park on the bed beside her and throw my arm around her shoulder.

"Don't worry, I won't forget about you," I say, giving her an affectionate squeeze. "We can be pen pals, or better yet, why don't you work on getting out of here and come to Coffs Harbour for a holiday." I slip my hand into my pocket and pass her a piece of paper with my sister's address written on it. "This is where I'll be staying until I can get back on my feet."

Becca reminds me of a younger version of my sister Jacqueline. They both have the same creamy skin and circular cheekbones. Jackie's eyes are far more outstanding, though. They're a swampy green, framed by long curly lashes—like mine—courtesy of our mother. Despite having jet-black hair and walnut skin, I, too, managed to inherit my ma's light eyes. I often get comments on them, especially from older women. They're the only decent thing my mother has ever given me.

Becca leans in and kisses me on the cheek, stunning me with the iciness of her lips. "I'm sure gonna miss you," she says. "You're the only one who sees me for who I am."

"Right back at cha, Darlin'," I reply.

We stand, and I give her a final hug before she waves and leaves, just missing Lindsay by a matter of seconds.

"So, this is it then? You're officially bailing on me." Lindsay folds her arms over her chest and leans against the doorframe, her face scrunched. Lindsay's not originally from Australia. She was born in Argentina, hence the accent. "Who's going to have my back now, WarHead?"

I hand her the second piece of paper with my sister's address written on it. "Stop acting crazy, and they'll release you, too." I cast her a pointed look. "Don't throw your life away for Dirty Dick, he ain't worth it."

She stabs a finger at my chest, eyes slitted. "He's got big plans for us; I'll have you know." Her scowl disappears, and her voice turns singsong. "He's going to leave his wife and take me to a tropical island where all of my problems will melt away."

And the award for best actress goes to Lindsay Mendez.

"Sure." Cynicism drips from my voice. "It sounds like a *real* fairy tale."

Lindsay punches my arm hard enough to leave a bruise. "Lecture me all you like, but I don't recall your 'so-called' girlfriend, Indi," she air-quotes, "coming to visit you once this past year."

I straighten, my muscles bunching. "That's different."

Indi wouldn't be able to come, even if she wanted to. She's trapped. The thought of her being held prisoner by her father has me worrying so hard I can barely think straight. I hate not knowing what's happened to her.

"Of course, it is." Lindsay rolls her eyes.

Her gibe stings more than ever, but I hide my hurt under a care-free smile. It's the last time I'll be seeing Lindsay for a while, and I don't want to fight.

Lindsay can be snarky and downright infuriating at times, but she isn't as crazy as she pretends to be. She's merely an ex-druggy with daddy issues and nothing to lose. The only reason she's clinging to Dirty Dick is because he's loaded and filling her head with big promises, which he'll never keep.

I've tried telling her he's full of it, but she won't hear it.

"Say... WarHead..." Lindsay's cockiness dries up, and she leans in closer, worrying her lower lip. "What were you talking to him about earlier? You didn't mention my name, did you?"

"Who?" I ask, brows puckered. "Dirty Dick?"

Her expression hardens with irritation. "His name is Jerry," she corrects. "You know I hate it when you call him that."

This isn't the first time Lindsay has accused me of speaking to Dr Richards. Clearly, she's paranoid.

"I think it's about time you got your eyes checked, Darlin'."

She hmpfs dismissively. "Don't 'Dar–lin'' me, I know what I saw."

Regardless of the accusation, her pitiful attempt to mimic my Australian accent makes me chuckle. She always over-rolls the Rs.

The first time Lindsay and I spoke, she called me WarHead. When I asked her why, she said, "You might look sweet like candy, but you're packed with a punch."

I'd lashed out hardcore for the first two months before realising the only person I was hurting was myself. No one believed Indi was real. Hence, they weren't looking for her. They believed I'd conjured her in my drug-induced state. Pressing the matter only made me

look crazier. So, I decided to shut my mouth, do my time, and tell Dr
Ross all the things she wanted to hear.

I planned to behave, get out of here, and then prove everyone
wrong.

So far, so good.

I just hope I can find Indi. Anything could've happened to her in a
year. Her father could've killed her and hidden her body.

"Here." Lindsay hands me a card she's made with a drawing of
the both of us on it. *The girl sure has talent.*

Inside reads:

Dear WarHead,
  I can't believe you're finally getting out, bastardo!
Thank you for being my eye candy this past year
and for making this place bearable. If it wasn't for
Indi and Jerry, I think you and I could've really had
something special. ;-).
This place won't be the same without you.
  love Lindsay

"You're a pain in the ass, but I'm gonna miss you something
fierce," I say, cupping Lindsay's shoulder and giving it a squeeze.

She cocks a brow and purrs suggestively, "I know you will,"
before embracing me with a bone-crushing hug.

My sister Jackie arrives in time to sign her part of my release
paperwork. She's responsible for helping me transition back into the
real world. When she mentions she's already got a job lined up for
me at The Hoey Moey, which is a pub/restaurant, she's met with a
frown by the sister in charge.

"Don't worry," Jackie tells her. "It's my husband's business. Raj
will be there to keep an eye on Monroe while he's on shift, and I'll be
the one dropping him off and picking him up. He won't have any
time to drink, I promise."

When we step outside, my entire body lightens and loosens. The sky is clear, and the sun shines warmly on my face regardless of the chilly winter breeze.

I inhale deeply, savouring the smell of freedom. It's sweeter than the hint of freshly cut grass rising from the newly mowed lawns.

Jackie presses a button on her keys, and a new, flashy Mercedes-Benz parked across the way springs to life.

The inside of Jackie's car looks and smells new, unlike any of the beat-up hunks-of-junk Ma ever owned. I sigh in relief when Jackie hops in beside me and turns the engine over. It's a good indication she's not having second thoughts.

"Thanks for still taking me in," I say.

She gives a genuine smile, her eyes crinkling up at the corners. "You don't know how glad I am that you're feeling much better. Raj and I have been counting down the days until your release."

My chest loosens. I was worried she'd be nervous about taking me in; *clearly not*. She still loves me despite what I've done.

After a long while of cruising in companionable silence, Jackie strikes up the subject of Ma. She was taken in and charged with drug distribution after my arrest.

"Leonie's appeal was last week. You'll be glad to know the judge didn't rule in her favour. She's still looking at another twenty years in prison."

My teeth grit. "Leonie could have been given the death penalty for all I care. I'm nineteen now. I don't need no parent."

Jackie's knuckles protrude as her grip on the steering wheel tightens. "Dad says the warden should do us all a favour and throw away the key."

Our conversation runs dry, prompting Jackie to switch on the radio. I'm not big on pop music. I prefer R&B, but as Jackie relaxes and sings along with Jewel's "Foolish Games", I can't help but smile.

My life could've been so different if...

No...

I shake off the thought. Dr Ross said, "There are no regrets in life, just lessons, and you need to focus on your future."

It takes eight hours to get from Rozelle Hospital to Jackie and Raj's property in Coffs Harbour.

Jackie and Raj's property, Yarramin, is set on fifty-five acres and backs onto the national forest. The first time I came here, I was twelve, and going from a dilapidated two-bedroom shack in Lismore–where we were living at the time–to a large property in Coffs Harbour with a pool and tennis court, was like being transported from the pits of Hell to the Heavens above.

Jackie's Mercedes passes through the gate, and I get out and swing it closed again, making sure to wedge the latch in properly so the cows don't escape.

My eyes lift to the white Brahman bull grazing in the middle of the paddock. It stands out like a beacon amongst the herd of Angus cows. The monster of a thing almost killed me the last time I was here. It'd tried crushing me against a fence.

I hop back in the car, and we follow the long gravel driveway, which comes to a wooden bridge crossing over a bubbling creek. I spent a lot of time in that creek the last time I was here and have the scars from the leeches to prove it. The car shudders as we drive over the metal cattle grid leading to their large brick five-bedroom house. This place hasn't lost its magic. I'm just as mesmerised now as I'd been when I'd first seen it as a tween.

Once parked in the garage, Jackie fixes me with a firm look. "Raj and I have discussed your situation, and we're happy for you to stay with us for as long as you need, *but* there are rules."

"No drinking, no drugs, no parties, no fights." I chant along with her, having had the list recited to me numerous times over the years.

"And no random girls," she tacks on at the end, making me blush. "We're trusting *you* to do the right thing by us."

"I'll behave myself," I assure her. "I'm not an addict like Ma. I only dabbled in drugs and alcohol because they were there, and I was looking for an escape."

"I know... And I'm certain you'd never hurt anyone on purpose," she adds after a beat. "I blame Leonie for all of it. She should have let us take you in years ago when we'd offered. She's a selfish junkie who doesn't deserve children."

My lips quirk.

Jackie might be right about Ma, but she's wrong about me. I did hurt Mr Walker on purpose, and I'd do it again in a heartbeat.

CHAPTER 10
JUNE 26TH, 1998
COFFS HARBOUR, AUSTRALIA
∞ MONROE ∞

I watch as Raj cuts through his tandoori chicken with precision. He gracefully pops the piece into his mouth and then closes his lips before chewing.

Having caught me staring, he says with a sharp edge, "It's proper etiquette. You should try it."

Raj was born and brought up in Woolgoolga by his Australian mother and Indian father, and considering the intricately carved wooden furniture spread throughout the house, along with the colourful patchwork sofas in the living room, it's clear he's proud of his heritage. There's a strong Sikh culture in Woolgoolga. The area even boasts a Guru Nanak Sikh Temple, large and majestic, painted in white and gold.

Raj and Jackie were very welcoming at first, but for the past couple of days, Raj has been short with me. I'm not exactly sure if I've done something personally to upset him or if he's not coping well under stress.

One of his employees went missing after her shift the evening of my nineteenth birthday and was found dead in a local barn on Tuesday morning—in what the police are calling a ritualistic homicide. Christine Taylor was her name. I'd met her briefly at my induction. A pretty young woman around my age, with olive skin and hazel eyes.

According to the detectives on the case, Christine was last seen leaving The Hoey Moey alone after finishing her shift. Raj and the staff on duty that evening were called in and questioned yesterday morning, but we haven't heard anything of interest since.

When Raj had initially told me the news, my thoughts had gone straight to Indi and the religious cult she'd been brought up in. I wondered how far their community extended. Suppose there were a group of them situated in Coffs Harbour, too. Thinking of Indi has me biting at the bit to get back to Coraki. I need to know what happened to her. I hope to God that her and Jerimiah's wedding was cancelled and that I've made Mr Walker think twice before ever raising his hand to her again.

I've had a lot of time to think things over during my stay at Rozelle Hospital, and I found myself wondering if the real reason young women like Indi are kept under ball and chain inside their community is so that nobody notices when they go missing. The local grocer said the group was into ritual sacrificing, and Indi said Jerimiah's first wife went missing without a trace.

If he or her father have... I shake my head, shooing away the dreadful thought. Until I know for sure what's happened to Indi, I'm still clinging to hope. That's all I've got.

"What happened to your hand?" Raj asks, watching intently as I try mimicking his table manners.

I wiggle my fingers out and grimace. My knuckles are sore, stiff, and a deep shade of purple.

Jackie's jaw drops when she catches sight of the nasty bruise. "You didn't get into a fight, *did you?*"

"No," I say, scoffing. "I tripped down the stairs."

"How?" Her eyes widen. "Oh my God, you had another blackout, *didn't you?*"

I roll my eyes in exasperation. "No. I tripped on my shoelace."

I don't really remember what I did to my hand. All I know is it started throbbing a couple of nights ago. Chances are I did have another blackout, but I'm not about to tell Jackie that. If she informs the hospital, I'll get re-admitted.

Noticing my frustration, Jackie quickly changes the subject. "What do you plan on doing this weekend?" She sips her wine. "Is there somewhere special you'd like to go? We could do the Mutton-bird Island Walk together and then grab some lunch by the Marina if you want. It'll be my treat."

This will be my last free weekend for some time. Raj had me undergo a bartending course over the past few days, and as of next week, I will be working part-time as a server at The Hoey Moey on a rotating roster. I know my sister is looking for an opportunity to hang out, and I feel awful about letting her down, but I need to take advantage of my one free weekend before it's too late.

"About that," I say, swallowing a mouthful of rice. "I was thinking of spending the weekend with a friend in Coraki."

The pair exchange anxious glances.

"Don't worry," I assure them. "I'll stay out of trouble. I promise."

I'm being mendacious, but a years' worth of therapy has taught me an invaluable lesson: people don't *really* want to hear the truth; they'd rather hear a white lie told convincingly.

Jackie cuts me a sharp look. "This isn't about drugs, is it? You promised you wouldn't—"

"It's not about drugs," I'm quick to assure her. "But if it'll give you peace of mind, you can test me when I get back. I'm merely looking to catch up with an old friend, is all."

She bites her lip in deliberation. "What if you have another one of your blackouts?"

Here we go again.

"I don't suffer from blackouts anymore," I argue, irrespective of the truth. "Not since I've stopped drinking and taking drugs. Come on, Jackie, I'm not a little kid anymore. I'm an adult, which means you don't need to keep an eye on me 24/7."

"I know that, but you're still my younger brother, and it's my responsibility to look out for you." It's clear Jackie's not happy about me going off on my own, especially to Coraki, but my eyes plead with her, and eventually, she concedes. "Okay, fine, but promise me you'll be safe. Bring the Nokia I gave you, and make sure you keep in touch while you're there."

"I will." I nod in agreement. "By the way, is there any chance either of you can drop me at the train station tomorrow morning?"

"I'll take you," Raj says. "I've got to head to The Hoey Moey in the morning, anyway. I'm meeting the detectives there. They're conducting further investigations."

I'M up bright and early the next morning, showered and dressed before six-thirty. The clothes Jackie bought me are clean-cut and well-fitted. Nothing screams "I've got money" like a legit pair of Guess jeans and a collared Calvin Klein shirt. Not to mention my new set of Nike Airs. I doubt if Indi will even recognise me without my gaunt face and tattered clothing.

I enter the kitchen to the inviting aroma of coffee. Raj is sitting at the breakfast bench on a swivel stool with a mug of coffee.

He points with a slice of toast, indicating the percolator. "It's still hot," he says.

I glance at the opal-faced clock on the wall behind him and shake my head.

Raj follows my gaze and gulps. "Golly, where'd the time go?" He takes one last chug of his coffee and then snatches up his car keys, leaving the rest of his toast. "We'd best hit the road."

When we step outside, he glances me up and down, brows puckered. "Say, how do you intend to get around in Coraki?"

My gaze lowers to my feet, and then back up at him.

"You're going to wear out your new soles." He gestures for me to get in the truck while he disappears around the corner for a moment and then remerges with a fancy, green BMX. He pops the bike into the back tray and then chains it down before hopping into the driver's seat beside me.

"You can borrow my bike, but don't lose it. When you leave it, remember to chain it up. The code to unlock it is your sister's birth date, so you shouldn't forget it."

I smile, truly grateful for the set of wheels. They'll save me a lot of time.

"By the way, I haven't told your sister about our altercation the other night," Raj says, and I scratch my head, wondering what altercation he's referring to. My gaze drifts to my bruised hand.

Did I hit him? Is that why he's been so crisp with me?

I don't want him or Jackie to know that I'm still suffering from blackouts, so I keep my mouth zipped and lower my head in shame.

"Jackie has gone out on a limb for you, so please don't let her down. We both want to see you turn your life around. You're a smart bloke with a lot of potential. You'll go places if you put your mind to it."

Guilt heats my cheeks for more reasons than one, and I squirm under his intense scrutiny.

As much as I want to do right by my sister Jackie, I can't turn my back on Indi. I'll do *whatever it takes* to get her away from the cult's clutches. Consequences be damned. I've already let her down once. I refuse to do it again.

THE TRAIN RIDE from Coffs Harbour to Casino takes two hours and forty minutes, and I spend the entire time staring out the window, thinking about Indi and what I might say if I *do* find her.

I'm so nervous about seeing her again, my palms are sweaty.

I hope she doesn't resent me for letting her down.

The township of Casino dates back to the 1840s, and the main roads are lined with heritage buildings that are old by Australian standards. A pang of guilt fills my chest as I pass some of the stores I've robbed. I don't like being back here. This town has memories attached to a life I'd rather forget. If it weren't for Indi, I would've never returned.

"There are no regrets in life, just lessons," Dr Ross' voice echoes in my ear.

If only I could believe her words.

By the time I arrive at my old street two hours later, my shirt and jeans are clinging to me with perspiration.

Thank God I remembered to put on deodorant.

I skid to a stop in front of the old, dilapidated shack, which had once been my home, and a sense of anxiety fills me. The front window has been fixed, but otherwise, it's still the same hellhole I was hauled away from a year ago. My eyes shift to the Walkers' place, and my gut churns. The blistered front door has been replaced with a new stained glass one, and the swing chair by the porch has been repainted with a fresh coat of white. From this angle, I can see Indi's bedroom window. It's partly open, just as it always used to be. This gives me a slither of hope she might still be living at home with her parents–and that she's still alive.

When Mr Walker and his wife were brought to the stand, they told the court that they didn't have a daughter. Plus, the authorities couldn't find any evidence of a young woman having ever lived in their house.

Indi's lifeless room springs to mind, and I can't blame the authorities for disregarding my claims. If I hadn't seen Indi slipping in and out of her window on occasion, I would have been sceptical, too.

Indi said Sergeant Adams was her uncle and that he and his wife were members of her twisted church group, but when he was put on the stand, he declared that he didn't have a niece. Furthermore, he claimed he thoroughly searched the house and found no signs of a young woman living inside.

When I mentioned Jerimiah and the satanic cult, I was laughed at, and immediately shut down.

My blood boils at the memory.

Not wanting to leave the bike right out the front, I pass by several houses before chaining Raj's bike to a telegraph pole, praying nobody comes by with a pair of bolt-cutters. My body thrums with adrenaline as I backtrack to the Walkers' yard on foot. I've been dreaming about this moment for over a year. I need to find Indi, prove she's real, and bring her father to justice.

A red Nissan sedan sits in the driveway. It's nothing flash, but it's a slight upgrade from the old beige Volvo that used to billow out thick, black smoke. The hunk of junk always left a hazy trail as it drove down the street. I wonder where they got the money for the trade-in. Mr Walker had cried poor on the stand, claiming his hefty medical bills were setting him back with his mortgage repayments.

And then a memory pops to mind. Jackie mentioned something about a fundraiser being put in place to save the Walkers from losing their house. I was heavily doped up on sedatives at the time, so my recollection is hazy at best, but it would explain the new door and car upgrade. I could've been the best thing that ever happened to Mr Walker. In injuring him, it seems I've set his family up in a comfortable position.

The irony of it.

My old driveway is empty, so I make my way down the side of the house to the backyard. I figure this way I'll be able to jump the fence without attracting the attention of the neighbours.

The old wooden fence still sags, but someone's knocked in a few star pickets and wound them to the posts with wire, stopping it from toppling right over.

As I hoist myself over the top, I catch sight of a swing set with an adjoined slippery slide.

Surprised, I land and stumble backwards, nearly tripping over a kid's yellow bicycle.

The Walkers didn't have a small child, and their yard was never this tidy.

My throat constricts.

Please don't tell me they've moved.

Without knowing their new address, I've got Buckley's chance of finding Indi before the weekend's out.

Plan (A) was to check her family home for her first.

If I couldn't find her, plan (B), was to threaten Mr Walker at knifepoint to lead me to Jerimiah.

Sergeant Adams is the only other cult member Indi mentioned, and I'm not about to go threatening him. He's one of the bastards who testified against me and contributed to my being institutionalised for a year.

I'm about to swing back over to my old driveway and head to the local grocer in search of answers when a tiny voice freezes me in place.

"The window," it whispers, sending chills down my spine. "Don't forget about the open window."

Forgoing all rationality, I race down the side of the house to Indi's bedroom window and use the latticework to hoist myself up. The weathered timber creaks, threatening to buckle beneath me. I'm twenty kilos heavier than I was a year ago. No drugs, decent meals, and mandatory exercise equals a brawnier new me.

A plastic sheet has been taped across the window opening, so I use a pocketknife I'd nabbed from Raj's desk drawer to slit around the edges before squeezing my shoulders together to slip through.

I'm only head and shoulders in when something solid smashes against my lower back. A curse word erupts from my lips, and I tumble back out, knocking my head on the window slider on my way out.

My body scarcely hits the grass when I receive another blow to my chest, leaving me gasping and winded.

A strangled yelp leaves my throat as I roll to avoid the next blow.

"Wait!" I yell, thrusting out a palm toward my attacker.

When I discover my attacker is a tall, raven-haired woman, my eyes bulge.

My breath catches as she elevates her muscular arms, ready to take her next strike. With a powerful thrust, the bat rushes towards me, and I brace myself for another painful blow. However, she stops short at the last second, her eyes flaring with surprise.

When I exhale in relief, she snaps back to herself, and her face hardens once more.

"Explain yourself," she orders, her tone harsh. "Or my next swing will take off your head."

CHAPTER II

JUNE 27TH, 1998

CORAKI, AUSTRALIA

∞ SHAINA ∞

H is bright eyes snap to mine, wide and pleading, and for a second, I nearly drop the bat. His complexion is hazelnut, yet his eyes are swampy-green with flecks of yellow. I've never seen such light irises paired with such deep brown skin. The contrast is striking, especially paired with a dark set of arching brows. No criminal has the right to look this good. It's a crime in itself.

He clutches his chest and winces, all the while keeping a wary eye on my bat. "I'm looking for my friend, Indiana."

My grip around the bat handle tightens. "There's no *Indiana* living here."

He manoeuvres himself onto his knees. "She used to live here. That there," he points to the window, "was her bedroom."

My eyes give a quick flick to the window before narrowing in on him in suspicion.

"*Really?* Because I've been living here a whole six months, and I don't recall having any housemates." I raise the bat threateningly. "The cops are on their way, so you may want to hurry up and rethink your story before you find yourself in the back of the paddy wagon."

"You called the cops?" The colour drains from his face. "You didn't have to do that. I'm not here to cause any trouble."

"Then explain yourself," I repeat. "And this time, I want the truth."

"I...ah." His gaze turns downcast. "I haven't seen Indi in over a year. I've been locked up in rehab for attacking her father under the influence."

My eyes flare in alarm.

"No, no, no... Please let me explain," he rushes to add. "Indi's father used to keep her hidden away in that bedroom..." Again, he points to the window. "Where he'd beat her and fill her head with nonsense. She said her family were a part of some sick religious cult, where the young women were kept under ball and chain." He swallows and then adds, "I was supposed to help her to escape, but our plans were derailed. You don't understand. I haven't seen or heard from her since the morning she disappeared from my bedroom, and I'm afraid her father or someone from her church group might have killed her as punishment for being caught with me. She said talking to boys outside of her church group was completely forbidden. They believed it would lead her straight to the Devil."

Rattled by his story, I ask, "If the man who lived here *did* have a daughter and he or the cult killed her, wouldn't townsfolk have noticed her disappearance and reported it? People don't generally tend to evaporate into thin air without questions being asked."

"Like I said, she and the other young women were kept under ball and chain."

Unconvinced, my gaze narrows in on him. "Where exactly are you from?"

He points to the dilapidated house next door, and I side-eye him in disbelief. He looks too clean-cut to have lived in that poverty-stricken hovel.

"Indi and I were neighbours," he insists earnestly. "She used to sneak out of her bedroom window at night to come and see me. I kept her safely hidden while her father was drunk and on a rampage."

"Tell me," I insist, needing something more solid than a tale to go on. "What was Indi's father's name?"

I should be sending him packing, not indulging him, but despite my reflex scepticism, something in his expression reads sincere.

"Mr Walker," he answers without hesitation. "Wyatt Walker."

My grip on the bat loosens as my thoughts spiral. Wyatt—the man who sold me this house—hadn't come across as the abusive type, and I don't recall him mentioning a daughter. I'd only been introduced to his wife and son.

Street angel, house Devil, comes a tucked-away thought. I, for one, know that folks aren't always what they seem. And what's more, I know what it's like to have an unhealthy father/daughter relationship. My father tried to kill me.

"You know him, don't you?" The intruder's face lights with hope. "You need to tell me where he is so I can find Indi."

Spine straightening, I ask, "What evidence do you have to back your claims?"

He swallows hard and lowers his face, appearing dejected. "You don't believe me, do you?"

"Do you have any proof to convince me otherwise?"

He shakes his head. "No."

"Well then, I think it's about time you left," I say, nodding towards the fence.

"What about the cops?"

I raise a curious brow. "Do you want to be arrested?"

"No."

"Then you'd best hurry up and get out of here before they arrive."

His eyes remain fixed on mine as he levers to his feet, his hand still clutching his chest.

I'm in the process of escorting him off my property when, to my surprise, my son, Isaac, calls, "Enzo. Hey, Enzo."

The intruder jerks around, wide-eyed, and I glance over my

shoulder to find Isaac's small, innocent face peering out at us from the open window. His face falters when he spots the bat in my hand.

I quickly slip the bat behind me, out of view.

"Isaac, what are you doing in there? You need to go back into the kitchen *right* now. I will be back inside with you shortly, okay?"

He ignores me, his eyes locked intently on the intruder. "Are you Enzo?"

"Indi used to call me Enzo," he says and starts making his way back over to the window.

A shiver runs through me, but I fight to stay in control.

"Don't even think about it," I warn, swinging the bat out in front of him like a barrier. "Who the hell are you?"

"I'm Monroe," he says simply. "Monroe Morgan, but Indi would call me Enzo."

"Allow me to rephrase..." My voice takes on a razor-sharp edge. "How the hell does my son know who you are?"

"It's okay, Ma," Isaac calls. "Indi has been expecting Enzo; she's left messages for him. You should come inside and check them out."

Indi's name circles inside my brain, failing to strike a chord. I glance between the pair, brows knitted. *How does Isaac know who Indi is, yet I don't? Clearly, I'm missing something.*

When the intruder looks to me for guidance, Isaac grows insistent. "Ma, please. Enzo needs to come inside."

My focus settles on the intruder, whose bright eyes are pleading with me, and my implacable façade crumbles.

He looks genuine, I tell myself, *and he's well-dressed. The least you can do is give him the benefit of the doubt.*

"Okay, fine, Monroe, Enzo, or whatever your name is," I concede, and his eyes brighten. "You can come inside. But you're not to touch anything, and you're not to stay. You are to take your messages and go. We never want to see you back here again; you got that?"

He gives a slow but eager nod. "Sure thing, Miss. And for the record, I prefer Monroe. Only Indi ever called me Enzo."

"Noted." I lead him across the yard to the back steps, all the while second-guessing my decision.

I must be insane.

The door bursts open before we reach it.

"Come on." Isaac bounces foot to foot. "Follow me."

As he leads us down the hall to "Indi's room", my nose crinkles in protest. The scent of mould and wood rot is *so* thick in the air, I can taste it. We usually keep the spare room shut off from the rest of the house—as though it doesn't exist. The window inside won't close. It's jammed open. It was like that when I purchased the place. It's how I got the property for a steal. I plan on fixing it eventually, but it's a matter of time and money.

Owen, my ex, helped tape plastic over the window opening so the rain didn't come in, and ripped out the musty, shagpile carpet. He did a bit of maintenance around the place to make it liveable, but I didn't want him coming around every weekend to help fix things. I needed to be self-reliant, and I had no desire for his company—or his pity.

My feet abruptly halt at the entryway, and my eyes dart from wall to wall, the burn of fear rising inside my throat.

"Holy Mother of..." All four walls have been painted—floor to ceiling—with cursive writing and eerie symbols. I stare at the rusty, reddish-brown colour of the lettering and gulp. "Is that...blood?"

Monroe accidentally rams into my back.

"Sorry, I didn't..." He stops short when he sees what I'm seeing and gasps. "Well, I'll be damned."

He rights himself and steps around me to take a closer look, and then after a long moment of staring incredulously, he says, in almost a whisper, "Psychosis diagnosis, my ass."

Panic shoots through me. This Monroe fellow isn't the first intruder to enter my property. His friend, Indi, has managed to break in and deface my walls in, God only knows what that substance is. I sincerely hope it's *NOT* blood.

Brain firing with alarm, I turn to Isaac for answers.

"How long has *this*," I gesture widely around the room, "been here?" When he stays mute, I persist. "Did you see Indi do this?"

Monroe's ears perk at the question, but Isaac merely lowers his head, keeping his eyes downcast.

Clearly, he's withholding information from me, but I don't continue pressing the matter in front of Monroe.

Monroe walks over to a section that says, "Save me, Enzo," and runs a finger along the name.

My gaze falls upon the sentence, "The Devil will rise out of me and set this whole blasted world aflame," and fear wins over.

"Okay, that's it," I say, "I'm calling the cops."

Monroe swings to face me, brows puckered. "I thought you'd already called them?"

I hadn't. I was using scare tactics.

Realising this, Monroe pleads with me. "Don't alert them yet. They'll only poke around and start asking questions again, putting Wyatt on high alert. We need to find Indi before he has a chance to hide her again. He needs to be stopped."

"There is no 'we'," I reply. "This is *my* house," I sling an arm around Isaac, "and *my* son. I can't have people sneaking into my house and vandalising it. I need to protect my family, and my property."

"Then help me to find Mr Walker so we can put a stop to this." Monroe clasps his hands together, pleadingly. "He's a bad man who needs to be brought to justice. He used to beat on Indi and tell her she had the Devil inside her."

Indulging him once more, my eyes flick wall to wall.

"Look," he urges. "Read what's been written. Indi is a victim, and she needs our help. Please, help me, to help her, and then I'll leave you and your son alone for good."

Monroe's eyes leave mine to roam over the symbols and sentences again. "There's got to be a clue in here, somewhere. Look for a hidden street name or landmark." He points to a large symbol and says, "I recognise this from somewhere, but I just can't place it."

As I scan over the sentence, "They can break my body, but they can't break my soul", I shudder.

Dark clouds hover in my mind, curbing my thoughts. *Street angel, house Devil.*

If Monroe's story about Indi is true, and I turn a blind eye, then I'm as guilty as Mr Walker.

"I, ah..." The words feel thick, and stick in my throat. "I may know where the Walkers have moved to."

Monroe's face snaps to mine, interest piqued. "Where?"

My spine steels with caution. "What exactly do you plan on doing with this information?"

"I plan on doing whatever it takes to get Indi out of her father's clutches."

He stares at me expectantly, but I don't offer up the address right away. I've got a few questions I want answered first. I could very well be opening a can of worms.

"If what you're saying is true, then I know someone who might be able to help us."

Monroe's brow crinkles. "Who?"

"The 'who' isn't what's important. Why don't we make our way to the kitchen, and I'll fix you a drink while you fill me in on the backstory of the Walkers."

Hope glitters in his eyes as he accepts my offer.

I give Isaac's hair a light ruffle, hoping to Christ I'm making the right move here.

"You need to go to your room and play for a bit, okay? And don't come out until I say so."

CHAPTER 12
JUNE 27TH, 1998
CORAKI, AUSTRALIA
∞ MONROE ∞

The woman offers me a seat on the couch. I rest a cushion behind my back and rehash the same story I've repeated to the doctors and authorities over a hundred times since the day of my arrest. I start with the first night I met Indi and gradually work my way up to the day of her disappearance.

My eighteenth birthday. The day we were supposed to be making our big escape.

I refrain from mentioning anything about Indi's ex-boyfriend, Enzo. I'm afraid it'll destroy my credibility given I'd made it sound as though Indi had nicknamed me Enzo when, truthfully, it was just a case of mistaken identity. Needless to say, I don't share how gutted I was to discover that my name wasn't even written *once* on any of the four walls. Indi is all I've thought about this past year, yet it's clear she's still caught up on Enzo. If I were smart, I'd jump on the next train to Coffs Harbour never to return. It's heartbreakingly obvious now that Indi was just using me, but regardless of the fact, I can't bring myself to leave without knowing what's happened to her.

The raven-haired woman interjects here and there, reiterating some points, and asking pertinent questions, showing she's actively listening and engrossed in my story. Her face is refined with a straight nose and high cheekbones, yet her shoulders are broad like a rower's, giving the appearance of equal strength and beauty.

I wonder how old she is. She looks to be in her early twenties, but her kid is at least five, which means she would've been awfully young when she'd had him.

If he hadn't called her Ma, I would never have placed him as her son. They share no resemblance bar their hair colour. She has creamy-coloured skin with European features, while he has dark skin with Polynesian features.

I conclude my story with the saga of my violent encounter with Mr Walker, and she stares fixedly, making me squirm.

"So, you mean to tell me that you shot Mr Walker through the leg with a spear gun, all because he wouldn't tell you where he was keeping his daughter hidden? Are you insane?"

Agitated and somewhat uncomfortable under her scrutiny, I lean forward and take another sip of the water she's given me.

"The jury thought as much and saw to it that I was locked up. But the truth is Mr Walker deserved far worse than a punctured leg. The man is the epitome of evil. He clearly got pleasure out of beating his wife and daughter, and I wasn't about to let him get away scot-free."

"But he still got away with his crimes while you found yourself locked up. In hurting him, you only managed to hurt yourself. Had you kept your cool and explained the situation to the authorities, they might've taken your allegations more seriously."

"According to Indi, the local sergeant is a bad egg, so it was no good asking him for help." I cross my arms and fall back into the cushion. "Mr Walker is lucky I didn't kill him for all he's done. I wanted to. Christ, I wanted to."

The raven-haired woman leans forward and places a warm hand on my knee, taking me by surprise. I figured she'd be gearing up to throw me out, not comfort me.

"I'm sure the local Sergeant isn't as bad as you think. Next time, strike with your brain, not with your brawn. If Mr Walker is hiding his daughter, I can help you to find her, but we need to handle this situation with caution."

My stomach flips.

She believes me, I realise. *And what's more, it sounds as though she is willing to help me.*

"Well... What do you propose we do?" I ask.

She ponders a moment before snatching her hand back and rising to her feet.

"Wait here. I'll be back in a minute." Without another word she heads to the hallway and disappears from my sight.

After several moments of sitting and not-so-patiently waiting, I stand and wander around the room. Flashes of Mr and Mrs Walker enter my mind, making my pulse quicken. Had I not been too worked up to think straight, I might have seen through Mr Walker's trickery and outsmarted him, but the sound of Indi's blood-curdling screams had me lost in a frenzy.

Just off the living room is the kitchen. It has lime green bench-tops with laminate-wooden doors, courtesy of the '70s.

I spot a pile of letters on the benchtop, and my innate curiosity draws me to them. I flick through the envelopes and come across late notices and an overdue electricity bill addressed to Shaina Anderson. Going by the sole name on the envelopes, I'm guessing Shaina's a single mother. It's also clear she's struggling.

I wonder what her story is.

She's been gone awhile, which makes me wary, so I slink into the hallway to see what she's up to. It's hard to say if she's being real with me or setting me up for a fall. While she seems genuine enough, I've been tricked by pretty faces before.

I head to the door, which sits open ajar, and halt outside. When I catch wind of Shaina's voice, I edge closer, pressing my ear to the gap to listen.

"I'm not calling you for the third degree, Owen. I'm calling you for a favour, so will you help me or not?"

A beat passes.

"That's so typical. I'm sure if it were *Victoria* asking you for the favour, you wouldn't hesitate." She spits the name "Victoria" with venom.

"I just want to know what Mr Walker's story is; what it says in his records, that's it. I think some very awful things happened in this house."

Another beat passes.

"And you didn't think to say anything before now?"

Going by Shaina's response, I'm guessing Owen knows something.

Owen must apologise and offer up something of interest because Shaina's tone softens.

"I won't share it with anyone, I promise. You can trust me."

One last beat.

"Okay, sure. I'll see you at seven."

The click of the phone being set back in its cradle has me backtracking into the living room. I don't think Shaina would take too kindly, knowing I was eavesdropping on her conversation.

I make it back to the couch in the nick of time. As she re-enters, I twiddle my thumbs, giving the illusion that I've been waiting patiently all along.

"I have someone looking into Mr Walker." She doesn't take a seat. "But I won't have any answers until tomorrow."

"Who?" I ask, hoping to get more details on Owen. If he's a cop, I'm screwed. The authorities have nothing on Mr Walker, and Sergeant Adams is linked with Indi's church group. The finger will only be pointed back in my direction.

"As I said, the 'who' isn't important. You should come back tomorrow afternoon, and I'll share what I've discovered." She pauses a moment before adding, "Make it around two in the afternoon. I have a few errands to run in the morning."

Her face is tight and irritated. It seems this *Owen* guy, whoever he is, has gotten under her skin.

I want to ask if we could speak with her son again. There are some questions I'd love to run by him, but I realise I'd be pushing my luck. She's already been far more understanding than I deserve, given the circumstances. I'm lucky she's helping me at all.

Taking her cue to leave, I stand and nod appreciatively. "Sure thing, Miss."

"My name is Shaina," she offers.

She walks me to the door and watches closely as I leg it to Raj's bike. I'm relieved to find it's still chained up where I'd left it. Had it been pinched, Jackie would've been *very* disappointed in me.

I groan at the thought of having to convince her that I need to stay in Coraki until Monday morning. I'm supposed to be starting my first shift at The Hoey Moey tomorrow evening, but there's no way I'll even get to Casino Station by tomorrow evening if I'm meeting Shaina back here at two.

I'll have to think long and hard about what excuse I'm going to give, but first, I need to work out where I'm sleeping for the next two nights. I wish I really did have a friend to stay with. It's been a long while since I've had to sleep on the streets.

CHAPTER 13

JUNE 27TH, 1998

CORAKI, AUSTRALIA

∞ SHAINA ∞

After seeing Monroe off, I head straight to Isaac's room. There are so many questions running through my head right now, and I'm hoping he can answer some of them.

When I open the door, he's sitting on his bed, playing with a set of Ninja Turtle figurines.

I pop down beside him, and he offers me Raphael. "Do you wanna play?"

Eager to win his trust before jumping straight into interrogation mode, I accept the turtle and mimic the fighting stances and sounds he's exhibiting with Leonardo.

He shoots me a stern look and snatches the turtle back off me.

"Raphael doesn't fight like that. He uses twin sai, not a sword. He fights like this." He does a quick demonstration of how the weapons are supposed to be used before handing back the figurine.

I give it another whirl, but his frustrated expression tells me I'm not meeting his expectations as a sparring partner.

Sighing in defeat, I set the figure down.

"I was actually hoping to talk to you about Indi."

Isaac continues playing with Leonardo as though I haven't said anything.

I place my hands on his arms, bringing Leonardo's swing kick to a halt.

"I need you to tell me more about Indi," I insist. "When and where did you see her?"

His eyes lower to his bedspread. "I've seen her lots of times. She comes in and out through her bedroom window."

"But we have plastic taped across the window," I point out.

"Don't you ever wonder how it keeps coming undone?"

A sense of unease spreads through me. "It only comes undone when it storms," I maintain. "And I fix it straight afterwards, every time."

"That's when I see her most," he says so casually, it gives me goosebumps. "When it's storming."

My anxiety peaks, but I work hard to keep my composure.

"When you see Indi, does she speak to you?"

He nods, prompting me to persist.

"What does she speak to you about?"

"She says her father gets real mad and hits her when he's been drinking, so she jumps out the window and hides before he gets home. She also says that Enzo was going to save her, but he left without a word. She talks about running away to find him, but she's scared that if she does, and her father catches her, she'll be punished for giving in to the Devil." He glances up at me. "That's why I was glad when he came back. If he saves her, she won't have to jump out the window anymore, so we can finally close it."

The hairs at the back of my neck stand to attention. Isaac's story lines up perfectly with Monroe's story, even down to the fact he said Indi called him Enzo. What I don't understand, though, is why Indi keeps coming back to her old room.

Taking a minute to process my thoughts, I pause before asking, "What does Indi look like?

"She has really white skin." His brows furrow in thought a moment before adding, "Like milk."

"What about her hair and eyes?"

"Her hair is orange," he answers promptly. "Like fire. And her eyes are white... no..." He shakes his head and ponders a moment before correcting himself. "Light blue. Like an iceberg."

She's Caucasian with light eyes and orange hair, I repeat in my mind. *Just like Wyatt.*

This is all the confirmation I need to start digging.

"Say, why don't you go and see what those Jones boys are doing?" I suggest. "I have to go to the supermarket soon, and I'm sure taking a bike ride with the neighbours beats meandering the grocery aisles with your Ma."

Isaac's eyes meet mine, sparkling with excitement. "Really?"

I nod. "After the morning we've had, I think a bit of fresh air will do you good."

After walking Isaac to the Jones' and okaying the bike ride with the boys' mother, I go back home, grab my camera, and then head to the Walkers' new address.

I don't need any groceries. I need more answers.

CHOOSING A GOOD VANTAGE POINT, I pull to the curb diagonally across from the Walkers' residence, place my car into park, and then open my street directory, pretending to look inside. Meanwhile, I'm peeking above the open book, scoping the property for anything out of the ordinary. I note that all the windows on this side of the house have dark-coloured curtains covering the windows. It seems a bit odd to have blackouts drawn during the middle of the day unless they have something inside to hide. I'd really like to get out and investigate the property closer, but there's a car parked in the driveway, so I'm presuming they're home.

While the Walkers' new home is a definite upgrade from the

run-down shack I'm currently occupying, their property upkeep hasn't improved any. The grass on their front lawn is unkept, while the neighbours' yards are trimmed and neat. As I zoom my focus in on a neglected garden with overgrown shrubs, I discover a life-size statue of Jesus hidden in the tangle of red and white rose bushes.

The holy display collaborates with Monroe's claim about the Walkers being religious, although whether they are truly a part of a cult or not, I'm yet to determine.

I've carefully lifted my camera above the book to take a few snaps when a tap on my driver's window startles me, and I accidentally drop both the book and camera in a knee-jerk reaction.

Heart racing, I twist around to find James, Wyatt's son, peering in at me through the glass. He's broader with more facial hair than the last time I'd seen him, but his blue, downturned eyes are the same as I remember.

He stares questioningly as I wind my window down.

All the while, I berate myself for not being more cautious. Owen would have a field day if he were here to witness my screwup. I'd never hear the end of it.

"Can I help you there?"

When our eyes meet, recognition lights James' face. "Beg my pardon, Mrs Adams, but I thought you were—" His eyes lower to the camera, sitting skewwhiff on my lap, and he frowns. "What exactly are you doing here?"

I no longer go by Mrs Adams. I've reverted back to my maiden name, Anderson, but I don't correct him.

"My apologies," I say, thinking fast. "I've come to pay your parents a visit. I want to inquire about joining their church group."

Noting James' disbelieving gaze, I quickly gesture to the front yard and add, "And then when I pulled up and saw their glorious garden, I couldn't help but take a picture."

James' eyes flick to the overgrown garden, and I can tell by the crease of his brows he still isn't sold, so I tack on, "I've taken up

photography recently. I've been told it will help with my anxiety."
And the lies keep rolling off the tongue.

"Right." There's a hint of scepticism in his tone, telling me I
wasn't quite as convincing as I'd hoped. "Well, my parents are
inside."

There's no worming my way out of this one without it looking
even more suspicious, so I suck in a deep breath, open the car door,
and follow James up the front porch to the entryway.

This could work to my advantage, I tell myself. *The answers I'm
looking for are inside.*

James unlocks the front door and leads me down an olive-
coloured hallway to the kitchen. I note all the religious ornaments on
the sideboard and an enormous crucifix hanging on the wall directly
above them. My nose crinkles as we proceed down the hall. There's a
pungent smell in the air, which only intensifies as we round the
corner to the kitchen/dining area—and I soon discover why.

Ruth, Wyatt's wife, is by the kitchen countertop, hacking a whole
pig's hide with an overly large kitchen knife. I pause by the table and
swallow my nerves. She sure knows how to put her shoulder into it.

"Mrs Adams." She greets me with an enquiring smile. "What
brings you here, my dear?"

James continues striding through the kitchen, exiting out the
back laundry door.

"I'm looking for some extra guidance," I say, feeding the lie. "And
I remember you mentioning that you were a part of a church group. I
was wondering..." My fingers twiddle at my sides. "Is your denomination open to newcomers?"

Ruth sets her knife down, putting me mildly at ease.

"Why, of course, dear. There's no need for a formal invitation.
Our Church is open for mass every Sunday. God welcomes all."

I place a hand over my chest, acting pleased. "That's wonderful. I
was—"

Wyatt hobbles in through the laundry, looking like a Golem, and
kicks off his mucky gumboots.

"Why, hello, Mrs Adams. It's good to see you." The smile he gives is warmer than his wife's. He's round and friendly-faced. He doesn't strike me as an abuser. However, they do say it's often the ones you least expect.

Street angel, house Devil.

"James tells me you're looking to reconnect with The Lord."

We never had a connection to begin with, I think, although I keep my mouth shut and nod eagerly.

"Well, it seems you've caught us at the perfect time," he continues. "I'm about to wash up and then head over to the chapel. I promised Father Divine if I caught enough crabs, I'd bring him some over this evening, and I caught myself plenty." He glances at his wife while still speaking to me. "I'm sure Ruth will fix you with some fresh orange juice while I get cleaned up."

I'm about to decline the juice when Ruth promptly places a couple of glasses down and starts pouring.

"Come and take a seat," she says, leaving the board of half-chopped pig's hide to join me at the table.

We run through the usual small talk and niceties; however, the way Ruth's eyes bore questioningly into mine suggests she wonders what my agenda is. Just popping in out of the blue seems suspicious—and for good reason, but I'm sus of her, too. When she tries digging deeper to see what's really brought me here, I tell her I'm still struggling with my and Owen's break up and that I'm finding it hard to move forward. It's far from the truth, but I do my best to make it sound believable. The only thing that's stopping me from moving forward in life is money.

In Owen's defence, he has offered me far more help than I've accepted these past few months, but I don't like the feeling of being indebted to anyone, and Owen has a way of making me feel *just that*.

Eventually, Wyatt rejoins us in the kitchen, smelling of sandalwood instead of muck and fish. I swallow down the rest of my juice—praying I haven't been drugged—and then ask to use the bathroom.

The pair share a furtive glance before Wyatt points down the hallway and says, "The toilet is the second door to the right."

The hum of their whispers carries as I make my way down the hall, but their words are indistinguishable. This, combined with their stiff body language and furtive glances, suggests they really do have something to hide.

When I get to the first door on the right, I glance behind me to see if they're following. They're not, and James is still outside, so I take the opportunity to snoop with my one and only chance.

I grab hold of the doorknob and attempt to twist it, but the knob won't budge. It's locked. My heart thumps as the idea of Indi being locked inside becomes all too real. I glance over my shoulder again, and when I see that nobody has rounded the hall, I give the door a light tap. There's a slight scratching sound.

"Indi," I whisper.

Nothing.

I place my ear against the door and call her name under my breath once more.

Nothing. Damn it!

I rush to try the other two doors and they both open with the slightest of squeaks, revealing ordinary but dated bedrooms, smelling of must and mothballs.

Wyatt catches me closing the second bedroom door on the left, and I jump. "I've never been any good with my lefts and rights," I say, playing it off and then scoot across the hall to the correct door.

When I've finished sifting through the bathroom cabinet, I flush the toilet and run the tap for a moment–keeping my cover–before making my way back to the kitchen. There were some drugs I hadn't recognised, so I'd written their names down on the notepad inside my purse, but as for all the other items inside, they all seemed unremarkable.

"Are you ready?" Wyatt asks, plucking his keys from the bench with a jingle. I nod, and he leans over the kitchen countertop to kiss his wife on the cheek. "We'll be back before supper."

Out front, James slips through the side gate, carrying a small green cooler, which he places into the car's boot.

Wyatt reaches up to cup James' shoulder. He isn't a particularly tall man, plus his bad leg causes him to slump to the right, making him appear even shorter.

"Thanks, Son, you're such a good help. I'd be lost without you."

I riffle through my bag for my keys, preparing to follow him.

"No point in us taking separate cars," Wyatt says, putting me ill at ease. "I'll drive."

His logic makes perfect sense, but I can't say I like it.

I assume James is coming with us, but as Wyatt and I hop into the car and buckle up, James slips back through the side gate. My lungs decompress with a puff of relief. If Wyatt were to attack me, I'd stand a good chance of fighting him off. James, on the other hand, is tall and broad. Owen may have shown me a handful of self-defence moves, but I'm no Lara Croft.

"He's a good kid," Wyatt says proudly, following my line of sight. "He comes home from college one weekend a month to help with the lawns and other maintenance. No matter how old and busy he gets, he's still willing to give his old man a helping hand."

My thoughts slip to the locked bedroom.

Could Wyatt really be so cruel as to sit here and lovingly praise his son while keeping his daughter locked away in a bedroom?

The face of my father appears in the forefront of my mind, and hateful energy burns within me, but on the surface, I smile and say, "You're a lucky man, Wyatt."

"What about your son? Isaac, isn't it?"

I give an anxious nod, not wanting to talk about my son.

"How's he doing? I bet he's getting big."

"He is," I say, keeping it short.

Once we're on the road, Wyatt switches to tour-guide mode, which I'm far more comfortable with. He points out a few of the neighbours' properties and gives me the low down on the residents. He's familiar with a lot of the locals through the church, and if I didn't know any better, I would believe they were a close and caring community who looked out for one another.

The car Wyatt drives is manual, and as he reaches for the stick, I can't help but glance at his hand. His knuckles are silvery with scars.

"What happened to your hand?" I ask.

If he'd received the scars from beating up his daughter, he'd never admit it, but I'm interested in hearing what he comes up with.

"I got my hand caught in a broken crab trap." He glances my way momentarily with a look I can't decipher. "It wasn't pretty either; I can tell you that."

Eventually, we make it to the front of the Church. The building is red-bricked, with tall piers and a gabled roof. A set of symmetrically placed pointed-arch windows line the façade, matching the shape of the pointed-arch doorway. There's also a quartet of circular windows, set in a large circular stone feature towards the peak, which looks—to me—like a clothing button. I've passed this church countless times over the years, but I've never paid it any mind. I've never had a reason to.

When Wyatt finishes filling me in on the history of the Church and the primary school that backs onto it, he exits the car, and I follow suit. He pops the car's boot and asks if I would mind grabbing the cooler for him to save him from struggling with it.

Peering inside the cluttered space, I see knives, scissors, pliers, lines, ropes, nets, and a tacklebox, which are all used for fishing, *but could they be used for something else without raising suspicion?*

My thoughts darken with sickening scenarios.

"Are you coming?" Wyatt calls, having started off without me.

I shake away the disturbing imagery, snap the boot shut again, and follow.

As I step through the set of pale blue double doors, I'm surprised to find that the inside of the church feels warm and friendly. I'd been expecting it to be dark and sinister. If there *is* any pain and suffering going on inside these holy walls, it's being well hidden.

We find Father Divine sitting at a desk in the vestry, sorting through a pile of books and paperwork. He looks to be in his late sixties with papery skin and white hair.

When he sees us coming, he stands and greets Wyatt with a friendly smile, all the while shooting me a questioning glance.

"Who do we have here?" he asks, looking me up and down in a way that makes me feel inadequate.

"This is Shaina Adams," Wyatt answers before I get the chance. "She's the woman who bought my old property a couple of years back."

Just like with Wyatt and Ruth, the men exchange a furtive glance.

"What brings you here this evening, Shaina?" Father Divine asks.

I give him the same spiel I'd given Ruth, stealing the line James had fed Wyatt to seal the deal.

"I'm looking to reconnect with God."

Father Divine asks me about my religious beliefs, making my insides squirm. I may not be a woman of faith, but answering these questions dishonestly "in the house of God" still feels somewhat scandalous and wrong. In the end, I swallow my qualms and remind myself that I'm here for a greater purpose. I'm here to help save Indi and all the other young women who are being mistreated in the name of their religion.

After a brief tour of the chapel and surrounding yard, Wyatt and Father Divine slip off, telling me they need to discuss a private matter.

I nod and take a seat on a nearby pew, bowing my head as if in prayer. However, once they're out of sight, I launch back up again, taking the opportunity to peer inside one of the rooms they'd skipped during the tour.

The door squeaks when I open it. It's dark, like the evening sky outside, making it hard to see more than two feet inside. I try flicking on the light switch, but it appears to be broken. A shiver runs through me.

Perhaps they skipped this room for a reason.

"Hello? Is anybody in here?" I call in a whisper.

Silence. No answer doesn't mean no one's there. If what Monroe says is true, then these young women could be drugged, gagged, or worse.

Erring on the side of caution, I hold my arms out in front of me and use them as feelers as I carefully step further inside.

A few feet in, something brushes against my shoulder, and I yelp instinctively before slapping a hand over my mouth and cursing at myself for the outburst.

Now on edge, I feel around with my other hand, assessing the area. When my fingers tangle in a soft, stringy mane, my heart just about bursts out of my chest.

"Someone's really in here!" My brain screams in a panic.

It's not until I tap my way down to a long wooden stick that relief washes over me with a dizzying effect.

It's just the woolly end of a shag mop, you idiot! Get a grip on yourself.

Further examination by touch tells me it's held in a rack with what feels like a broom, dust-busters, and other cleaning essentials.

I'm in a storeroom.

Despite discovering this and having uncovered the culprit of my outburst, I'm still sweating profusely under pressure.

I'd make a terrible detective.

Finding my voice again, although a little more choked up this time around, I repeat, "Is anybody in here? Don't be afraid. I'm here to help."

Dead silence. Chances are this is just a regular storeroom with a blown light bulb, I tell myself, backpedalling towards the door. *There's no resounding evidence to prove otherwise.*

To stay and investigate further without the use of a flashlight would be a waste of time, and I'm under a time constraint.

Besides, had I found someone, what was I planning on doing with them? Did I think I was going to just carry them out to Wyatt's car and demand he take us to the Police Station? The Walkers and Father Divine are the only ones who know I'm here. If I were to threaten to expose their secrets, I could end up becoming their next victim.

It's blindingly obvious I have no idea what I'm doing. I should have waited until I'd spoken to Owen before approaching the Walkers, not that I'd *actually* planned on approaching them. I only wanted to scope out their house.

What are Wyatt and Father Divine secretly discussing, anyhow? How I'm to be dealt with?

Coming here alone with Wyatt might've been a huge mistake.

I get back to the pew before Wyatt and Father Divine notice I'm missing, and I'm glad when Wyatt eventually returns and says it's time to go.

He's unusually quiet on the way home to the point where it's unnerving. I catch his face twitching on several occasions, as if he wants to say something but then thinks better of it.

When we pull into the driveway, I reach to unplug my seatbelt in a hurry. However, Wyatt covers my hand with his, trapping the button beneath.

My eyes snap to his in alarm. "Wha—"

"Just because I talk slow don't mean I'm stupid." He lets the words hang in the air a moment before adding, "I know why you're here, and it ain't got nothing to do with reconnecting with God. I've heard the stories circling the neighbourhoods, and I know there are folks out there who still believe the accusations made against me, even though I've been proven innocent. There are always young folks sneaking around our property at this time of year, peeking through the windows and taking pictures. Why do you think we got blackouts put up?"

He sighs. "They say if you throw enough mud at someone, it'll stick, and my family are victims of that-there saying."

My hand squirms under his. "I'm not sure what you're—"

"James saw the camera," he says over the top of me. "And Father Divine and I tested your sincerity, and you failed."

The intensity of his gaze has me glancing away. I can't face the indignity of being caught in a lie.

"I need to go," I say, admitting to nothing. "I have dinner to make."

Wyatt releases my hand but adds firmly. "Don't be fooled by the rumours, Shaina. My family and I are good, honest people who stay true to God's commandments—*unlike some.*"

The accusation behind his words grazes me.

"Goodbye, Mr Walker," I manage before closing the car door behind me.

CHAPTER 14

1968 - 1978

SPRINGWOOD, AUSTRALIA

∞ ENZO ∞

It was the evening of the Winter Solstice, June 21st, 1968, that I decided I needed to leave the Blue Mountains. I'd thought that participating in Jerimiah's "Ageless Sacrifice" ceremony with reluctant acquiesce would've bought my mama and me more time and peace for several years to come, but I'd been wrong. Jerimiah stayed in Australia. He got a transfer from Austin State Hospital, Austin, Texas, to Callan Park Hospital, Lilyfield, Sydney. He spent his weekdays working in Sydney and the weekends socialising in Springwood. It was his way of taunting me. Of never letting me forget he was there. I was at his mercy.

Sitting at the kitchen table, I stared at the front door, a bottle of whiskey clutched in my hand. My heart was racing, and sweat dripped from my temples. It was the middle of winter, but my body was on fire. I was afraid that at any moment Jerimiah would come knocking on the door to drag me out for another one of his ceremonies.

The nights were getting harder, and I'd taken to drinking. Sleep evaded me. I would toss and turn, trying desperately to catch a little shut-eye, and even if I succeeded, my mind would torture me with hellish visions and dreams. The shadow around me had increased tenfold, and I could feel it smothering me with its darkness. I was suffocating.

To my relief, Jerimiah never came to get me that night, but I knew it was only a matter of time until he would call upon me again. I couldn't handle the thought of knowing he was close by. I could feel him watching me like a lion watches its prey. He was toying with me.

Mama and I put our place on the market, and I hunted down a place by the Richmond River in Coraki, located in The Northern Rivers.

Mama had struggled during the cold winters in the Blue Mountains, so I'd figured a move north was exactly what she needed.

Coraki was a small, friendly town, much like Springwood, but it was more remote.

Despite having moved far away from Jerimiah, my hellish dreams and visions escalated with the months that passed. They were a constant reminder of him. Some nights I drank myself to sleep while other nights I laid there sweating and shaking.

Come January 1970, dread rocked me to my core when Jerimiah strutted into the Coraki Hotel and took a seat next to me at the bar.

He called the bartender over. "Say, can you pour another whiskey for my old friend here? It looks like he could use another drink." He placed a twenty-dollar bill on the bar. "And I'll take a gin and tonic."

I accepted the drink because I needed it to steady my nerves.

"What are you doing here?" I asked coldly. I knew he wasn't here for the Winter Solstice. It was midsummer. "Have you come to torture me some more?"

"You don't look too good, my old friend," he said, eyeing me over. "Your face might be youthful, but your eyes are rheumy, and your skin is blotchy. It looks as though the years have taken a toll on your health."

"You mean you've taken a toll on my health."

A sly smile curled his lips. "What if I were to tell you, I have a plan that could ease the darkness from your mind?"

I downed the drink and slammed the tumbler on the bar, standing to leave. "I would say I wasn't interested."

"Even if it meant bringing you back to your former self?"

I hesitated a moment. The idea of being well again was a dream come true, but I didn't trust Jerimiah and his sly smile.

"All I want is for you to leave me and my Mama alone," I said, and then left.

In the months that followed, the nights grew worse, and my health faded rapidly. Worst still, Jerimiah managed to catch me everywhere I went, getting up in my face and pushing his proposal onto me. He wanted to start another Church of Salvation in Coraki, and he said he needed my help to get it up and running. Still, I refused.

By the time June came around, I felt close to death. Instead of me taking care of my elderly mama, my elderly mama was taking care of me. For a woman who couldn't see, she seemed to see everything and manoeuvred through the house like a woman half her age. It was as though her sixth sense had kicked into overdrive.

"Think about what you're doing, Enzo," she'd said, without me having told her anything about Jerimiah and his somewhat tempting proposal. "Your health is fading because you've been using dark magic, which means if you let any more darkness in, it'll consume you completely, just like it did, your pa."

It's already consuming me, I'd thought.

"Jerimiah is still using dark magic, and he doesn't appear to be feeling the effects of the darkness."

"He is still transferring his darkness onto others, forcing innocents to suffer in his place. The man is pure evil in my book." Mama put a cold cloth to my forehead. "Promise me you'll never stoop to that level again. You may have been naïve the first time around, but you know better now."

I closed my eyes, unable to meet hers. It was getting to the point where I would willingly sell my soul to the Devil to rid myself of the torture I felt.

Later that week, the "Devil" found me by the bar with a whiskey in hand.

"Well, my friend, it's time to make your decision," Jerimiah said. "I can use this coming Winter Solstice to do a ceremony to heal you, but in return, you *will* help me to start a Church of Salvation here in Coraki. What do you say?"

I said yes and woke up the next morning to discover Jerimiah had hung his symbol on Mama's porch, marking her, or perhaps both of us, as his property.

"Don't pretend to be surprised," my mama said, reading my mind. "He marked me as his property long before he marked my house. *He* knows where I am and where I've been, and he can inflict whatever he wants on me, yet I'm unable to do a thing about it. The connection only goes one way, and it's irreversible. You, however," her tone was biting, "Chose to partake in evil dealings of your own free will."

She placed a suitcase in front of me.

"You're my son Lorenzo, and I'll always love you, but while you're associating with Jerimiah, I want nothing to do with you. You've chosen the selfish path, and I can't forgive that. I think it's time for you to find somewhere else to live."

She paid a man down the road to paint her porch ceiling haint-blue and to hang blue glass bottles upside down from the trees in the front garden, as a talisman to ward off evil spirits.

Meanwhile, I moved into an old caravan on Jerimiah's sixty-acre property. He spent his weekdays in Sydney, working at Callan Park Hospital, so I only saw him on the weekends. In exchange for my board and lodgings, my duties were to take care of his cattle and his property, as well as aiding with the sermons for the new Church of Salvation. It'd seemed a reasonable enough deal, and there were even times when Jerimiah would invite me in for supper of a Sunday evening, showing me a shred of kindness and humanity. Afterwards, he would pour us a couple of drinks and put on his charm. We would sit and chat about our week and whatnot. Sometimes, we would even share our secrets.

The part of me that still craved his friendship stupidly forgot how evil and vindictive he truly was, and we reformed a tenuous friendship.

The ceremony Jerimiah performed on me was successful at keeping the darkness at bay, but the strength and radiance I was feeling eventually came at the cost of my own humanity. I was no longer consumed with guilt for the things I'd done, let alone the things I had yet to do.

When I visited Mama's place on occasion to bring her some fruit and vegetables from our garden, I found I could still cross the protective threshold, but it made me weak and sick. She'd only cry when she saw me and refuse the food I'd brought, so eventually, I stopped going to save her the heartache.

The years seemed to pass by in the blink of an eye, and by the mid-'70s, The Church of Salvation had a strong following.

Welcome to The Church of Salvation, where your soul checks in but never checks out, was a personal slogan I chanted in my head whenever newcomers entered the double doors.

The people of our church hadn't been a bunch of dregs like our previous followers. Most of our new followers were good people with hopes and aspirations, so we needed to proceed at a much slower pace when it came to draining them. Besides, Jerimiah's narcissism and inflated sense of self-importance had made him more interested in the power he held over these people than sucking the life out of them. He wanted to keep the people around so they would continue to worship him. Jerimiah's powers had increased tenfold since he'd sacrificed those young women.

He was a control freak who would influence and dominate his desires, and yet he was charismatic and seemed to possess an uncanny ability to warp people's minds into believing his every word. His egocentric nonsense caused much pain and suffering, especially for the young women of our church group, yet I stood by his side, allowing it to happen. I lost my conscience, and I was in the process of losing my soul.

It was during the mid-'70s that Jerimiah married Caitlyn, a pretty young woman from our church group, only to have me help sacrifice her a couple of years later when he'd grown tired of her. He told our followers she'd given in to the Devil's persuasion and had followed Lucifer on the path directly to Hell. This should've been a red flag for everyone, but instead, they all blamed his wife for not having faith.

In truth, Jerimiah had started having an illicit affair with one of his patients from Callan Park Hospital.

"Her name is Rebecca Brown," he told me over a bottle of whiskey. "And she's the prettiest thing I've ever seen. I think I might actually be in love."

I wasn't sure I believed him. I'd never known Jerimiah to love anyone bar himself.

After partaking in the "Sacrificial" spell on Jerimiah's wife, my protective shell began to crack, allowing me to experience real emotions again and see Jerimiah for who he truly was. I'd felt the darkness trickling back in and was troubled at the thought of going back down the road of self-destruction when, to my surprise, small rays of light managed to filter through the cracks. A young woman named Indi Adams had started showing interest in me, and in turn, I felt a giddying sense of affection towards her, too. She was only young, so I never acted on my feelings. We merely met up on Sunday evenings by the Richmond River and talked. Indi's father was an abusive drunk who'd used the biblical nonsense Jerimiah fed him to punish his wife and daughter in the name of God's will. It'd crossed my mind to punish him in return, but Jerimiah liked to keep the Adams brothers onside. They were important men in town and well respected amongst the townsfolk.

Indi had told me, "As soon as I turn eighteen, I'm gonna marry you," and I'd made the mistake of repeating her words to Jerimiah during one of our more amicable moments, not realising he would begrudge my happiness.

Before I knew it, he and her father had organised an arranged marriage. Indi and Jerimiah were set to get hitched the following year on the evening of the Winter Solstice.

As soon as I caught a whiff of the news, I marched into the church, grabbing one of the candelabras along the way. I flew at Jerimiah, clocking him square across the temple. I would've kept swinging it at him—I'd wanted to kill him—but I'd made the mistake of confronting him in front of our followers, and the Adams brothers immediately jumped to his aid and restrained me.

The tenuous relationship Jerimiah and I had reformed quickly disintegrated after that. It was the straw that broke the camel's back.

I left his property and managed to stay with a family of our community for a couple of weeks, but it hadn't taken long for Jerimiah to clue onto my whereabouts and spread lies about me. He told the family I was untrustworthy and unstable and that if I was to continue staying with them, I'd end up leading them down the path to eternal damnation.

My reputation fell to tatters as the news spread through the community.

Jerimiah had grown ultra-powerful, thanks to the latest sacrifice we'd performed on his wife, and he no longer needed my help with casting the spells anymore.

He could've just let me go and allowed me to live out the rest of my years in peace, but for some sick reason, he was vindictive and intent on turning my life into a nightmare.

The proposed wedding arrangement hadn't stopped me and Indi from meeting on the sly. I'd warned Indi never to trust Jerimiah, that he had an evil agenda and a black heart. I'd also made her a promise, telling her that as soon as she turned eighteen, I would take her away from Coraki and The Church of Salvation, but fate intervened, causing me to break my promise.

As the weeks rolled over, the darkness closed in hard and fast.

The "Protection" spell Jerimiah had put in place to guard me had entirely disintegrated.

After exhausting my welcome with the few locals who were still willing to take me in for a night, I needed to come up with alternative sleep arrangements before Jerimiah stepped in and punished them. I resorted to spending my nights sleeping in a local horse barn. Sadly, I wasn't able to shower, and by the mornings I stunk of manure. I looked and felt like a derelict, and I hadn't wanted Indi to see how low I'd sunk. I was too ashamed, so I stopped going to see her at our usual meeting spot and went back to drinking again instead.

CHAPTER 15
JUNE 27TH, 1998
CORAKI, AUSTRALIA
∞ SHAINA ∞

After making quick and easy omelettes for dinner, I remain seated at the table, sipping a cup of chamomile tea–trying to settle my nerves. My insides bunch and squeeze repeatedly, threatening to bring my dinner back up. I stuffed up *big time* today. I really should have waited until I'd spoken to Owen before taking action.

Wyatt's speech of innocence and victimisation circles inside my brain, scattering my thoughts. While he'd justified the dark window coverings and the furtive glances I'd witnessed, I still have no answer for the locked bedroom inside his house or the fact that my spare bedroom has become a desperate cry for help.

There's a knock at the front door, and Isaac rushes to answer it.

"Dad," he cries, diving into Owen's arms.

I glance at my watch and hmpf. He's over an hour late.

Typical.

Owen's green eyes lift to mine. "I'm sorry I'm late, I got–"

I raise a palm, disinterested in whatever story he's crafted. After years of being with him and receiving nothing but bullshit excuses,

I've run out of patience. I'm just glad he's not *mine* to worry about anymore.

"Have you got the information I asked for or not?"

"That I do..." He places Isaac down and hands me a small stack of manilla folders, eyeing me questioningly. "Where's this all coming from anyway? I'm not exactly sure what you've heard or where you heard it, but the allegations made against Mr Walker were false. He's clean. It's the neighbour who was the concern, but he's being institutionalised down in Rozelle Hospital, so you needn't worry about him."

I glance down and take a sip of my tea without arguing the point.

Wyatt Walker's file sits atop the stack, thick with paperwork. I flip it open and scan through the paperwork, desperate to find a discrepancy that will pull the plug on his innocence. My eyes flick through the statements and medical reports, and I stop short at the graphic photos of his wounds.

As I stare at a set of gaping holes on Wyatt's chin, my pulse quickens. Monroe hadn't mentioned anything about gauging Wyatt's chin. He'd only mentioned stabbing his leg.

In Wyatt's statement, he refers to Monroe as being erratic, agitated, and confused on the day of the attack.

Wyatt says Monroe was insistent that he and his wife Ruth had a daughter named Indi, and that they were hiding her somewhere in the house. He said he'd been cooperative and pretended to help find this imaginary girl in fear of losing his life.

Further down the page, Wyatt mentions "strange happenings" going on in their spare room and says he suspects Monroe had been sneaking in when they weren't home.

A wave of doubt washes over me. "So, the Walkers *didn't* have a daughter?"

Owen pulls out the chair next to me and takes a seat.

"Nope." He shakes his head. "The neighbour made it all up. His mother was a junkie, and it seems the apple didn't fall far from the tree. According to his statements, his mother had multiple partners over the years, too. The poor boy doesn't even know who his real father is."

Pushing Wyatt Walker's file aside, I pick up Monroe Morgan's file and pluck out the paperwork.

At the top of his rap sheet is a mug shot, although the teenager in the picture looks very different from the young man I met today. The photo shows him to be gaunt and unkept, with the righthand side of his face back-and-blue and swollen like a balloon. The only recognisable feature is his distinct swampy-green eyes.

His list of convictions includes drug possession with intent to sell, break and enter, aggravated assault and grievous bodily harm.

Beneath the rap sheet is his statement, which reads similar to the story he told me, only it's more detailed with some shocking family history tacked on to the end. There turns out to be several statements in the pile, and each of them reads more or less the same. As I read his statement, Indi's name bounces off the pages, smacking me in the face, and I no longer know what to think.

Is this girl real or the case of a drug-addled brain?

Monroe and Isaac insist she's real, and the blood-smeared cries for help plastered across all four walls of the spare bedroom down the hall suggests the same.

"Clearly, Monroe has a criminal record, and from what Wyatt suggests, he was high at the time of the attack, but that's not to say his allegations aren't true. How do the authorities know that Indi doesn't actually exist?" I ponder out loud. "Could she exist?"

Owen snatches up a handful of folders and flicks through the pages, tossing several police reports, testimonials and neighbours' statements at me.

"They found no evidence of the Walkers ever having a daughter. Furthermore, not a single neighbour could recall ever having seen a young woman enter the Walkers' house. If anything, the neighbour on the other side reported spotting Monroe speaking to himself on multiple occasions. The kid has been suffering from mental illness and blackouts ever since he was six. It says so in his medical reports."

He tosses more pages at me, and I'm seeing phrases like:

Post-Traumatic Stress Disorder
Reactive Attachment Disorder
Borderline Personality Disorder
Depression

"The Psychologist told the court that Monroe was suffering from drug-induced psychosis," Owen continues, handing me yet another sheet of paper. "The kid was high as a kite and losing it. 'Indi' was all in his head. He made her up."

A comment Monroe made earlier flashes to mind, putting it into context.

"Psychosis diagnosis, my ass."

Evidently, he doesn't agree with the diagnosis he was given.

Meanwhile, I don't know what to think. I'm conflicted.

"He wasn't making her up, Dad," Isaac pipes in, and I shoot him a glare. He'd promised not to bring up today's events in front of Owen. "Indi's real, I'm sure of it."

Luckily, Owen laughs off Isaac's comment. "Why don't you run along to bed, Son? This here is grown-up talk."

Isaac's gaze falls on mine, eyes large with desperation. "Tell him about the room, Ma."

"Your father told you to go to bed," I say firmly. "You should do as he says."

"But Dad won't help us if he doesn't believe Indi's real."

Owen glances between us. "What room? Am I missing something here?"

I sigh. There's no use in denying the matter any longer. Especially when Owen might have a way of figuring all of this out.

"Somebody broke into our spare bedroom and defaced the walls, but don't worry, I'm handling it."

"You're handling it?" Owen raises a sceptical brow.

"Come, Dad." Isaac reaches for his hand. "I'll show you."

Reluctant and somewhat frustrated, I set aside the paperwork and follow them down the hall.

Isaac opens the bedroom door, and Owen's nose crinkles as he steps inside. "Sweet Jesus!"

"See, she's real, Dad, and she needs our help."

Ignoring Isaac, Owen glances over his shoulder at me. "How long has this been here?"

"I'm not entirely sure," I answer honestly. "I only came across it today."

Owen reaches for his flip phone. "I need to call this in."

I leap forward, placing my hand over his to stop him. "No, don't. Not yet, anyway. Let's give it a couple of days."

He jerks to face me, brows puckered. "Why? What's going on here? Are you up to something?"

I'd planned on keeping Monroe's visit a secret, but now that Owen knows about the room, it's probably better I come clean. "Monroe's out," I say, "and he came here earlier today looking for Indi."

"Shit, Shai. Why didn't you tell me this before?" His eyes leave mine to glance about the room. "Was Monroe the one to tell you about the room?"

"No." I shake my head. "Isaac brought our attention to it. He told Monroe that Indi had left messages inside for him. Believe me, Monroe looked just as shocked as I felt when we entered the room."

Owen's gaze snaps to mine again, his eyes nearly popping out of their sockets. "Are you telling me you let the kid in? What are you, stupid?"

I blanch at his comment. "Refer to me as stupid again, and you can see yourself out."

"You can't be letting strange men into your place, especially with our son being here. Forgive me for saying so, but it ain't smart."

"A second ago, you were referring to Monroe as a kid, but now that you're looking to put me in my place, he's magically a man?"

"I bet the boy's grown some in a year."

"He wasn't here long," Isaac says in my defence. "And Ma had a bat on him at first, so he didn't cause us any trouble. He's okay, Dad. Really. Indi says so."

When Owen doesn't respond, Isaac continues, and I cringe internally.

"He's coming back at two tomorrow if you want to meet him."

Owen's jaw tightens, his cheeks reddening with anger.

"Tomorrow," he repeats. "Is that why you got me to bring the paperwork around?" His eyes bore into mine. "Did Monroe ask for it?"

"No. I wanted to know more about the case," I retort. "He seemed genuine. It didn't seem to me like he was making Indi up."

"He seems genuine because he *genuinely* believes it. Like I just showed you, the kid was diagnosed with drug-induced psychosis. Do you even know what that means?"

I roll my eyes in answer.

"Don't be giving me those eyes. If you know what it means, then you shouldn't be questioning the case. It's closed. I've given you all the answers you need in black and white."

"Well then, how do you explain what happened to this room?"

"Who's to say Monroe didn't do all this?" Owen says, narrowing his brow. "Don't you find it the slightest bit strange that your spare room magically wound up this way before he came knocking at your door? The boy was desperate for affirmation."

Owen's comments hit me with a wallop.

What if he's right? Did I catch Monroe trying to sneak in or out of the spare bedroom window?

I think about what Isaac's told me and immediately shake off the idea.

"But Isaac says he's seen Indi. He described her as having red hair and blue eyes, just like Wyatt."

"First of all, this town is full of redheads, my dad and his side of the family included, so you can't go putting that down to evidence. And secondly, there isn't a single person in this neighbourhood who doesn't know who Monroe is. His story of drugs, violence, and the mysterious young woman made it into all the local papers. He was the talk of the town." He glances down at Isaac. "I bet those Jones boys down the road have a tale or two to tell, am I right?"

Isaac's face falls in response.

Owen reverts his focus back to me. "I'm surprised it took you this long to catch up. Maybe if you went outside more and–"

I cut him off with a look of warning. "Don't."

"Our son needs stimulation," he continues regardless. "Why don't you try taking him to the park and throwing a ball around instead of sitting inside wallowing in self-pity? It's been nearly a year since–"

"STOP!" The sheer volume of my voice appears to startle him.

I'd like to throw the lines *"Isaac isn't your son, he's mine, so back off"* in Owen's face, but we both know it's not true. While Isaac might not be Owen's biological son, Owen *is* his father in every other sense of the word. Not to mention, he has the adoption papers to prove it.

Noticing tears welling in my eyes, Owen steps closer and puts his hand on my arm, giving it a rub. I'm pretty sure he's trying to comfort me, but it feels belittling, just like everything he's said.

If he thinks I'm still wallowing over him, he's sorely mistaken. While I might still be bitter about what happened between him and Victoria, I wouldn't take him back if my life depended on it.

I jerk my arm back, and he frowns a moment before saying. "Don't you worry your pretty little head about Monroe. I'll swing by at two tomorrow and sort everything out."

I swallow, trying to still my thoughts. "But what's if?"

"But what's if nothing. The case is closed. Monroe ain't got no right coming around here, bothering you, and you shouldn't be indulging him. If he keeps it up, I'll see to it that they re-admit him into Rozelle Hospital."

Isaac tugs at Owen's shirt. "Dad, you can't–"

"Don't be doing that." Owen swipes his small hand away before crouching to his level. "I know exactly what's going on here, and I don't like it one bit. If you keep on telling fantastical stories, you'll find yourself being thrown into a hospital like Monroe. Do you want that?"

Isaac shakes his head.

"Then look your Ma in the eyes and tell her the truth. Indi isn't real."

Isaac hesitates a moment before turning my way, eyes lowered. "Indi isn't real."

"Now, that's better," Owen says, glancing at me, his face smug with satisfaction. "You see? Isaac is five years old and fighting for your attention. Of course, he's going to jump on something like this. He pulled a similar stunt a couple of years back–or have you forgotten?"

Resentment burns inside me. Owen *always knows best,* right or wrong.

"It's getting late," I say, dismissing him. "And I have errands to run in the morning. So, if you don't mind..." I incline my head towards the door.

Owen pushes off his knee to stand. "I'll be here tomorrow like I said. If the troublemaker arrives any earlier, don't be opening the door."

"Look, if you're going to insist on being here, fine." I throw my hands up. "But let me do the talking. We all know you have no tact, and I don't want this turning into another one of your shitshows."

Clearly offended, he shoots daggers at me before storming out of the room.

Isaac chases after him. "Dad, wait."

I'm glad when I exit to find them hugging. "Do me a favour and look after your ma, okay? Make sure she doesn't do anything stupid."

If it wasn't for Isaac being in his arms, I would've considered putting my boot to Owen's head.

Disappointment floods me when Owen snatches up the paper-work before leaving–slamming the door behind him. I was hoping to spend the night skimming through the files, looking for cracks.

"I'm sorry, Ma," Isaac says, staring at his feet. "I didn't mean to cause any trouble." Tears roll down his cheeks.

I kneel before him and dry his tears with my sleeve.

"About Indi," I say gently. "Is she real or not?"

He shakes his head in the negative, but I'm not sure I believe him. Only hours ago, he'd been the one to convince me *she was real*.

I lift his chin with my pointer and look him straight in the eyes. "You're not afraid to say otherwise because of what your father said, are you?"

Again, he shakes his head. "No. Do you forgive me?"

"Of course," I say, taking his small hand in mine and squeezing it. "Come on, it's time to get ready for bed."

CHAPTER 16

JUNE 28TH, 1998

CORAKI, AUSTRALIA

∞ OWEN ∞

I show up at Shaina's place half an hour early, only to have her greet me at the door with a snarl.

"And here I was, banking on you arriving late, as usual," she spits. "Trust it, the one day I actually want you to arrive late, you arrive early."

"You might wanna wipe that *God-awful* snarl off your face before the wind changes," I quip. "Otherwise, you'll spend the rest of your life looking like a Shar-Pei."

The creases along her forehead deepen. "Isn't there somewhere else you've got to be?"

"I'm exactly where I need to be."

"According to *who*, exactly?"

I snort. "When did you become so bitter?"

"I don't know... Perhaps it was when I found out my husband was a lying, cheating arsehole."

"Watch it," I warn, blanching at her comment. "If it wasn't for me, you'd be living on the street."

Shaina's eyes cut to mine, sharp and resentful. "My hero."

It's clear she's mocking me, but I keep my cool and let it

slide. It's the jealousy talking, not her. She can't help it if she's still in love with me. In all fairness, I still have a soft spot for her, too. It's exactly why I'm here. When we got married, I swore to protect her and her son until death do us part, *and I ain't dead.*

I'd briefed my father and uncle on what transpired here yesterday, and they believe Monroe has sinister motives for being back here.

"Find a way to get rid of him once and for all," my uncle said. "The tell-tale little prick is out for vengeance and will only bring disgrace to you and this town."

Monroe tried implementing me in his twisted tale last year, telling the court I was involved in the same religious cult as the Walkers and that I, too, had daughters whom I was keeping under ball and chain. Thankfully, that's where his whole testimony came undone. Neither I nor the Walkers have any daughters; we only have sons.

I'd never mentioned the sordid case to Shaina because I hadn't wanted her to delve too deeply into my family history. She can be like a dog to a bone when she gets an idea in her head, and it would've only been a matter of time before she ended up sticking her nose where it didn't belong. From the very first time Shaina met Uncle Harold, she's had it out for him, saying he's the carbon copy of her father. I'm sure she would've done anything she could to burn him.

Some things in life are better left unsaid, I'd convinced myself. Besides, Shaina and I were living in Evans Heads at the time–a quaint beach town about thirty minutes from Coraki–and we were having marital problems. I thought it best not to add to them.

I glance at my watch. It's 1.50 PM.

Not long now.

Shaina and I take a seat at the kitchen table, and I use what little time we have to shoot off a game plan. She nods along agreeingly as I speak, as though she's listening, but I can tell her mind is elsewhere.

It's obvious she doesn't want me here when Monroe arrives, and I'm curious as to why.

What exactly has he told her? Has he mentioned my family at all?

When the knock finally comes, Shaina launches off her seat and races to the door like an excited puppy.

She only opens the door ajar, trying to cut me out, but I grab hold of the door and tug it wide open.

I startle a moment before recomposing myself. The young man standing in front of us looks mighty different to the gaunt drug-head I'd dealt with last year. It's obvious now why Shaina hadn't wanted me here. It seems she's been bedazzled by this delinquent.

The young man glances me over, wide-eyed, before returning his attention to Shaina.

"Your friend is Sergeant Adams?" he says warily.

He recognises me.

It seems those drugs didn't do his brain too much damage.

Shaina glances between the two of us, biting her lip in agitation. Well, if she's not going to answer his question, I sure as hell will.

I step forward, puffing my chest out with authority. "You mean her husband is Sergeant Adams."

I catch Shaina rolling her eyes at me in my peripheral, and I give her an elbow in warning. She is still my wife on paper, after all. Neither of us have filed for divorce.

The delinquent glances between us questioningly.

"Monroe, I'm sorry," Shaina starts, "but I–"

"She can't help you," I cut in. "And if I catch you lurking around here again, I'm going to see to it that you're arrested and locked up for good, you hear?"

The young man's face falls. "But your son," he says, eyes pleading with Shaina. "He knows something. Can I at least–"

I stab my pointer at his chest, nearly knocking him off balance. "You dare bring up our son!"

A look of confusion crosses his face, which is quickly replaced by sheer desperation. "I'm not here to cause no trouble, I promise. What you do behind closed doors is your business. I just want to find Indi. If you'd only hear me out–"

"There's nothing to hear. The case is closed, dead, and buried, just like you're gonna be if you don't leave our property."

"Owen!" Shaina jumps between us, squaring up to me, eyes full of rage. "What the hell are you doing? This is not *at all* what we discussed. Why don't you go back inside and let me handle this?"

"To hell, I will! I'm doing exactly what you should be doing. Getting rid of him. The kid's mentally unstable, and he's got no right being here." I shift my focus back to the young man in question. "And don't think for one second that I don't know what you're up to. I know it was *you* who snuck in and defaced them walls. I bet if I ring them in, we'll find your fingerprints all over the joint."

Without another word, the delinquent turns his back, mounts his bike, and shoots off down the driveway–proving I'm right.

"See, Shai," I gloat. "The kid's as guilty as sin."

"Monroe, wait!" She lunges forward, but I grab hold of her upper arm to prevent her from chasing after him.

"Don't even think about it," I warn.

She struggles and hits me with the heel of her fist. "Stop it, Owen. Let me go."

Once he disappears around the corner, I finally relent and release my grip–satisfied there's no way she'll be able to catch him.

Shaina rounds on me, her eyes flared. "What in God's name was that? You said you were going to handle this professionally. I told you I didn't want another one of your shitshows, but you just couldn't help yourself, could you?"

I stoop forward, forcing our faces nose to nose. "Don't think I don't see through you, too," I growl. "Going all gooey-eyed for a delinquent."

"Please." She pffts. "He wasn't here to pick me up for a date. He was here asking for my help."

"I'm sure that's not all he'd be asking for. Young men like him are like dogs in heat. You're lucky I sent him packing now–before the neighbours' tongues start wagging. The last thing Isaac needs is for his Ma to be labelled a 'Cradle Robber' to a delinquent."

"That's rich coming from you, the 'cradle snatcher' himself. I'd only just turned eighteen when you took me in. There's a far bigger age gap between us than there is between me and Monroe."

My blood pressure spikes, turning my face to fire. "That's different. I took you in for your own protection. *You* needed me."

"Well, times have changed." Her shoulders square. "And I don't need you anymore, so why don't you run on home to Victoria and let me handle my own business."

Lashing words sit at the tip of my tongue, threatening to spill, but instead of taking my rage out on Shaina, I stalk over to my truck, hop in, and belt up.

The engine barely clicks over when I shove the vehicle into reverse, and squeal out of her driveway, onto the road.

That delinquent has no idea who he's messing with!

CHAPTER 17

JUNE 28TH, 1998

CORAKI, AUSTRALIA

∞ MONROE ∞

The roar of an engine approaching fast behind me has me quickly pedalling to the side of the road for safety. I expect the vehicle to zoom on past, leaving dust in its wake. Instead, it veers off the asphalt and gravel flies as it screeches wildly in my direction. Panic grips me as the back wheel of my bike is clipped, and I'm launched over the handlebars. I fly several feet into the air before landing on the unforgiving road with a crash.

Winded—but miraculously not too wounded—I scramble to my feet, adrenaline pumping. I spin around, shocked to find Shaina's husband, Sergeant Adams, charging towards me. His face is ablaze, and his fists are balled at his side.

I should high tail it—it would be the smart thing to do—but this cop is playing dirty, and my gut tells me it's because I'm right about him. He *is* a part of the religious cult that Indi was brought up in.

I know it.

I hadn't realised that Owen was Sergeant Adams' Christian name. If I had, I wouldn't have agreed to involve him.

Does Shaina not know what kind of man her husband is? Or was she playing dumb the whole time in order to set me up? Indi said that Sergeant

Adams and his wife were a part of her church group, so Shaina would've known about Indi and the cult, at the very least.

Clearly, she was upset with the way Owen was speaking to me, but perhaps she just felt guilty after the fact.

I'm disappointed. Out of everyone I've spoken to about what happened with Indi, Shaina was the only one who seemed to believe my story, so I was *really* counting on her help. She's the one person who I'd thought–*maybe, just maybe*–I could trust.

As Owen approaches, I stand my ground. "You know where Indi is, don't you." It's a statement, not a question. "You're tied in with the cult."

Blanking my accusation, Owen swings a left in line with my cheekbone. I swiftly duck the blow, only to be surprised by an uppercut from his right. My teeth give a painful clank, and I stumble backwards, losing my footing.

Shock waves roll through me as I hit the ground hard and heavy for the second time in a matter of minutes.

I should have run.

Owen towers over me, rage written on his features.

"Where is she? Where's Indi?" I press, heedless of the vulnerable position I'm in. "I don't care about your involvement; I just want to know where she is."

A dangerous glint sparks in Owen's eyes, and he reaches for his firearm. He draws the gun from its holster and racks the slide before pointing the muzzle directly towards the centre of my forehead.

I swallow.

There's nowhere for me to go.

"Please," I blurt, having nothing to lose. "At least tell me if she's still alive."

Owen's hand tremors ever so slightly as his finger closes around the trigger.

As if snapping back to himself, the spark in his eyes ebbs, dimming to a low burning ember.

"Listen here, you twisted little fuck," he says, choosing to kick the boot in instead. "Indi doesn't exist."

I open my mouth to argue, but he silences me with another vicious boot to the gut. A wisp of air crackles through my throat down to my lungs as I gasp for breath.

"Come back sniffing around in these parts again, and I *will* kill you," he warns. "Make no mistake about that."

CHAPTER 18

OCTOBER 7TH, 1978
ROZELLE HOSPITAL, LILYFIELD, AUSTRALIA
∞ ENZO ∞

It was a stormy night. I'd had one whiskey too many, weeks of no sleep, and I was burning with pent-up rage. A fragmented plan formulated in my mind, and I hitched a ride to Lilyfield. My heart was broken, my funds had run dry, and my health was failing. All I wanted was revenge.

Jerimiah made the mistake of bragging about how he was able to sneak Becca in and out of Callan Park Hospital through tunnels undetected. That was Jerimiah's problem; he was vain and liked to boast about just how clever he was.

I found the entrance to the secret underground tunnel system without too much difficulty and managed to break in successfully. The air smelt musty inside and reminded me of a dark and dank rabbit warren, which came as no surprise considering it had been built under Callan Park Hospital back in 1885. I explored the twists and turns of the labyrinth, finding dead-end passages with ornate arches and empty chambers. I came across the section where the underground cells were and shone my flashlight inside. The iron doors still hung, grim and forbidding. A dark energy radiated from the walls, fuelling the darkness inside my head. I was certain terrible things had happened in there. I could feel it in my bones, and yet here I was, planning to do something terrible myself.

I finally stumbled across the set of stairs that led up to the storeroom. I used the lockpick to open the door, and once I was inside the hospital, I moved through the corridors with stealth. Jerimiah had mentioned there were only skeleton staff on duty in the evenings, so it was easy enough to sneak around undetected if you were quick and quiet.

I eventually found the ward Rebecca was confined to and crept over to her bedside. I recognised her from the photo Jerimiah kept of her in his wallet.

Staring down at the peacefully sleeping Rebecca, I could see why Jerimiah had been so taken by her. She had the face of a porcelain doll, smooth, perfect... innocent.

Everyone was asleep, some of the women snoring loudly, like rolls of thunder.

My hands hung curled and shaking by my sides, and the air felt heavy in my lungs. *Don't do it,* I begged myself, *you're not like Jerimiah. You don't need to hurt an innocent girl to get back at him.*

My conscience was waging a war, right against wrong. Ultimately, my darker side won, taking over my body. I lost control, and before I knew it, my hands wrapped tightly around her throat, crushing her airways. She tried to scream, but all that escaped her was a gasping squeak that was drowned out by the loud snores. I held tight until the fight in her gave out.

Covering my tracks, I plucked a piece of rope out from inside my pocket and made a noose to go around her neck. I tied it to the head of the bed and dragged her body down over the edge, making it appear as though she'd taken her own life.

I was almost caught twice by the night nurses while leaving the hospital. I was shaking so hard, my limbs didn't want to cooperate, and my head was so messed up that my brain couldn't coordinate my exit strategy.

"What have you done, Lorenzo?" my mama's voice repeated inside my head. *"What have you done?"*

As soon as I got outside, I vomited, sickened by what I had done. I tried telling myself that Jerimiah made me kill her, just like he made me kill the other girls, but deep down, I knew it wasn't true. The darkness had consumed me, just like Mama said it would.

Eager to leave Sydney, I made my way back to the highway, hoping to hitch a ride to Lismore. I couldn't return to Coraki. Jerimiah was sure to figure out I killed Rebecca, and he would be out for my blood.

To my surprise, a truck driver pulled over within minutes of sticking my thumb out. He was heading to Ballina, which was close enough to Lismore.

Ten hours later, he dropped me off by The Australian Hotel on the main drag. I wandered over to the nearest servo, approaching the customers who were parked at the bowsers. When I asked the first two people if they were headed towards Lismore, they shook their heads and avoided any eye contact, but the third guy I approached simply grinned and said, "That just so happens to be my next stop. Jump on in."

He was a friendly, chatty young fellow who'd been happy to oblige when I asked to be dropped off at The Winsome Pub.

"The Winsome Pub," he repeated sentimentality. "Pop said back when that pub was first built in 1882, the land was damp and swampy, and the area was affectionately known as 'Sleepy Hollow'."

"Huh," I said, not the least bit interested.

All I knew was I only had a few bucks left, and I planned on spending it on whiskey.

When we pulled up outside the pub, I thanked the young driver and walked straight to the bar. My legs bounced in agitation when a blonde, scabby-looking broad plonked herself beside me, rattling on and on about some deadbeat who'd done her wrong.

She leant forward pushing out her cleavage. "I'm Leonie, by the way," she said, introducing herself with a slur.

I glanced at the sorry excuse of a woman sitting before me, and the cogs began turning.

I'd come across a spell in one of Jerimiah's books, which spoke about transferring a deceased person's spirit into the body of a newborn child. The only issue was that the baby had to be of flesh and blood to the deceased, and the connection needed to be made while the baby was still in utero.

Despite living like "The Walking Dead" and being surrounded by a darkness that was eating at me, I wasn't ready to say goodbye to the world just yet.

Leonie was rough around the edges, and it was clear she had a substance abuse problem, but she had pretty eyes and a nice smile. More importantly, it was obvious I'd taken her fancy.

I calculated that it was just over eight months until Indi's wedding. This would be enough time to bring a baby into the world if I were to act fast enough.

Suddenly, Leonie had my full attention, and I reached into my pocket for my last bit of change.

"Say, can I buy you a drink?" I asked.

She smiled widely and said, "Make it a bourbon and coke."

MY SCHEME WORKED. Within a matter of weeks, Leonie took a pregnancy test, which came back positive, and she flew at me, kicking and screaming.

"You bastard! How could you do this to me? I don't want no baby. You need to pay to get rid of it."

I refused and pulled her to me, acting overjoyed and telling her it was a blessing.

I'd been staying at her place ever since I met her at the Winsome Pub. She lived in a small fibro dump not far from the main street in town. The place was grimy, mouldy, and had cockroaches aplenty, but it sure beat sleeping in the horse stables.

I was literally broke. I didn't have a cent to my name, but Leonie confided in me that she made her money selling drugs, so I'd helped her, and in return, she shared her home and profits with me.

I cast the initial part of the "Linking" spell in the early stages of Leonie's pregnancy to ensure my second chance at life was already set in motion come the time Jerimiah caught up with me. I told Leonie I was performing a religious practice that had been passed down through the generations in my family to help keep the baby safe in utero. I had added an "Anti-Addiction" spell, which would help to curb Leonie's addiction throughout the pregnancy. The baby was my future vessel, after all, and I needed to keep it safe and healthy. For reasons I didn't understand, the "Linking" spell seemed to reduce the darkness that consumed me, and life became somewhat bearable again.

Leonie looked different once she was clean and had gained some meat on her bones. Some may have even called her beautiful. For a moment, I considered cancelling my plans of rescuing Indi and staying with her, but Leonie's wild, unpredictable personality made her too hard to tolerate. She would lose her temper at the slightest of inconveniences and kick and scream like a grown child.

It was during this time, she admitted that she had a daughter who'd been taken away from her as a baby, hence the fact that she hadn't wanted any more children.

At sixteen weeks, Leonie needed to have an ultrasound done. We were looking at the images on the monitor, trying to distinguish the body parts when, to our surprise—and dismay—the radiographer pointed out two babies. Leonie was pregnant with twins.

"They're both boys," the radiographer told us, which was something to be glad about, at least.

I wasn't sure I'd make a very good woman. Then again, I hadn't made a very good man.

The months passed by quickly, and Leonie and I fell into a routine. I would cook, clean, and sell the meth while she laid on the couch watching daytime TV and barking out orders. I put up with her demands and did whatever I could to keep her happy, knowing it was only a matter of months before the babies would be born, and I would be finalising the spell.

On the morning of the Winter Solstice, it was a fine day with clear blue skies. I slipped a potion into Leonie's breakfast to send her into an early labour. Once the magic worked its way through her body, she started screaming blue murder. Plates were thrown, and cups were smashed.

She pummelled me as I tried to soothe her, screaming, "You did this to me, you bastard. I hate you; I hate you."

She begged me to take her to the hospital, but I told her it was too late, that the babies were coming. Truthfully, I hadn't wanted her to go to the hospital. I'd done my research in the months leading up to the delivery, and I was planning on delivering our babies myself. I helped Leonie onto the foam mattress that I'd laid out on the living room floor. I could see the head crowning, and I gently helped guide it out of the birth canal. It was bloody and messy, and Leonie's screams echoed loudly against the walls. I gently tapped the baby boy's back to dislodge any fluid and then cut the umbilical cord and clamped it before placing the child on Leonie's chest.

She brushed the boy aside without care and screamed, "Hurry the fuck up and get the other one out, right now!"

The second child was much easier to deliver than the first, and I felt the connection right away. This was my boy. The boy I would soon become if tonight's plans went awry. When the hard part was over, and Leonie's screams had subsided, I'd taken the second twin to the bedroom, wrapped him up, and closed the door, hiding him inside.

Afterwards, I'd given Leonie a potion to drink, telling her it would take the pain away–which it would–but failed to mention it would alter her memories of what'd just taken place.

"You've given birth to our son, Monroe," I'd said, both of us having picked the boy's names before they were born.

I'd wanted to name one Elias, after my Pa, and Leonie had liked the name Monroe.

"There was no Elias," I continued. "The second baby died in utero at sixteen weeks, just after the ultrasound. He was reabsorbed by his twin Monroe, so there were no complications. You only delivered one baby boy, alone on your living room floor, because Enzo ran off and left you."

I went and grabbed Elias, then slipped out the back door. I jumped the back neighbour's fence and made my way down their driveway, crossing to the other side of the road where I parked my getaway car earlier that morning. It was a cheap, beat-up Holden Commodore with bald tyres and panel damage from front to rear. It would be good enough to get me to Coraki and then Casino, which is all I really needed it for.

I placed Elias in the capsule I'd picked up off the side of the road a couple of weeks back and buckled him in before hopping into the driver's side and heading to my mama's place in Coraki.

She'd seen me coming, of course, and was standing on the porch, arms crossed, when I arrived. When I pulled to the curb, she made her way down the steps, stopping mid-yard to speak to me.

"My son." Her voice had grown raspier with age. "To what do I owe the pleasure." There was a haunted look in her milky eyes, conveying a profound sense of anguish and despair. She looked much older than the last time I saw her. Deep groves ran down her cheeks, and long lines creased her forehead. Her hair was shaved short, revealing a short fuzz of salt and pepper curls knit tightly to her skull.

I opened the car door, unbuckled the capsule Elias was sleeping in, and entered the yard, ready to have a heart-to-heart. Instead, I accidentally dropped the capsule, gasping for air. It felt as though my body was being torn apart from the inside out.

Coughing and spluttering, I stumbled backwards.

My mother's trinkets, symbols, and special garden scents, which had been set in place to ward off evil, were disabling me. I fell to my knees and scrambled to the council strip on all fours like an old dog.

Elias screamed like I'd set him on fire.

My mama raced over to the capsule and picked it up, carrying it to the council strip just outside her property line.

Her eyes narrowed, and her brows furrowed as she traced her fingers over him. "You've instilled your darkness onto this poor child."

"No," I said adamantly, and then a thought snapped to mind.

It struck me that perhaps I unintendedly had. After I'd formed the "Attachment" spell, my darkness had lessened.

"I need you to take care of him for me," I said, not admitting she could be right. "Can you do that?"

"There's two of them," she stated.

I hung my head low, sensing my mama's disappointment in me. "I only have one of them."

"I'm a seventy-seven-year-old, blind woman, Lorenzo. How am I supposed to take care of a small child?"

"Blind though you may be, you can see more than the rest of us. And we both know you're worth more to Jerimiah alive than dead. His link to your powers is what helps to keep him strong."

Noticing the bitterness crossing my mama's face, I glanced down at the baby and added cajolingly. "I named him Elias after Pa."

"Wait here." She placed the capsule down carefully before taking off to the house.

Minutes later, she remerged with a glass of liquid filled with a mix of herbs, spices and whatnot. She dipped her finger in it and then into Elias's mouth for him to suck, repeating the process several times over before passing the glass to me and telling me to drink what was left.

"The effects will only last a few hours," she said.

I eyed the glass suspiciously. "What's in it?"

"That, my son, is a secret potion. All you need to know is it'll allow you to be in my house temporarily. I'll need you to come in and set up your old room for Elias if you expect me to raise him for you."

I chugged down the strange contents and handed the glass back to her, wondering how it was that she'd always been able to see the unseeable. It was a gift I wished I'd inherited. Perhaps if I had been blessed with it, I wouldn't have made so many mistakes.

While Mama took Elias inside, I popped the boot of the car to grab out the bags of stuff I'd carefully collected over the last couple of weeks. There were three bags. One filled with nappies, one filled with cans of formula, and another filled with a variety of baby clothes I'd bought from the Salvation Army store. I hesitated before re-entering her yard again, but whatever my mama had given me did the trick. I could cross the threshold without growing violently ill.

We spent the next few hours getting the room ready for Elias. Mama had an old wooden laundry tub the size of a bassinet, which we dragged in and then folded a thick continental quilt to form a mattress. It was hard to work out where to put everything, but luckily, the room had shelves floor-to-ceiling, so we'd been able to put all of the dangerous items on the higher shelves—out of reach of small hands—come the time Elias grew into a toddler. I made sure to explain where I was placing things so that Mama would know where to find them the next time she needed them. I also organised the individual items in a way where she could easily lay her hands on them without any trouble. When we finished babyproofing and sorting all that we could, mama made me a sandwich and told me my time was running out. She questioned me about Leonie and Monroe and asked why I didn't bring both children to her. I could see in her eyes she knew the answer, but she wanted to hear me say it. Her disgust in me was evident, and I couldn't bring myself to admit to what I'd done. Instead, I asked if I could use her shower.

After a refreshing wash and a clean shave, I put on a pin-striped suit I'd also bought from the Salvation Army store. It was slightly tight, but the sleeves were long enough, and it only had to last me a couple of hours while I attended the wedding.

When I entered the living room, Mama handed me my car keys. "It's time to go." As we got to the front door, she added adamantly, "I will love and protect this child, even from the likes of you. I love you, my son, but I don't trust that you have your child's best interest at heart. Once you leave, don't return. I don't want to see you again."

I wondered then if I'd made a mistake bringing Elias to my mama's house, but it was too late to turn back. What was done was done.

CHAPTER 19

JUNE 28TH, 1998,

CORAKI, AUSTRALIA

∞ SHAINA ∞

11.50 PM

I bolt upright, startled by a heavy bang, like a door being slammed, and my heart pounds erratically. There's a loud creak, immediately followed by the sound of thudding footsteps. I strain my ears to listen.

"Isaac?" I call out.

When he doesn't reply, full-blown panic sets in, snapping me straight into action. I catapult out of bed, grab my bat, and dash into the hallway, adrenaline pumping.

A burst of lightning illuminates the hallway as I enter, and I glimpse Isaac standing by the opening of the spare bedroom. The hairs on the back of my neck prickle as I register that the door is open, and Isaac's lips are moving as though he's speaking to someone inside. He'd specifically told me that Indi often visited during storms.

Is she here? Is that who he's talking to?

"Isaac?"

When the light vanishes, and blackness descends, I find myself second-guessing what I've seen.

I've had a horrendous night of tossing and turning, and my brain is groggier than usual. My botched investigation regarding the Walkers, closely followed by the inexcusable way Owen sent Monroe packing, has left me flustered and frustrated. I've barely slept a wink.

I knew Owen would go and run his mouth; he just can't help himself.

What's more, a fierce storm set in soon after Monroe left, and as if the constant thunder and lightning wasn't enough to keep me on edge, the wind has been howling wildly through the window gaps, causing the doors to rattle.

I race forward and flick on the hallway light to find Isaac standing alone, glancing up at me innocently, but I don't buy it. I hastily push past him and switch on the spare room light, only to find the room empty.

My arms prickle, not only with unease but at the sudden drop in temperature. Monroe had cut the plastic covering while trying to break in earlier, and now it's flapping about wildly, allowing the frigid air from outside to leak into the room. Droplets of rainwater trickle down from the windowsill, amplifying the rank smell of mould and wood rot. I make my way over to the open window, and my feet hit a puddle with a breath-stealing splash. The iciness of the water has me recoiling, but I continue to investigate.

I glance back at Isaac, who's standing all too innocently by the doorway, and ask, "Who were you just talking to?"

He glances away. "No one."

I don't believe him. I could've sworn I saw his lips moving.

"I heard you," I say, trying to catch him out.

"The wind blew the door open," he says. "I heard it banging, so I got up to shut it and... I said a naughty word. I'm sorry, Ma."

Unconvinced, I grab at the flapping piece of plastic and peer out the window. It's useless. I can't see a thing. The sky is jet black, and the rain is coming down in sheets. I run my finger along the swollen timber of the windowsill and groan.

"I can't re-tape the plastic covering now," I say to Isaac. "The area is sopping wet. I'm going to have to fix it tomorrow. Perhaps we can wedge the door with a stopper until then?"

Isaac nods agreeingly.

As I step across the sodden floorboards–leaving the room–my eyes roam over the eerie writing and symbols plastered across the walls. The letters look redder than earlier, taking on a new life in the yellow of the artificial light.

I stop dead in my tracks just as I'm about to exit. A sentence catches my eye which–I know for sure–was NOT there earlier. I read it over and over.

"I'm still here."

Chills run up and down my spine.

My gaze shifts to Isaac. "Did you write this?"

He lowers his head and slowly shakes it from side to side.

"Well, do you know who did?"

His chin lowers as he utters, "No."

"Did Indi do this?" I push, knowing the writing couldn't have just appeared out of thin air.

"No," he repeats.

An image of Monroe slipping through the window flashes into my mind, and I force the thought aside. I don't believe Owen's theory. Monroe looked as shocked as I'd felt when he'd entered this room. If he really *is* the one who wrote all this, then he deserves an Oscar for his performance.

I kneel in front of Isaac and take his small, cold hand in mine, and then, in a slower but more forceful tone, I repeat, "Did Indi do this?"

Isaac bites his lip, appearing conflicted.

"Have you seen Indi tonight?" I ask, trying a different angle. "Is that who you were just talking to?"

His teeth recede, and his lower lip quivers. Eventually he nods, a single tear escaping down his cheek. "Please don't tell Dad."

"Where's she gone now?" I ask. "Did she slip back out the window? You should've brought her in to see me," I continue before he has the chance to answer. "I would've liked to have spoken to her."

Isaac's gaze bounces nervously from me to over my shoulder. I glance behind me, but there's nothing to see.

A chilling thought sweeps over me, making the hairs up on the back of my neck stand on end.

"He pulled a similar stunt a couple of years back—or have you forgotten?" Owen had said.

"I won't tell your dad, I promise," I say, giving Isaac's hand a reassuring squeeze. "But there's something I need *you* to tell me, and I want you to be honest, okay? It's important."

Isaac's eyes meet mine, wide and cautious.

"Is Indi alive like you and I?" I ask, gesturing between us, "Or is she visiting you in spirit, like Coen?"

He flounders a moment before saying. "Indi's not visiting, she's trapped here. She doesn't even know she's dead." His eyes flick past me and then back again, and he leans in closer to whisper, "When I asked Indi what happened to her, how she died, her lips and eyes turned funny, so I don't ask those types of questions anymore."

"Funny as in, how?" I ask, curiosity piqued.

His head shrinks into his neck, and his body quavers as though rehashing a terrifying incident. "I don't want to talk about it."

I swallow around the lump inside my throat and then ask, "Is Indi still here now?"

He nods. "Yes."

"What does she want?"

"She needs Enzo's help to escape."

"Why Enzo specifically?" I ask. "Can't we help her?"

He shrugs. "I've tried helping her, but I don't know how."

CHAPTER 20

JUNE 29TH, 1998

CORAKI, AUSTRALIA

∞ SHAINA ∞

After an eventful night, with no sleep to be had, it's a struggle to roll out of bed the next morning, get ready, and drive Isaac to school. A double shot of coffee and a few splashes of water to my face finally kickstarts my limbs into cooperation, and I'm able to get him there just before the bell rings. While my body might be sluggish, my mind is abuzz with thoughts and ideas.

After closing the spare bedroom door last night and wedging it shut, I'd suggested to Isaac that he should hop into bed with me, and he readily agreed. Once he was snuggled securely in my arms, I'd brought up the subject of Coen again.

When Isaac first spoke about seeing his biological father, I was sceptical. I wasn't sure if his visions were real—as Coen had died before he was even born—or if it was his way of dealing with the fact we'd moved out of Owen's place and that he no longer had his adoptive father at his beck and call.

However, as the weeks passed and Isaac gave me more details about his visions, I grew less sceptical and eventually came around to the idea that Coen's spirit *was, in fact,* contacting him. Isaac's descriptions of

Coen were accurate to a tee, right down to the scar across his left temple and the way he kept his hair shoulder length. Isaac also mentioned things that only Coen and I could have known. Things we'd done together when Isaac was still a sparkle in my eye. I'd never spoken to Owen about those times, so the stories could only have come from Coen.

When I told Owen about Isaac's visions, he'd laughed and proceeded to scold me for encouraging such nonsense. He pointed out Isaac has a photo of Coen and that he'd sprung him flicking through an old diary of mine on several occasions, but despite his explanations and semi-persuasive argument, I wasn't entirely convinced.

The photo I'd given Isaac was taken on the day Coen got his learner's licence, and he was leaning on his father's old Commodore with his hair tied back for a change. His father had called to him just as I was taking the picture, and Coen had turned, leaving only his right profile visible, meaning the scar across his temple wasn't in the shot.

I swallow hard around the painful lump forming in my throat. They say time heals all wounds, but there are some wounds that no amount of time can heal. They continue to fester and rot until the day you die.

I never envisioned my life turning out this way. A broke single mother struggling to make ends meet in the small town of Coraki.

I grew up on a large cattle farm just north of Woodburn, so I know what it means to put in a hard day's work. My father would have me up and working at the crack of dawn. Some days, I was made to muster the cattle into the yard and ear tag them for buffalo flies; other days, I had to fix the barbed wire fences from where the bulls push and rub against them. The work was hard, tiring and constant, which meant I never caught a break. When I returned home from school in the afternoon, my father would be cracking the whip again.

Due to my father's high expectations and explosive temper, we experienced a high turnover of farmhands. He was extremely demanding and a difficult man to work with.

This meant we got stuck doing a lot of the work ourselves.

My mother died when I was only two, and I was brought up as an only child until the age of thirteen when my father remarried. To my disappointment, my father's new partner, Astrid, turned out to be a cold fish and a ball buster, just like him. Worse still, she had two strapping sons in their early twenties who were misogynistic pigs. They did take on some of the workload, though, easing my chores.

My world changed when I started high school that same year, which is where I met Coen. He was in my art and English class. His kindness and spiritual outlook on life were like a breath of fresh air after spending years being brought up in a loveless household with a father who was a street angel–who everyone in the community had liked and admired–yet a house Devil. The only folk in town who knew his true colours were our short-lived farmhands.

Coen spoke openly about his cultural beliefs that defied all laws of science. He was learning the guitar and would sing to me. He would also make me small gifts from Mother Nature's resources. For the first time in all my life, Coen made me feel loved and alive.

When my father found out I was pregnant with Isaac at the mere age of seventeen, he fell into a complete and utter rage. He waited behind the bushes on the corner of Duke Street, near the rugby fields, knowing full well it was the route we took home after Coen's footy training. As we rounded the corner, he slipped out from his hiding place and pointed his rifle straight at Coen. He shot and killed Coen point blank before turning his gun on me.

"You've disgraced my name," he hissed.

I instinctively dove for cover, and the bullet hit my shoulder. I was told in the hospital that I was lucky it didn't hit a vital organ.

When the trial was over, my father was sent to jail. Astrid took control of the cattle farm and told me I was no longer welcome on their property. She took everything and kicked me out without a cent to my name. I was left alone and homeless with expensive physiotherapy bills–which I couldn't afford to pay–and a newborn baby to raise on my own.

Owen was the leading senior constable at Woodburn Police Station at the time of the shooting and was the first to arrive on the scene. He came to visit me at Lismore Hospital every day for the long, painful weeks that followed, bringing me treats and presents for the unborn baby. I knew it wasn't protocol. It was obvious he fancied me, so when he suggested that I come and stay with him, I jumped at the offer. I had nothing to my name, and he was a meal ticket–a very handsome meal ticket at that. I'd hoped to fall for him the same way I'd fallen for Coen, but as the saying goes, you can't choose who you love. To my dismay, you can't always judge a book by its cover, either. Owen may have been a hardworking man, a good provider, and a decent father figure to Isaac during our time together, but he was also arrogant, pigheaded, and belittling. As time went on, I went from admiring him to resenting him.

I often wonder if Owen knew I never truly loved him, that–in a way–I was using him, and that's why he ended up seeking affection elsewhere. Lord knows I never gave him the ego-stroking he craved.

I snort at the thought.

In a way, I'm glad he left me for Victoria. I'm much happier without him, even with my financial struggles. I just worry about Isaac. I'd wanted him to have stability.

I suck in an anxious breath as I pull into the driveway and remain seated for a moment before shutting off the engine and exiting the car.

After a night's worth of rehashing yesterday's events on repeat, the only rational conclusion I can come up with is that the Walkers *did* have a daughter named Indi and that Mr Walker killed her as punishment after he caught her fraternising with Monroe.

Ultimately, I think Indi *is indeed* dead and that her spirit is still here because she has unfinished business.

Owen is adamant that the case is closed, "dead and buried," as he so eloquently put it, so I'm back to investigating on my own.

It's probably for the better. I tell myself. *He's too damned arrogant and pigheaded to work with, anyhow. Look at how he treated Monroe.*

If I knew of a way to reach out to Monroe, I would do so in a heartbeat, but I don't know where he's staying or if he's even still in Coraki. He's probably caught the train back to Coffs by now.

The best I can do is keep looking into his story. I'm not feeling quite as confident in my detective skills after my botched investigation of the Walkers, but I'm also not ready to give up until I've acquired the answers we're both looking for.

I think back to when I was in the Walkers' house and jot down my memories for clues I might've missed. Chewing the lid of my pen, I examine my notes. The fact that the Walkers are keeping one of their rooms locked is a major red flag. Indi might be deceased, but who's to say they don't have another daughter or church group adolescent that they're keeping locked away? When I tapped on the door, I distinctly heard a scratching sound, which means there was most definitely something or someone in there.

I'd like to go back to the Walkers' property and investigate further, but my stupid stunt would've put the Walker family on high alert. Monroe was afraid if Wyatt caught a whiff of someone looking into him again, he'd hide all evidence, and quite likely, he was right. I'm sure the Walker family will be keeping an extra eye out. My second-best bet is to dig up more background information on the Walkers by speaking to their old neighbours–my neighbours–which is precisely what I'm planning on doing right now.

While making my way up the neighbours' front steps, I mentally gather a list of questions I want answered. Sally greets me at the door with a look of surprise. Besides the odd wave over the past few months, I've done my best to avoid her. She's known as the town gossip.

I explain how I've recently learnt about the crime that took place in my house a year ago and then proceed to ask her what she knows about the case.

Sally's story is on par with those I'd read in the case files, painting Monroe as a psychotic junkie and Wyatt and his family as the victims of his vicious crimes. When I ask her if she's ever seen a young girl at the Walkers' home, her answer is a flat-out "No".

"Are you absolutely sure that the Walkers weren't hiding–"

"Now you listen here," she cuts me off sternly. "The Walkers are good people and upstanding members of our family church. I won't have you–" she waggles a finger at me "–or anyone else dragging their names through the dirt again over some 'he said, she said'. You can ask any of the neighbours on this street, and they'll give you the same story. That Monroe boy and his Ma were all kinds of trouble, and we're glad to be rid of them. They deserve to be locked up for good."

It's clear I've offended Sally, so I apologise for my forwardness and politely wrap up our conversation, telling her to have a great day.

Undeterred by her abrasive response, I follow suit with the next few neighbours, opting for a gentler, less accusing approach. To my disappointment, their answers all align. Not a single person can recall ever having seen a young girl in the Walkers' household. And what's more, they all believe the Walkers to be "good" people.

As I'm saying my final goodbyes, Shelby–one of the neighbours on the far end of the street–jars me by saying, "I wouldn't be bothering with the old woman next door. She's as blind as a bat." She leans forward and, in a hushed tone, adds, "Plus, folks around here say she's into that whole witchy hocus pocus–if you know what I mean."

Intrigued, I glance over at the old woman's front yard. Her property had piqued my curiosity when I'd first moved to Coraki. Colourful bottle trees line her garden, and the ceiling of her porch has been painted sky blue. When I'd pointed it out to Owen, he said that an African American woman lived there, and word on the street was that she'd moved here from New Orleans, Louisiana, back in the late '60s. The rare setup was said to be a part of an old superstitious practice set to ward off evil spirits and other haints. When I'd asked

Owen if he believed in spirits, he'd laughed it off, declaring superstition to be a bunch of nonsense.

Shelby stares at me expectantly, blue eyes gleaming as though she's just let me in on some big secret.

Disregarding the witch comment, I say, "The old woman might be blind, but I'm sure she still hears things. She might know something of value."

Shelby's eyes dim with disappointment. She was obviously expecting a different reaction.

"You can go ahead and door-knock if you'd like, but if you wake up tomorrow with a nasty rash or worse, don't be saying I didn't warn you."

I laugh off her comment as though I think it's a joke, yet all the while, I'm slipping into caution mode. *It's clear Shelby truly believes the woman is a witch.*

"Thanks again for all of your help," I say, waving politely as I leave her porch.

As I cross the invisible line between the neighbouring yards, my skin prickles with apprehension. I can't say I'm overly familiar with witchcraft and those who practise it, but I'm open-minded enough to keep wary.

Beyond the colourful bottle trees lies an overgrown garden that smells of sage and dill. Woven grass and wool trinkets with bells and wind chimes hang from the porch, swaying and dinging in the light breeze.

One of the trinkets spins in my direction, and I halt mid-stride, my breath catching. I recognise the symbol from my spare bedroom wall. I stare a moment, wondering what it stands for...what it means. It's all a little too coincidental for my liking.

This woman must know something.

Suddenly filled with a new sense of purpose, I take the porch steps two at a time, determined to unearth the answers I've been searching for.

I rap my knuckles against the wooden door and step back. My eyes lower to find a strip of earthy-red grit lining the doorway.

What's the purpose of it? I wonder.

The door creaks open ajar, the safety chain stopping it from opening further.

"Who's there?" It must be the old woman speaking because her voice is raspy, and I can hear her breaths crackling in and out as though there's a ball of phlegm at the back of her throat.

"My name's Shaina," I offer. "I'm one of your neighbours."

The door doesn't budge. Instead, she clears her throat and asks, "What do you want?" Now that her voice is clearer, I can distinctly hear a Southern American accent.

"I purchased a house down the road a couple of months back," I say. "And it's just been brought to my attention that a violent crime took place before I bought it. I was wondering if you knew anything about the case?"

The door closes slightly while the safety chain is removed, and then she opens it. I gasp at the sight of the short, paper-skinned woman with salt and pepper hair standing before me. She looks frightful with inflamed circular sores surrounding her lips, protruding like tiny volcanos spread intermittently. Her eyes are milky white, like those of a blind person, yet I get the distinct impression she's assessing me.

"I'm sorry," I say, immediately regretting my intrusion. "I didn't... I wasn't..."

"Come in, Child," she says, moving aside for me to pass.

I gaze beyond her figure, and my feet freeze in place. Shelves upon shelves line the hallway. One side is like an apothecary, with herbs and potions, whilst the other side is cluttered with candles, animal parts, raw bones, and strange handmade objects.

"Oh no, no, no," I say, taking a step back instead. "I just have a few questions; it won't take long."

"If you want any answers, you'll need to enter," she insists. "Or else, I have nothing to say."

I hesitate a moment, considering my options.

You've already come this far, I tell myself. *Either leave and learn nothing, or bite the bullet and see this through.*

I've barely crossed the threshold when the woman grabs hold of my arm and rasps, *"Malum ostendet verum faciem tuam."*

Panic-stricken, I snatch my arm back. "What are you doing?"

"I'm just making sure you ain't one of them. They have ways of slipping through my barriers from time to time."

"Who's they?" I ask, but she ignores me and stalks off down the hall.

Disregarding my self-preservation instincts, I follow the woman, glancing about nervously, not knowing what might jump out at me.

Unsurprisingly, the kitchen is just as creepy and cluttered as the hallway. There are liquid jars of organs, and God knows what! Swap out the candles out for Bunsen burners, and I could swear I just stepped into my year nine biology classroom.

The woman's hands clatter around the kitchen cupboards. She appears to be looking for something with those unseeing eyes of hers.

"So, *do you* happen to know any information regarding the case of the Walkers versus Monroe?" I prompt, eager to get my questions answered quickly and then get out.

The woman looks up at me—like, *right at me*—and her lips start twitching as though she wants to say something, only her mouth won't part. I stare, baffled. The small volcanoes around her lips tug and pull, appearing as if they've been sewn together with an invisible piece of string.

My breath hitches, and I stagger backwards, ready to make a run for it.

Shelby was right. I've made a terrible mistake in coming here.

The woman seems to find what she is looking for, clasps it in her hand, and then, as though reading my intentions, she reaches out with lightning speed, grabbing my arms and locking them in a vice-like grip. For an old woman who's frail and blind, she certainly doesn't lack strength or balance.

Using the self-defence moves Owen taught me, I point my elbows up and slice my arms downward, trying to forcibly escape her grip, but she's far stronger than I'd given her credit for.

Supernaturally strong comes an unbidden thought.

My heart hammers in my chest. I *really* should've listened to Shelby.

I work to keep my voice strong and steady.

"Let me go," I command, tugging against her grip.

"Quit struggling, Child," she says, dragging me over to a chest of drawers. "I have the answers you're looking for."

She thrusts me in front of the dresser and shoves a cold item in my hand. "I need you to open the top drawer for me."

I glimpse at my palm to find an antique key with an intricate pattern woven into the brass head.

"Why?" I ask sceptically. "What's in there?"

"The answer to your questions."

I glance over my shoulder, side-eyeing her. "Why don't *you* open it?"

"I can't," she answers flatly, which I find hard to believe. "Not while you're here."

"Fine," I say, slotting the key into the lock and then twisting. "But this better not be a trick." Despite my bravado, my pulse quickens.

What the hell am I doing? I've got a son to worry about. If I die trying to find answers for Monroe, then what's going to happen with Isaac? Owen doesn't understand him like I do. He won't be able to support him emotionally.

When I delay opening the unlocked drawer, the woman nudges me. "Open it."

"Okay!" I take hold of the handle and pull slowly, afraid of what I might find.

To my bewilderment, the drawer is empty, bar an old, faded

wedding photo. It's a group photo of fifteen or so people, all of them dressed in dated formal attire, the women with puffy hairdos.

"Do you see it?" The woman asks.

"See what?" I ask in return. "There's only an old photo inside."

The woman gives me another nudge. "Yes, that's it. Pick it up."

Frowning in confusion, I pluck the photo out of the drawer and examine the newlywed's faces, wondering what it is, *exactly*, I'm looking for. The groom is blond with fair skin and a chiselled jawline. He looks to be in his early twenties with a self-assured smile. His eyes are dark and empty, like bottomless pits.

The bride, on the other hand, only appears to be in her late teens. Her complexion is milky, and her face is sweet and angelic. Her hair is long, red, and plaited in a loose, puffy side braid with–what appears to be–gypsophila woven through it. Her eyes are round, doll-like, and an icy blue.

Isaac's description of Indi flashes to mind, and my skin prickles, but this girl can't possibly be her. This photo is too old.

"Whose wedding is this?" I ask.

"Read the back, Child."

Indi and Jerimiah
June 21st, 1979

"INDI AND JERIMIAH?" I read aloud. *What the...?* My brain boggles. *She can't possibly be the "Indi" Isaac and Monroe have been talking about.*

I swing around to confront the old woman, my mind a jumble of confusion. "This can't be right." I insist. "It says right here–" I point to the date, irrespective of the fact she can't see, "–that this picture was taken in the late '70s, but Monroe said Indi was only a year older than him when they met. If Indi was married in the late '70s, then that would make her much older than him." Another inconsistency occurs to me. "In fact," I say, driving in my next point. "Monroe said

Indi wasn't married when they first met. He said she was set to marry Jerimiah the following June."

The old woman listens but doesn't say a word, which I find infuriating.

"Well? What does this all mean?" I demand.

The woman's lips twitch, causing the small volcanos to tug aggressively against the invisible thread. It's a chilling sight and one I can't fully comprehend.

What's wrong with her?

Appearing to ponder a moment, she takes a breath and then asks, "Have you heard of the 'Time Loop' spell or the 'Keep My Secrets Binding' spell?"

I shake my head. "No. Why, what are they? What do they do?"

"They are two *very* powerful spells that remain binding even after death. Rather than doing the workings of God's will, there are some spellcasters who abuse magic and take it to a dark place. The only way of breaking such spells is by killing the spellcaster with this." She reaches into her pocket and hands me an intricate, jewel-encrusted dagger.

I stare down at the beautifully constructed weapon in my hand, feeling both fearful and fascinated all at once. It appears very old, and I'm guessing it was hand-crafted, going by the blackened silver and small imperfections.

"Daggers have been known throughout the ages as being used for ritual and ceremonial purposes," the woman says. "But they can also be used to restrain evil and harmful occult forces."

"I don't understand," I say. "Are you implying that the 'Time Loop' spell and the 'Keep My Secrets Binding' spell were used on Indi, and in order to free her from them, someone needs to kill the spellcaster with this?" I hold the jewel-encrusted dagger up for emphasis, hoping for an answer.

The woman's lips tug, but she doesn't answer. Frustrated, I stare back at the wedding photo. Judging by the timelines, I can only assume that Indi was dead when Monroe met her. He'd been seeing a ghost but hadn't realised it. It'd also suggest why none of the neighbours can recall having ever seen Indi at the Walkers' house. Not everybody sees ghosts.

Another major thought springs to mind.

This would mean Wyatt isn't Indi's father. The man could very well be as innocent as he claims.

My stomach twists with guilt. If Indi truly had died years ago, then I was wrong about him.

I study the photo, trying to piece together my strewn thoughts when it occurs to me that I recognise one of the faces. *Bruce?* Make that two of the faces. *Harold?* No, three. *Monroe?* I stare incredulously.

No, I realise. *It's not Monroe. The man in the picture has a darker complexion and brown eyes.*

"Who's the man on the far right," I ask, fully aware that I'm asking a blind woman. Ironically enough, I'm not at all surprised when she answers.

"That's Enzo."

"Enzo?" I repeat in confusion. "Monroe said that Indi called him Enzo."

"Enzo is Monroe's father," she says, "and my son."

As soon as she says it, I can see the resemblance to her, too. I hadn't picked it up right away because I was thrown by her eerie eyes and lips.

A curious thought occurs to me, and I frown. "I'm surprised Monroe didn't mention he had a grandma who lived down the road."

"That's because he doesn't know about me."

"Why?"

"Because my son is selfish." The woman's tone is biting.

It's clear I've touched on a delicate subject, so I move on to my next question. "What about the man standing next to the groom? Is that Bruce Adams?"

"Sergeant Adams." The old woman snorts in disgust. "Did you know him?"

"Not all that well." I choose not to admit that Bruce is my father-in-law. I don't particularly like the man. He used to be the local Sergeant in town, but he was forced to retire five years ago because he had a stroke. That's when Owen put his hand up for the position. He got a promotion from a Senior Constable to a Sergeant and was able to work closer to home.

Is Bruce connected to all this? Is Owen connected to all this?

"I don't understand what all of this means," I say, voicing my thoughts aloud. "Who cast the spells on Indi, and who killed her? Was it her father?" I stare at the two familiar redheads in the photo and cringe before adding. "Who is her father?"

"Harold was her father. He was a beast of a man, but he wasn't the one to cast the spell on her, nor was he the one to kill her."

Harold is Bruce's brother, Owen's uncle. *If Owen had a cousin named Indi, who married a guy named Jerimiah, wouldn't Monroe's story have struck a chord with him? More importantly, does that mean Owen's uncle used to live in my house? I'm mystified as to why Owen wouldn't have mentioned any of this when he helped me to buy the property.*

Does he have something to hide?

"Then who did it, do you know?" I ask, frowning. "Who killed Indi?"

Once again, the small volcanoes around her lips tug, forbidding her from answering. Suddenly, a comment Isaac made about Indi pops to mind.

"When I asked Indi what happened to her—how she died—her lips and eyes turn funny, so I don't ask those types of questions anymore."

That's why Monroe's grandmother can't give me the answers I'm seeking, I realise. *She's had the "Keep My Secrets Binding" spell placed upon her, too.*

Both women have been bound.

A loud crash, followed by the tinkle of glass shattering, startles me from my train of thought. Next comes a chilling shriek.

"Is there someone else here?" I ask in alarm.

The woman nods, appearing unrattled by the sound. "That's my Elias."

"Elias?" I repeat in question.

"I must see to him," she says, ushering me away from the open drawer. "You need to go."

"Oh..." Caught off guard, I stammer. "Okay." I clasp the photo tightly between my fingers as she hurries me back through the kitchen and into the hall. I'm not ready to give the photo back just yet. I want to study it.

"Would I be able to borrow this picture?" I ask.

"By all means, take it. The answer you're seeking is hidden in plain sight."

I offer the dagger back, but she places a hand over mine, pressing the handle into my palm.

"Keep it, Child. There is danger all around you."

The shrieking intensifies, and I can't help but wonder who Elias is and what in the world has happened to him. It sounds as though he's being tortured.

As I step out onto the porch, I ask, "What's your name?"

"Dawn," the woman answers before slamming the door shut on me.

CHAPTER 21

JUNE 21ST, 1979

CORAKI, AUSTRALIA

∞ ENZO ∞

I left my mama's house in my pin-striped suit and headed straight to Jerimiah's property for his and Indi's wedding ceremony. I meandered around the property, taking in the ambience. It was alight with twinkling fairy lights, flickering candles, and a couple of large firepits. A large marquee was pitched beside the church, with an arbour at the entrance decorated with green leafy branches, red ribbons, and flowers. Inside the marquee were long white cloth trestle tables and chairs, with silver cutlery, crystal champagne flutes, and place tags for the guest seating.

The people of the community were mingling around the firepits as hors d'oeuvres were being served by hired waiters. Slowly, they started noticing me, and gasps and grunts echoed as they whispered amongst themselves. None of them were brave enough to approach me, let alone speak to me. They'd all been warned that associating with shunned community members comes with consequences.

They kept a wide berth like I was the plague sweeping through the area to infect them.

It didn't take long for my presence to be reported to Jerimiah, and before I knew it, he came strolling out of the church in his white, pressed suit to greet me.

"Enzo, my old friend, I wondered if I might see you here tonight. We've all been praying for you, hoping that you would see the light and return to us." He put his hand on my shoulder in a false show of affection when, really, it was a warning. "You've been dearly missed."

I snuffed out a laugh. "Is that so?"

Jerimiah's lips curled into a smug smile. "Tonight is going to be a beautiful and memorable evening. I'm so glad you've reformed enough to attend. I wouldn't have wanted you to miss it."

I nodded politely, keeping up with his performance. "I wouldn't have missed it for the world." Meanwhile, my eyes shot daggers at him with an inaudible message that said, *"Fuck you."*

On his way back into the church, Jerimiah stopped by the steps and spoke to Bruce and Harold. As both men turned my way, I got the distinct impression that Jerimiah was asking them to keep an eye on me. They were strong, burly men, the types you wouldn't want to cross, and it seemed they'd since become Jerimiah's bodyguards of sorts.

They weren't going to intimidate me. I followed Jerimiah into the church, taking a seat on one of the front pews, closest to the aisle on the bride's side. Jerimiah's eyes narrowed as I sat. His jaw ticked, but he said nothing.

The ceremony wasn't set to start until six-thirty, which was half an hour away, but I wanted to make a statement. As the minutes ticked over, the church slowly began to fill with guests. Bruce gave me a filthy look as he and his son, Owen, passed. I was aware that the front pew was generally reserved for the family members of the bride and groom, but I was exactly where I wanted to be, and I wasn't about to budge. Before Bruce got the chance to rebuke me, his wife beckoned him and Owen to sit on Jerimiah's side with her and their two daughters. Jerimiah hadn't needed to reserve the pew for his family members. They'd long since died by his hand. I was the closest thing to a relative he had, and he was intent on destroying me, too.

When the song "What a Wonderful World" by Louis Armstrong started playing, my heart hammered wildly in my chest. Not only had Jerimiah stolen my girl, but he'd also stolen my favourite song. He must've been counting on me turning up and had vindictively gone one step further to drive the knife deeper. For the first time since arriving, I wondered if I could honestly sit through the charade. Watching Jerimiah marry Indi, just to spite me, was my worst nightmare come true.

When Indi entered the church, I gasped. She looked more beautiful than I could ever have imagined. Her dress was simple but elegant, with pearl-like beads stitched on the bodice, enhancing her milky complexion. Small white flowers adorned her long red locks, which were held neatly in a side braid, and thin tendrils had been left out at the sides, framing her angelic face.

When she caught sight of me, she stumbled, but Harold's firm grip steadied her as they continued to walk down the aisle.

As far as weddings go, this one was gloomy and bordered on the heartache of a funeral. It lacked any genuine love, joy, and excitement. Jerimiah used a celebrant of the church group to officiate their nuptials, and it was obvious the young man had been heavily coached on exactly what to say.

I gritted my teeth and forced myself to sit tight while Indi and Jerimiah exchanged their vows. It was clear Indi's vows had been written for her. She read the words with no emotion, flat and lifeless, as though they had no meaning.

When the celebrant said, "Should anyone present know of any reason that this couple should not be joined in holy matrimony, speak now or forever hold your peace," both Indi's and Jerimiah's heads turned in my direction.

Indi's doe eyes were round and pleading, but for my plan to work, I needed to bite my tongue. It would be much easier to slip away with her while everyone else was tipsy and busy celebrating at the reception. To drag her out of the church against the will of Jerimiah and her family would certainly be the death of me.

When the ceremony finished, Indi and Jerimiah made their way over to the far end of the marquee, where a woman from the church stood, holding a camera.

"Can I get all family members over this way, please," she called.

I waited until Indi's family took their positions and then went and stood on the far right. I did it to annoy Jerimiah, but it had more of an effect on Harold.

"Hey," he spat, shoulders squaring. "You're not a part of the family,"

Jerimiah placed his arm on Harold's. "Now, Now," he said, his southern drawl still strong even after a decade of living in Australia. "I'm sure we can allow him to be in this one shot."

While they finished getting their photos taken, I strolled around the marquee, checking out the place cards on the tables. My name was nowhere to be seen.

Eventually, Harold's wife came across to speak with me.

I was certain she was going to ask me to leave, but instead, she said, "I'm so sorry there's not a designated spot for you. Jerimiah hadn't mentioned you would be joining us."

He knew I would show up, I thought, but instead, I said, "I thought I would surprise them."

Mrs Adams leaned in closer, her lips nearly touching my ear. "I wished you'd come sooner like you promised. I never wanted this for her." Her eyes flicked to Jerimiah momentarily with a look of disgust. "My husband's spellbound by him, just like the rest of these mindless sheep, but my daughter and I can't be brainwashed. And we're forever being punished for it. Jerimiah told my husband that my daughter and I need to be contained or else the Devil will rise out of us and set this whole blasted world aflame."

My prayers were answered in the name of Mrs Adams. Quick to take advantage, I whispered, "Tell Indi to pretend to slip off to the bathroom after dinner. I will be waiting out the front in the beat-up

Commodore, with the keys in the ignition, ready to go. I have a getaway plan."

Mrs Adams gave a quick nod and then strode off.

As the guests made their way to their designated seating, I went back to my car and waited restlessly, glancing at the clock every other minute to gauge the time. Sweat poured from my temples, and I needed to take off my jacket and tie because my neck and chest felt as though they were being constricted.

As the time ticked by, I sent myself into a panic, wondering if Jerimiah had cottoned on to my plan and stopped Indi from leaving, but then I saw her pale figure racing to the car, and my chest loosened in relief.

I smiled at her as she jumped into the passenger side, and I immediately reached to turn the key in the ignition.

"Wait." She grabbed my arm, stopping me. "My mother's coming, too."

What? Taking her mama hadn't been a part of the plan, but I accepted her appeal without arguing and said, "Okay."

A quarter of an hour later, I was biting at the bit to get a move on. It was only a matter of time before Jerimiah grew suspicious of Indi's whereabouts and came searching for her. It felt as though the car was closing in on me.

"Where is she?" I asked.

Indi shrugged, her brows furrowed with concern. "I don't know. She said she'd be right behind me."

I clasped my hand around Indi's, imploring her to look at me. "We can't keep waiting," I said. "We need to leave."

Indi shook her head. "No. We have to wait. She can't stay here."

"There's no time," I argued. "You've been gone too long. Jerimiah will come searching for you, and if he finds us—"

Indi tugged her hand back. "I'll go and find her, and I'll come back after dessert."

"Indi, no," I begged.

I reached for her hand, but she was already halfway out the door.

I jumped out after her and called out softly, "Indi, no, please come back."

She glanced over her shoulder. "I'll be back," she said, before dashing off towards the festivities.

I felt so sick I began to heave. If it wasn't for her mama, we would've been well and truly gone by now.

The next half-an-hour dragged by slowly and painfully, each second like a minute and each minute like an hour. Dessert would've come and gone already, and I had a sickening feeling that something had gone terribly wrong.

I heard a nearby crunch, and my eyes darted to my side mirror. I was hoping to see Indi. However, I wasn't at all surprised to discover it was Jerimiah. My plan was foiled. This was the end.

He opened the door, and I braced myself, waiting for the knife or gun.

"I'm sorry, my friend," he said, his voice void of sympathy, "But Indi is, and always will be, mine."

Before I was able to react, he opened his palm and blew red dust on my face, which burned like acid powder. I howled as it singed my eyes and scorched my skin. The effects were immediate. I tried wiping my eyes, but I couldn't move a muscle. My body had gone limp, and I started falling sideways toward the door. Jerimiah stepped back as I toppled toward the gravel. Though I tried, I wasn't able to move a muscle. I'd been rendered paralysed by the substance, and yet I still felt excruciating pain. The burning sensation spread throughout my body from head to toe, and I wanted to scream, but I was unable to open my mouth. It felt as though I'd been tied above a fire ants' nest, and they were all feasting upon my body.

"Goodbye, Enzo," Jerimiah said coolly, before striding off into the night.

Whatever Jerimiah had done to me left me dangling there in complete torture. Unable to move or scream or see anything bar a blur, my mind begged for the Lord to take me. I believed death would be a blessing by comparison.

The hours dragged on, the music died down, and eventually, the guests started making tracks. I was hoping someone would have seen me on their way to their car and called an ambulance, but I'd deliberately parked across the road, away from the guest parking, ready for a quick escape. Hence, nobody saw my slumped body hanging out of the driver-side door.

I imagined the powdered substance Jerimiah used on me was going to kill me slowly, but as the evening rolled around, I felt it easing. It was past midnight before I could lever myself upright. My limbs felt stiff, my neck throbbed, and my vision was still slightly blurry.

It was pitch black before I finally mustered the energy to drag myself across the yard to Jerimiah's property. A dead man walking doesn't care about danger. Besides, it was easy to be reckless and take risks, knowing that I wouldn't stay dead for long. Even if this body was killed, my soul would go on. I'd come to Coraki with a backup plan.

The marquee was all but lost to the darkness. The firepits and candles had been doused, and the fairy lights switched off. The only place which was still aglow was the church.

Fear clutched my heart. The only reason the candles would still be burning at an ungodly hour was if Jerimiah was performing a ritual.

I raced to the steps, my feet practically tripping from under me, and held on fast to the rail as I climbed the staircase. I held my breath as I pushed open the double doors, hoping my fear was groundless. It was dark, and I couldn't see properly due to my blurred vision, but I detected a faint glow of candles alight on the floor in front of the altar.

I forced myself forward, my knees growing weak.

He wouldn't. Not yet, I'd thought. *She still has time.*

But as I grew closer, it soon became apparent that I was wrong.

"No," I cried out, falling to my knees in despair. "No."

Indi's pale body laid lifelessly, atop a chalk drawn pentacle inside a ring of candles. Blood-red rose petals were spread over and around her body, and just like the other young women we'd sacrificed over the years, her lips were sewn together, and her eyes were bleached. Jerimiah didn't want his secrets shared, especially among the dead.

I took Indi's hand in mine and squeezed it, tears streaking my cheeks.

"Why?" I asked. "Why did you have to go back?"

The sight of her disfigured face seared my soul like a branding iron.

My anguish quickly morphed into a rage I couldn't control. I stormed back out of the church like a madman and marched over to Jerimiah's house, adrenaline fuelling my movements.

"Jerimiah!" I shouted. "Jerimiah!"

When he didn't come out, I went to the back door and twisted the handle, surprised to find it unlocked.

I raged through the house, yelling Jerimiah's name on repeat and smashing his belongings as I passed. I searched high and low, but the monster of a man was nowhere to be found.

Frustrated and heart still hammering, I hurried back to my car and took off into town. I pulled up out the front of Indi's old house and bashed on the door. Mrs Adams was the one to answer. Her husband Harold was out cold from drinking too many beers at the wedding.

"Indi's dead," I said bluntly. "Jerimiah killed her."

"What?" She shook her head, not wanting to believe me.

"She went back for you," I spat, pointing my finger in her face. "I could have taken her away from this, but she went back for you."

"Harold caught up with me," she spluttered. "He knew I was up to something. I couldn't get away."

"Well, you'd best leave with me now while he's passed out, or your daughter's death will be in vain."

"We should pick up my sister and her daughters on the way. I don't want to leave them behind."

"Your sister's husband is a cop," I pointed out.

"He's a bad cop. Jerimiah has corrupted him."

I sighed and tossed her the keys. "Here, take the car, pick them up, and get the hell out of here. There's two grand in the glove box. It should be enough to get you started. Choose somewhere safe where they won't be able to find you."

She glanced between me and the keys in her hands, eyes questioning. "What about you?"

"I'm going to do something I should've done a long time ago. Now go," I urged, "before it's too late."

She didn't need to be told a third time.

Once she'd safely driven out of the street, I started pounding on the neighbours' doors. Most of the people around this side of town were a part of Jerimiah's church group, and I wanted them to know exactly what kind of man they were following. Every time someone opened their door, I inundated them with the facts.

"Indi's dead. Jerimiah killed her. The church he's running isn't Godly. You've been lured into a satanic cult."

The Church of Salvation wasn't a satanic cult, strictly speaking, but it came close. Jerimiah was as evil as Satan, and I wanted the community to fear him. I wanted them to question their blind faith in him.

People were coming out of their houses to find out what the commotion was about when the wail of sirens blaring filled the night air. The paddy wagon squealed to a stop across the driveway of the house I was leaving, and Sergeant Adams jumped out with his gun raised.

"Lorenzo, put your hands up," he shouted, pointing his gun straight at me.

There were plenty of neighbours out in the street watching and whispering. Whether I'd gotten through to them or not, I didn't know, but I hoped I'd at least planted a seed of doubt. Nothing meant more to Jerimiah than power and the faith of his followers. Without his followers, his power would diminish.

I didn't resist Sergeant Adams when he came over to cuff me.

Instead, I continued to call out at the top of my lungs, "Indi's dead. Jerimiah killed her. The church he's running isn't Godly. You've all been lured into a satanic cult."

I assumed Sergeant Adams would be taking me into the station, but as we headed in the direction of Jerimiah's property, a replay of Harold's wife's words repeated in my head.

"He's a bad cop. Jerimiah has corrupted him."

This is it, I thought. *After all this time, I'm finally going to meet my end.*

Bruce drove to the far end of Jerimiah's property and parked before forcing me out the back of the wagon. I looked around, waiting for Jerimiah to appear from the shadows, but he didn't show.

"This is for Indi, you sick son of a bitch," Bruce said, before aiming his gun at my chest.

His finger closed around the trigger, and the gun fired. My ears rang with the resounding echo as the sheer force of the bullet penetrating my chest sent me toppling. I hit the ground with a surge of searing pain and put my hands to my chest. The warmth of blood gushed around my fingers, thick and sticky. Then mercifully, after a few gasping breaths, my soul floated away from my body.

CHAPTER 22
JUNE 29TH, 1998
CORAKI, AUSTRALIA
∞ SHAINA ∞

As I descend the porch steps, I catch sight of Shelby next door, peeking through her window shades. Noticing me, notice her, her face disappears. Next thing I know, she's bursting out her front door and bailing me up.

Shelby's eyes are alight with anticipation. "What just happened in there?" It's obvious she's not asking because she's concerned. She's after some gossip.

Elias' shrieks die down into faint, uncontrolled sobs, which can only just be heard from the front lawn where I'm standing.

"You were right," I say, blowing Shelby off. "Dawn didn't know anything."

"But... but..." Shelby spies the dagger in my hand and her jaw slacks. "Did you?"

Not in the mood for her games, I hurry on past, waving politely with my free hand. "Have a nice day, Shelby."

I can feel her eyes burning a hole in my back as I make my way down the street back to my house. I'm sure all the neighbours' tongues will be wagging with an embellished version of this morning's events soon enough.

I glance at the photo again, and a million and one questions circle my mind. My first instinct is to contact Owen and demand answers, but after careful consideration, I decide against it. I'm afraid he won't be honest with me. He'll play it off like I'm being ridiculous and ruin any chances I have of finding additional answers elsewhere. He had the opportunity to share what he knew about the case of the Walkers versus Monroe with me, and he didn't take it. All he managed to do was scare off Monroe and make me realise that I *really* can't trust him.

I slip my hand into my pocket and pull out my car keys, now certain of what my next move should be.

As soon as I pull up outside the front of the Walkers' place, bile rises in my throat. The last time I'd come here, I'd been certain that Wyatt was guilty, and now I'm the one left drowning in self-reproach.

I hide the dagger in my glovebox but take the photo with me, hoping against all odds that they are forgiving, and I can convince them to share what they know about Harold with me.

When I get to the front door, I knock twice, loudly but not aggressively.

"Hold on there just a sec," Wyatt's voice calls from inside.

I hear him shuffling up the hallway before unclicking the lock. When the door swings open, a flash of surprise crosses over his face.

"Shaina?" His questioning tone holds a wary edge. "What are you doing here?"

"I owe you and your wife an apology," I say. "I made a big mistake coming here the other day and taking pictures. I was searching for answers in all the wrong places."

"Oh... Well, that's mighty decent of you to say so. I'll pass the message on to Ruth." He nods politely and starts to close the door. "Good day, Shaina."

"Wait." I thrust a palm against the door, startling him. "Can I come in?"

His eyes roam over me cautiously. "I don't know that it's such a good idea. Ruth is busy."

"Please," I beg. "I'd really like to apologise to Ruth in person."

He opens his mouth to say something, but instead, he sighs. "Very well."

Wyatt leads the way down the olive-coloured hallway, stopping halfway at the door which was locked the last time I was here. Despite knowing the Walkers aren't Indi's parents, my heart still races.

Why was the door locked?

Wyatt knocks softly. "Ruth, we have a guest. Shaina's back."

I stare at the ground, settling my nerves and pretending not to notice the uneasy edge in his voice when mentioning my name.

"Just a minute," Ruth replies.

The sounds of scuffling and scratching, followed by Ruth's warning, "Now, now, stop that," sends my heart rate spiking.

"Come." Wyatt beckons, pressing on towards the kitchen. "I'll fix you with a drink while we're waiting."

I should let it go, but I can't. I stay fixed to the spot.

"What's in that room?" I ask.

Wyatt glances back at me, disappointment written over his face.

"Why exactly are you here, Shaina? And don't go feeding me the same nonsense as last time. I was under the impression that you're here because you wanted to make nice and apologise."

"I'm sorry, I do want to make nice." I swallow hard before adding. "I'm just on edge. A lot has happened in the past few days, and I no longer know who I can trust. Last time I was here, this door was locked, and I heard scratching, and now..."

The door swings open, and Ruth steps out with a ringtail possum curled in her arms.

"And now, what?" she asks contemptuously.

"It's a possum," I say, more to myself than to them.

Ruth's brows narrow into a V. "What? As opposed to our make-believe daughter?"

"About that," I glance between the pair. "I know for a fact Indi wasn't your daughter, and I have proof." I hold up the photo.

Ruth leans forward, squinting at the picture in my hand.

"The photo was taken in 1979," I say, flipping it over so she can see the writing on the back. "And as you can see, it says Indi and Jerimiah."

"Where did you get this?"

I flip the photo back around, deflecting Ruth's question with one of my own. "Do you recognise anyone in the picture?"

As she scans along the line of faces, a glint of recognition flickers in her features. "Enough of this," she says, not giving me an answer. "I think it's about time you left."

"No, please," I beg. "I need your help. I believe the bride–" I point to Indi "–was killed many years ago and that she's haunting my house. My son has seen and spoken to her, just like Monroe. Only my son knows Indi's a ghost. Isaac says she's scared of her father, and she asks him to help her hide so that she doesn't get a beating. I've since found out that this man–" I point to Harold, aware that I'm rambling at this point "–is her father, and I've seen him enough times to know what a beast of a man he can be. What I don't know, though, is if my ex-husband is connected to all this, and what's more," I add, "I don't know who killed Indi."

A long and painful silence ticks on while Ruth and Wyatt share a measured glance. *Should we, or shouldn't we?* Their eyes communicate.

To my relief, Wyatt folds. "Come on then." He beckons me towards the kitchen once more. "Why don't I fix you with a hot cup of tea."

"I'll put Percy back away," Ruth says matter-of-factly and slips back into the room, closing the door behind her.

"Ruth does volunteer work for Wires," Wyatt says, setting me straight. "She helps to nurse the joeys that've lost their mothers. She's a good woman."

I nod in acknowledgement. "I'm sorry. I see that now."

By the time the pot of tea is ready, Ruth comes and joins us at the table. Her negative energy is thick and fills the room, threatening to suffocate me where I sit. I can tell she isn't keen on helping me, and for good reason. I did deliberately deceive her and her family the last time I was here.

Ruth pours us tea while Wyatt pops his spectacles on.

"Would you mind passing me that picture of yours? I'd like to take a look now that I can finally see it." He scans over the people in the photo before using his finger to point out the faces he recognises. "That there is Harold, as you know, and Bruce, and Owen–"

"Owen?" Shocked, I zoom in closer.

Wyatt's finger hovers over a young, gangly kid around the age of eleven.

"My Owen?"

Why the hell am I saying, "My Owen?".

Wyatt glances up at me questioningly. "You didn't know?"

"No. He looks so different. I've never seen any childhood photos of him."

Wyatt moves on. "Those there are his two older sisters, Grace and Willow."

I stare down at the two young women in the photo, gobsmacked. Grace looks around fourteen with sandy blonde hair like Owen. Willow, on the other hand, looks about sixteen and has dark hair, like the woman standing alongside her. When Wyatt identifies the woman as being Terri, Owen's mother, I'm not at all surprised.

"I've never met Owen's mother or sisters," I say. "He told me that his mother up and left with the girls when he was eleven, and he and his dad have never heard from them again since that day."

"Didn't you find it the least bit strange that he never showed you any childhood photos or photos of his family?" Ruth asks, passing me the jug of milk.

I shrug. "I've never really thought about it. I don't have any photos of my family to show. My mother died when I was two, and my father wasn't big on cameras. I actually don't even know if I have any childhood photos."

For the first time since meeting her, Ruth's expression softens. "That's very sad, dear."

Wyatt continues to point out a few of the other faces he recognises, but none of the names ring a bell with me. "So that's Jerimiah," he says, staring at the groom. "I've always wondered what he looked like." His gaze shifts to the bride. "And that's Indi."

"Hold on a sec," I say, perplexed. "If you knew of Jerimiah and Indi, wouldn't it have sparked your curiosity when Monroe mentioned their names in court?"

"Now, hold on just one second." Wyatt holds a finger up. "I never said I knew a girl named Indi. The first time I'd ever heard Indi's name was when Monroe said it, the day he broke in. And I've only ever known *of* Jerimiah. When I bought the house off Harold, he was a single man. He said his wife had left him and that he was looking for something smaller. He never, once, mentioned anything about having a daughter, let alone her name."

As always, with more answers comes more questions. "When did you buy the house?" I ask.

"Nineteen years ago." Wyatt expels a deep sigh before continuing. "Truth is, there were a number of houses available in that particular area back then, but that old shack was cheap and all we could afford with a child on the way. We hadn't known it at the time, but some of the locals later said that Richmond Terrace, Bridge Street and Nolan Street had once been inundated with cult members."

"Those types tend to live in clusters," Ruth cuts in.

"I don't exactly know what happened, but something must've gone down because, apparently, the group split. A couple of the members who were born and bred here—like the Adams brothers—stayed put and returned to their normal lives, but most of the community moved on."

"The Adams brothers," I repeat. "So, Owen's family were a part of the cult?"

"Yes, the Adams brothers," Ruth says pointedly. "They were important members of the cult, Bruce being of authority and all."

I push the unwelcome revelation aside a moment, needing more answers to get a better understanding of what exactly I've gotten myself into.

"Did you notice anything unusual about the house when you bought it?" I pry. "Or did anything strange happen in the north-facing bedroom while you were living there?"

Wyatt had mentioned "strange happenings" going on in their spare room in his police report, but I can't exactly admit that I've read it.

Wyatt ponders for a moment, "Sure, we had a few issues with the room, but we didn't see any ghosts if that's what you're asking. We're not superstitious people. I believe it was the neighbour interfering with our things. He was always high and talking to himself. The kid and his mother were trouble."

"He's out of rehab now. Did you know that?" I ask. "He came to the house on Saturday looking for Indi. He still believes Indi is your daughter and that you were the one mistreating her. He doesn't realise he was talking to a ghost, let alone a ghost from a different time. He may have been high and troubled, Mr Walker, but I don't think he was crazy. I believe he was misguided by Indi's spirit."

Ruth scoffs.

"Now you listen here," Wyatt says, growing sharp with me. "That kid *was* crazy. He wouldn't listen to reason. When I told him I didn't know who Indi was but offered to still help him find her, he gouged my throat and fired a spear into my bad leg." His voice rises as he continues. "I had to get physiotherapy for a good twelve months before I could walk again!"

"I'm not saying that I agree with his actions," I say, waving my hands in surrender. "I don't. All I'm saying is that Monroe legiti-mately thought he was attacking Indi's father, a man who'd repeatedly abused his daughter. Wrong though it may be, it makes perfect sense."

"What do you want from us, Shaina?" Ruth asks. "First, you come here with false motives, sneaking around and treating us like criminals, and then you say you're back to apologise and that you need our help, only to insult us yet again."

"I'm not trying to insult you. I'm trying to uncover the truth. I believe Indi was murdered." I tap the image of her with my pointer. "And I believe someone in this photo killed her." In a much more controlled tone, I add, "Monroe told me, when he reported that Indi was in a religious cult, he was immediately shut down by the authorities and, later, the judge. They'd pinned him as crazy. Why? If everyone in town knew about the cult overrunning the area, then why didn't they speak up? Is it because the Adams brothers were a part of the cult and Bruce was a cop?"

Monroe had mentioned as much, but I want to hear the words come from Wyatt's mouth.

"Why don't you ask your ex-husband, Owen, for the answers?"

"Because I'm afraid he won't tell me the truth," I answer honestly. "If Owen finds out I'm looking into this, and he and his family really were a part of the cult, as you've said, then he's likely to stonewall me and squash any remaining evidence."

"Or he'll squash *you*," Ruth says in all seriousness. "Just like Gary."

I raise a brow. "Gary?"

"Now, now. Don't be bringing that up to her." Wyatt tsks. "She might repeat it to the family."

"She wants answers," Ruth insists. "I'm just giving them to her, plain and simple." She shifts her focus to me. "Folks say Gary was a local who was 'mysteriously' run over by his own tractor after spilling allegations that Jerimiah, the cult's pastor, was involved with several minors. And then there was Roger, who mysteriously ran his car off the East Coraki Bridge on his way home from work after spilling allegations that Jerimiah killed his first wife. And then there was Kevin, who was impaled by his own machinery after making accusations that the local Sergeant was disregarding residents' allegations. And then there was—"

"Okay, Love," Wyatt interrupts. "I'm sure she gets the picture."

"Rumour was, folks around here were terrified of the cult," Ruth continues, delving down a different path. "They believed if they too spoke out against the cult, they would also die by a 'mysterious' death. Some say it was black magic that killed them, but we believe it was the Adams brothers. They had the power and the means to cover up the crimes."

My mind boggles. Once again, with more answers comes more questions.

I'm not at all surprised to discover that Harold and Bruce are caught up in this mess. I would, however, be surprised if I were to find out that Owen is covering for them. While he can be an utter bastard at times, I'd hate to believe that he is an evil bastard.

Something Monroe said to Owen springs to mind, making me re-evaluate everything I once believed about him.

"What you do behind closed doors is your business."

What has Owen been doing behind closed doors?

I wish I had a way of contacting Monroe. I want to share what I've learnt, and perhaps together, we could puzzle in the missing pieces.

And then, like a flash, another elusive memory pops to mind. Monroe said he was starting a new job this week.

What was that pub called again? The Holy Moley? No... think, think.

The Hoey Moey.

CHAPTER 23

1979-1997

CORAKI, AUSTRALIA

∞ ENZO'S SPIRIT ∞

L ittle had I known the spell I'd cast, which was supposed to give me a new lease on life, would ultimately be my curse. While my spirit was able to enter Elias' body, the link was diluted given he was a twin, so I was unable to stick.

Mama was right when she said, "You've instilled your darkness onto this poor child."

I felt an overwhelming sense of darkness as soon as I entered Elias' body, and what made matters worse was the way he reacted to me possessing him. Every time I made the connection, I could literally feel him rejecting me from his body. He would scream and thrash hysterically until Mama came rushing in to settle him down.

Mama was able to feel my presence through her gift, and she did all she could to block me from entering Elias' body and their home. The spells and potions she used would work for certain periods of time, and during those times, my spirit laid dormant, almost fading into oblivion. As soon as the spells wore off, though, I would try again, hoping Elias would come to accept my spirit within and we could live as one. Without him, I ceased to exist. I couldn't move about freely and do as I wished. My spell had tied my spirit to him, much like a dog on a short leash.

I managed to catch a glimpse of Jerimiah before Mama banished me the first time. I watched through the window as he left a large yellow envelope in Mama's mailbox. I was worried he would pick up on my spirit through his connection with Mama, but her gift of spiritualism must've remained hers solely.

Mama opened the envelope and plucked out a photo. She gasped and quickly dropped it, shaking her fingers as though they'd been zapped. As it fluttered to the floor landing face up, I saw it was the family portrait I'd intruded on the night of Indi and Jerimiah's wedding. Why Jerimiah had chosen to taunt Mama with my final photo was anyone's best guess. Even after all the years we'd spent together, I still couldn't comprehend the inner workings of his psyche.

After many years of trying, yet failing to connect my spirit with Elias' body, I began to wonder if I could make a connection with Monroe's body instead. Within seconds of the thought, I was standing in front of him, transported by the forces of magic. To my delight, I was able to connect with Monroe's body easily, the only drawback was I couldn't maintain the connection for any more than a few hours at a time.

I could feel the mind-altering effects of dark magic plaguing Monroe's mental stability, courtesy of his link to me, but it was nothing in comparison to the darkness that had invaded Elias' entire body.

I stayed with Monroe throughout his younger years, and in some ways, I protected him. Leonie had slipped back into her junkie ways and would bring home scumbags who treated her and Monroe terribly.

Monroe was never aware of the events that took place when I was in possession of his body. I would get him to do all manner of underhanded things to make these guys' lives difficult, until they left. Sadly, Leonie would only replace one scumbag with another, and so the cycle continued. A revolving door for scumbags.

As Monroe grew older, Leonie started noticing odd behavioural patterns with him and accused him of losing his mind.

She would blame him for doing the things I'd done while possessing him, and he would argue the matter black and blue, resentful of her accusations.

Monroe was having a hard time at school as well as at home, so I stepped in to help there, too, hoping to make things better for him. Instead, I made matters worse. While possessing him, I fought the bullies who tediously picked on him and threatened them to back off. When they didn't get the message, I resorted to dark magic which inadvertently left a black mark on Monroe's soul. I didn't want Monroe to be a walkover like I was. I'd wanted him to be strong.

Monroe wouldn't remember any of the awful things I'd gotten him to do and would always deny any fault. The school staff collectively agreed there was something off about him and suggested that Leonie got him medically assessed.

I WASN'T ALWAYS able to reach Elias during his younger years because of the magical barriers my mama put in place to block me. However, as he grew older, she grew laxer with the upkeep, and my spirit was able to zap back to him occasionally. I was glad Elias had my mama to take care of him. I don't know that he would've lasted long under Leonie's care. He was a unique boy with genuine mental and physical health issues, undoubtedly rising from the darkness within him. He needed the extra love and care my mama provided, and over the years, the pair had grown extremely close. They were like two peas in a pod.

I didn't try entering Elias' body again until he was at the ripe age of seventeen. He must've gotten somewhat used to my presence as I came and went over the years, because he only screamed and thrashed momentarily before giving in to my spirit and allowing me to stay. My goal wasn't to possess him permanently, I just wanted to borrow his body to learn the ins and outs of what'd taken place in Coraki since I'd left.

I went down by the Richmond River and spoke to an old drunk who was sitting on the park bench. He was swigging a bottle of bourbon and puffing on a cigarette.

In my experience, drunk people loved a good yarn, and this old boozer was no exception.

I steered the conversation in the direction I wanted information, telling him I'd heard rumours about there being a cult in town.

"Those crazies are long gone, boyo," he raved. "And thankfully, they moved on when they did. They just about destroyed this town with their Satanic nonsense. They had everyone corrupted, even the police. I just wish the Adams brothers had moved on with the rest of them."

"Someone mentioned the name Jerimiah," I'd said, probing for information. "Was he their leader?"

"My word." He nodded. "I heard that cocky bastard went back to the US where he belongs. Good riddance, I say, although folks insist, he still owns the property over on Casino Road. Apparently, he's leaving it to his son in his will."

"His son?" I enquired, interest piqued. "Who's his son?"

"Word on the street is Jerimiah got his first wife pregnant before she took off, and the kid has since reached out to him, but I don't know much about the bloke, nor do I care to."

I knew for certain this couldn't be true, given I'd helped to sacrifice Jerimiah's first wife, and she wasn't with child. This must've been the story Jerimiah had spun so that he could make a return to The Church of Salvation in the future, posing as either his son or his grandson, depending on how long he stayed away. He'd made his mark on this town and would be back to claim it as his, once and for all.

"I'd be careful about bringing Jerimiah's name up in public," the drunk warned. "He's still got some folks around here spooked. They believe if you speak ill of him or The Church of Salvation, you'll die a mysterious death."

"Do you believe that?" I'd asked.

He laughed. "Hell no. Magic is for fairy tales, boyo, and I've outgrown those."

~

BEFORE HEADING BACK to Mama's, I went for a stroll to Indi's old place, feeling nostalgic with a sick sense of guilt.

I was staring at the front porch, lost in memories, when a vision of Indi materialised before my very eyes. She was leaning by the side rail, looking as beautiful as ever.

"Enzo," she called when she spotted me, excitement in her voice. "You're back. You came back for me."

She raced down the porch steps and threw herself into my arms with such enthusiasm that the impact made me stagger backwards.

I gazed down at her, gasping in shock. I could see her, feel her, smell her, and yet I knew it couldn't actually be her, because she was dead. I'd seen her lifeless body with my own two eyes. Jerimiah had killed her.

It wasn't until she drew back to meet my gaze, and I saw she was in her wedding dress, and hadn't aged a day, that realisation hit me like a freight train. Seventeen years had passed, yet Indi didn't look a day over eighteen.

I was seeing her ghost.

Shock forced me out of Elias' body, and when his senses came to, and he found a girl in his arms, he panicked. He threw her off him, sending her crashing to the lawn.

Worried, I rushed to her side.

"Are you okay?" I'd asked, but she took no notice. Instead, she watched on in bewilderment as Elias stood there, appearing confused and hyperventilating.

My eyes flicked between the two of them, trying to gauge what'd just happened. While Elias and I had a strong resemblance, we were by no means identical. He had paler skin and light eyes like his mother.

How had Indi so easily mistaken him for me? Was it my essence in Elias she'd sensed as opposed to physical appearance?

Before I could come to any conclusions, a disgruntled man with a pot belly and a cane opened the front door and stepped out onto the porch.

"What's going on out here?" he shouted, and Elias took off like a flash, dragging me along with him.

I was desperate to visit Indi's place again, but after Elias returned home blubbering incoherently and quivering like jelly, my mama had been quick to block me again.

Before drifting off into oblivion, as I'd done in the past, I made the switch to Monroe, hoping I would be able to see Indi again through him.

He and Leonie were living in Woodburn, which was only a forty-five-minute bike ride from Coraki. Luckily for me, Monroe's body was fit enough to make the ride there and back with relative ease. Although, it was always much trickier getting back to Woodburn from Coraki because Monroe had a habit of pushing my spirit out of him mid-ride. His sudden disorientation caused a number of stacks, but they only resulted in bruises and scratches. This "strange" ongoing occurrence quickly caused Monroe to question his sanity. He thought he was having blackouts again due to alcohol and drugs.

While I may have been responsible for his "mental health issues" and for introducing him to alcohol during my time in his body, I liked to blame Leonie for the latter. The good thing about Monroe was he'd never fallen into full-on addiction territory like his mama. If anything, he'd only seemed to dabble with substances here and there as a way of dulling out reality.

I often wondered if Monroe was subconsciously aware of the things I did while being inside his body and if those things affected him mentally. When Weasley came to within an inch of his life after being beaten by thugs, I knew Monroe was willing him to die. Therefore, I took it upon myself to enter Monroe's body and make sure that the beast of a man never woke up again.

INDI ACCEPTED that Monroe was me, the same as she had done with Elias, and I enjoyed speaking to her in my natural Louisianian drawl. The Strine accent was challenging, and I often struggled with my words while speaking through Monroe. There were even times when Leonie mistook Monroe for being drunk because of it.

After a few unusual conversations and much confusion on my part, it quickly became clear that Indi didn't know she was dead. Jerimiah had put a "Keep My Secrets Binding" spell on her, amongst other things. So not only could she not talk about what'd happened to her, she also couldn't remember what'd happened to her. I did find it surprising that she was still able to speak about Jerimiah and everything that had happened before the wedding, though.

She spoke about the engagement and the upcoming nuptials, not realising that the event had already taken place.

During one of our visits to Indi's rundown shack, I noticed a newly stationed "For Lease" sign on the neighbouring lawn, and it sparked an idea. Leonie had been complaining about the high rent she was paying for weeks. She was running out of drugs and money fast and was scared shitless of thugs bashing down the door. The thought of not having to do long and hazardous bike rides on a regular basis would be a blessing, so I wrote the real estate number down and talked Leonie into calling them, telling her the place was cheap, and it was a deal too good to pass up. It was partly true. The place *was* cheap, but it was because it was falling apart.

I gave myself a pat on the back when it all went through,

believing I'd made life easier for everyone and that I would get to spend more time with Indi. Little had I known she would end up communicating with Monroe himself in the times he pushed me out and that the two of them would form a bond. I wasn't happy about sharing Indi with my son, but he didn't know about me, and Indi struggled to differentiate between us. Even when Monroe told her she was mistaken–that he wasn't Enzo–she only seemed to understand it momentarily. By the next time she saw him, she would slip back to believing he was me again. When I'd tried explaining to her that I was using my son's body to communicate with her because we were both dead, her face flashed with the horrifying ramifications of the "Keep My Secrets Binding" spell, and I could tell my explanation was lost on her.

Her sole focus was to be saved, and given Monroe thought she was alive and in danger, he promised to rescue her. I'd made a similar promise decades ago, yet I'd let her down, and now her soul belonged to Jerimiah.

When Indi mentioned again how she'd hoped Enzo would come back for her, Monroe said in no uncertain terms exactly what he thought of me. His opinion was prickly, and the more I thought about it, the more it stung because I could see what he was saying was true. I should have fought for Indi, consequences be damned. She'd deserved much better. I really was "chicken shit".

On the day of Monroe's eighteenth birthday, Monroe awakened with a start to the sound of Indi's screams coming from next door. I was alarmed too, but then I'd rationalised it had something to do with the spell that Jerimiah had put on her and that whatever was happening to her would eventually pass. Monroe, however, genuinely thought Indi was being attacked by her father and charged next door to save her. I knew that Mr Walker wasn't Indi's father and that he had nothing to do with her bloodcurdling screams. Regrettably, I couldn't tell Monroe this, so I tried frantically to enter his body. I wanted to stop him from making a terrible mistake. His emotions were heightened–fuelled by alcohol and adrenaline–which made it impossible for me to make the connection.

In the weeks that followed, after Monroe threatened and attacked Mr Walker, his sister Jackie paid his bail, and they holed up in a motel whilst awaiting his trial. In the meantime, she had taken him to see a psychiatrist, who prescribed him a heavy dose of sedatives, which kept him in a zombified state.

During the trial Monroe looked haggard, and his senses were dulled down due to the sedatives. It was soon proven that Mr Walker didn't have a daughter named Indi–because he didn't–and the rest of the information Monroe provided was decades out of date, which only hindered his case.

It was easy to see how those of the jury who weren't familiar with Jerimiah and The Church of Salvation believed Monroe was having a psychotic episode.

It was also easy to tell which folks were familiar with the cult and afraid of the ramifications of dark magic. They kept their eyes lowered and their trembling hands clasped in their laps.

Lastly, ex-cult members like Harold, Bruce and his son Owen showed no signs of remorse and kept their heads held high. They squashed all allegations, making a laughingstock out of my son.

It took me a moment to recognise Owen. He'd gone from a gangly kid to a strapping stamp of a man. He'd also taken his father's place as Sergeant, making him the new–and hopefully improved–Sergeant Adams.

I overheard Bruce on a phone call during the adjournment–when he thought no one was listening–and the mention of my name quickly caught my attention.

"He's definitely Enzo's kid," he said. "He looks just like him, and he knows things only Enzo would've known."

He paused a moment, listening to the person on the line before adding, "I called him yesterday, and he said he'll be here to assess him. I've already got it covered."

Another pause. "Okay, I'll let you know how it all pans out."

I hadn't known what the second part of the conversation meant until I saw Jerimiah strutting through the court doors, introducing himself as Dr Jerry Richards, the Lead Psychiatrist of Rozelle Hospital. It seemed Old Adams had pulled a few strings to get him called upon to do the psych evaluation for Monroe's case. "Dr Jerry Richards" ended up diagnosing Monroe with drug-induced psychosis. Given Monroe's long list of mental health disorders, he recommended he would benefit from being admitted to Rozelle Hospital, where he would receive full-time psychiatric care from some of the best medical health professionals in NSW.

My heart sank when the judge and jury ruled in favour of "Dr Jerry Richards'" professional opinion, declaring Monroe would serve time at Rozelle Hospital.

CHAPTER 24

JUNE 29TH, 1998

COFFS HARBOUR, AUSTRALIA

∞ MONROE ∞

Jackie pulls to a stop at the rear entrance of The Hoey Moey, placing the car into park but leaving it idling. When I unclick my seatbelt, she turns to face me, her expression stern.

"I'll be back here to pick you up at ten sharp, you got it? Now remember, no drinks, no drugs, no parties, no fights. You're not some young thug living on the poverty line anymore. You're a young man who's been given a second chance at a bright future. I know you've never been taught to be reliable or responsible, but if you want to continue making this arrangement work, then you need to be considerate of others and adhere to rules."

"But I didn't get in a fight, I accidentally–"

Jackie thrusts her palm out, face tight. "Stop with the phoney excuses. I don't want to hear them."

She's livid because I arrived home on Monday instead of Sunday like we'd agreed, and yesterday was supposed to be my first shift.

"Not only are you letting us down—you'll be letting the entire team down," she scolded when I'd rung her about staying in Coraki an extra night. *"There should be no reason for you to stay until Monday. Just buy your ticket tomorrow morning and come home like we agreed."*

I gave her the answer she wanted and hung up, knowing full well I was staying, regardless of her approval. There was no point in mindlessly arguing the matter, and I didn't want her driving to come and get me, which is something she'd likely do.

I knew she would be cranky with me for disobeying her orders, and I was prepared for an earbashing, but I wasn't planning on returning home battered and bruised. Not to mention, Raj's fancy BMX is completely totalled. The frame's badly scuffed, and the back wheel is buckled beyond repair.

I tried convincing Jackie and Raj I'd stacked it at the skatepark, but they wouldn't have a bar of it.

"The major damage is to the rear of the bike, while all your injuries are anterior," Raj was quick to point out. *"The bike looks as if it's been hit by a semi-trailer, and so do you."*

Jackie spent the next twenty minutes trying to draw the truth out of me, but I kept to my guns and wouldn't budge. There's no way I could tell her that I was taken down by a cop. She'd jump straight on the phone to Coraki Police Station demanding answers, and then Owen would deny the incident ever took place, making me look like a liar. Besides, I don't want Jackie to know I went back to Coraki to find Indi. She'd only worry that I was losing it again because, like everyone else, she doesn't believe Indi is real.

"Don't worry, I'll be on my best behaviour today," I say, hiding how sore I feel.

Jackie's posture relaxes, and her tone lightens to one of concern. "You do know I'm only being hard on you because I want what's best for you, right? I love you. You're my little brother, and I want to see you make something of yourself." She leans across and kisses my cheek as though I'm a child being let out at school drop-off.

"Shoot," she says, rubbing the area she'd kissed with her thumb, attempting to wipe off the lipstick stain she's left behind.

She didn't want me to look like a thug on my first shift, so she forced me to wear concealer over my bruises.

Embarrassing much.

"We don't want any of the employees, or patrons, making precon-ceived judgements," she said.

I didn't want to wear it. I would've preferred to rock up on my first day looking like a thug than a drag queen. At least people don't pick on thugs–they're scared of them. Regardless, I couldn't afford to upset Jackie any further, so I bit my tongue and sat there like a child getting their face painted.

I open the car door and swat her hand away. "Stop fussing. Everything is going to be fine. I promise."

After grabbing my bag from the boot, I make my way to the back entrance. Jackie's car remains idling on the spot even after I've entered the double doors. She's been keeping a close eye on me since I destroyed her trust.

An employee glances up from the bar. He's tall and lanky with thick brown sideburns.

"Hey, I'm Monroe," I say, keeping my head angled to hide the bruises. "I'm here for my first shift."

"Welcome, I'm Sawyer," he replies, offering me his hand to shake. His strong grip makes my tender knuckles scream, but I do my best to keep my expression neutral. "You'll find Raj in his office, out the back."

"Cheers."

Raj hasn't spoken a word to me since last night, so I'm not at all surprised when he gives me an icy greeting. He hands me a uniform to change into and runs me through all the protocols and proce-dures. He treats me as though I'm a regular, fresh-faced employee. There's no warmth or informality. It's all business.

I'm taken to the floor and introduced to the other staff, although I can only recall a few names. I immediately take a liking to the bartender, Daniel, who offers to show me the ropes. He's dark-skinned with Indigenous features, which he says are compliments of his ancestors. The Gumbaynggirr people of the Mid-North Coast.

I glance around at the mass of tables, jam-packed with chatty patrons, and feel slightly overwhelmed. Raj had mentioned The Hoey

Moey was a popular pub, but I hadn't realised just how busy it would be. It'd been closed when I did my induction.

At the Coraki Hotel, having twenty people inside was considered a crowd.

"The reason The Hoey Moey is so popular is because it's situated parallel to Park Beach with direct access to the beachfront through the sand dunes. Plus, it also has a backpacker's hotel behind it, which attracts a diverse and cheerful crowd," Raj had said.

I'm just getting into the swing of things when a small child charges in front of me, almost tripping me over. I narrowly regain my balance in the nick of time.

That was way too close, I think, taking a steadying breath.

The plate of fish and chips I'd been on my way to serve almost ended up on the lap of an unsuspecting patron.

I can't afford to mess anything up. Not tonight.

Witnessing my near catastrophe, Daniel heads across and asks, "Are you right there, mate?"

"The kid came out from nowhere," I say.

"Here, hand me those." He gestures to the plates. "Why don't you head behind the bar instead? There's a bit of a lineup, but at least there's no kids running around your feet."

I accept his offer, grateful for the change of scene. "Cheers."

The rest of my shift runs far smoother than I'd anticipated, which I'm hoping will win me brownie points with Jackie and Raj. The only complaint I received was from an elderly gentleman who said I served his beer with too much head.

"Don't worry about him," Daniel assured me. "That old geezer is always complaining about something. It's his favourite pastime, I'm sure."

I'm heading to Jackie's car when Daniel calls out to me. I stop as he jogs over.

"Someone named Shaina just phoned, looking for you." He slips me a piece of paper with her name and number scrawled on it. "She asked if you could call her back ASAP. It sounded like it was important."

"Cool," I say. "And thanks for helping me out today. I really appreciate it."

He pats me on the back, "No problem, brother. It's what I'm here for."

Once Daniel disappears inside, I scrunch up the piece of paper and toss it into my bag with no compunction. I can't believe Shaina had the audacity to try contacting me after setting me up for a fall. I wish I hadn't given her so much information about myself. At this point, I trust no one.

CHAPTER 25
JULY 11TH, 1998
COFFS HARBOUR, AUSTRALIA
∞ MONROE ∞

The next week-and-a-half flies by in the blink of an eye, and although my bruises have faded, the memory of Owen pulling his gun on me still lingers in the forefront of my mind. Shaina has called several times since my first shift, leaving messages with random staff members for me to phone her back ASAP.

It's not going to happen.

Owen made it clear that if I were to return to Coraki, I was a dead man, so speaking to his wife–for whatever reason–seems like a dangerous move.

I want to let go of my past and become the person Jackie yearns for me to be, but I need to know what became of Indi before I can move on with my life.

There are nights when Indi haunts my dreams. "You've failed me," she accuses. "You promised you would save me, but you've left me here scared and alone, just like Enzo."

The prospect of returning to Coraki anytime soon is completely out of the question. Jackie has barely let me out of her sight. It feels like I'm nineteen going on ten. Things with Raj are worse still. I'd hoped that working with him at The Hoey Moey would help to bring us closer, but he has remained distant towards me ever since I returned from Coraki. Nowadays, he only converses with me out of necessity. Jackie says he's still angry about the stunt I pulled and that he doesn't completely trust me, but I'm beginning to question whether he even likes me at all anymore.

Working evening shifts at The Hoey Moey has since become my escape. Raj is the only one who knows about my colourful past, and he's keeping a tight lid on it.

Daniel and I have become great mates. Not only do we share witty banter behind the bar, but he really goes out of his way to help me whenever he can.

He says, "Bros stick together."

I've fallen into a routine and even managed to familiarise myself with some of the regulars at The Hoey Moey.

When they say, "The usual", I can pour their drinks on autopilot.

I've heard a few whispers about Christine Taylor, the employee who went missing after her shift and was later found dead in a local barn. A few of the employees have speculated over some of the patrons they suspect could've killed her, while others are just praying that the predator is found.

Daniel asked me if I knew anything, being Raj's brother-in-law and all. If only he knew how little Raj spoke to me about anything these days, let alone disclosing confidential information.

Tonight, we have live music playing, and the place is abuzz with good vibes, laughter, and cheers.

"The weekend spirit," Daniel calls it.

I'm relaxing in the tearoom on my dinner break, chugging down an orange juice, when Daniel peeps around the corner, snapping my attention.

"You've got a pretty girl out here asking for you," he says with a suggestive arch of his brow.

My heart sinks.

Shaina's here.

I leave my orange juice and follow Daniel back out onto the floor, wondering why the hell Shaina's so eager to get hold of me. I doubt she's here to apologise. A worrying thought penetrates my mind.

Perhaps Owen regrets not killing me when he had the chance so he's using his pretty wife as bait. He's hoping to lure me out so he can finish the job.

I've barely made it to the bar when Lindsay launches herself into my arms, wild with excitement.

"WarHead," she squeals. "Oh, God, I've missed you."

"Lindsay?" I blink, trying to make sure I'm seeing right. "When did you get out?"

I've only been out of Rozelle Hospital a matter of weeks myself, and there'd been no talk of her release before I left.

"I couldn't bring myself to stay in that hellhole without you, so I spoke to Jerry, and he took care of my release. He's even helped set me up in an apartment not far from here so that you and I can hang out together."

Concern stops me from sharing her enthusiasm. "Who's paying for the apartment? Please don't tell me it's Dirty Dick."

She hits me across the arm with her purse. "Will you quit being a buzzkill already? I just told you I'm out and that I'm living close by. Where's your excitement to see me?"

"I'm sorry. I *am* excited to see you," I say, and I mean it, but I can't understand how she's so blind to the issues with this setup. There's no such thing as a free ride, and if Dirty Dick is paying her way, she'll lose her independence. He'll think he owns her.

"How long until you're finished? We should get a drink and catch up."

"You know I'm not supposed to drink," I point out. "And you shouldn't be drinking either."

"We'll get a ginger beer then," she counters, eyes alight.

"I'd love to, but I really can't," I press. "My sister always picks me up at the end of my shift."

Lindsay looks crestfallen, and the disappointment on her face just about kills me.

I really am a buzzkill.

"I'll speak to my sister when she gets here at ten," I rush to say. "I might be able to persuade her into having a ginger beer with us."

This immediately puts a smile back on Lindsay's dial. "Cool, I'll wait around until you're done."

I glance over at the clock on the wall. "There's still another two hours until ten," I say.

Her lips curl in a suggestive grin. "I'm sure I can find someone else to entertain me until then."

I laugh, realising just how much I've missed her sass. "I'm sure you can."

I give her another hug and then head back into the tearoom to finish my juice with the two minutes I have left until my break ends.

"Oh, hey, you just missed your dad," Sawyer tells me as I pass him. "He came into the tearoom looking for you."

I frown at his comment. "I don't have a dad."

Sawyer laughs as though I'm joking. "Everyone has a dad."

Clearly, he's mistaken.

Perhaps it was Daniel's dad.

It certainly wouldn't have been my dad. I doubt the douchebag even knows of my existence.

Waving it off, I carry onwards and chug down the rest of my juice. A sour flavour burns my tongue as I finish it, making my lips twist. Someone ought to check the used-by date on the drinks we're serving. The OJ must be close to expiry.

When I return behind the bar, Lindsay gives me a wink from a nearby pool table and then leans over, squeezing her arms together to reveal her busty cleavage as she takes a shot.

Daniel notices and glances my way with a look that says, *"Damn, she's hot!"*

There's no doubt about it, Lindsay is all sex appeal, like Salma

Hayek in "Dusk Till Dawn", but there's never been anything sexual between us. We're just friends.

I serve a handful of patrons as normal, but as the minutes tick by, my vision begins to swim. I accidentally drop a schooner while trying to pour a beer, and shards of glass go flying.

"Are you alright there, mate?" Daniel calls from the far end of the bar.

I try to answer, but my words are slurred.

What's happening to me? I'm struggling to keep upright.

I grab hold of the bar to stabilise myself, but I can feel myself waning.

Daniel excuses himself from the patron he's serving and rushes over to help steady me. Noticing there's a problem, Lindsay drops her pool cue and comes rushing over, too.

"What's going on?" she asks, voice shrill with alarm.

"I don't know," Daniel shrugs. "He was fine just a moment ago."

When I look over the bar at Lindsay in confusion, I spy a familiar figure standing by the far wall. "Dirrrtty Diccck?"

Lindsay glances about. "Where?"

I blink and he's gone.

"I don't see him," she adds.

Daniel raises a brow, which appears like a blurred spitfire arching itself up on his forehead.

"Have *you* been sneaking some of the sauce?"

"I... no... I...," is all I manage to slur.

He wraps an arm around me and drags me to the edge of the bar, motioning for Lindsay to follow. They meet at the end, where he swings my arm over Lindsay's shoulder.

"Sawyer," he calls.

A second later, Sawyer is at my other side, his wiry arm helping to shoulder most of my weight.

"Take him back to the tearoom before his brother-in-law sees him," Daniel tells them.

I want to say that I'm sorry, that I don't know what's happening to me, but my lips won't cooperate. The space around me blurs in and out as they lead me away from the crowded bar and into the tearoom.

"Monroe. Monroe, snap out of it." I've never heard Lindsay call me Monroe before. "He's not okay," she says, most likely to Sawyer. "Come on, help me get him to my car."

It's the last thing I recall before everything fades to black.

CHAPTER 26
1997-1998
CORAKI, AUSTRALIA
∞ ENZO'S SPIRIT ∞

Monroe's first couple of months in Rozelle Hospital were tough. He was heavily sedated to begin with. Whenever the doctors lowered his meds, he'd lose control easily and lash out, especially at the mention of Indi.

Rozelle Hospital was originally called Callan Park Hospital. However, it underwent a makeover in 1994 and was renamed.

Given I couldn't stay in possession of Monroe at all times, I made good use of the periods when I was in control. I spoke to patients, nurses, and his assigned therapist, Dr Ross, and I learnt that Dr Jerimiah Richards resigned from Callan Park Hospital in 1980 and had since returned in 1995 as the fresh-faced "Dr Jerry Richards Jr, the estranged son of Jerimiah". How no one thought it was strange that Jerry had a Louisianian accent, given he was brought up with his Australian mother, baffled me.

Jerimiah came to speak with Monroe a few times, glancing over him in wonder. He seemed intrigued by the fact he hadn't known of his existence and did his best to sus him out. When he asked Monroe questions about his father, as in me, Monroe told him, as far as he was concerned, he didn't have a father.

When Jerimiah enquired, "What would make you say something like that?"

Monroe grunted and replied, "The deadbeat left before I was even born."

It stung hearing him speak the truth, but it was better—for his sake—that he knew nothing about me.

"Dr Jerry Richards" wanted to know exactly what Monroe knew about Jerimiah and the cult and kept pushing to find out where Monroe obtained his information. When Monroe kept insisting he'd gotten his information off his neighbour, Indi, Jerimiah loosened his collar, seeming flustered. It was a side of him I'd never seen before. Jerimiah always seemed either cool, calm, and collected or completely savage. He wasn't the type to get flustered or show weakness.

Monroe made two friends during his stay at Rozelle Hospital, Lindsay and Rebecca; only little did he know that Rebecca Brown was a ghost. I recognised Rebecca as soon as I saw her, and froze in disbelief. It was clear by her casual expression; however, she didn't recognise me in return.

It was dim in the ward the night I'd killed her, so she wouldn't have gotten a good look at me, I rationalised. However, I quickly discovered this wasn't the answer. Just like Indi's predicament, Rebecca had no idea she was dead. I couldn't fathom why this would be. I hadn't cast any spells on her. It had been a spontaneous, alcohol-induced kill fuelled by vengeance.

It wasn't until I noticed a small tattoo of Jerimiah's symbol on her inner wrist that I realised Jerimiah must've already marked and cursed her before I killed her.

Rebecca had become his possession, just like the girls we sacrificed in the past, only he must've wanted to bind her to him as his lover for life. It wasn't about stealing her soul.

This revelation made me wonder if he honestly believed he *was* in love with her. The Jerimiah I knew seemed incapable of truly loving anyone bar himself. But then again, there were many dimensions to Jerimiah, and the more I learnt about him, the less I understood him.

He was an enigma.

Heartbroken or not, Jerimiah had long since moved on. Monroe's friend, Lindsay, had become his new plaything, and the details she would share about their secret trysts were enough to make a grown man blush. Monroe despised the man because of it and nicknamed him "Dirty Dick", which made me smile. I only wished I'd thought of it first.

WHEN "DR JERRY RICHARDS" requested for Monroe to visit his office out of the blue one day, my skin prickled. As soon as we entered his office, and I spotted the red and black candles burning, I knew in an instant Monroe was in trouble.

Monroe glanced curiously at the candles but said nothing.

"Take a seat," Jerimiah insisted. A completed psych evaluation test, signed by Dr Ross, sat on his desk. "I've brought you in to discuss your progress."

Monroe's teeth were clenched. I could tell by the look on his face he wanted to confront Jerimiah about the illicit affairs he was having with his patients, but my boy was smart enough to hold his tongue.

When Jerimiah asked to see Monroe's arm I panicked and rushed to make a connection, afraid of what he might do. I hurriedly snatched Monroe's hand back from his clutches, somehow revealing myself in the process.

Jerimiah's eyes darted to Monroe's, and for the first time, it was as though he could see me. Not Monroe, but me.

The corners of his lips curled into a faint, malevolent smirk.

"There you are, my old friend; I knew you had to be inside somewhere." His fingers scratched at the smooth surface of his chin, each movement deliberate, almost predatory as if he was savouring the twisted plans forming in his mind.

"I must admit, I'm rather impressed. I didn't know you had it in you to play smart. Of course, you weren't quite smart enough, or else you wouldn't have landed yourself in here." He leaned forward in his chair. "Tell me, what was the point of your little fiasco in Coraki, hmm? What were you hoping to achieve?"

"I had nothing to do with the 'little fiasco', it was all Monroe. He'd spoken to Indi, and she'd told him everything."

"Indi is dead," Jerimiah bit back sharply.

"And so am I," I retorted. "The dead can speak, and they do. So, it'll only be a matter of time until all of your secrets unravel."

"My spells are binding, even after death."

"Your spells are flawed," I said, "just like your new identity," and then I stood from the chair and left his office.

Things grew more complicated after that, and Jerimiah was intent on asserting his dominance. Although Monroe wasn't aware of what'd transpired during his visit to "Dr Jerry Richards'" office, he was switched on enough to be wary of him.

Jerimiah's new love interest, Lindsay, wasn't shy and outrageously flirted with Monroe. While Monroe laughed and took it all in good fun, I wondered if Lindsay's affection was growing stronger for Monroe, than for Jerimiah. I would watch Jerimiah observing their interactions from afar, and I could feel burning jealousy radiating off him in waves.

If I were a good father, I would've found a way to end their friendship, which would've gotten Jerimiah off Monroe's back, but I took pleasure in seeing the man suffer.

One afternoon, while Monroe and Lindsay were out in the garden, I spotted Jerimiah watching the pair like a hawk from the shadows of the second-story window. I relished in witnessing his jealousy and saw an opportunity to goad him, so I entered Monroe's body and began shamelessly flirting with Lindsay.

I waited until the nurse on watch was busy with other patients before luring her to the garden shed, where she eagerly stripped me down.

When we re-emerged twenty minutes later, grinning and dishev-elled. Jerimiah was still at the window watching, so I gave him a salute.

I told Lindsay that it was a one-time thing and our little secret we were never to speak of.

"You have Jerry, and I have Indi," I said. "And we wouldn't want to hurt either of them over something that happened in the heat of the moment."

Lindsay inclined her head in agreement, but it was clear by the gleam in her eyes she wanted more.

In the weeks that followed, I waited for the backlash of my indis-cretion. I kept an eye over Monroe's shoulder, waiting for Jerimiah to make his move, but to my surprise, he kept clear. More unexpectedly still, Dr Ross brought up the subject of Monroe's release.

It wasn't until the morning of Monroe's release that I saw Jerim-iah. When he looked into Monroe's eyes, and saw I was in control, he came over to give me his parting words.

"Until we meet again, *my friend*." While his voice was as smooth as caramel, the warning in his words was unmistakeable.

"Until then," I'd said fearlessly.

$\sim$

ON THE NIGHT of Monroe's birthday, which was only a matter of days after his release, he woke to loud beeps, alerting him to a message on his new Nokia phone. The text read:

To MY FRIEND *of many years, I've brought you a present where the mountains meet the sea. Who would have thought we'd HERD cattle together as a pair of SIXTY-NINE-year-old BUCKS?*

I'm hoping to still meet you at Barney's tonight for the exchange.

• • •

MONROE STARED at the text message, eyes blinking and brows furrowed, before typing back:

SORRY, *I think you've got the wrong number.*

MEANWHILE, I sat there cursing Jackie's name for updating Monroe's new number on his file with Rozelle Hospital.

Monroe may have been quick to pass the text message off as a case of the wrong number, but I knew exactly who it was from and who it was for. What I didn't know, though, was what it all meant. As Monroe curled up under the blankets to fall back asleep, I made the connection with his body and took charge.

Switching the phone screen back on, I read the message over again. "My old friend of many years" was obviously a reference to me, and Coffs Harbour was a place where "the mountains meet the sea", but I'd struggled to understand what "HERD, SIXTY-NINE" and "BUCKS" stood for.

Monroe's brother-in-law, Raj, had an office set up down the hall from Monroe's room, so I got up quietly, opened the door, and tippy-toed down to it.

When I pushed the small round button on the computer tower to switch it on, it startled me by making a loud running-fan noise, along with continual ticking. I hadn't realised just how much the sound would carry in the dead of the night. When it finished opening, it made an ultra-loud musical sound that echoed inside the room. I cursed under my breath before hurriedly bringing up Yahoo.

I typed into the search bar, "Coffs Harbour herd sixty-nine bucks," and up popped a residential address on realestate.com.au.

"69 Herds Road, Bucca, NSW".

My heart pounded. Jerimiah was in town and wanted to meet up with me *tonight*. It wasn't lost on me that it was the evening of the Winter Solstice.

The "present" he had for me was sure to be something terrible.

I didn't know if Barney was the name of the property, the name of the person who owned the property, or something else entirely. I added it to the search bar to see what came up, but the extra word didn't change anything. The results remained the same.

I wrote the address down on a sticky note and then cleared the search history before closing the computer down and making sure everything was exactly as I found it.

Next, I went to the kitchen, where I knew Raj always left his keys and grabbed them from the bench before slipping outside and heading to his car.

Driving a car while possessing Monroe's body posed a huge risk. If he were to wake up mid-drive, we would most certainly crash, but I was too intent on finding out what Jerimiah had in store for me to worry about "what ifs".

I used the street directory in the glovebox to get to Herds Road and made sure to kill the lights before rolling up to the property. All the lights in the house were off, leaving the area pitch black. There was a small flashlight in the glovebox, which I grabbed and aimed down to avoid attracting attention. While carefully making my way down the gravel driveway on foot, I detected a small glow of light flickering from an old barn. Suddenly, the last piece of Jerimiah's cryptic message fell into place.

"I'm hoping to still meet you at Barney's tonight for the exchange". It wasn't the name of a person or a place. He had been referring to an actual barn.

Clever.

I made my way over to the old, sheet metal barn and stepped inside, expecting to find Jerimiah inside. Instead, I found a ring of burning candles surrounding a young woman dressed in white. Long dark tendrils fanned out from her crown, and blood-red rose petals were scattered across her body. Another young victim—dead at the hands of Jerimiah. I moved in closer to see If I recognised her, but I didn't. I stared in confusion, wondering who this young woman was and why Jerimiah had brought me out to see her. It wasn't as though he brought me out to help kill her. It soon struck me that perhaps there was no significance. He was merely setting Monroe up to take the fall and, in doing so, would punish me.

I glanced about warily, waiting for Jerimiah to pounce, yet he was nowhere to be seen. I made sure not to touch anything and quickly left, listening out for sirens in the distance. In a way, I was disappointed. I wanted to see Jerimiah. Now that he'd become aware of my existence, I wanted to fight things out.

The drive back to Yarramin was uneventful. I didn't pass any emergency vehicles in my travels, and I managed to stay in control of Monroe's body the whole way home.

Before entering the front door, I punched the brick wall in frustration, picturing Jerimiah's face. Because of him, I'd become the type of man who could easily look at the dead body of a stranger without any feelings of dread, sympathy, or remorse. I'd killed with him, and I'd killed without him. Even with the darkness inside me ebbed, empathy evaded me. All I felt was anger and resentment that Jerimiah was back to taunt me, and that he had outwitted me once again.

"Where have you been?" Raj's voice startled me, pulling me from my thoughts.

"Out," I said, pushing past him.

"Excuse me?" He grabbed my arm, Monroe's arm, and I could feel my spirit starting to detach from Monroe's body. "Where have you been all night?" He studied Monroe's eyes. "Are you high?"

"No, I'm just not feeling well," I said. "I went for a drive because I needed some fresh air, and now all I want to do is go to bed."

I tugged out of his grip and made a beeline for the stairs.

"Touch my car without permission again, and there will be consequences, do you hear me?" he called out after me.

I managed to make it all the way to Monroe's room before the connection broke, and Monroe's body went tumbling onto the carpet.

CHAPTER 27
JULY 12TH, 1998
COFFS HARBOUR, AUSTRALIA
∞ MONROE ∞

I awaken to a thumping sensation inside my head, and the world around me sways and bobbles.

Stop, I plead. *Stop, stop.*

I place my arm over my eyes and groan, blocking out the brightness of the downlights above me.

What's wrong with me? Do I have food poisoning?

I slip in and out of consciousness for the next few hours until, eventually, my migraine disappears and my head clears.

Vague memories from last night's shift slowly form shape in my mind. I was on my tea break, having a burger and an OJ, when Lindsay dropped by The Hoey Moey to see me.

It must've been the juice that took me down. It had tasted a little more sour than usual. I'll have to speak to Raj about it right away before it makes someone else sick.

I peel my eyes open and force myself to sit up, dying for a cold glass of water. Blinding light assaults my eyes for a moment before my pupils zoom into focus. Still partially dazed, I glance about in the brightly lit room in confusion.

This isn't my room.

I spot a tangled trail of mine and Lindsay's clothes spread across the floor, and my heart hammers.

No, I shake my head. *My mind is playing tricks on me again.*

I reef back the blankets to discover that I'm completely naked, and my stomach turns.

I didn't, did I? Please tell me I didn't. Lindsay is my friend.

I swallow hard and pat the mattress beside me, afraid I'll find her sleeping beneath the covers. To my relief, the lumps are merely two fluffy pillows.

I take a second to calm my scrambling thoughts before hopping out of bed and quickly chucking on my pants. I'm desperately hoping I've misread the signs.

I didn't... We didn't... I would never... I try to assure myself. *She would never...* Unsure, my brain halts before finishing. True, Lindsay likes to play the flirting game with me, but she's with Dirty Dick and I'm with...

I'm not with Indi, comes another interrupting thought.

It's clear from the messages Indi left on the walls of her old bedroom that she's forgotten about me and is still in love with Enzo. That was a sucker punch after a year of worrying about her, but I still need to know what's happened to her.

I slip on my shirt and pause at the bedroom door, bracing myself for the world's most awkward encounter *ever.*

If we did sleep together, then how am I supposed to act?

I don't want to be an arsehole and blow her off, but I also don't want to give her the wrong impression.

We're good as friends. Just friends.

I fiddle with the door handle, procrastinating.

If only I could remember what happened.

The door creaks as I open it, and I spy a flickering orange circle in the semi-darkness. The scent of melting wax is thick in the air, along with a more pungent smell I don't recognise.

What in the world is she trying to do out there? Burn the house down?

"Lindsay?" I call but receive no answer.

Puzzled, I feel for a nearby switch and flick the lights on.

When my surroundings become fully visible, I blink like rapid-fire, convinced my eyes are deceiving me.

They must be. They have to be. Because if they aren't...

My breath catches, and stabbing pain slices through my heart.

"Lindsay?"

Her body lays whimsically in the middle of a chalk-drawn circle upon a bed of blood-red rose petals, in stark contrast to her lacy white dress. A ring of red and black candles surrounds the circumference of the circle, and her long, dark hair flows around her shoulders in luscious waves. Her face is tilted to the side, and as I rush over to check on her, my stomach heaves. Her lips have been sewn together with string, and her eyes which were once reddish-brown, have been bleached of all colour. My body tremors, and my head shakes in protest.

No... No... It's in my mind. It's all in my mind.

I close my eyes a moment and re-open them again, hoping that the scene before me is a hallucination. A nightmare.

It isn't.

"Lindsay?" I drop to my knees and nudge her, hoping to magically rouse her. "Lindsay, Lindsay."

Her skin, which was once olive, is ashen and cold to the touch. Tears sting as I avert my eyes from her maimed, lifeless face. Reality sinks in with a nauseating effect.

She's dead. She's most definitely dead.

I turn away and crawl on my hands and knees to the corner of the room where a large pot plant sits. Last night's meal leaves my stomach in a rancid stench of pulpy-orange and burger chunks.

When I'm done emptying my guts, I force my tremoring body upright and scramble to my feet. An alarming thought penetrates my mind.

Who did this to her?

Glancing about, I note that the living area is neat and tidy, and all the doors and windows are closed with no sign of forced entry.

The entire apartment appears to be untouched all except for this disturbing ritual-like display. There's no evidence whatsoever of a break-in or a struggle.

Was she killed by someone she knew?

For a horrifying split-second, I question whether I've done this to her, but then I know *I couldn't, I wouldn't, I would never.*

A flash memory pops into my mind, causing a more viable answer to hit me like a sledgehammer.

Dirty Dick. It had to have been Dirty Dick.

He was at The Hoey Moey last night, I'm sure of it. I'd seen him with my own two eyes. Plus, he was the one who rented Lindsay this apartment, so he'd certainly have a key.

Is he still here?

I rush to inspect the unit, opening all the doors and cupboards, peering under the beds, and pulling the shower curtain across. Next, I exit out onto the balcony to scan the area. It's pitch-black outside, making it impossible to see much of anything.

Unsurprisingly, I find no sign of Dirty Dick or any other culprit.

Back in the kitchen, the clock reads 10:10 PM.

I must've lost a whole day sleeping.

I pick up the phone and dial 000.

As the ringtone buzzes, my gaze drifts to the mess I made in the pot plant, and I grimace. I've got a strong suspicion that I'll get the rap for this. I would've been the last person to be seen with Lindsay and my prints and DNA are all over her place. Plus, everyone thinks I suffer from blackouts and mental issues.

If I were smart, I'd hang up and make a run for it, but I can't just leave my friend here to rot. It wouldn't be right.

The lady on the phone asks for my name, but I don't give it. She also asks for my location, which I can't give her either, because I don't know where I am. Her gentle voice grows frustrated, and she responds cynically instead of attentively, as though she believes I'm some dumb kid playing a prank on her.

"Look, I don't know where I am," I insist. "All I know is my friend is dead, and I think Dr Richards, the Head Physiatrist from Rozelle Hospital, killed her. I'll leave the line open so you can trace it."

I place the phone on the bench and walk away, snatching up the set of car keys I'd spotted on the side table by the door.

Squatting down by Lindsay's side, I take one of her hands in mine and kiss it, tears stinging the corners of my eyes.

I wish she'd listened to me. I told her time and time again that Dirty Dick was bad news and he'd break her heart. I just hadn't realised he would go so far as to kill her.

"He won't get away with this," I promise her. "Dirty Dick will pay for what he's done."

As I push off my thighs to stand, my eyes catch sight of a familiar mark written inside the circle, although it's partially obscured by flower petals. Curious, I brush the pedals aside to get a better look. It's the same symbol from Indi's bedroom wall. I swear I've seen this symbol somewhere else, too, but I just can't place it.

What does it mean? Is there a connection?

My mind shifts into overdrive. I hurry to brush the rest of the petals out of the way whilst simultaneously blowing out the candles. The inside of the circle is filled with multiple symbols, including a few more that I remember seeing on Indi's bedroom wall.

What the?

At that moment, I see the flash of a small tattoo on Becca's inner wrist.

It's the symbol.

Shit! She could be next.

Sirens blare in the distance, telling me I need to go. I've spent far more time here than I should've.

I book it to the door, open it, and race down the five flights of stairs that it takes to get me to ground level. Lindsay's car key has a Toyota symbol written on it, so I scan the parking area for a vehicle that fits the bill. Spotting a small red Camry on the far left, I race over and insert the key, twisting it until it clicks.

Bingo, it unlocks.

I haven't got a licence, but I've done enough paddy bashing in my time to know how to handle a car. Lance, one of Ma's many boyfriends, loved paddy bashing and dirt racing and taught me everything he knew. He was the best of the scumbags, but he didn't last very long. He was smart enough to get on a winner and get out.

I make a right at the end of the driveway, heading in the opposite direction to the sound of the sirens. From there, I zig-zag down several more streets before pulling up by a street sign and checking the glove box for a street directory.

I scan through the letters until I find a name that matches the street sign, shedding light on my current location. Next, I map out which way I need to go to get to the Pacific Highway. I need to get to Rozelle Hospital, Lilyfield.

It's a long way to Sydney, and I've never driven long distances before, let alone long distances in the dark, but I have an important report to make and a friend to warn.

CHAPTER 28

JULY 13TH, 1998

ROZELLE HOSPITAL, LILYFIELD, AUSTRALIA

∞ MONROE ∞

I diligently survey the road and beyond as I drive, my eyes zooming in on any vehicles that look suspiciously like road patrol. The pressure of having to stay awake and continually evade cops is intense. I feel like a shaken-up soda can that's ready to pop.

I stick to the speed limit, like a law-abiding citizen, even though it hurts to do so. No doubt, Lindsay's car has been reported as missing, so I only make one quick stop along the way to fill up. I don't have any money. My wallet is still in my locker at work, but I find fifteen dollars' worth of coins in the centre console. I use the cash for fuel, and then nab a pair of sunnies and a cap off a whirly-stand on my way out. I need a disguise for when the sun comes up.

I can't believe my luck, when I arrive at Rozelle Hospital the next morning having missed all road patrol. Coffs to Sydney is an eight-hour drive, and I was certain I'd run into trouble at some stage of the game. Perhaps it was a good thing I had to travel through the evening. Fewer cars, fewer cops.

In order for my allegations against Dirty Dick to be believable, my story needs to be watertight. I've been sorting through my memories from last night, trying to make sense of them.

"Oh, hey, you just missed your dad," Sawyer said when I was heading back to the tearoom to finish my OJ.

At the time, I thought he'd confused Daniel's dad as being my dad, but now I'm beginning to wonder if Dirty Dick told Sawyer he was my father so he could slip into the tearoom and spike my drink without arousing suspicion. That would explain why my orange juice tasted so bad. Whatever Dirty Dick used to sedate me must've been potent.

I exit the vehicle, sore, mentally drained, and absolutely busting to pee.

The double-story, sandstone-bricked building that stole a year of my life catches my eye, and a sense of resentment brews inside me. It would've stolen even more than that had I not learnt the art of telling people what they wanted to hear.

People don't really want to hear the truth; they'd rather hear a white lie told convincingly.

Nobody believed a word I said about Mr Walker and the cult, and chances are nobody's going to believe a word I have to say now, either. Regardless, I need to do this. I have a strong suspicion Lindsay and Becca aren't the only patients foolish enough to have fallen for Dirty Dicky's charm. He is chiselled and clean-cut, with a presence that commands attention. When he walks into a room, everyone turns. This hospital is full of confused, fragile women, and Dirty Dick is a practised predator who has a way of promising these broken young women the world. It's no wonder they fall so willingly into his web of deceit.

I can't let anyone else face the same fate as Lindsay, especially not Becca.

Dirty Dick needs to be exposed for the slime bag he truly is. Even if nobody believes my allegations right off the bat, once the spotlight has been shone on Dirty Dick proclaiming that he sexually assaulted two of his patients, people will grow cautious of him.

After relieving myself behind a bush, I make my way inside to the reception area and tell the middle-aged woman who's running the desk that I'm here to file a report against Dr Richards.

She peers above her oversized glasses, eyeing me with piqued interest. "What exactly is this regarding?"

"Dr Richards is having an affair with two of his patients."

The receptionist all but scoffs at me. She doesn't believe a word of it, as I suspected.

"Can I get your name, please?"

I consider giving a false name but immediately decide against it. If I want my allegations to be credible, then I need to be honest about who I am and how I've come to obtain this information. Lying will only discredit my claims if I'm caught.

My thoughts shift to Becca, and my name leaves my lips in the fight for justice.

"Monroe Morgan," I say, hoping with all my heart that I can at least save Becca, if no one else.

"Okay, Monroe. Well, why don't you take a seat while I track down the superintendent."

Having been left to sit for a long time, so begins the trickle of fear that the authorities have cottoned on to my whereabouts and have warned the staff to keep me put until they arrive. My legs bounce with agitation, and I'm just about to do the runner when my name is called by a familiar face.

I stand and make my way over to Mrs Hill. She is a tall woman with a curved nose and greying hair.

"Follow me," she says and leads me down the narrow hall.

Feeling paranoid, I scan my surroundings as I walk, keeping on the balls of my feet, just in case it's a trap.

She offers me one of two armchairs while she takes a seat on the chair behind the desk, facing me. Her computer sits to the side of the desk at an angle, and her fingers tap vigorously on the keyboard as she speaks.

"Monroe Morgan, isn't it?"

I nod, nervous energy building inside me. I bet she's bringing up my file.

She won't believe you, says the voice inside my head. *You've made a big mistake by coming here. They'll only lock you back up again and throw away the key.*

"I hear you wish to file a report against Dr Richards. Is that correct?"

My throat crackles hoarse with dryness. "Yes."

"Dr Richards is currently on leave, but by all means, do tell."

"I was a patient here up until recently," I say, telling her what she already knows. "And I made good friends with Lindsay and Becca, who both admitted to having a clandestine affair with Dr Richards."

Mrs Hill's fingers take to the keyboard again, and she focuses her attention on the screen rather than me. "How long ago did you learn about these clandestine relationships?"

"About six months ago," I admit.

Her eyes flick to mine, narrowed with suspicion. "If that's the case, why have you waited until now to report this?"

Guilt courses through me. "I didn't want to violate my friends' trust, but Dr Richards has since hurt Lindsay, and I want to make sure the same thing doesn't happen to Becca."

"When you say Dr Richards hurt Lindsay, are you talking physically or emotionally?"

"Physically."

The woman's eyes narrow as she types. "The patient you're referring to would be Lindsay Mendez. Is that correct?"

I nod.

"I'm sorry to inform you, Monroe, but Miss Mendez is no longer a patient of ours," she says, telling me what I already know. "She was released two days ago. So, unless she's willing to come back and file a report herself, there's nothing I can do to help."

It's too late now. She's already dead. I think, but don't say.

"What about Becca?" I ask. "I want to know that she'll be protected."

"Becca," she repeats, "as in Rebecca...?"

She draws out her first name, prompting me to continue.

"Rebecca Brown."

After a few clicks of the keys, her eyes flick between me and the screen, brows furrowed.

"You must be mistaken. We haven't had a Rebecca Brown on our books since 1978."

"No," I shake my head. "That must've been another Rebecca Brown. The Rebecca Brown that I know is still a patient here," I insist. "Check again. She's around 5'8 with blonde hair and green eyes..." Grasping for straws, I add. "I'm pretty sure her middle name was a type of purple flower. Lilac, lavender—"

Mrs Hill's eyes snap to mine. "Violet?"

"Yeah." I nod agreeingly. "That's it."

Her face contorts. "Is this some kind of sick joke?"

"What?" I frown. "No, I—"

"Rebecca Violet Brown is long deceased."

"Long deceased?" Confused, I argue, "But it's only been a matter of weeks since my release. If Dirty Dick..." *Oops*...I shake it off. "I mean, Dr Richards has already killed her. He could've only done it since June 19th."

Mrs Hill's annoyed expression suddenly morphs into one of concern.

Uh-oh, I recognise the look she's giving me. She pities me, believing I've relapsed. That I'm talking crazy.

"Monroe, have you been drinking or taking illicit drugs?" Mrs Hill asks, confirming my fears.

I shake my head. "No."

However, if they were to test me, I'm not sure what they would find. I have no idea what Dirty Dick slipped into my drink.

"My mistake." She hands me a piece of paper and pen and, with a gentle, plastic smile, says, "Why don't you write down everything you just told me while I go and check our filing system out back? Computers aren't always the most reliable sources of information."

I nod, playing along, and put pen to paper. Meanwhile I see right through her performance. She's looking for a way to reincarcerate me and needs help to do so.

Dr Richards was-

Writing the word *was* instead of *is* feels like a knife to the heart.

-having an affair with two of his patients, Lindsay Mendez and Rebecca Brown.

When Mrs Hill leaves, I quickly add:

Dr Richards killed Lindsay in her Coffs Harbour apartment, which is an apartment he rented especially for her.

Check his financial records and his whereabouts for last night. I saw him at The Hoey Moey when I was on shift.

I'm not sure what's happened to Becca. Mrs Hill says she's dead too.

There's more I would like to write, but I don't have the time. I drop the pen and scoot around the desk to the computer. My file is on display, but I'm not concerned with it. Everything these people know about me is a lie. I close the tab to reveal Becca's file. It's not a normal file. It's an incident form that's been handwritten and scanned into the computer. The date jumps out at me, smacking me in the face. *October 7th 1978*. As does the word *"suicide"*.

An image of Becca dressed in her usual 1970s knee-length pink dress, along with a matching headband, springs to the forefront of my mind, and my head spins. She'd had—what I thought was—a small quirk where she thought it was the year 1978, but it says here that she'd died in 1978.

I don't understand. Was Becca already dead? No... She couldn't be. Someone on the inside is trying to mess with me.

There's a full report, and I really want to read it. I want to know what they say happened to her, but I can't stay here any longer. I need to get out while I still can.

I dash for the door and book it down the hall as fast as my feet will carry me.

"Hey," the receptionist calls as I dart past her. "Wait!"

From the corner of my eye, I see her reach for the phone.

Not a chance, I think, before coming to a skidding halt.

My heart leaps into my throat. "Lindsay?"

It can't be. My mind is playing tricks on me.

She greets me with one of her trademark sultry smiles. "Hey, WarHead."

"But you were..." I shake my head disbelievingly, my mind swirling in confusion. "I saw you at the apartment. You were..." I can't bring myself to say dead.

She laughs. "Did you forget your meds this morning?"

I stare, dumbfounded. Her skin is back to a glowing olive, and her eyes and lips appear untouched. She's as radiant as ever.

"What's up with you?" She punches my arm in a playful manner. "You're acting stranger than normal."

Was she playing a trick on me? If so, it wasn't funny.

"I thought you were dead," I say accusingly. "I thought Dirty Dick killed you. Why would you do that to me?"

Her eyes flash milky white, and nasty red sores surround her mouth where the stitching had been. Startled, I curse and stumble backwards, right into someone's grasp.

Panic overtakes me, and I struggle away from the person's grip.

"It's okay, Monroe," Dr Ross says, her voice soft and assuring. "Everything is okay."

She tries clutching my arm again, but I shrug her off.

She's wrong. Everything is *most definitely not "okay"*.

Lindsay's face is back to normal again.

No, not normal. It's not Lindsay. Lindsay's dead. You're hallucinating from the drugs Dirty Dick slipped you, I rationalise. *They're still in your system. Either that, or I'm talking to a ghost*. I shake off the thought. *I don't believe in ghosts*.

I catch movement in my peripheral and swivel to find two security guards moving in on me. They want to lock me back up again, but there's no way in hell that I'm going to let that happen. I spin toward the exit and bolt as though the "Hound of the Baskervilles" is after me. Fast and heavy footsteps thud behind me, but I'm much faster. I'm able to get out, cross the parking lot, leap inside Lindsay's car, lock the door, and then turn the key before anyone can get near the vehicle. As I screech out of the bay and into the open parking lot, the security guards dive aside to avoid being hit.

That was close. Too close.

I zip down a maze of streets until I hit a secluded location, pop on my stolen cap and sunnies, and then dump the car.

"Flat Street," I say, taking the street directory with me to study it as I walk. My fingers flick through the pages, which are listed alphabetically. I search up L for Leichhardt Station. Once I've marked the spot, my pointer traces along the streets from my current location to the station, navigating the quickest route. The Leichhardt line runs directly to Central Station, which is exactly where I need to go to catch a train back to Coffs.

When I get to the station, I see a middle-aged gentleman dressed in a suit with a briefcase, and doing the unthinkable, I pretend to stack it on the stairs, intending to pick-pocket this poor unsuspecting gentleman if he's kind enough to help me up. When he bends down to lend me his arm, I swipe his wallet from his pocket and then slip it into my back pocket in one quick, precise movement.

"Are you alright, buddy?" he asks.

I nod, keeping my head down. "Yeah, cheers."

Once he and I have gone our separate ways, I pull out his wallet, hoping there's cash inside.

Two greenbacks.

Bingo.

I've got my train fare back north and then some. My excitement is quickly overshadowed by an overwhelming sense of guilt. Stomach churning, I pluck out the gentleman's licence and glance at his photo. His friendly face stares back at me, kind and caring, and my heart sinks.

I don't want to steal from this person, but what choice do I have? I don't have any money of my own, and I can't ring Jackie for help in case the cops are there.

"Mathew Henderson, 1 Ivory Street, Leichhardt, NSW 2040."

I read the gentleman's name and address several times over to make sure it sticks in my head.

If I ever get out of this mess, I will repay you, I vow.

Sliding the licence back inside its card sleeve, I leave the wallet on a nearby bench seat, hoping some decent person—unlike myself—will hand it in.

CHAPTER 29
JULY 13TH, 1998
COFFS HARBOUR, AUSTRALIA
∞ MONROE ∞

T
he train ride back to Coffs Harbour is long and exhausting. I keep my head down and mouth shut the entire journey, not wanting to arouse the attention of fellow passengers. I had the forethought of buying a sandwich and coke for my lunch, and once my hunger is satisfied, I try to relax and rest my eyes, but my mind is working in overdrive. The image of Lindsay's disfigured face won't leave my mind, and it's brought back a memory that I filed away years ago—never to be thought of again—until now. The last time I saw Indi, her face had flashed disfigured like Lindsay's, and the similarities don't end there. The symbols written on Shaina's wall and the ones inside the chalk circle where Lindsay's body was laid out are identical. And then there's Becca's tattoo, and Christine, the young employee from Raj's work who was found dead in a local barn in what the police called "a ritualistic homicide".

Everything seems to be connected, and somehow, I'm in the centre of it all.

By the time the train arrives at Coffs Harbour station, my joints are stiff and sore. I'm bleary-eyed from a lack of sleep but there's no time for rest. It's only a half-hour walk to The Hoey Moey, so I head straight there, needing to ask Sawyer a few questions about the person he'd mistaken as my father. If the man he saw matches Dirty Dick's description, it will certainly work in my favour when I'm brought in and questioned by the cops. I'll also need to speak to Jackie about getting a good lawyer.

I can't be put away. Not again. And certainly not for life.

When I get close, I notice a cop car out front, forewarning me to stealthily slip around the back. As I head to the rear of the building, I hear voices drifting from the back carpark, cautioning me to duck behind a parked van for cover. Carefully inching along behind three parked cars, I get close enough to spy several of The Hoey Moey staff gathered in a group, including Daniel and Sawyer. I see Raj off to the side, speaking with two uniforms.

I wonder what he's telling them.

I haven't made a very good impression on him so far. If the authorities believe I killed Lindsay, he's more than likely to help lead them straight to me.

My sister's car is parked on the other side, which means she's here, but I can't spot her at the gathering.

I chew my lip in deliberation, wondering how in the world I'm going to be able to peel Sawyer away from the rest of the group. I'm also second-guessing whether I really should. If he believes I killed Lindsay, there's no guarantee he'll even want to speak to me, let alone help me.

I'm stuck crouching for a long time, but as luck would have it, Sawyer leaves the group momentarily to grab a bag from his Corolla.

Poor kid, I think, as I catch a glimpse of his lobster-red nose and cheeks. He's really feeling the pressure.

I'm not fast or slick enough to catch him this time around, but at least now I know exactly where to wait for him.

When Raj and the authorities migrate inside, I quickly take advantage.

It's a challenge to move to the next couple of cars unnoticed, given the empty car spaces between them, but I move swiftly and quietly like a ninja.

After a few minutes of waiting behind Sawyer's Corolla, I hear footsteps heading towards me, and I'm thinking, *you beauty*. However, when I poke my head around to sneak a peek, I see that Sawyer's still with the group.

Crap, it's not him.

My breath catches.

I'm about to be busted.

There's a loud thud as something heavy is dumped inside the back tray of the ute parked alongside the Corolla, where I'm crouching. I glance up to see Daniel staring down at me.

"Pssst, you shouldn't be here," he says, surprising me with the casualness of his tone. "Cops are all over the joint, and they're all asking questions about you."

"Do they think I killed Lindsay?" I ask, my voice catching on her name.

"It sure appears that way, but for what it's worth, I know you didn't do it."

By straight-up warning me rather than giving me in, Daniel has shown I can trust him, but his absolute faith in me—without question—comes as a shock.

"How do you know I didn't do it?" I ask, stunned.

"Lindsay and Sawyer couldn't get you to the car on their own. You were too heavy, so Sawyer came back in and manned the bar while I basically carried you to the car. Trust me, mate, you were out cold. Nobody comes back from that kind of state sharp enough to kill someone the way Lindsay was killed."

If Lindsay couldn't carry me because I was out cold, how had I woken up in her apartment? Did she call Dirty Dick to help carry me up? If so, it meant she knew he was here in Coffs.

I have so many questions and not enough answers.

The image of Lindsay's disfigured face enters my mind again, and a sick, heavy feeling fills my stomach.

Noticing me swallow back the bile in my throat, Daniel quickly adds, "I'm sorry, man, you must be devastated." There's another thud as he tosses something else into the back tray, probably for cover. "Do you have any idea who *is* responsible? It's got to be the same guy who killed Christine, right?"

"It was Dr Richards," I say with certainty, "But I need more time to gather evidence in order to prove it. In saying that," I add, "Did Sawyer mention seeing a man who told him he was my father."

"Yeah, why?"

"Did he give you, or the police, a description of this man?"

Daniel cocks his head, interest piqued. "Yeah. Why? Do you think it was Dr Richards?"

"I do." I nod. "I think he deliberately posed as my father so he could gain access into the tearoom and spike my drink. If you get a chance, use the computer inside to look up Dr Richards. He's one of the leading psychiatrists at Rozelle Hospital. Show his picture to Sawyer and see if he recognises him."

"Sure, I can do that." Daniel glances at the group of staff members huddled across the way and shuffles where he stands. "I'd better go before someone gets suspicious. If anyone asks, I never saw you here today."

When he turns to leave, I hush-call, "Wait! Is there any chance you could do me one more favour?" I hate putting him in a precarious position, but right now, he's all I've got. "Can you grab my bag for me?"

He shakes his head. "Not a chance, the cops are all over your stuff. What are you after? Money?" He slips his hand into his pocket and hands me a fifty-dollar note. "This is all I have on me, but it's yours."

"No," I say, waving him off.

He pushes the note firmly into my hand.

"Take it." He insists. "Oh...and by the way," He hands me a piece of paper from his other pocket. "Shaina called again. She said she's sorry about Owen's behaviour and that she *really* needs you to call her back. It's important."

He shrugs. "I don't know what the story is between you two, but you should really call her back, even if it's only to tell her to stop calling."

"Thanks, Daniel. I owe you one."

His lips tug up at the corners in a sympathetic smile. "Good luck."

I stay put, sweating it out, while I wait for the crowd to disperse. Sawyer doesn't return to his car, which is probably for the best. I don't know if he has as much faith in me as Daniel. He didn't look as though he was coping under pressure. There's a chance he'd give me up out of fear alone.

When I finally lever myself up to leave, I catch sight of my sister storming out of the restaurant. Her hands are fisted by her sides as she makes a quick beeline towards her car across the lot. At first, I think I've struck gold. I'd hoped to catch her alone, but just as I'm about to circle around to her car, Raj charges out after her, calling for her to wait. I duck slightly, keeping my eyes on them through the windows of Daniel's ute.

"Jackie, wait!"

Jackie whirls on him, her eyes full of fire.

"I can't believe you," she says, voice raised. "Talk about handing my brother over on a silver platter."

"All I did was tell them the truth. There's something very wrong with your brother. I know it, and you know it, whether you're willing to admit it or not. I'm sure whoever he got in a brawl with up in Coraki knows it, too. Monroe has been known to hurt innocent people in the past. He has severe mental issues. It's not a secret."

"Why didn't you tell *me* that you caught Monroe taking your car out during the night or the fact that your credit card has mysteriously gone missing? Why tell the police but not me? I am his sister. If I knew there was a problem, I would've addressed the situation. He listens to me."

"Does he, though?" Raj argues. "Because as far as I can tell, the boy does what he wants with no consideration for others, including you. He's been nothing but a menace since he arrived."

"I know my brother. He may have done some terrible things in his time, but he didn't kill that girl. I would swear my life on it. Deep down, he's a good kid."

Raj hmpfs. "What about me, Jackie? Have you taken a second to think how I might be feeling about all this? One of my employees is dead, last seen leaving here after her shift, and now I've found out that my credit card has been used to pay three months' worth of rent on the apartment for the girl who was just killed—*who, may I add,* was also last seen leaving here with *your* brother. Do you have any idea how this looks for me and my business? I could lose everything that I've worked so hard to achieve."

Raj's words repeat in my head, and confusion follows.

How was Lindsay's rental paid for with his credit card? Does he think I've stolen his credit card? It most definitely wasn't me.

"I know how this looks, but in case you weren't listening, Daniel and Sawyer said that Monroe basically needed to be carried to the car. It doesn't sound, to me, like the state of someone who would have the capacity to kill someone in an orchestrated manner. I'm sure there's an explanation. I just need to find Monroe," my sister says.

"Daniel and Sawyer didn't even inform me that Monroe left. They covered for him. They could very well still be covering for him."

"They're teenagers, not criminal masterminds. Daniel knows about Monroe's substance abuse issues. I told him about it before Monroe even started. I asked him to show Monroe the ropes and to keep an eye on him. He said he covered for Monroe because he 'liked the guy and didn't want to see him get in trouble'."

"Well, where is Monroe, huh? The cops said they found his DNA all over Lindsay's apartment. He was there, and now he's gone."

"He's probably scared or in shock. Lindsay was his friend. He's spoken about her many times. Now, I'm going to find him," she says, putting an end to the conversation.

She turns away from Raj and continues to her car.

"Innocent people don't run," Raj calls out after her.

Ignoring him, my sister slips into the driver's side, revs the engine, and squeals out of the parking lot.

I manage to get out of The Hoey Moey car park without being seen and hit the street power walking. It's just on dusk, and the sky has begun to darken.

Jackie and Raj's argument rattles through my brain. I have no idea why Raj believes I took his car out during the night.

Could it have been Dirty Dick who took his car?

I'm one hundred percent convinced Dirty Dick is the one who stole Raj's credit card, although I have no idea how he got his hands on it.

It's clear he's trying to frame me for Lindsay's death, *but why me in particular?* It feels like a personal vendetta.

Did Lindsay happen to mention all the derogatory things I'd said about him? To seek revenge–to this extent–over a few lousy insults is absolute madness.

Whatever the reason, he has well and truly managed to screw me without even getting in my pants.

I want to call Jackie to tell her I'm okay, but I shouldn't. It'll only make her an accessory. Going by the argument she had with Raj, I'm already destroying their relationship and the business' reputation. I've done enough damage. I can't expect her to keep digging me out of trouble. Besides, if my own brother-in-law believes I'm guilty, it'll be hard to convince a jury any differently, no matter how good my lawyer is.

I'm on my own.

With no one to turn to and nowhere left to go, Shaina's number starts burning a hole in my pocket.

I should call her. What do I have to lose? My life? I've lost it anyway.

I'm better off dead than rotting in a prison cell or psych ward for the rest of my days.

There's a payphone further along the road, and when I get to it, I step inside the booth. While slotting in the coins, I pull out Shaina's number and stare at it for a long moment before punching in the numbers.

"Hello," she answers, sounding uncertain.

When I don't reply, she repeats herself.

"Hello? Is anyone there?"

"It's me," I force out. "Monroe."

"Monroe?" Surprise fills her voice. "Oh, thank God. I've been calling and calling."

"I know."

"Why has it taken you so long to get back to me? I have important information I want to share with you."

Hope fills me. "You do?"

"Yes, I do. But I'd rather not get into it over the phone. Are you coming back to Coraki anytime soon? There're some things I need to show you."

My sense of hope is quickly replaced by doubt.

"Are you setting me up?" I ask outright. "Are you trying to get me back there so that your husband can finish me off?"

"Finish you off?" she repeats. "What? No. Don't be ridiculous. Owen was just talking big with the whole 'dead and buried' thing. He was trying to scare you off, not finish you off. And for the record, Owen's my ex-husband. I didn't even want him here, but Isaac let it slip that you were coming. I'm sorry about the way he treated you, I really am, but Owen runs his own show, irrespective of what I have to say. He's an arse like that."

When I remain quiet, soaking in what she's said, Shaina asks, "Are you still there?"

She mustn't know that Owen ran me off the road and pulled a gun on me.

A comment Indi made surfaces to the forefront of my mind. *"Ser-*

*geant Adams and his wife are a part of our church group, and they've got
their own two young girls they're trying to keep the Devil out of."*

"Do you have any daughters?" I ask.

"What?" I note the confusion in her voice. "No. I only have Isaac."

I'm curious as to how Isaac fits into the picture. He doesn't look
anything like Shaina or Owen, but that's a question for another time.

"In that case, does Owen have any daughters from a previous
marriage?"

A non-humorous laugh escapes her. "Not that he's told me. Why
do you ask?"

"Indi mentioned that Sergeant Adams had daughters."

"Oh... I see," she says, as though I've triggered a thought, but she
doesn't offer to share her thought with me.

The remaining time on the phone is ticking down fast, so I
rummage through my pocket in search of more coins. I find three
twenty-cent pieces and pop them in. They're chewing up quickly.

I need to get straight to the point.

"Listen, Shaina, I'm in a world of trouble down here. The cops are
after me, and I have nowhere to go."

"What? Why?" she asks incredulously. "What did you do?"

"I haven't done anything, but someone's gone to a lot of trouble
to make sure I look guilty."

Aware that she deserves more of an explanation, I sigh before
elaborating. "I can't fully explain everything over the phone, but
someone killed my friend Lindsay, and they're doing everything in
their power to frame me for it."

Shaina gasps. "Are you serious?"

"I found her this morning." My voice cracks. "She was laid out
like a human sacrifice inside a chalk-drawn circle with burning
candles surrounding it. It was like a scene from The Craft, only
worse. Her eyes were... and her mouth was..." Unable to bring myself
to finish, I recompose myself and get back to the point. "This didn't
all start with Lindsay, and it probably won't finish with her either.
Just over a week ago, before I came to Coraki, a local girl named

Christine was murdered too, in what the cops are calling a ritualistic homicide."

"Holy shit."

"She worked at my brother-in-law's pub, The Hoey Moey. I'm surprised you didn't see it on the news."

"I don't watch the news."

"You should keep an eye over your shoulder because I think that the person who's trying to frame me for the murders of Christine and Lindsay has been in your house or, at the very least, has a connection with the person who has been in your house. I don't believe it was Indi who drew those things on the walls. I think the room was staged. The symbols drawn inside the chalk circle where Lindsay's body was laid out are identical to the ones drawn on your spare bedroom wall. And I bet my bottom dollar that the same symbols were drawn in the barn where Christine's body was found. I'd ask around if I could, but I can't. It'd only end up being used as evidence against me."

"Do you have any idea who's behind the killings? From what you're telling me, it sounds cult-related."

"I know for certain Dirty Dick is using my mental illness and colourful past as a weapon to frame me, but I'm not sure if he was the one who murdered both young women or if he's involved with the cult somehow."

I've found myself wondering if Indi's ex, Enzo, has it out for me and is collaborating with Dirty Dick. He could've easily helped to stage her old bedroom. Perhaps that's why it'd only been his name written on the walls.

I don't mention this to Shaina. I've already told her that Indi used to call me Enzo, and I don't have time to explain the details fully, nor do I have anything solid to back my claims. It's just a wild theory I came up with on the train ride back to Coffs.

"There's one particular symbol that's caught my attention, but I don't know what it means. All I know is that I've been placed dead centre in this unholy mess, and I need more time to figure out the details before the cops get hold of me. I've got a whole lot of theories to go on, but I can't quite connect the dots to prove my innocence."

"Dirty Dick," Shaina says as though in thought. "That's the psychiatrist from Rozelle Hospital, am I right? Didn't you say that he was having an affair with Lindsay?"

Wow. She really must've taken in everything that I'd said to her the first day I met her.

"Why do you suspect him?"

"I know for a fact that he's a predator," I say, "And I saw him at The Hoey Moey the night I was drugged and Lindsay was killed."

"You were drugged?"

The phone screen flashes urgently, prompting me to glance at the timer again.

"Shaina, I'm fresh out of coins, and I've got less than a minute left."

"Where are you now? I'll come and get you," she says, surprising me with her calmness and generosity.

I literally just told her that I'm suspected of homicide.

"I'm on Park Beach Road, but I can't stay here. There're cops out and about looking for me."

"Where's somewhere safe I can meet you?"

"I'm not far from Brian Navin Park. I could hide out there for a few hours. There's a small shopping centre with a car park that backs onto Brian Navin Park. I'll stick back there amongst the trees. The shopping centre is located on Park Beach Road across from Phillip Street."

"That sounds like a good plan. I'm leaving now." I hear the jingle of her car keys being lifted. "I'll see you soon, okay?"

"Okay."

CHAPTER 30
JULY 13TH, 1998
COFFS HARBOUR, AUSTRALIA
∞ SHAINA ∞

By the time I pull up at the shopping centre that backs onto Brian Navin Park, the sky is pitch black. I double-park at the far end of the carpark, facing the trees and flick my high beams a couple of times to alert Monroe of my arrival. A few minutes pass, and I flick them again, but he's nowhere to be seen. I grab my bat and flashlight from the passenger seat and step out of the car, making sure to keep the door open in case I need to make a quick getaway.

One can never be too prepared.

Most people would think I'm crazy, driving three hours during the night to pick up a near-stranger who's been previously institutionalised for violent crimes and is now being accused of two murders. Never mind the fact that I'm about to enter the dark shadows of bushland alone in search of him.

"What are you, stupid?" Owen's patronising words echo in my mind, and I snort.

I'm doing this because I believe Monroe's story and think he's innocent. According to him, he doesn't have anybody else. Plus, he doesn't know the truth about Indi and the cult—whereas I do. Even then, I don't know everything.

I'm still not sure what Owen's connection to the cult is. Hence, I've been super friendly to him the last two times I've seen him, buttering him up so he'll give me the answers I want without him realising it. I never ask anything directly. I always dance around the questions, but he's arrogant and foolish enough to have let a few things slip. He thinks I'm still in love with him and that I want him back, which is the reason he's indulging me.

I shake off my nerves and put on my brave-girl hat. Now that I know exactly what these members of the cult are capable of, it's got me spooked. If they're targeting young women for ritualistic kills, I could very well become their next victim and be perceived to be "Monroe's" next kill.

Serial killer, here I come.

When I get to the tree line, I flick on my flashlight, shining it through the gaps between the trunks.

"Monroe?" I call in a whisper. "Monroe, are you there?"

Footsteps crunch within the shadows, the sound growing louder as the person's feet move in my direction. My heart pounds erratically as I position my bat over my shoulder, biceps tense and ready to strike.

Seconds later, Monroe exits through the trees, looking dishevelled and shaking.

"I saw the car lights," he says, glancing warily between my face and the elevated bat. "But I wasn't sure if it was you or not."

His eyes are hooded, and his face is drawn.

I wonder how long it's been since he last slept.

Relieved to see he's still in one piece, the tension in my shoulders eases.

I relax my stance and lower the bat. "I wasn't sure what else I might find out here," I say, diffusing the tension.

"You can never be too careful," he agrees.

"Come on. Let's get you out of here, shall we."

Monroe shivers all the way to the car. It's only 6°C outside, and he's wearing a thin cotton shirt.

Once we're safely inside and the doors are shut and locked, I crank the heater up full blast.

"When's the last time you slept?"

"Saturday night," he answers. "The evening Dirty Dick spiked my drink."

"How'd he get to your drink without you noticing?"

"I was mid-way through my break when Daniel called me out of the tearoom, saying there was a pretty girl looking for me." He glances my way. "The funny thing is, I'd thought it was going to be you, but it turned out to be Lindsay. Dirty Dick gained access into the tearoom by telling Sawyer that he was my father and then slipped something into my OJ while I was distracted."

Boy, am I glad it's dark inside the car.

Monroe's offhanded compliment has my cheeks flushing. It's been a while since anyone has paid me a compliment. Owen used to say sweet things back when he was trying to woo me, but these days, he prefers to belittle me or insult me instead.

"You know," Monroe continues, "if Lindsay hadn't been killed, I'd *almost* believe she was in on it. Cleverly distracting me while Dirty Dick spiked my drink. But Dirty Dick drugged me so that he could kill her and then frame me for it, so there goes that theory. Besides, I know she'd never do anything to hurt me. She could be rebellious and a royal pain in my arse, but we were friends. Good friends."

"Perhaps she was in on it but was led to believe they were playing a harmless prank?" I say, and immediately regret it.

I should be steering him away from these kinds of ideas. No good will come of them now that Lindsay's gone. It'll only cause more heartache.

"Or perhaps she didn't even know Dirty Dick was there, and it was all just a coincidence."

"I guess I'll never know," he says, voice thick.

"How did you end up in Lindsay's apartment?"

"The last thing I remember is feeling woozy at the bar and then seeing Dirty Dick before passing out in Lindsay's arms. When I popped by The Hoey Moey this afternoon, Daniel, a fellow employee, told me that he helped carry me to Lindsay's car. He said I was completely out of it and a dead weight. This means Lindsay must've had another strong set of hands to help get me inside her apartment, considering it was located on the fifth floor with access via stairs only."

Monroe's face hardens. "It had to have been Dirty Dick who helped carry me up, and then killed her. I should've filed a complaint about him as soon as I was released from the hospital, but I was so busy worrying about Indi that everyone else came second." He laughs, a dark, hollow sound that's void of humour. "The worst part is, I still have no idea what became of her or if she's even still alive."

I glance across momentarily and detect the glisten of tears rolling down Monroe's cheeks. "I'm sorry," is all I say.

Guilt claws at me as I hold on to the truth. Now is not the time to share what I've learnt with him. He's not ready to hear it. He needs time to grieve his friend, Lindsay, and have a good night's sleep before I reveal the earth-shattering information I've uncovered about Indi.

Meanwhile, Monroe swallows hard, stammering on his words when he gets to the devastating part about finding Lindsay deceased and on display on her living room floor. He elaborates in greater detail what he'd briefly mentioned on the phone. Describing a ring of lit candles, rose petals, and a chalk-drawn circle with symbols inside.

"If it wasn't for her disfigured face, she would've looked beautiful," he says. "She was dressed in a white lace gown and carefully laid out on a bed of red rose petals, with her long dark hair flowing around her in luscious waves. She'd looked like a bride on her wedding night."

When he describes the way her lips had been sewn together with string and how her eyes, which were once a reddish-brown, had

been bleached of all colour, Dawn's face flashes to mind–his grandmother's *face–a grandmother whom he knows nothing about.*

I shudder.

He's right. Everything is most definitely connected to the cult
somehow. We just need to work out how and why.

He tells me about his impromptu trip to Rozelle Hospital to file a
complaint about Dirty Dick and to warn his friend Becca, who was
also having an affair with him.

"I'm not sure if it was Dirty Dick or someone else on the inside,
but they managed to botch up Becca's paperwork to make me look
crazy. There wasn't any file on her, only a scanned document dated
back to 1978, stating she'd killed herself." He swallows. "I mean,
it's either that or I'm seeing..." He shakes his head. "I think that
whatever Dirty Dick slipped in my drink is messing with my mind
because when I was leaving the hospital, I thought I saw Lindsay.
She spoke to me like nothing had happened, as if it had all been
just a nightmare, but then her face changed and I... I... I don't
know what's real or what's not. If I saw her or not. Maybe I am
crazy."

"I don't think you're crazy," I say. "I think you need some sleep.
You're safe now. You should try resting."

"You're probably right," he agrees.

I reach back and hand him one of Isaac's stuffed toys from the
rear seat. "Here you go, you can use this as a pillow."

I spend the rest of the journey rehashing everything I've learnt so
far, trying to work out the connections, but I can't understand Dirty
Dick's involvement unless he is a member of the cult.

*Where is the cult now? Coraki? Coffs? Sydney? Have they spread out
into other areas?*

When we arrive at Coraki, I rouse Monroe with a soft shake to
the shoulder. He startles and throws his arms up as though ready to
take me on.

"I'm so sorry," he says when he comes too. "I thought..."

"It's okay," I say, waving it off. "I understand."

We make our way inside, and I show to him Isaac's room. "Isaac is with Owen tonight, so you can take his room."

"Are you sure? I don't mind taking the couch or the floor."

I scoff. "*Please*, just take the bed."

His eyes grow soft and puppy-dog-like. "Thanks, Shaina, you've been very kind."

My cheeks heat. "Rest well, Monroe."

CHAPTER 31
JULY 14TH, 1998
CORAKI, AUSTRALIA
∞ MONROE ∞

(EARLY HOURS OF THE MORNING)

A clap of thunder—as loud as a bomb exploding—jolts me into consciousness, and my eyes dart open to find I'm standing in a dimly-lit room. Confused and in a semi-dazed state, I glance about bewildered. A bolt of lightning strikes, illuminating pale walls covered in rusty-coloured writing and symbols, and only then do I realise I'm in the middle of Shaina's spare bedroom. Rain hammers down on the tin rooftop and splashes through the open window, creating a puddle across the floor.

Goosebumps prickle my arms. I have no recollection of entering this room.

Icy fingers clasp my arm from behind, and I whirl around, stumbling on wet, frozen feet.

My heart skips a beat when I see Indi's face. I stare mouth agape, wondering if it's really her or if I'm dreaming.

"Indi?" I glance her up and down, still suspended in disbelief. "Are you okay? Where have you been? Did you escape? What happened with Jerimiah? Did you still have to marry him?"

I'm flooding her with questions without giving her any time to answer them, but I can't help it. Seeing her here in front of me has set my mind into overdrive.

"I was afraid something terrible might've happened to you," I continue to ramble. "The cops couldn't find you, and your father denied your existence. Everyone thought I made you up."

Indi stares back at me wide-eyed and face tilted. "I'm gonna be married soon, Enzo," she says, giving me an overwhelming case of déjà vu. "The date's already booked. June 21st, in line with the Winter Solstice."

Only then does it occur to me that she looks exactly the same as she did when I last saw her a year ago.

I must be dreaming. I pinch myself hard and wince. It hurts, *but who's to say it wouldn't still hurt in a dream?*

"Monroe? What's going on?" My eyes dart in the direction of the voice to find Shaina standing by the doorway with her trusty bat in hand. She glances about the room as though looking for someone.

"Who are you talking to?"

My eyes flick between Shaina and Indi, and I find myself questioning my own sanity.

I swallow hard before saying, almost pleadingly. "Tell me you can see Indi too, that I'm not losing my mind."

Shaina bites her lip and stares, focusing solely on me with a look of sorrow in her eyes. I know that look, and I don't like it one bit, especially coming from her. She places the bat down and moves towards me, slowly, like I'm a small animal she's afraid to startle.

I regret saying anything.

She thinks I'm crazy, and perhaps I am.

I'm about ready to have myself re-admitted, when Shaina surprises me by saying, "Ask Indi if she knows anyone by the name of Dr Richards."

My mind boggles. *Why doesn't Shaina just ask Indi herself.*

My gaze shifts back to Indi, who's staring absently.

They're both acting mighty strange. Surely, I must be dreaming.

"Do you know someone by the name of Dr Richards?" I ask anyway, knowing full well Indi would have heard Shaina asking me to ask this. It takes me a second to remember Dirty Dick's real first name. "Dr Jerry Richards?"

At the mention of his name, Indi's face morphs. Her eyes glaze white, and her lips tug and distort. I jerk back in fright, cursing while backpedalling to the door.

She looks like Lindsay... No wait... She looks the way she did the night before my eighteenth birthday when I asked her to run away with me.

"What's wrong?" Shaina asks in alarm. "What did she say?"

Are you freaking blind? I think. *Then, it hits me like a sledgehammer. Shaina mustn't be able to see Indi. That's why she's talking through me as the third person. But why? I don't understand what's happening. Is she messing with me?*

My gaze returns to Indi, and her face magically morphs back to normal. My blood runs cold.

"I'm dreaming," I say more to myself. "For sure and certain, I must be dreaming."

"No," Shaina assures me. "You're not dreaming."

"Then it's the drugs," I argue. "It must be the drugs. They're still in my system. They're playing tricks with my mind."

Shaina moves closer and gives my bicep a reassuring squeeze. "You're not dreaming, and it's not the drugs. Indi is here, and you need to ask her more questions before she leaves."

"Can you see her?" I ask again, certain she can't.

"No, I can't," she confirms, "but Isaac can."

I glance between the two young women, heart pounding.

"I don't understand. How is that possible? Unless she's..." The thought turns my stomach, and I'm instantly plagued with a strong sense of guilt.

"Indi is dead, isn't she? That's why she hasn't aged. They killed her. They killed her because of me."

Between my freezing feet and shock setting in, my knees buckle from under me. Shaina tries to support me, but I'm too heavy, and we both end up falling. We hit the floor heavily, snapping a few of the rotted wooden boards with the combined weight of our bodies when we land.

Shaina scrambles to her knees and takes my face in her hands.

"Monroe, listen to me. None of this is your fault, okay? Now, I know this is hard, but you need to keep it together. To prove your innocence, we need answers, so you need to keep asking questions."

"Indi's dead," I repeat, struggling to process it. It's my worst nightmare come true. When I was first admitted to Rozelle Hospital, I told Dr Ross that I was afraid Indi's father might kill her because of her association with me, a young man who wasn't a part of their church group. I didn't want my prediction to be true. I wanted to believe she got away.

"Yes, Indi's deceased," Shaina says firmly, but not without compassion, "and we need to find out who killed her."

My brows knit. "Have you known about this all along?"

"No," her voice softens. "Not all along. I've learnt a lot since you were last here, but now is not the time to elaborate. You need to ask Indi what that symbol means." Her hand leaves my cheek to point to the symbol in question. "And more importantly, you need to ask who killed her."

I nod agreeably, knowing she's right. I need to pull myself together so I can discover the truth.

Shaina takes me by the arm and levers me upright. Not only is she strong-minded, she's also physically strong.

"I'm here," she assures me. "You're not alone."

Indi stares my way blankly as though she's a TV presenter who's been put on pause.

I open my mouth to speak but struggle to formulate any words. My mind is reeling.

I'm speaking to a ghost. Indi's ghost. Ghosts are real, not the work of fiction.

"The symbol," Shaina prompts.

I nod once more and step across the room to point out the large symbol placed dead centre on the wall.

"See this symbol," I say, capturing Indi's attention, "What does it mean?"

A knife twists inside me when her eyes glaze over, and her lips tug and distort while she tries desperately to open her mouth to speak. I turn away, sickened by the sight of her once sweet face, gruesomely disfigured. It breaks my heart.

Shaina tugs at my arm. "What did she say?"

"She can't speak." I swallow back the bile rising up my throat. "It looks as though her lips have been sewn together like Lindsay's."

"'Keep My Secrets Binding' spell," Shaina says under her breath, and I glance at her questioningly. "I had a feeling she wouldn't be able to tell us who her killer was. That's why I didn't start with it, but I was hoping, at the very least, she'd be able to tell us what the symbol means."

"Are you suggesting she's been put under a spell?" I ask sceptically. "As in magic?"

"Now's not the time," Shaina says. "Don't question me, question her."

"But she can't say anything, her lips are..." An idea formulates in my mind, and I turn to Indi, bracing myself for the frightful sight.

"Did somebody hurt you?" I ask. "You don't have to say the person's name aloud. You can use the letters on the wall to tell us."

Indi lifts her hand and points out the letters D A D.

"Wyatt Walker," I mutter. "I knew it."

"That can't be right," Shaina argues. "Did she really just write his name?"

"She wrote dad, which amounts to the same thing."

"Wyatt isn't Indi's father, Harold is, but that's not what's important right now. We already know that her father used to hurt her. It's not a secret. What we need to know is who killed her. Be specific."

Once again, my mind is reeling. Everything that I thought I knew is being turned on its head.

Why hadn't Shaina told me any of this during the car ride last night?

I feel as though I've been thrown into the deep end without floaties.

Building the courage to ask the question, I take a deep breath and then say, "Who was the person that took your life?"

Indi lifts her hand, but before I can figure out what letter she's pointing to, her arm tremors violently. A blood-curdling screech emits from the small gaps in her lips, a sound so ear-piercing it causes the room to shake like an earth tremor has erupted. The light bulbs explode, and the windowpane shatters, sending small shards of glass flying across the room. I throw myself in front of Shaina like a human shield to protect her as glass slivers rain down over us. Stars dance in my vision as they slice across my arms and back. The rotted floorboards crack and buckle beneath us with quake-like movements, and before we can even register what's happening, they've given out on us completely, sending us crashing down amongst the foundations.

We both cough uncontrollably as disturbed dirt and mould particles rise into the air, filling our lungs.

Eventually, the screeching ceases, as does the quaking, and the debris around us starts to settle.

My ears remain ringing, and my back and arms burn from cuts and scrapes.

"Shaina." I feel around for her in the darkness. "Are you okay?"

Our trembling hands find one another, and I have a sudden urge to pull her to me tightly. It's as though I've just woken up from a bad dream, only it wasn't a dream.

"What the hell was that?" There's a tremor in Shaina's voice.

"I have no idea," I say, feeling as shaken as she sounds. "All I know is we need to get out of here."

We manage to crawl to the edge of the foundations, which leads into her backyard. The rain patters against my skin with a biting freshness, instantly reducing my stress levels and bringing me back to myself. The neighbours' lights are on, and we see their silhouettes peering out the windows, appearing like blurred shadows through the heavy sheets of rain.

"They must've woken in fright with the noise," Shaina points out.

"We should get back inside before they start asking any questions," I suggest, knowing we have no rational way of answering any of them.

I follow Shaina to the back door, where she lifts the corner of the coir doormat and plucks out a key.

She unlocks the door, and I reach for the handle. "I should go inside first and make sure it's safe."

She grasps my hand and grips it tightly. "We'll go together."

Once inside, Shaina flicks on the laundry light switch, startling me with the brightness. I imagined *all* the light bulbs would've shattered with that hell-raising sound.

"It looks untouched in here," Shaina says, glancing about, brows narrowed.

The same can't be said for her. She looks as though she's been in a war zone, covered in muck from head to toe. Her mud-spattered hair and clothes, soaked from the rain, are leaving dirty drip marks on the floorboards.

"Your arm," she says, inspecting me too. "It's bleeding." She rotates me around for a full body scan and gasps. "Your back!"

"It's from the window shards," I say.

She lifts my shirt and runs a finger along my skin, making me shiver. "It looks bad. We need to get you cleaned up."

CHAPTER 32

JULY 14TH, 1998

CORAKI, AUSTRALIA

∞ MONROE ∞

(EARLY HOURS OF THE MORNING)

We stick close to one another as we make our way through the rest of the house.

Shaina flicks on every light switch as we pass, checking for any damage and making sure that all the floorboards are still intact. Only the spare bedroom seems to have been affected by the supernatural occurrence. The rest of the house is untouched. Shaina doubles back to the kitchen and grabs a flashlight from one of the drawers before returning to the doorway of the spare bedroom.

My chest twinges at the thought of seeing Indi's distorted face again but I put on a stoic front.

"What are you doing?"

"I want to quickly assess the damage before shutting the room off from the rest of the house."

I reluctantly follow Shaina's lead, and together we peer inside.

"What a disaster," she says, voicing my thoughts.

"It looks like a demolition site," I add.

"This room has always needed work, but I can't afford to fix it. Owen offered to pay for the repairs, but I flat out refused to take his money."

"I don't have much money, but I'm good with my hands, and I'll help if I can," I offer. "I just don't know what the future holds for me. Chances are I'll be locked up soon."

"In that case, if I help to prove your innocence, you can repay me by helping to fix my spare bedroom. Deal?"

The hint of a smile curls her lips, but it fades just as quickly as it comes. "Do you see her," she urges. "Indi, I mean. Is she still in here?"

I shake my head, saddened that I'm relieved. "No, she's gone."

To think, I've spent over a year waiting for that very moment, desperate to see her again or—at the very least—find out what happened to her, and now... Indi's disfigured face fills my mind, and guilt rips me to my core.

She's dead, and I'm afraid it's my fault.

What hurts even more is that the encounter felt empty. She didn't seem to remember me at all. She thought I was Enzo again.

I'm coming to the realisation that the words and symbols she'd painted on the wall were *solely* for Enzo. I didn't even get a look in. I was merely her escape plan.

Once Shaina and I have wedged the door shut, she goes to the linen press and hands me a towel.

"You should take a shower and get cleaned up so I can tend to your wounds." She gazes down at the floorboards and playfully adds, "I can't have you dripping blood all over my squeaky-clean floor."

I glance down to find crimson spots adding to our dirty footprints. The floor is wet, muddy, and blood-stained, just like my clothes.

I look at her in consternation and bite my lip. "I don't have any other clothes."

She eyes me up and down. "I have a pair of loose trackies that might fit you. Give me a sec." She disappears into her room and comes out with a pair of black tracksuit pants. "Try these on. Hopefully, they'll fit."

When I'm tossing my pants aside in the bathroom, I hear something drop to the floor. My heart stills when I spot Raj's credit card lying on the tiles.

Jackie's words replay in my mind. *"Why didn't you tell me that you caught Monroe taking your car out during the night or the fact that your credit card has mysteriously gone missing?*

Shit! Was it really me who took Raj's car and card?

I can't have been the one who paid three months' rent on Lindsay's apartment, though. I didn't even know she'd been released until the evening she showed up at my work. My mind spirals with confusion.

I don't take long in the shower, mindful that Shaina will need a rinse off too.

The dirt washes away easily, but my cuts are still bleeding when I'm finished, making a mess of the towel. It turns out Shaina's "loose" tracksuit pants are a snug fit on me—not that I'm complaining. They're clean and dry and do the job.

I keep the towel around my shoulders while Shaina showers, taking a seat on one of the kitchen chairs while I wait. She'd given the floors a quick mop-over while I was in the bathroom, and I don't want to mess them up again.

She comes out looking fresh with the towel wrapped around her head like a turban and goes straight for the kitchen cupboards. I watch as she rummages through the supplies in the first aid box.

She pops a handful of packaged dressings on the table, as well as cotton wool balls, butterfly stitches, Band-Aids, and a bottle of Dettol.

"Alright," she says, positioning herself behind me. "Show me the damage now that you're clean."

I slide the towel off and drape it on the chair beside me.

The wounds mustn't look pretty because she makes a sucking

noise through her teeth. "A few of these could really use stitches, but I know a hospital visit is out of the question."

She picks up the disinfectant bottle and soaks a cotton wool ball with the solution before dabbing it on my skin. Her touch is soft, but the sting of the disinfectant has my teeth gritting.

"How are you doing? Are you okay?"

"The disinfectant burns a bit, but I've been through worse."

"I can only imagine," she says, "but that's not what I was asking."

"Oh..." The meaning behind her question is clear now, but the answer is much more complicated.

"Guilt plagues me over what happened to Indi... And yet..." It's hard to share my true feelings with Shaina when I haven't told her the whole truth, so instead, I say, "Every time I close my eyes, I see flashes of Indi's and Lindsay's disfigured faces, and it's like I'm trapped in a nightmare. I can't unsee the horrifying things I've seen, and I can't wrap my brain around what just happened in your spare bedroom. My mind is struggling to process everything."

"It's a lot," Shaina agrees. "And yet, there's more I need to share with you."

She finishes wiping down my arms and back with more Dettol and then plucks out a couple of fresh cotton balls to pat down the section of my back with the deepest cuts. "I'm not sure how well these are gonna stick," she says, turning her attention back to my wounds. She discards the used cotton balls and opens the packet of butterfly stitches. "But I promise to give it my best shot."

I feel the pressure of the tape tugging where she pulls the skin together before sticking it down. All up, she uses thirteen butterfly stitches on my back and shoulders. I'm not particularly superstitious, but with the luck I've been having lately, I'm hoping that "thirteen" isn't a bad omen.

"They seem to be holding for now," Shaina says, sounding satisfied. "But I can't guarantee it'll stay that way. I'm almost finished. I've just gotta pop a couple of Band-Aids on the smaller cuts."

I crane my neck to face her. "Thank you."

"I'm the one who should be thanking you for jumping in front of me like you did. I've managed to come out of the bizarre encounter with only minor bumps and bruises."

"I couldn't have you getting hurt. I'm just sorry that I've dragged you into this mess."

"Truth is, I was caught up in this mess long before I ever met you. I just didn't know it."

I frown. "What do you mean by that?"

"Let's go to the living room and get comfortable. There's a *lot* I need to tell you." She raises a finger in thought. "Actually, I think I'll pour us some drinks first. We're *definitely* going to need them."

I'm not supposed to drink, but after everything that's happened in the last forty-eight hours, I'm not about to knock back her offer.

Shaina brings in two tumblers of whiskey. She hands me mine, telling me not to bend in case the plasters come unstuck, and then slips down on the couch beside me.

We sit in companionable silence, swigging our–much-needed–drinks before she begins.

"I've done a lot of digging since I saw you last, and I've discovered that Owen's family were a part of the cult. In fact, Owen's uncle, Harold, was Indi's father."

Given what I've seen of Owen, I'm not surprised to discover he is linked with the cult, but the part about his uncle being Indi's father doesn't line up.

"If Harold is Indi's father, then why was she living with the Walkers?"

"She wasn't." Shaina throws back the rest of her whiskey and then pops the tumbler down on the coffee table, appearing apprehensive. "Come with me. There's something I need to show you," she says.

She leads me to her room, and I stand by the doorframe while she walks to the side of her bed. Her room is basic, with minimal furniture and a teal bedspread, but it's tidy. She opens the top bedside drawer, takes something out, and brings it over to me. It's a wedding photo and an old one at that. It looks to be taken in the late '70s if the fashion they're wearing is anything to go by. Plus, the photo itself looks aged with discoloured edges.

My eyes are drawn to the bride, who stands out from the crowd, and when I recognise Indi's face, the world closes in around me. She looks utterly miserable, on the verge of tears. Despite knowing that she was using me, my heart still breaks for her.

There's no way she could've been a ghost when I met her, I think, trying to puzzle everything together. *We spent time together, we shared stories, and she hadn't been married yet. She has to have been killed after I left.*

Something's not adding up. This is an old photo, I remind myself. Lost in confusion, my gaze drifts to the groom, Jerimiah, and time stands still.

It's only when Shaina's hand touches my arm that I realise I'm shaking.

"Monroe, what's wrong? What are you seeing?"

"It's Dirty Dick," I say, my voice catching in my throat. "Jerimiah is Dirty Dick. Dr Jerry Richards, the predator."

Her gaze darts straight to him, and she stares in disbelief.

I stagger back to the living room and flop into the armchair. My gut is churning to the point where I think I might throw up.

"When was this picture taken?"

"Turn it over," Shaina says.

When I flip the picture over to check the back, a familiar date hits me square in the face.

June 21st, 1979.

This photo was taken on the exact same day I was born.

There's a loud knock on the door, which startles me out of the dark place my mind was spiralling.

I glance at Shaina with alarm. "Are you expecting someone?"

"No," she says, alert and ready to act. "Not at this hour."

She retrieves her bat and makes a move for the door, but before she can reach for the handle, I grab hold of her hand, stopping her in her tracks.

"Don't open it," I whisper. "You don't know who's out there."

Another loud knock jolts us with a start.

"Open up. It's the police," a male voice calls from the other side.

"Shit," we both curse in unison.

Shaina points frantically in the opposite direction. "Hide."

I stall, afraid of leaving her alone. I've never trusted cops, and even less so nowadays, since finding out about Owen's family's involvement in the cult. I've already lost so much. I don't want to lose Shaina too. She's the only person who's ever taken me seriously. I need her.

"What are you doing?" she scolds under her breath and then gives me an irritated shove. "Get out of here. Go."

Making a snap decision, I hurriedly slip inside her room, which is closest to the entry. Not only do I want to hear what's going on, I need to be able to get to her in a flash if things turn ugly.

I hear the click of the door opening and the pitter-patter of rain hitting the porch.

"Sam," Shaina says, familiarity in her voice. "What are you doing here?"

"Sorry to bother you, Shaina, but we received a report about a disturbance at this address. The neighbours said they heard a deafening scream, followed by the sound of shattering glass."

"Guilty as charged," Shaina says playfully. "As Owen's likely told you, I've had major issues with the window in the spare bedroom since I bought the place. It won't close, and the room gets waterlogged every time it rains. I tried hammering the damn thing shut during the storm tonight, but the decayed floorboards gave out from under me." She lets out an embarrassed chuckle. "I screamed and accidentally sent the hammer through the windowpane as I fell. It was silly. I should've just left it alone, but I can be stubborn when I want to be."

"Owen hasn't said anything about the window, but he may have mentioned the latter once or twice," the cop says and then laughs.

Shaina continues to chuckle along with him, but it sounds forced. "I bet."

"Would you like me to come and take a look?" the cop asks. "I have some ply at home. I could help board the window up at the very least."

My muscles clamp in panic. If the cop sees the state of the room, her story won't hold.

"No, it's fine, honestly," Shaina says, flooding me with relief. "I've only just closed the door and wedged it shut. Besides, the storm has died down now, so I'm looking to get a little shut-eye."

"Fair enough. You take care, Shaina."

"Yeah, you too, Sam."

As soon as the door clicks shut again, I exit, wiping the sweat from my brow.

"I take it you knew the guy."

She nods. "Thank goodness it wasn't Owen on tonight, or he'd make it his business to stay."

I snort. "You haven't finished telling me what you managed to dig up on Owen."

"It wasn't so much about Owen himself, but about his family. Wyatt and his wife, Ruth, told me that Owen's dad and uncle, Bruce and Harold, played a major role in the cult. Apparently, if anyone spoke ill about any of the cult members, they would mysteriously wind up dead. Bruce is corrupt and he used his power as a cop to help cover the murders up, making them look like accidents. Owen knows something. I can tell that much, but I don't know how deep in it he is."

"He's in deep enough that he threatened to kill me."

Shaina waves my comment off. "As I said before, he was just talking big and trying to scare you off. He can be an arse, but I don't think he's capable of truly killing anyone."

"You say that, but you don't know the half of it," I bite back. "The guy ran me off the road, roughed me up, then pulled a gun on me and threatened to kill me if I ever came back to town. My brother-in-law's bike was totalled, and I was left black and blue, so forgive me if I'm more than a little convinced that he's as evil and twisted as the rest of those monsters."

"He did what?" Shaina's fists ball at her sides. "I can't believe it. That son of a bitch."

"I'd thought you knew about it. That's why I never called you back. I was convinced you'd deliberately set me up."

Her eyes snap to mine, round with shock and hurt. "I would never dream of doing something like that. When I said I would help, I meant it. And I've stuck my neck out investigating the case every day since. Owen was never supposed to find out that you came here. I kept my lips sealed. Isaac was the one who told him, believing his dad would help you, not run you off the road."

"Clearly, I was wrong about you, and I'm sorry," I say, my tone softening. "I have serious trust issues, which've only gotten worse as I've gotten older." I step closer and take her hand in mine. The warmth of it is comforting. "I really appreciate everything you've done for me. You're the only person who's ever believed my story and gone out on a limb for me. You're all I've got, and I need you."

For a second, I worry that I've gone too far, that I've said too much. I sigh in relief when her frustration melts away and her eyes flood with warmth.

"I need you too. I no longer know who I can trust, either."

"Trust no one until we know more," I say. "And be careful of your neighbours. Some of them might still be affiliated with the cult."

"On that note..." Shaina's top teeth graze her lower lip. "I've actually already gone door-knocking along the street, and strangely enough, I met an old woman down the far end who claims to be your grandmother."

"What?" I hmpf in disbelief.

"Stranger still," Shaina continues, her hand slipping from mine as she waves it around for effect while she's speaking, "her face looked the way you described Lindsay's to look when you found her. Her eyes were glazed over and white, and her lips had tiny holes around them that puckered like tiny volcanoes. They pulled and tugged when she tried answering my questions about Indi. It looked as though her mouth had been sewn together with an invisible piece of string. Only they hadn't been... well, not physically anyway, more like supernaturally."

My brows dip in question. "Supernaturally?"

"Oh, come on..." Shaina rolls her eyes at me. "Don't give me that look. After everything you've seen recently, is the idea of the supernatural really that unbelievable? My spare room was just annihilated by Indi's ghost, for Christ's sake. How much more supernatural can you get?"

"Okay, okay." I raise my hands in surrender. "Point taken. I know what I've seen, but I'm struggling to believe what I've seen. My brain hasn't caught up yet. Up until tonight, I thought ghosts were the work of fiction."

"Your grandmother didn't blow me off like the other neighbours did," Shaina continues emphatically. "Instead, she invited me into her house and showed me the photo of Indi's wedding. I tried asking her a load of questions about it, but she couldn't answer. The supernatural string would seal her lips shut every time she tried. After several attempts of desperately trying but failing to get through to me, she mentioned something about a 'Time Loop' spell and a 'Keep My Secrets Binding' spell, which would explain why she, Indi, and Lindsay all look the way they do when someone brings up a forbidden topic."

Shaina goes and picks up the photo from the coffee table where I'd left it, bringing it over for me to take another look at.

"I did manage to get a couple of things out of her, though, like who Indi's father was." She points Harold out. "And who this man was."

Her pointer moves to a man who shares a similar resemblance to me. I hadn't noticed him before; I'd been so caught up on Indi and Jerimiah that all the other faces had blurred into the background.

"Your grandmother says this man is her son, which would make him *your* father."

"No," I say, immediately rejecting the idea, even though I can see the resemblance myself. "He couldn't be."

"Look at the guy, Monroe," Shaina urges. "It's blindingly obvious you're related to him somehow. At first, I thought he was you. Apparently, his name is Enzo, which I found strange, especially since you told me that Indi used to call you Enzo. Do you think, perhaps, she was confusing you with your father? I mean, going by the photo, he was from her era."

My heart skips a beat before thrashing wildly, and I curse. The thought sickens me to my core.

Shaina steps forward. "I'm sorry, I shouldn't have—"

"It's okay," I say, sharper than anticipated. It's not okay, but it's also not her fault.

I glance at Dirty Dick again and point him out before saying, "Do you know what's even more disturbing? Dirty Dick looks as though he hasn't aged a day. He looks exactly the same now as he does in this photo."

Shaina's brows pucker. "What are you thinking? Is he a ghost, too? The world was scary enough when I thought I was dealing with the evil living, never mind the evil dead."

"That's where my thoughts initially went, but everyone at the hospital could see him, so there has to be another explanation. Perhaps Jerry is Jerimiah's son, like I'm Enzo's son." I examine the photo more closely, only to second guess the theory.

It's Dirty Dick. I know it's him. I just don't know how it's him.

"Can you stay with me tonight?" Shaina asks, glancing towards her bedroom. She rushes to add. "Just for comfort. I don't really want to be alone right now."

"Of course," I say, feeling much the same. "I don't want to be alone either."

CHAPTER 33
JULY 14TH, 1998
CORAKI, AUSTRALIA
∞ SHAINA ∞

I'm awoken by a loud knock at the front door, and I groan, not yet ready to face the world. Monroe rouses beside me, semi-dazed and blinking back sleep.

"What time is it?" he asks.

I glance at the clock. "It's 7.30 AM."

Although we'd retired to my bedroom at 3 AM, neither of us had gone back to sleep until 5 AM. We'd laid awake, mulling through the bits and pieces of information we'd both gathered, trying to put it together like a jigsaw puzzle. So many of the pieces fit together, but we just need a few more bits to figure out the whole picture.

The sheet is wrapped low around Monroe's waist, allowing my eyes to roam over his naked chest and muscular arms with admiration. A dizzying sensation threatens to overwhelm me. I know it's outrageous. He's four years younger than I am, and we barely know each other, but from the first moment I saw him, I felt an instant attraction.

Not only am I attracted to him, but the more I get to know him, the more I'm growing attached to him. There's a quiet strength yet a gentleness about him that reminds me of Coen. Monroe might look bad on paper, but in my heart, I believe he is a good person who's been dealt a bad hand. Most of his issues stem from his shitty childhood and the fact that he's been misguided by Indi's spirit. I can't bear the thought of him being locked up for life for crimes he didn't commit. He's being framed and I'm prepared to do whatever I can to help clear his name.

The persistent knocking converts to hammering. "Shaina, it's me, open up."

"Shit, it's Owen," I tell Monroe. "I'd better go and get the door before he knocks it off its hinges. You stay in here, okay? Don't come out, no matter what."

I slip through the door, making sure to close it firmly behind me. I don't trust Owen not to force his way down the hall to check out the spare room.

Clearly, Sam's rung to tell him about the early morning disturbance call.

Why else would he be here at this hour?

My breath catches when I open the door to find Owen holding two takeaway coffee cups and a brown paper bag of goodies. The delicious aroma of coffee and sweet pastry fills my nostrils, and my taste buds dance. Meanwhile, my heart is pounding.

Since when does Owen bring over breakfast?

"Well, are you gonna just stand there, or are you going to invite me in?" he asks impatiently.

I reluctantly step aside, allowing him in. He has his uniform on, which tells me he's on the clock. Hopefully, that means he won't be staying long.

"What are you doing here?"

He shakes the brown bag in his hand. "What does it look like I'm doing? I've brought us breakfast."

Us. My stomach sinks. I thought I was being clever buttering him up to get information, but his ego has read more into it.

He takes a seat at the kitchen table and pushes one of the coffees in my direction. "Go on, get into it. You look like death warmed up."

I roll my eyes. "Complimentary, as always."

"I'm just saying you look tired. What's wrong with that?"

"I look tired because you woke me."

"Sam told me about what happened to the window in the early hours of this morning," he says, taking a bite of his cinnamon roll. "And he got me to pop around and pick up a piece of ply he had lying around so I could get the window boarded up. I figured I'd get it done this morning while it's blue skies out."

A string of curse words soar through my mind.

"Tell Sam, thanks. But you don't need to board up the window. Leave the ply down the side of the house, and I'll fix it myself later."

"Nonsense, I'm happy to do it for you. It'll only be a temporary fix, of course. I'll organise a proper window replacement in a couple of weeks when Ted gets back to town. Now sit down with me and have your breakfast, won't you?"

"I don't need your help. I'm a capable woman, and I can take care of myself."

"Can you, though? Don't think I don't see the pile of unpaid bills sitting on your kitchen countertop and the second-hand clothes you're sticking our kid in. Face it, you're sinking without me."

"Oh, go fuck yourself."

Shocked by my outburst, his brows raise. "What's got up your nose?"

He can't be serious.

I snort. "You're such an arse."

"You'd better watch what you're saying." He tsks. "I went out of my way to come here this morning. Hell, I even bought you breakfast. A little gratitude wouldn't go astray."

If he thinks he's getting any gratitude out of me, he has another thing coming. The only reason he's here at all is because he still thinks of me as his possession.

I sit at the table opposite him, struggling to bite my tongue. If Monroe is listening, which I'm sure he is, the last thing I want to do is get into a heated argument with Owen.

Owen grins and shoves a cinnamon roll my way, believing he's won the argument.

God, he irks me.

I don't want the roll, but I bite into it anyway, figuring the quicker we get breakfast over with, the quicker he can board up the window and be on his merry way.

I keep quiet and nod politely while he tells me about all the antics he and Isaac have gotten up to these past few days. As much as I resent Owen for the way he treats me, he is an active dad, and I know that Isaac loves him, even if he can be tough on him at times.

Once we've finished eating, I help Owen to unstrap the ply from the top of the paddy wagon and carry it inside.

"I need to put this down for a sec," I say when we get to the spare bedroom. Owen nods, and we rest the piece of ply against the hallway wall. I un-wedge the spare bedroom door and hold my breath as I turn the handle, praying the room has magically repaired itself overnight.

Here goes, I think.

No such luck.

Owen enters and gasps. He surveys the room from top to bottom, his jaw swinging open in disbelief.

"Shit, Shai. What in the world did you do in here?" He scans the busted floor, and my eyes follow his line of vision. I swallow nervously at the sight of glass glittering across the bedroom floor like confetti. Dark spots of Monroe's blood have soaked into the wood, staining it burgundy.

If only I'd mopped in here, too.

Owen's eyes rove over me. "Did you hurt yourself?" he asks.

"A little," I lie. "It's nothing serious."

His gaze lowers to the floor again. "That's a lot of blood for nothing serious."

I watch as the invisible cogs tick over in his mind.

"Say, why is there glass scattered across the room? If you smashed the window from the inside, it would've—"

"You see," I bite, "This is exactly why I didn't want you helping me. I knew you'd pick holes in my story, and I didn't want you to know just how badly I messed up. I locked myself outside, and I had to break in, so I smashed the window. It needed to be replaced anyway, so it's not a big deal."

"I thought you kept a key under the back doormat?"

"I used to," I agree. "But I forgot to put it back after the last time I used it."

He frowns, not completely sold on what I'm telling him. "What were you doing going outside at that time of morning? What was it– one, maybe two, in the morning?"

"A crack of thunder startled me awake, and I remembered I still had washing hanging on the line, so I quickly rushed outside to gather the clothes and bring them in before the rain hit. I forgot to use the back doorstop in my haste, and a gust of wind blew the damn thing shut before I could get back inside again." The lies keep pouring out of my mouth. "It was foolish, and I regret it, okay? Now, can we quit with all the questions and get the job done already? I'm tired, and I want to go back to bed."

"Fine," he agrees, and I nearly fall over. I thought, for sure, he'd grill me further. "I'll go and get the drill."

He leaves the room, and I take a steading breath. If I'd been strapped to a polygraph test, my stats would've given me away in an instant. I'm sweating, and my pulse is racing so hard that my whole body thrums with the beat. I really need to take tutorials on how to become a better liar.

I suck.

I hear the squeak of an interior door opening and I panic.

Oh, crap!

I dash out to find Owen standing at the entrance of my bedroom.

What the hell is he doing? I thought he was going to grab his drill from the car.

And then it hits me; he's not getting his drill; he's getting my drill he'd given me.

266 ∞ SHAINA ∞

"I picked up a spare tool set which I'm going to leave here," Owen had said, shoving a sizeable toolbox under the foot of my bed. *"It'll come in handy for you, and it'll save me carting my stuff back and forth every weekend."*

That'd been four months ago, and we'd gotten into a massive fight that evening, putting an end to the weekend visits. In a fit of rage, I'd told Owen that I didn't want his help anymore and that his persistent weekend visits were suffocating for me and confusing for Isaac.

"We should only see each other at drop-offs and pick-ups," I'd insisted. *"You have your mistress living with you now, so go and play Mr Fix-It with her."*

Owen, being Owen, never fully stuck to my request, but he did ease off on the weekend visits and quit playing Mr Fix-It with me. It wasn't until I asked him here to show me the files on Wyatt Walker that the boundaries have blurred again. I should never have involved him. And more importantly, I should never have spent the last two visits buttering him up.

Owen falters in the doorway, looking dumbstruck. My heart beats a wild staccato as I step up beside him. I watch nervously as his eyes scan over Monroe, examining his bare torso with my track pants sitting low on his hips.

Instead of flying at him in rage, like I'm expecting, Owen's face blanches, and his eyes swivel to mine.

I'm even more stunned to find there's genuine hurt behind them. Tension fills the space around us, making the air thick and hard to breathe.

"What the fuck, Shai?"

Did he really think there was a chance of us rekindling things? Is that what breakfast was all about? He's still with Victoria, for crying out loud.

And then, like the flick of a switch, the Owen I'd been expecting rears his ugly head. Like a bull seeing red, he charges at Monroe, fists clenched and eyes ablaze.

"Owen, don't," I call after him, but he doesn't listen, fuelled by a primal force of rage.

Monroe doesn't hesitate or hold back, either. He leaps straight into action, lunging forward and closing the distance between them with a lightning-fast jab to Owen's nose. Owen grunts and staggers backwards, eyes wide with surprise. He'd been too blinded by his own fury to see the hit coming. Blood trickles from his nostrils down into his mouth, but he quickly recovers. He bounces back onto the balls of his feet and takes to Monroe with a powerful right hook. Grunts soon mingle with the sound of fists meeting flesh as they pummel into one another blow by blow.

"Stop it!" I shout, "Owen, Monroe, stop it."

I try breaking them up, only to receive a painful hit to the forearm.

Monroe pushes me out of the way with an apology written in his eyes. "Stay back, or you'll get hurt," he warns.

While his attention is turned on me, Owen strikes him across the chin with a crack.

I gasp and then backpedal, realising I've only made matters worse.

Blood and sweat glisten from both men as their bodies move in a blur of motion, neither of them willing to back down.

After receiving a breath-stealing uppercut to the ribs, Owen loses his footing, and his arms fly up for balance. Monroe sees the opening and takes it, unleashing a series of quick and agile strikes to Owen's face.

Aware that Monroe has the advantage, Owen snatches up his gun from his holster and jabs it against Monroe's temple, bringing his fists to a halt.

"Owen, no!" I shout.

"I know who you are and what you're trying to do, but you won't succeed," Owen growls into Monroe's ear. "Trust me, when my uncle is through with you, you're gonna be wishing you were six feet under like your father."

"What do you know about my father?" Monroe asks.

"Your father was a cold-blooded killer, and apples don't usually fall far from the tree."

"Well, I guess that makes us both rotten apples then, doesn't it?" Monroe retorts.

While they're busy exchanging insults, I slink around the side of the bed to grab my bat.

Weapon now in hand, I quietly make my way back over, levelling the barrel of the bat with the back of Owen's skull. The floorboards creak as I'm about to swing, and Owen jerks around to face me, his eyes wide like saucers.

Monroe uses Owen's moment of distraction to knock the gun out of his hand and kick it under the bed.

"I really don't want to hurt you, Owen," I say, and I mean it. "So please, just go."

Monroe eases off and hangs back, allowing me to take control of the situation.

"It's clear to see why you were so eager to get back to bed," Owen spits with venom. "But listen, Shai, you have no idea who you're getting involved with. This boy is dangerous."

"More dangerous than the cult you're involved in?" I ask.

He snorts. "What cult?"

"The cult that's run by Jerimiah... Dr Jerry Richards... Indi's husband. The 'Indi' that you'd told me was a figment of Monroe's imagination."

"You don't know what the hell you're talking about."

"I might not know everything, but I know what kind of man your uncle is and what he's capable of. I also know that your father is corrupt and has used his power in the police force to help cover up the murders of those who spoke out against Jerimiah and the satanic cult. Why didn't you ever tell me that your family was a part of a cult?"

It's clear I've struck a chord because he doesn't answer, nor does he argue.

Instead, he says, "If you want me to leave, then I need my gun."

"Step outside, get in your car, and I'll bring it out to you," I insist.

Owen's gaze swivels towards Monroe, shooting him a look that could kill.

"The fight's over," I urge. "Now, walk away."

"If you hurt her—" He stabs a finger at Monroe.

"Owen, please..." I tug at his shirt. "It's time to go."

He's on his way out the bedroom door when something catches his eye, and he backtracks. It seems the picture of Indi's wedding has caught his attention.

Owen snatches the photo off the bedside drawers and brings it to eye level, staring at it incredulously.

"Where did you get this?"

"What does it matter?"

Frustrated by my response, he bends the photo in half and shoves it into his back pocket before storming out of the room.

I retrieve Owen's gun from under the bed and head to the door, glancing towards Monroe before I exit. "Stay inside," I say, tossing him my bat. "I'll sort out Owen."

Owen is already in the driver's seat with the window down by the time I get out to his car. As I'm passing the gun to him through the open window, he grabs hold of my arm and tugs me closer.

"I sure hope your night with him was worth it because you've just lost all rights to our son."

His eyes dart to something behind me, and he releases his grip, allowing me to snatch my arm back.

"If I were you, I'd sleep with one eye open," he warns, and then squeals out of the driveway, leaving black tyre marks on the road in his wake.

When I turn around, Monroe is standing in the doorway watching. I stomp up the stairs and shove him back inside.

"What are you doing? I told you to stay hidden. Owen could've easily shot you from there."

"If he really wanted to shoot me, I'd be dead already. That's twice he's threatened me now, yet he hasn't pulled the trigger."

My heart sinks at the sight of Monroe's battered face.

"Are you okay?" I run a finger over his bleeding lip, and he flinches. "I'm sorry. I thought you'd be safe in my room."

"I was leaning against the door listening when I heard his footsteps stop outside. As soon as I felt the door handle twisting and realised what was happening, I jumped back, but it was too late to hide." Monroe's eyes command my attention. "The way he talks to you is disgusting, you know that, don't you? The man is arrogant and controlling. You shouldn't stand for it."

"I know he can be an arse," I agree. "But there was a time when he took care of me. Plus, we have a son together, so I'm stuck with his bullshit whether I like it or not."

"Forgive me for saying, but Isaac doesn't exactly look like either of you."

"Isaac's biological father died when I was pregnant with him, and when Owen and I got married, he legally adopted him."

Monroe's expression is open like he's waiting for me to elaborate, but now is not the time to get into the nitty gritty of my messed-up family life. We have bigger problems at present.

"It's not safe for you to stay here anymore. Once Owen discovers you're wanted for murder, he'll be straight back over here with a set of cuffs." Tears sting my eyes as the weight of the world comes crashing down on my shoulders. "I'm so sorry, Monroe, I messed up."

"It's not your fault." He closes the distance between us and wraps his arms around me. They're slick with blood and sweat, but I don't care. I lean into his chest and breathe him in.

"Remember that, okay," he urges. "Whatever happens to me, it's not your fault. You're not the one who put a target on my head. You've done your best by me, which is more than I can say for anyone else."

"What's going to happen now?" I ask, feeling helpless. "Where can you possibly go that's safe?"

"I don't know," he muffles in my ear. "But I'm sure I'll figure it out. I'm street savvy, and I know how to survive on next to nothing." His grip around me tightens. "It's you I'm worried about. You shouldn't have brought up the cult with Owen. I'm afraid you might've put yourself in danger."

"Owen won't let them hurt me."

"Because he's still in love with you?"

"I'd say it's more like he's protective of me. I'm Isaac's mother, which, to him, makes us family."

As soon as the word family leaves my lips, an idea sparks.

"That's it!" I blurt, startling Monroe with my abrupt enthusiasm. "I think I know somewhere safe that you can go."

CHAPTER 34

JULY 14TH, 1998
CORAKI, AUSTRALIA
∞ OWEN ∞

I flick the paddy wagon lights on and zoom through the streets like a rally car driver, committing the *exact same* offence that road patrol continues to fine other drivers for on a daily basis. Only, I can get away with it.

I'm untouchable.

As far as anyone watching is concerned, I'm just a police officer on his way to an emergency.

My temples are pulsating, and I'm seeing red. Shaina has pushed me to the brink this time. To think, I was actually worried about her. I'd gone over there with the good intention of helping her. She wears a hard exterior and acts tough, but on the inside, the woman is as weak as water. That scumbag is taking advantage of her, and she's allowing it. He's bewitched her with his boyish good looks. Anyone would think she was a teenager with a schoolgirl crush by the way she's acting.

Hopeless fool.

I've shown her the boy's profile. He's all kinds of screwed up, with an extensive criminal record and nothing to his name.

What could she possibly think she's going to get out of this?

She's looking at a lifetime of debt, drug abuse, and domestic abuse—assuming he doesn't kill her straight off the bat.

Shaina needs to be with someone strong, like me. A man who can take care of her and dispose of the trash she naively invites in.

Her stubbornness—especially towards me in recent months—is exasperating. Every time I've tried helping her, she's gotten all snappy with me. She's like those stubborn toddlers who want to do everything themselves, even though they're not fully capable. I've tried telling her repeatedly that I'm not offering my time and money solely for her benefit, I'm doing it for our son, too. He's gone from a decent home with everything he could possibly want to living in a dilapidated shack with the bare minimum.

My father had convinced me to give Shaina the deposit to buy the house on Richmond Terrace back when we first separated. He'd said it was cheap and had loads of potential. It'd been my uncle's place back in the day, so it'd made sense. It was familiar, and it'd been a part of my family.

I'd planned on spending the weekends fixing the place up. Dedicating my time and money was a no-brainer. I wanted our son to live in a decent dwelling. I managed to get several things fixed, but instead of thanking me for my hard work, Shaina snarled and snapped and insisted on doing things herself.

Victoria had moved into my place a month after Shaina had moved out, which had caused a fuss. I ended up finding myself in the doghouse with both women. I'd have Shaina whinging and bitching in one ear—asserting her independence—and then I would get home, and Victoria would jump straight on my case, telling me if I kept spending my weekends over at Shaina's, she was going to leave me. She said she refused to be treated as anyone's second choice ever again.

"I've already been the mistress once," she'd complained. "And I refuse to be that person again."

When I'd told Victoria I was only over there fixing the place for my son, she had bitten back, saying, *"He's not even your real son."*

I lost my temper and called her all sorts of names. I wanted to hurt her, just like she'd hurt me. Neither of us spoke to each other for a week after that, but I ended up forgiving her and keeping my distance from Shaina, knowing it was the only way to move forward.

Victoria was speaking from a place of jealousy. She wants kids of her own, but sadly, I can't give them to her. I got into a terrible accident with a horse when I was a teenager. I came off the saddle during a wild trail ride, and when I tried chasing after the beast, it'd bucked me in the balls. The damage was so bad the doctors told me there was a chance I would be sterile, and further testing in later life proved their prognosis correct.

This is one of the main reasons I pursued Shaina all those years ago, even though she was much younger than I was. She was an attractive pregnant woman with no partner or family members to turn to. She was in need of a man like me to provide for her and her child, and I didn't want to miss out on the chance of becoming a father. More importantly, Shaina wouldn't need a child from me because she already had one of her own. As soon as I saw her cradling Isaac in that hospital bed, I knew for certain I wanted to marry her and be the father to her son.

Our son.

Once we were hitched, I made it official and legally adopted Isaac as my own.

I turn the lights off and ease my foot off the accelerator before turning into the driveway of my father's overrun farm. It looks like a car wreckers' business with rusted old car scraps and used threadbare tyres littering the property. I can only imagine how many brown snakes, red bellies, and redback spiders are hiding amongst the scraps.

Ever since his stroke, my father has struggled with the upkeep of the place. I've tried convincing him to sell up and get something smaller, but the man is as stubborn as a mule.

I step inside to find him lounging in an armchair with the TV blaring. The coffee table in front of him is littered with mugs and dirty dishes, as well as half a dozen empty biscuit packets.

"Hey, Son." He greets me with a lop-sided grin, which disappears instantly the second he catches sight of my face. "What in the bloody hell happened to you?"

"Monroe's back in town, and we got into a scuffle."

"Well, it serves you right, I told you to get rid of him the last time he was here, but you were too piss weak to do it. How'd you go this time? Did you get rid of him?"

The way in which my father talks about getting rid of Monroe is so casual. It's as though he's merely asked me to swat a fly.

"Police records still state Indi as a missing person," I say, having checked the system again recently. "Which is what you had me believing, until Monroe dragged my name all through the court, saying that I was involved with the cult."

I shoot him a pointed glance.

"When you finally told me the truth about Enzo sacrificing Indi and you putting an end to him for the greater good, I accepted your actions without argument."

My father tries to cut in, but I keep going, determined to say my piece.

"Furthermore, when you convinced me to keep a lid on anything to do with The Church of Salvation and those affiliated with the old community, I willingly obliged, no questions asked." I throw my hands up. "Hell, I never even pressed for details. But if you're asking me to pull the trigger on someone, then I need to know exactly what happened, where the bodies are buried, and what I'm up against."

Questions of doubt flood my mind.

"What exactly has this kid done that's *so* terrible, you need me to kill him? I won't shoot someone blind. In fact, I won't pull that trigger unless it's 'kill or be killed'. I have a son to take care of, and I can't do that from behind bars if I'm caught."

"If you think you're doing right by your son by letting that kid walk, then you're in for a nasty surprise," my father warns. "Monroe's father, Enzo, gave into the Devil's persuasion, lost his mind, and then killed your cousin in cold blood. I needed to kill him before he killed anybody else from the community, and now I'm asking you to do the same with Monroe."

"But why? Monroe hasn't killed anyone from the community, has he? As far as I'm aware, all he's done is drag mine and a few church members' names through the dirt."

"Monroe knows I'm responsible for his father's death because his grandmother—who happens to live down the road from Shaina—has been in his ear. She's known as a witch and is into the whole Devil worshipping, hocus pocus."

"You mean that frail, blind old bitty with the messed-up mouth?"

"She might be old and frail these days, but it doesn't stop her from stirring up trouble and dredging up the past. She's put the Devil in that kid and put you in the line of fire." He slams his fist on the coffee table to stress his point. "As long as that kid remains in town, we're all in danger. There's no saying what he'll do to you or your boy in the name of revenge."

"Isaac is gonna be staying with me permanently for a while. I won't let Monroe touch him."

"That's good to hear, but what about the rest of us?"

"Monroe maintains that our church group was a satanic cult and insists you used your power in the police force to cover up the murders of those who spoke out against it."

Shaina was the one who brought it up, not Monroe, but I don't mention her name. I don't want my father to discover she's fraternising with the enemy and insisting I take her out of the equation, too. I could never do that. I still love her, regardless of what she's done.

My father lets out a guttural laugh.

"And you believe that nonsense? Come on, Son, I thought you were smarter than that. The kid's trying to get inside your head." He uses two fingers to tap the side of his temple in emphasis. "He's a whack-job and a mind-twister just like his witch of a grandmother.

The Devil's persuasion is a powerful thing. Satan plants ideas in the minds of trusting individuals, which then spreads like an infectious disease, bringing about hatred, jealousy, fear, and panic."

He clears his throat. "The group we were involved in was a non-denominational, ecumenical religious organisation, not a cult. The only reason anyone in town believed otherwise was because Enzo spread lies about our community. He was jealous of Jerimiah and his relationship with your cousin, so he demonised our denomination, labelling it as a satanic cult–when in reality–he was the one following Satan."

My father's face reddens with frustration and his eyes grow bloodshot. "The heathen took it upon himself to kill Indi in a ritual-istic act, hoping that when the townsfolk discovered her disfigured body left by the altar, they'd believe our religious community were responsible. Thankfully, Jerimiah was the one who found her, and in his rage, he called upon me to capture and kill Enzo, assuring me that God forgives those who seek his forgiveness and that I will be rewarded in Heaven for eliminating those who seek to do the Devil's work."

For all his talk of God and worship, my father's actions don't reflect those of a true Christian.

Suppressed childhood memories tumble disjointedly through my mind, making me shift uncomfortably where I sit. I get flashes of candles, minerals, and symbols, and people huddled in the middle of the circle while we chanted in Latin. I recall how the storms would light the sky, and objects and minerals would fly across the church, in what Jerimiah called "God's response to our prayers".

I remember the way the young boys and young girls were kept separated and told they were not allowed to mingle with each other in the church or its grounds. There came a point where I wasn't even able to play with my sisters or my cousin anymore.

For the very first time, I find myself questioning if I really was brought up in a satanic cult and if I've made a terrible mistake by protecting the community.

"Both bodies are buried under your uncle's old place–Shaina's place," my father admits. "You can see now why I was so keen for you to snap up the property as soon as it became available on the market again. I'm keeping it safe in the family." He clicks the side of his mouth and winks at me.

I readjust my collar, loosening it, suddenly in need of more air.

"Monroe knows where the bodies are buried," my father continues, "That's why he's been sniffing around the property recently. He wants them exhumed."

The image of Shaina's spare bedroom flashes into my mind, and my blood runs cold. The floorboards had been smashed in, and the foundations were exposed.

He's planning on digging them up himself.

As more childhood memories flash through my mind a troubling thought occurs to me.

I pluck out the photo from my back pocket and shove it at my father with angst. I watch as his eyes bulge when he recognises the familiar faces from our past.

"What about them?" I say, pointing out my mother and sisters. "Did they really leave us, or are they buried somewhere, too?"

I had a shock when I spotted the family photo at Shaina's. I haven't seen or heard anything from my mother or sisters since the day they left, back when I was eleven years old. There have been times when I wondered why my mother didn't take me with them.

Had she not wanted me? Or was it the whole "boys stick with boys and girls stick with girls" scenario?

My father scoffs. "For Pete's sake, Owen. Your mother ran off with the girls in the middle of the night, taking all the savings we ever had. Your mother wasn't a committed woman, and neither was your aunt. They'd lost their faith in God and encouraged others of our small Christian community to follow them down the path of damnation."

CHAPTER 35

JULY 14TH, 1998

CORAKI, AUSTRALIA

∞ MONROE ∞

As we climb the steps to my "grandmother's" house, I glance up at the blue porch ceiling, and a wave of nausea hits me. My entire body breaks into a cold sweat, making my skin prickle.

"Look, it's the symbol," I say, pointing to a woven trinket that swirls our way in the breeze.

Flashes of Indi's and Lindsay's distorted faces flicker through my mind, and the world around me begins to glitch. I pause, trying to right my senses. There's a sharp pain growing in my stomach, making me feel nauseous.

Noticing my body swaying in rhythm with the trinkets, Shaina takes hold of my arm. "Monroe, are you okay?"

Bells ding, and wind chimes dingle—*in welcoming or warning?*

"I don't think this is where I should be going?" I splutter. "I mean, why does my grandmother have a trinket with the same symbol that was drawn on Lindsay's floor and your wall dangling from her porch? Don't you find that the least bit strange?"

"There's a *lot* that I find 'strange' about your grandmother and her home, but she did guide me to the wedding photo, which I believe was her way of steering me in the right direction of Indi's murderer."

My breathing becomes laboured, and I bow forward, my eyes fluttering.

"You don't look so good," Shaina says, putting a hand to my face. "And you're breaking out in a sweat. I think you might have a concussion."

There's an old raw iron chair at the edge of the porch, facing the garden, and Shaina ushers me over to it, aiding me to sit. "You wait here. I'll see if your grandma has a cold cloth I can use to cool you down."

The smell of sage and dill is thick in the air. It irritates my inner nostrils and the back of my throat, making me gag.

Shaina knocks on the door, and a woman with a raspy, Louisianian drawl answers. Shaina told me my grandmother was originally from New Orleans. It was a bit of information she'd gleaned from Owen. I try listening to their conversation, but my hearing and vision fade in and out.

Shaina enters the house and comes out moments later with a glass of water and a cool cloth. She hands me the glass and squeezes cold water from the cloth over the back of my neck before patting down my exposed skin. Eventually, the world rights itself again, and the woman, "my grandmother", comes outside.

She makes her way over to the chair where I'm sitting, cradling a handful of herbs or something of the like. Without any guidance, she sprinkles the dried plant-like contents into the glass of water I'm holding, and I wonder how she can move with such accuracy when she's blind.

I glance at the sediments at the bottom of the glass, my nose shrivelling.

I'm not so keen on drinking the water now.

"My dear child." Her milky, glazed-over eyes project a sense of seeing all. "After all this time, you're finally here."

An eerie sensation spreads over me from head to toe, making me shiver. Shaina was right. My grandmother's disfigured face is similar to that of Indi's and Lindsay's.

"Hi," I manage. "I'm Monroe."

"I know who you are, and I know why you're here."

Unnerved by her statement, I examine her face, looking for a slither of myself in her features. Her skin is papery and thin, with deep creases along her cheeks. She looks ancient, as if she could be my great-grandmother. If she was to say she was a centenarian, I wouldn't bat an eyelash.

"Should we take him inside?" Shaina asks.

My grandmother shakes her head. "No. Fresh air is what he needs right now. Leave him out here, dear. I'll take care of him."

Shaina stammers a moment, seeming thrown.

"Oh... Okay then."

Taking my grandmother's cue, Shaina steps around the chair and squats in front of me, levelling her face with mine. "I should go now before any of the neighbours see us here together, and gossip spreads. I don't want Owen to discover your location."

She places the wet cloth over my knee and cups my hands in hers. Her top teeth graze her lower lip, and she stares deeply as though there's more that she wants to say but doesn't feel comfortable with an audience.

My grandmother clears her throat, and Shaina lowers her gaze.

"I'll keep digging and see what I can come up with."

"Don't," I warn. "It's too dangerous."

"I'll be careful." Shaina's hands squeeze mine reassuringly. "And you be safe, too. I'll sneak back here after dark if I can, okay?"

She pushes off my knees to stand and whispers a thank you to my grandmother.

"Remember what I told you, Child," My grandmother says in dire warning. "Now, more than ever, you should be keeping the gift I've given you on your person at all times."

CHAPTER 36

JULY 14TH, 1998
CORAKI, AUSTRALIA
∞ OWEN ∞

I t's 11 AM by the time I arrive back at the station, lugging in a cuffed, kicking, and cursing Barry Brown. I'd received a domestic abuse call-out on the way back from my father's place. I hadn't needed to punch in the address I was given. It was one I knew all too well. Barry Brown is a recurring offender who needs to be taken off the street permanently, but his wife won't officially report him, so we can't press charges. The man is a fifty-six-year-old junkie and a drunkard. When I looked at Sharon Brown's battered and bruised face, it had saddened me to think this could be Shaina's future if she doesn't wake up and pull her head in. A broken housewife who's too afraid to file an official report on her husband because she knows she'll cop it worse the next time around.

Constable Daryl glances up from his desk as I pass him on my way back from locking Barry Brown in one of the holding cells. "What in the world happened to you?"

"Fuckin' junkies," I say open-endedly.

Daryl takes the bait. "Well, the one good thing is, we'll finally have something solid to pin on the son of a bitch."

I nod agreeingly, without commenting, and make my way over to my desk. My face is throbbing, and I need a second to recoup. I pluck the old wedding photo out of my back pocket before taking a seat. My eyes linger on the groom, Jerimiah Richards, and a sense of unease spreads through me. His, was a name that'd sat at the tip of many tongues. The almighty Jerimiah who would save us from a life of eternal damnation.

I don't remember him well. I was only a child when he used to preach his sermons. What I do remember, though, was the feeling of his almighty presence, especially when he was standing on the pulpit. He was in all his glory, with the congregation mesmerised. There was a charisma about him that people were drawn to, and when he spoke, it was as though his words had everyone spellbound. The teenage girls of our church group had all fawned over him, regardless of the strict lifestyle he'd forced them to follow. And the young men of the group had all wanted to be him. He was textbook handsome and possessed the power to command the attention of his followers with a single glance.

After my cousin Indi was killed, everything changed. Many of the women in the group took off, never to return. A short while later, Jerimiah left, too, making his home in Sydney his permanent place of residence. During his time as our pastor, Jerimiah had also worked part-time as a psychiatrist at Callan Park Hospital, which meant he was always flying in and flying out. He still owns the property in Coraki, where The Church of Salvation was built and still stands, but he locked the doors before he left, putting an end to the gatherings.

I wonder what it was that made Jerimiah so influential.

It seems strange, on reflection, to think a mule like my father could be so influenced by the words of a young man with no authority. Since speaking with my father this morning and learning of his lies, secrets, and deceit, I find myself questioning everything about my past and the community I was involved in. I especially find myself questioning who this Jerimiah guy really is.

Some have said they've seen Jerimiah on and off over the years, insisting he came back for short stays, but to my knowledge, he never tried reuniting the remaining community members for gatherings.

In recent years, his estranged son, Jerry, has taken over the property. Jerry was born to Jerimiah's first wife, who'd mysteriously gone missing a few short years after their wedding.

I hadn't met Jerry until I was dragged into court. Uncle Harold introduced him to me as Jerry Junior, and I was told he was the leading Psychiatrist at Rozelle Hospital, which I've since discovered is Callan Park Hospital, renamed. Jerry's resemblance to his father was striking, but I hadn't realised just *how striking* it was until now.

I click into Yahoo and type "Dr Jerry Richards" into the search bar. A professional portrait of Dr Jerry Richards fills the screen, and I hold the photo up alongside the image for reference. Jerry Junior is the spitting image of his father, Jerimiah. In fact, they look so similar with their self-assured expression, blonde hair, and black penetrating eyes that it's hard to believe they are two separate people.

They're identical. Doppelgängers.

"The cult that's run by Jerimiah... Dr Jerry Richards... Indi's husband. The "Indi" that you'd told me was a figment of Monroe's imagination," Shaina had spat accusingly, as though she was referring to one man.

"Hey, Daryl," I say, beckoning him over. "Come here a minute."

He strides across and peers over my shoulder, glancing at the photo I'm holding up to the screen.

"What do you make of this?"

Daryl is still young and new to the force. He may have heard whispers of the name Jerimiah circling through town, but he would've never met him.

His eyes dart between the two photos, and he frowns. "I dunno, who is he?"

"He". Daryl believes he's looking at *one* person.

"That's what I'm trying to figure out," I say.

"By the way..." Daryl reaches across to his desk to grab something. "We got a fax while you were out."

He passes me a sheet of paper with Monroe's picture on it. The words, "Wanted suspect, deemed dangerous, in connection with two homicide cases," smack me in the face.

"Shit!"

"What is it?" Daryl asks, but I don't have time to answer him.

I whip out my flip phone at lightning speed to call Shaina.

CHAPTER 37

JULY 14TH, 1998

CORAKI, AUSTRALIA

∞ SHAINA ∞

T'm in the spare bedroom, searching for a hidden answer in amongst the script and symbols, when the phone rings.

I can only imagine who's calling, so I leave the phone to ring out.

When the incessant bring-bring stops, I exhale, grateful for the much-needed silence, but not a moment later, it starts up again.

Teeth grinding, I let it ring out once again. However, when it starts up for the third time, the mother in me begins to panic.

What if it's not Owen? What if it's Isaac's school? Something could've happened to him.

This time, I race to the phone, the sound of glass shards crunching under my boots. The dagger Dawn had given me jiggles within the sheath inside my left boot, irritating me, but I'd promised I would keep it on me at all times. The boot sheath was the only place I could think to put the dagger where it wouldn't be a complete and utter nuisance. I wasn't about to carry it around in my bra strap or my jeans pocket, that's for sure. The piece of ply Owen had brought over this morning still leans against the hallway wall, obscuring my path. An unwelcome reminder of this morning's events.

I dive for the phone just before the last ring dies out.

"Hello."

"For fuck's sake, Shaina," Owen's voice booms through the receiver, "you had me worried out of my mind."

I groan, wishing I'd stuck to my original instinct.

"What do you want, Owen?"

"Is Monroe still there with you?" he asks.

"That's none of your business," I retort.

"Don't play games with me, Shaina. Is Monroe still there or not?"

I pull the phone a few centimetres away from my ear. Owen must be in his paddy wagon with the police sirens going because they're blaring loudly through the receiver.

"Would it make any difference if he was?"

I wonder if he's on his way over here to arrest him.

"Listen to me, the boy's dangerous. We just received a fax at the station. He's wanted for the murders of two young women."

"Trust me. It's not what you think," I say, knowing full well I'm speaking in vain. "Monroe didn't commit those murders; he's been set up. Besides, he's gone now, *okay.* You scared him off. Are you happy?"

"I'm sure he's told you he's innocent. That's what he wants you to think, but trust me, Shai, you don't know who this kid's father is or what his family is capable of."

"The same could be said about you," I remind him.

"I know I haven't always been open and honest with you, but I can explain. Stay put. I'm coming to grab you."

"What?" I balk. "No."

There's a knock at the door, and I jerk upright.

"It's that you?" I ask. "Seriously?"

"Is what me?"

"Are you at my door already? Forget it, Owen, I'm not coming with you. You can keep Isaac for another week. That's fine. With everything that's happening, he's probably safer in your neighbourhood, but if you try keeping him away from me for longer than that, we *will* have issues."

"Shaina, it's not me at the door," Owen insists. "Don't answer it."

When I don't reply right away, he repeats himself. "I'm serious, don't answer it."

Refusing to listen, I pop the phone down and grab my bat, Owen's voice blasting my name repeatedly in the background.

I pull the door open, slowly and cautiously, to find Monroe standing on the other side. My eyes bug at the sight of him.

"What are you doing here?" I whisper in a panic. I place my bat down, resting it alongside the door frame. "Owen's on his way over here right now. You need to get back to Dawn's place, pronto." Before he has the chance to respond, I hold up a finger and say, "One sec," before dashing back to the phone.

I don't want Owen to hear Monroe's voice.

I pick up the phone and put it to my ear, turning away from the front door. Owen is still on the line, cursing and carrying on.

"Calm down," I say.

"Calm down," he repeats, sounding more outraged than ever. "I told you not to answer the door, and then you disappear off the line. Who was it at the door? Was it him?"

The sound of Monroe's footfalls echoes behind me. I spin around to shush him before he has the chance to say anything, and I drop the phone, startled by the sight of my bat in his hands.

"My apologies, Shaina," he croons with a Louisiana drawl.

What the fuck's he doing? And why is he talking like that?

I should run, punch, kick, but I can't move. I'm frozen in shock.

The bat flies towards my skull, and the last thing I see is stars upon impact before slipping into unconsciousness.

CHAPTER 38

1998

CORAKI, AUSTRALIA

∞ ENZO'S SPIRIT ∞

When Raj mentioned that one of his employees went missing after her shift on the evening of the Winter Solstice, I immediately wondered if she was the girl Jerimiah had left for me to find. My suspicions were confirmed when the officers on the news announced that Christine's body was found in a local barn, in what they suspected was a ritualistic homicide.

It seemed Jerimiah hadn't just picked a girl at random after all.

The way Raj kept glancing at Monroe's bruised and swollen knuckles gave me the impression he was putting two and two together and growing suspicious of him. Thankfully, Monroe had no memory of that night, so he hadn't come across as guilty or challenging. He never remembered any of the things he did when I was in control of his body. As far as he was concerned, he still had a mental condition that caused black spots in his memory.

I was glad when Monroe insisted on going to Coraki for the weekend, not only because it was a good time for him to get out of town, but because I was hoping we'd see Indi again. As it turned out, a lot had changed in a year, and Indi was nowhere to be found.

Wyatt, the man Monroe attacked, had since moved on, and a young woman named Shaina had taken up residence. I was surprised when Shaina's son, Isaac, called my name, grabbing Monroe's attention.

Furthermore, I was absolutely gobsmacked to discover all four walls of Indi's old bedroom had been painted from floor to ceiling in symbols and scripture. Jerimiah's mark stood out like a sore thumb, painted large and positioned dead centre on the side wall.

My first thought was that Jerimiah had played his next move, and Shaina's home had been marked. However, as I read what'd been written on the walls, I quickly realised that the messages had to have come from Indi, not Jerimiah. Most of the sentences were Indi's personal thoughts and feelings.

The symbols and verses, however, were identical to the ones Jerimiah and I had used in sacrificial circles. It seemed Indi finally remembered something about the day she was killed, and she'd found a way to communicate it within the parameters of the "Keep My Secrets Binding" spell.

I'd been interested to discover that Shaina was the wife of Owen Adams, Bruce Adams' son. I wondered if Owen remembered much about his childhood in the cult and whether he knew it was his father who killed me. When he ran Monroe off the road and then threatened to kill him if he kept sniffing around, I felt I got my answer.

THE WEEKS FOLLOWING Monroe's trip to Coraki passed by without any drama. I was expecting evidence to pop up, putting Monroe at the scene of Christine's murder, but it seemed the case had gone cold. I wanted to feel relieved, but deep down, I knew Christine's sacrifice was only the tip of the iceberg. Jerimiah wouldn't have planted a body just for it to become a cold case. He was cool and calculated, and he wasn't the type of man to let things go. The more I obsessed about what Jerimiah was planning, the more paranoid I grew, and with the paranoia came delirium.

On the evening of July 11th, 1998, I had a gut feeling that something terrible was looming on the horizon. I sensed Jerimiah's presence lurking, preparing to play his next move.

Monroe was working a shift at The Hoey Moey and was on his tea break when his co-worker, Daniel, beckoned him out, telling him there was a pretty girl there to see him. As soon as Monroe exited the tearoom, he was so enthralled by the sight of Lindsay standing in front of him that he hadn't noticed Jerimiah slink behind him through the "staff-only" door. I barely recognised Jerimiah myself. He was dressed in a black sweater with jeans and a Billabong cap. In all the years I'd known Jerimiah, I'd never seen him dressed so casually. He was always streamlined, smart, and proper. I followed him a short distance, but my tight link to Monroe stopped me from moving too far from him.

I tried possessing Monroe, but between his excitement and my state of panic, there were too many heightened emotions at play to make the connection.

While Lindsay stood there flirting, I scrutinised her, wondering if she was in on whatever Jerimiah was doing, but the way Jerimiah had angled himself away from her when leaving made it evident he hadn't wanted her recognising him either.

When Monroe went back to the tearoom to finish his meal, I glanced about frantically, wondering what Jerimiah had done. It wasn't until Monroe started growing woozy that I realised Jerimiah must've spiked his drink.

After Monroe was carried out and placed in Lindsay's car, she called Jerimiah and asked if he was still in town.

"I went to visit Monroe at work, and something strange happened to him," she rattled off in a panic. "I need you to help me carry him upstairs to my apartment. If his sister sees him in this state, she might think he's relapsed and get him re-institutionalised. He needs somewhere safe to rest until he's feeling better."

Fear enveloped me as I pictured snippet scenarios of what Jerimiah had planned. Monroe wasn't in a state to be possessed, so there was nothing I could do to help him.

Jerimiah was already waiting at the car park of Lindsay's apartment when she arrived, looking suave in a suit with his hair slicked back.

Talk about an impressively quick change.

Once Lindsay parked the car, he opened the back door and heaved Monroe out. He threw him over his shoulder like a ragdoll and lugged him up the five flights of stairs, sweat beading his brow.

I watched in confusion as Jerimiah headed straight to Lindsay's room and dumped Monroe on her bed before turning to face her.

"I take it that's where you want him? In your bed?" The cool accusation in his tone made Lindsay flinch. It was as if the man who'd spoken to her on the phone and helped to get Monroe up the stairs was an entirely different man altogether.

His eyes narrowed in on hers. "Are you in love with him?"

"What?" She backed up a step, a spark of fear in her eyes. "No. Of course not. I'm in love with you. Monroe's my friend, and he was in trouble. I just wanted him to be safe."

For every step Lindsay withdrew, Jerimiah took another step forward. "Safe at your place, not his."

"He's still under surveillance, you know that. He can't be caught with any alcohol or drugs in his system, or they'll send him back." Lindsay's back connected with the hallway wall behind her, and she gulped, aware Jerimiah was closing in on her. "What's going on?"

"Who was better?" he asked, leaning in and closing the gap. "Him or me?"

Realisation registered on Lindsay's face, amplifying her fear. "It only happened the once, I promise. It meant nothing. We're just friends."

Jerimiah placed his hands on the wall, either side of her face, trapping her. "That's not an answer."

Lindsay's eyes flicked to Monroe's limp body momentarily before saying, "You. You were better."

Jerimiah brushed his lips against her ear and whispered, "Wrong answer."

He whipped his arm down and plucked out a syringe from his pocket, swiftly flicking the cap off before injecting her with its contents.

She started to scream and thrash, but he pressed his body firmly against hers and smothered her face with his hand. She struggled hard, but it wasn't long before her fight gave out, and she collapsed against him, alive but unconscious.

I watched as Jerimiah laid her down on the floor. He disappeared a moment, returning with a box of candles, chalk, and other occult goods. It wasn't like him to perform a sacrificial ceremony outside of the Winter Solstice, but it seemed he'd made a special exception. I tried to possess Monroe again, but he was still too out of it to make the connection. Instead, I sat there pathetically, watching while Jerimiah did Lindsay up beautifully, before sacrificing her soul in an act of revenge.

When he came back to Lindsay's room, I imagined he was going to kill Monroe too. Surprisingly, he just stripped him naked, slipped a credit card into his back pants pocket, and trailed his and Lindsay's clothes across the floor.

"Goodbye, my friend," he said, before exiting and closing the door behind him.

It felt like hours waiting for Monroe to wake up. He'd start to come to, and I'd try to possess him, but then he would fall unconscious again, and the connection would break. I paced the room in paranoia, waiting for the sirens to come.

I couldn't switch to Elias for safety because ever since I took over his body and he came back blubbering, Mama had upped the blocking spells again on a regular basis.

I feared the idea of being fixed alongside Monroe while he served a lifetime of imprisonment, but it was either that or oblivion.

∾

BY THE TIME Monroe finally awoke, I was too worked up to make the connection.

It'd been a damn shame, too, because Monroe handled the situation very differently from how I would've handled it. I hadn't, for the life of me, understood why he would call the police, let alone make a quick dash down to Rozelle Hospital to file a report against "Dr Jerry Richards". If his idea was to come across as completely insane, it worked. The superintendent looked as though she was ready to lock him up and throw away the key.

Going back to The Hoey Moey was another foolish move on his part, although at least he saw Daniel, who convinced him to get back in contact with Shaina.

While staying at Shaina's that night, I finally saw Indi again.

Ever since discovering the scripture and symbols painted across her old bedroom walls, I'd been dying to get in touch with her again. I assumed she'd found some clarity and was finally aware of what'd been done to her, but I was left disappointed when she spoke as if it was still pre-wedding. I pointed to all the symbols and things she'd written, pushing her to remember what'd happened, but all it managed to do was upset her. A storm started brewing, and her face became distorted. It wasn't a natural storm, either. I felt the electrical build-up of spiritual energy in the air.

The wind picked up dramatically and whistled through the gap of the open window. The useless strip of plastic had pulled away from the tape and it flapped ineffectually, allowing droplets of rainwater to flow in with the wind.

A bolt of lightning cut down through the sky, hitting the neighbouring fence with a flash of orange sparks. I made a futile attempt to soothe Indi in order to prevent the storm from intensifying, but another earth-shattering bang shook the ground.

To my dismay, the sound woke up Monroe with a start, forcing me from his body.

Things only got messier from there. Shaina awoke from the sound of the thunder, too, and found Monroe speaking to himself in Indi's old room.

Strangely enough, Shaina immediately grasped the situation and accepted that Monroe was speaking to Indi's spirit. In fact, she encouraged him to ask her questions. It appeared Shaina knew things that Monroe was still unaware of.

Later that evening, Shaina shared everything she'd learned since she'd last seen Monroe. She even spoke of my mama.

Shaina also showed Monroe a picture of Indi's wedding. It'd been the photo Jerimiah had left in my mama's mailbox all those years ago.

When Shaina pointed me out as Monroe's pa, I wondered what was crossing his mind. He blew the idea off instantly, so it was hard to gauge his thoughts and feelings.

As an outsider looking in, it was blindingly obvious that Shaina was keen on my son. Women appeared to be naturally drawn to him, and it was easy to see why. He was a good-looking young man with dark skin, a brawny build, and bright eyes like his mama's. He'd taken the best from both of us, along with the love and compassion of my mama.

While Shaina had her sights set on Monroe, it soon became obvious that her ex, Owen Adams, was still in love with her. I watched as Owen beat Monroe in a jealous rage after finding him in Shaina's bedroom, and an evil plan formulated in my mind.

If Shaina's body was to be found at the property of "Dr Jerry Richards", it would create a stir amongst the Adams brothers as well as the locals. And if the Adams brothers turned on "Jerimiah's son", the rest of the town might be brave enough to follow.

Perhaps Monroe's quick dash to Rozelle Hospital had proved useful after all.

The more uncertainty there was surrounding "Dr Jerry Richards", the more the authorities would investigate him, and I was certain they'd find incriminating evidence. Jerimiah had eighty years' worth of transgressions to hide, and most people don't go on that long without making a slip-up.

I tried possessing Monroe once Owen left, but his adrenaline was still pumping from the fight, so it was mission impossible.

When Shaina suggested taking Monroe to my mama's place to keep him hidden from Owen and the authorities, I felt like killing her there and then. With both of my sons blocked from me, I'd fade off into oblivion, and Jerimiah would win once again.

As soon as Monroe stepped over the council strip and onto my mama's property, the effects of the darkness I'd instilled upon him rose to the surface, trying to escape him. He hadn't screamed like Elias or nearly choked to death like me, but he'd broken out in a sweat and started to stumble.

I couldn't follow them past the council strip without feeling as though my soul had been set ablaze.

My ears perked to listen as they spoke. Meanwhile, my spirit was waning with each step Monroe took. I tried reaching Elias, but the blocking spells that prevented me from entering him were a powerful source. My choices had come down to sheer agony or oblivion.

Shaina had been quick to put Monroe's symptoms down to a concussion, but Mama knew better. She went and fetched Monroe one of her special concoctions, unaware it would be a huge mistake on her part. My mama had never been an easy woman to catch off guard, but because she'd blocked me, she hadn't felt my presence nearby.

More importantly, she wasn't aware I could enter Monroe, so she hadn't blocked me from entering him.

Shaina didn't stay long, and once she left, mama coaxed Monroe into drinking her special concoction. He'd turned his nose up at first, appearing revolted by the sediments at the bottom of the glass, but Mama assured him the drink was full of healing properties, which would make him feel much better.

With those magical ingredients floating around inside of

Monroe, keeping his darkness at bay and easing his mind, I'd effort-
lessly been able to make the connection.

Immediately sensing my presence, my mama's spine steeled.

"Hello there, mama," I said, laying the Louisianan accent on
thick. "Long time, no see. Pardon the pun."

My mama bristled. "You're not welcome here."

"And yet here I am."

A look of conflict crossed her face. It was clear she wanted me to
leave, but on the contrary, she didn't want to throw her grandson
out. Her problem was with me, not Monroe. She was probably
hoping she would get to know him and that the boys could bond.

"What have you done to this child?"

"Well, that's my business now, isn't it?"

"I always had hope for you," she said, her voice breaking. "Just
like I had hope for your pa, but you've passed the point of no return.
There's no good left in you. Even with your darkness at bay, you still
reek of rot."

"Like father, like son," I quoted.

"You didn't have to turn into your father. You chose to, even after
all of my warnings. The twins are good boys, and they deserve much
better. You need to let them go."

The front door creaked open, and Mama whipped around.

"No, Elias. Stay inside."

Elias seemed determined. He stepped onto the porch and shuf-
fled over, eyes downcast and body twitching.

"Can't you see what you've done to this boy?" My mama's milky
eyes scrutinised me. "Does it make you proud?"

I ignored her. "Hello, Son."

In turn, I am ignored. Elias just stood there, staring into my eyes.
His hand slowly slipped into his pocket as though to grab something.

"No, he doesn't deserve it," Mama said, her voice catching.

Elias tremored, appearing conflicted, and when his hand
reemerged, I was surprised to find it empty.

What didn't I deserve?

Elias continued to stare, tears streaming down his cheeks, until Mama put her arms around him and ushered him inside, whispering, "It's okay, Child, it's okay."

She glanced my way. "It's time for you to leave now, Lorenzo," before following Elias inside and shutting the door.

I was only too happy to oblige. I hit the pub for one quick drink before heading back to Shaina's place and surprising her with a whack across the head using her own trusty bat.

CHAPTER 39
JULY 14TH, 1998
CORAKI, AUSTRALIA
∞ OWEN ∞

I screech into Shaina's driveway and reef up the handbrake, taking note that her car is no longer parked under the carport. Her front door is wide open, too, so I'm hoping it means she made a quick getaway. I unholster my gun and make my way up the steps to the porch, surveying the area with caution.

The living room and kitchen are clear. Everything appears in proper order, and there are no signs of a struggle. I keep the gun aimed ahead as I make my way down the hall. The piece of ply I'd brought around earlier still leans against the wall, untouched. Shaina's and Isaac's rooms are clear, but when I get to the spare room, I see a dark figure and holt, lining my gun with the person's head.

"Where is she?" I growl before fully registering who I'm seeing. As my eyes adjust to the dimness of the room, I blink in confusion.

The man standing before me looks scarily similar to Monroe, but he couldn't possibly be him. Not only does his face not have any traces of this morning's scuffle, but this young man is gaunt and sickly looking, with dark shadows under his eyes. His hands tremble at his sides, one clutching onto something rectangular-shaped.

"Drop what's in your hands, and let me see them."

The young man kneels and places a small box down on the floor before struggling back to his feet and raising his unsteady hands. His movements are jittery and uncoordinated as he moves towards me. "H...he."

"Stay back," I warn.

I have a flashback of Monroe from a year ago, drugged up and malnourished. This is exactly how I would've expected Monroe to turn out. However, I'd only seen him recently, healthy and built, so this person couldn't possibly be him.

Could he?

I'm worried my mind is playing tricks on me.

"Where is she?" I repeat, keeping my voice strong.

The young man keeps his eyes downcast. "He's t...taken her."

"Who's taken her?"

"M...my father. He's t...taken her t...to The Church of Salvation. I... I reversed the barrier spell, s...so I can feel him."

I frown. Monroe's father is dead. My father admitted to killing him.

I take a step closer, keeping the gun pointed at his head. "Who are you?"

"I'm E...Elias. Monroe's t...twin brother."

This was news to me. Never, in any of Monroe's paperwork, was there a twin brother mentioned. My father never mentioned a twin brother, either.

"Where is Monroe?"

"H...he's not Monroe right now. M...my father has possessed him."

I struggle to fathom what he is telling me, but I don't have time for details. I need to find Shaina.

I lower the gun and spin on my feet to exit, no longer deeming the young man as a threat.

"W...wait. I need to come. I...I know a way to e...end this."

I glance over my shoulder, eyeing his scrawny frame. He'll only slow me down. I'm about to refuse when it occurs to me that I have no idea what I'm walking into. My father was talking Devil worshipers and mind-benders, and now this young man is talking spells and possession. Either everyone around me has gone crazy, or the world has gone crazy. I feel like my whole life up until now has been a lie.

"Fine. Hurry up," I say.

He kneels back down to pick up the box, and I put my hand out for it, concerned he might be concealing a weapon.

He hands the box to me without argument and says, "T...that's for Monroe. You need to g...give it to him if he survives."

I take off back to the wagon and wait by the wheel while Elias struggles to the driveway and hops in the passenger side.

"You need to c...call the ambulance and tell them a m...man has been shot on Casino Road," he says.

"Why? Who's been shot?"

"N...nobody yet. I...I need you to shoot Monroe."

CHAPTER 40

JULY 14TH, 1998

CORAKI, AUSTRALIA

∞ SHAINA ∞

(40 MINUTES EARLIER)

My body bounces against a hard, inflexible surface that rattles and vibrates beneath me. Confusion washes over me as my eyes flutter open, revealing nothing but darkness. My heartbeat thuds in my temples, triggering the memory of the bat in Monroe's hands swinging steadfastly towards me. I want to scream, but I've been gagged. I reach to remove the piece of material and find my hands have been bound. Now aware of the rope, I can feel its constricting pressure around my feet, too.

It's painful.

The rumble of an engine tells me I'm in a car, the boot of a car. It's my car, I recognise the smell.

The car takes a sharp turn, and my body slides sideways.

Next, I hear the tink, tink, tink of loose gravel. It seems we've left the asphalt and are either on a back road or someone's driveway.

When the car pulls to a stop, I hold my breath, stay stock still, and listen.

I hear the car door click open, followed by a clunk, and the hood of the boot clicks ajar. A small stream of light filters through the gap. My eyes have barely adjusted when a set of hands pull it wide open, allowing me to see a dark shadow standing above me. Those hands slide under me and lift me out. I buck and squirm, trying to break free, but they hold fast. It's virtually impossible to fight my way free with the restriction of the restraints, and I exhaust easily, giving up the struggle.

I glance up to see Monroe's profile, and my heart shatters. I'd been hoping my memory had been playing tricks on me—that he hadn't really been the one wielding the bat.

I curse myself for being so stupid as to trust him, but in my defence, he *had* put on a convincing act. I truly believed he was the innocent victim in all this, even with all the incriminating evidence piled up against him.

Owen was right. I'd been blinded by his sob story and strikingly good looks.

I'm an absolute fool.

He carries me roughly to a small wooden church set on the property and plonks me down on the bottom step. I watch as he climbs his way to the gothic-arched, double doors and fiddles with the chains.

It seems he doesn't have a key, so while he's occupied picking the lock, I take the opportunity to try and wriggle free.

The dagger!

I yank against the restraints reaching for my boot. The rope fibres are rough like sandpaper and scrap my wrists as I contort myself into position. Just as my fingers brush the dagger's handle, Monroe comes back for me, foiling my plans. He reefs me up like a sack of potatoes and throws me over his shoulder.

I buck and thrash wildly, determined not to be a helpless victim.

"Stop that, now." He smashes his fist hard against my thigh. That's twice now he hasn't spoken with his usual Aussie accent.

I thrash even harder, making it difficult for him as he carries me up the stairs.

While hauling me down the aisle, he pivots, and my left ankle bone clips the corner of one of the pews. A jolt of excruciating pain shoots through me, stilling my body momentarily.

When we reach the altar, Monroe unceremoniously drops me to the floor and plants his foot on my chest to hold me in place. Tugging open the inner draw of the pulpit, he pulls out a slim, wooden box, and opens it. He haphazardly places the box down beside my head, revealing three daggers.

My stomach lurches, and I cry out again, the sound muffled by the gag.

He kneels beside me and removes one of the daggers.

"My apologies, Shaina," he says. "Know that this is nothing personal. I just can't have my son spending a lifetime in prison, you understand? Sacrificing you will save him."

My head spins a moment, trying to make sense of what he's said. *"My son,"* ticks over in my brain, making me question what's really going on here. I consider how Monroe said Indi would call him Enzo, and an incredulous thought formulates in the back of my mind. I'm not entirely sure how possession works, or even if it's a real thing, but still, I say, voice catching, "You're Enzo."

While the gag may have muffled my words, it's clear by the glint in his eyes he's understood what I've said.

"You're a smart girl," he says, sounding impressed. "I can see why my son likes you. It's a shame you had to marry into the wrong family."

Knowing it's Enzo hurting me, not Monroe, does take the sting of betrayal away, but it doesn't change the fact that I'm about to be sacrificed. Enzo's mention of the word "son" makes me think of Isaac. Tears formulate in the corners of my eyes.

What will happen to Isaac once I'm gone? He needs me around for emotional support.

Enzo straddles me, pushing my bound arms above my head. He extracts one of the daggers and drives it towards my wrists, causing me to buck like a wild stallion.

"Stop it," he warns, pinning my wrists down with his other hand.

I expect to feel the painful burn of the dagger as it penetrates my skin, but instead, he shoves the dagger through the tight gap in the rope between my wrists and then uses the handle of another dagger to hammer the blade into the floorboards. Once my hands are trapped in place, he straightens my body out and, using the second dagger, repeats the process with my feet. He's busy hammering the dagger into the floorboards when the figure of another man steps through the double doors.

Enzo stops pounding and looks up, appearing startled.

The man wanders towards us, and I realise, with a jolt, I recognise him. He's the man from the wedding photo.

He's Jerimiah, or as Monroe calls him, Dirty Dick.

Something Monroe said floats to mind, and I understand now *exactly* what he meant.

"Do you know what the most unsettling part of this photo is? Dirty Dick looks as though he hasn't aged a day. He looks exactly the same now as he did back when this photo was taken."

"I wasn't expecting company," Jerimiah says. His voice sounds like Mathew McConaughey's, only deeper, smoother. Melodic like a crooner.

Enzo straightens himself. "I hadn't realised you'd be here, but I suppose it's better this way. As you can see, I've brought you a present."

"A little birdie told me you were in town, so I made a special trip. It's not a long drive from where the mountains meet the sea. You did well to figure out my cryptic message, by the way. I hadn't been entirely sure if my plan would work."

"You've been a very busy man," Enzo growls. "I'd love to know how you acquired Raj's credit card without being noticed. Paying for Lindsay's apartment and then planting it on Monroe was a clever touch."

Jerimiah steps closer and glances down at me.

"Who have you brought me?" he asks, not bothering to enlighten Enzo with any explanation.

"Shaina," Enzo says simply before adding, "Sergeant Adams' wife."

Jerimiah's jaw ticks. "I see."

"I thought you'd be impressed. I know you still have ties with the family."

"Killing her won't save you," Jerimiah says in warning. "The cops know who killed those other women."

Enzo jumps to his feet with the third dagger and launches it straight at Jerimiah's neck.

"You mean the cops think they know," he says, pressing the blade against his skin threateningly.

"You drove me to sacrifice Lindsay," Jerimiah growls. "Her blood is on your hands."

"Perhaps." Enzo's expression grows smug. "But why kill Christine?"

"Christine was a case of being at the right place at the right time, or should I say, the wrong place at the wrong time. I needed Raj to suspect Monroe of foul play, hence the stolen credit card and luring you to the murder scene in the middle of the night. Raj's testimony against his own brother-in-law was paramount to my plan."

Enzo forces the blade harder against Jerimiah's neck, nicking the skin. "Too bad you won't be around long enough to see your plan through."

A trickle of blood dribbles down Jerimiah's neck and a bitter laugh escapes him.

"Kill me, and your mother dies too."

Suddenly, the blade begins shuddering, as though it's been taken over by a magical force.

Enzo clasps the handle with both hands, holding fast. "My mother is already dead to me."

The sound of tyres crunching over gravel echoes through the church, and both men glance towards the window.

A glimmer of hope fills me.

Please be Owen.

While Enzo tenses, momentarily distracted, Jerimiah takes advantage, and in one swift move, he disarms Enzo of the dagger.

"You're sloppy, my friend," Jerimiah says, rotating the handle of the dagger between his fingers. "And you're uncommitted. You and I could have had the world at our fingertips, but you never trusted me or stuck by me, and because of that, we lost everything."

"You stole Indi from me, so why the fuck would I commit to you?"

Jerimiah shakes his head. "You were never committed. That's the problem. I took you under my wing, gave you a place to stay, and made you somebody. Yet when it came to the sacrifices, you shied away and turned your back on me. You ran from me at every chance you got, and you tried encouraging Indi to run from me, too."

His jaw ticks. "I was privy to the tales you shared with her, including what your plans were. She confided in Melissa, who, in turn, told me. You were waiting until she turned eighteen, and then the two of you were going to run away together, so if anything, you were planning on stealing Indi off me, off the community."

"It wasn't a community. It was a cult."

Dread overwhelms me when Bruce Adams walks through the door with a hunting rifle in his hands and points it directly towards Enzo. "Hands up, Monroe."

CHAPTER 41
JULY 14TH, 1998
CORAKI, AUSTRALIA
∞ MONROE ∞

(ENZO'S POV)

I glance between Jerimiah and Bruce, feeling like a mouse caught in a trap. Bruce doesn't look as tough or as able as he once was. His gut hangs down over the waistband of his jeans and his left side appears to be lame and drooped, as though he's had a stroke.

"Hands up," Bruce repeats with a slight slur, and fresh out of options, I comply. His eyes flick to Shaina, who's squirming and crying out against the gag, and his right brow raises. "Is that Shaina?"

"I believe so," Jerimiah answers. "I'll stay and untie her while you take him outside."

Shaina thrashes, shaking her head in protest, but Bruce doesn't notice. His gaze is fixed on me.

"You heard what the man said." Bruce motions with his rifle. "Outside."

I scan my peripheral, searching for anything that could be used as a weapon.

Damn Bruce, for distracting me. Now Jerimiah has the one dagger while the other two still anchor Shaina down.

This wasn't how my plan was supposed to play out.

Bruce moves in closer, nudging me with his rifle. "Move," he says.

If it wasn't for the gun and two against one, I would've considered putting up a fight. Instead, I grit my teeth and reluctantly comply.

We descend the stairs, and Bruce pokes me in the back with his rifle, forcing me to walk out into the open.

"You know," he says, "This is feeling a little like déjà vu."

If only he knew, no truer words were said.

"This is for Indi, you sick son of a bitch," he'd said before aiming his gun at my chest.

My pulse accelerates at the memory.

"Alright, turn around," he orders.

"You're going to Hell for this, you know that, don't you?" I say, using his faith against him. "Thou shalt not kill."

"God forgives those who seek his forgiveness, and I will be rewarded in Heaven for eliminating those who seek to do the Devil's work," he replies, feeding me a line straight from Jerimiah's mouth.

He points the rifle towards my chest. "Any departing words?"

I give a nonchalant shrug before making my move, knocking the barrel of the rifle upwards. Bruce pulls the trigger a beat too late. The shot misses me and hits the bow of a nearby gumtree. The blast of the shot makes my ears ring, and Monroe's body threatens to throw me out, but I fight with all my might to stay in control. My will to survive is strong. I've got both of my hands on the rifle, and Bruce and I wrestle for it. Bruce isn't the man he used to be and is no match for Monroe's young and capable body.

It doesn't take long to overpower him. I knee him hard in the stomach and he doubles over, loosening his grip. This allows me to snatch the rifle from his slippery fingers and take charge.

I point the tip of the rifle towards his chest, and the colour drains from his face.

The tables have turned.

I look him dead in the eye, savouring the moment.

"This is for Enzo, you sick son of a bitch," I say, parroting his own words back to him, and then I pull the trigger.

I'm charging back to the church to kill Jerimiah when I see a paddy wagon turning into the property.

"Fuck!"

The wagon roars up the gravel driveway, sending dust and gravel flying.

I point the rifle at the vehicle's widescreen and shoot. The glass shatters, but I can't tell if I've hit anyone.

Jerimiah comes to the double doors to investigate, sees the rifle in my hands, and makes a hasty retreat.

The wagon squeals to a stop as I'm running up the stairs, and Owen launches out of the vehicle, his gun aimed my way.

"Stop right there," he warns.

I turn and fire wild shots in his direction. A few of the bullet's spray into Jerimiah's car and the passenger tyre squeals as the air hisses out. Not stopping, I gung-ho inside the church.

Jerimiah has his arms wrapped around Shaina, holding her in front of him like a human shield.

"Now, Now, my friend," he says as I move towards them. "Think about what you're doing. You can kill me, and then the cop will kill you, or you can kill the cop, and we can both escape. This doesn't have to be the end. We can start over and have everything we've ever wanted."

As much as I want to kill Jerimiah, I can see he has a point.

"The only problem is this isn't my body. It's Monroe's, and when he regains control again, he has the potential of ruining everything. I've been stuck sharing this body with him for nineteen years, and I'm sick of always being pushed out at the drop of a hat. Help me to cast a spell to bind my soul with this body, and then we will call it a truce," I offer, knowing full well I have every intention of killing him once the spell is complete.

"You have my word," he says. "Now get the cop."

I rush back to the doors just in time to take a shot at Owen. The bullet clips his arm before he jumps the side rails out of the line of fire, disappearing from sight.

I make my way to the doors and scan the area, holding the rifle out in front of me with my finger hovering over the trigger.

"Shaina's still in here," I call, "and she's still alive. If you want her, come and get her."

A loud crash inside the church startles me as one of the leadlight window's shatters, and Shaina screams. I turn to find a sizeable rock on the floor amongst the shattered glass. Another blast follows closely on its heels, and I'm struck by immense pain. The rock was a distraction. I've been shot in the back. Crying out in pain and rage, I point the rifle toward the doors and fire the remaining bullets, hoping that at least one of them makes contact.

I can feel Monroe trying to push me out again, but I resist, afraid that we are both about to meet our end. I need Monroe to live so I can exist. Without him, I'll fade into oblivion.

Shaina's still screaming hysterically around the gag, and I watch as Jerimiah tosses her aside like a ragdoll and makes a beeline for the broken window to make his escape.

Adrenaline waning, I fall back against the back row of pews.

Owen enters through the archway, brandishing his firearm. When he sees I'm down, he rushes past, heading straight for Shaina.

My eyelids are flickering when I see a vision of Elias walking towards me. At first, I think I'm hallucinating, but when he kneels by my side and places his hand over mine, I sense it's really him through his touch.

"M...Monroe isn't going to make it," he says. "C...come to me."

"I'm blocked," I say.

"N...no, you're not. L...let go and come to me."

If Monroe dies, he's no longer of any use to me, so making the switch to Elias' body is the logical move. I release myself from Monroe's body and allow my spirit to enter Elias' body.

Before I've fully made the connection and have control, I feel a slight resistance. Elias slips his hand in his pocket, fumbling for something and I watch in horror as he pulls out a jewel-encrusted dagger. He turns the tip of the dagger towards the left side of his chest, aligning the sharp point between his ribs.

Realising his intention, I try to extract myself, but Elias anticipates my move and locks in our connection before falling forward and impaling his heart with the dagger.

He deceived me into believing he was saving me, only to sacrifice the both of us. Sheer agony flares briefly inside my chest, followed by a bitter coldness as I feel myself slipping away. Everything fades to nothingness, into oblivion.

CHAPTER 42

JULY 14TH, 1998

CORAKI, AUSTRALIA

∞ OWEN ∞

I rush over to Shaina, who's bucking and crying out hysterically. Her face is flushed, and tears are streaming down her cheeks.

I unfasten the gag from her mouth and the first thing she says is, "Where's Monroe? Is he okay? He's not dead, is he? You didn't kill him?"

I'm fine, I think begrudgingly. *Thanks for asking.*

"I shot him," I tell her, "But I had no intention of killing him. I just needed to put him out of action. The ambulance has already been called and should be on their way."

"Your arm," Shaina says, glancing at it with concern. "How bad is it?"

My bicep burns from where a bullet grazed it, leaving my arm-sleeve coated with blood.

"The bullet only nicked me," I say. "I was lucky. It could've been much worse."

I cut through the rope that's tied around her hands and feet with a dagger I've found lying on the floor.

"Thanks," she says, giving them a quick rub to bring the circulation back before racing off to Monroe's side.

I snatch the parament from the pulpit and follow.

Monroe is staring at Elias, lying dead in front of him. It's clear he's in shock. His pupils are dilated, and his skin is clammy. A look of total incomprehension is written all over his face.

"Monroe, is it you?" Shaina asks before touching him.

I'm guessing she must've known about him being possessed by Enzo. I wonder how long she has known about all of this hocus pocus. Elias gave me a brief rundown on what he knew about Enzo, Jerimiah, and The Church of Salvation, informing me that the two men were able to stay young and spritely over the years by using the power of dark magic to drain the lives of their followers. This confirmed my suspicions that Dr Jerry Richards and Jerimiah *are* the same person–as mind-boggling as that may be. I found myself wondering how much life these sick sons of bitches have stolen from our congregation over the years. I don't seem too affected, but I wasn't chosen for the circle often, and I was only eleven when the gatherings ceased.

My father and uncle, on the other hand, look in poor health for men in their late fifties, and they were only chosen for the circle on special occasions, so I can only imagine how the people who were chosen regularly may have fared.

Elias said Jerimiah persuaded Enzo to participate in human sacrifices in a bid to gain power, and then turned on him when he no longer needed him.

"Shaina–" Monroe glances up at her, voice stricken, "–I don't know what's happening. I think I'm hal–"

She slides down beside him and puts her arm around his shoulder. "Shhh... Shhh... it's okay. Everything is going to be okay."

Watching her fawn over him makes me green with jealousy, but I have scruples and hand her the parament, telling her to press it firmly against his wound. If he dies, she'll blame me for shooting him, and Shaina isn't one to let things go easily. She'd never forgive me, and I can't have that.

Shaina's eyes flick to Elias, and her face pales with horror. Clearly bewildered, she glances up at me for answers.

"It's Monroe's twin brother, Elias," I say. "He told me his father had the ability to possess both him and Monroe."

"Elias," she repeats, and I can almost see her mental gears grinding. "He was at their grandmother's house the day I door-knocked," she says.

"She was the one who raised him," I confirm. "He said his grandmother was a powerful witch who helped to protect him from his father's spirit, but Monroe wasn't as lucky because he was raised by his junkie mother."

Shaina nods, comprehension written in her expression, but I'm still mind-boggled with the insanity of it all.

"Will you be alright here?" I ask, "I need to find Jerimiah before it's too late."

Shaina eyes Monroe over warily.

"According to Elias, the dagger he used to sacrifice himself put a permanent end to Enzo's spirit, meaning he can no longer possess Monroe. You should be safe here with him now."

Shaina clicks her fingers, her eyes gleaming with a lightbulb moment, and then she hurriedly digs into her boot, pulling out a jewel-encrusted dagger.

"If you find Jerimiah, you need to kill him with this. Their grandmother said the only way to break Jerimiah's spells is by killing him with this dagger. Otherwise, the spells will remain binding even after death." Shaina hands the dagger to me, and I give it a cautionary look over before tucking it into the holster on my belt.

"By the way, Jerimiah was the one who killed your cousin, Indi," she says. "Not Enzo."

"What?"

"Apparently, Enzo was in love with Indi and intended to run away with her, but Jerimiah found out what he had planned and put an end to it by stealing Indi from him and then killing her. He said Enzo wasn't dedicated enough to the community, to the cult."

My stomach heaves, knowing my cousin had been a victim of their power struggle.

Jerimiah had everyone in the community fooled with his biblical nonsense–including my father, who he corrupted.

I'm turning to leave when Shaina reaches up and grabs my hand, squeezing hard. "Please be careful," she says, eyes full of worry. "Isaac needs you."

I squeeze lightly in return and give a weak smile before letting go. Isaac still needs me, but she doesn't, and that's something I need to come to terms with before I lose her completely.

I leave the church and hit the yard in search of Jerimiah. To my relief, all four vehicles are still parked outside, one of which belongs to my father. His lack of whereabouts has me concerned. He's not the kind of man who runs and hides during a shoot-out. He likes to stand his ground and fight.

The front paddock is clear grassland, with only cows in sight, so I make my way to the main house, hoping Jerimiah's inside hiding. I search high and low only to find it empty. I leave via the back door and scan the yard. There's a large barn, which I check out next, and then I circle around a set of water tanks. There are numerous gumtrees on the block, and I zigzag my way across the yard, checking behind them as I make my way over to an old tin shed at the rear of the property. Behind one of the thick trunks, I come across my father. His shirt is soaked crimson, and his eyes are open and glassy, devoid of life.

A painful lump forms in my throat. He wasn't always the best father. He could be a hard man with unreasonable expectations, but I loved him anyway.

Pushing my emotions aside, I hurry onwards. If Jerimiah gets away, more innocent people are at stake.

Stepping into the dim shed after being outside in the bright sunlight turns everything pitch black. My eyes haven't fully adjusted when I feel a swoosh of air followed by something hard smashing across my forearms. My gun goes flying out of my hand and crashes to the ground with a clank. I grunt before launching in retaliation, my arms bringing Jerimiah into a headlock. He yelps and pivots, managing to break free of my grip.

"You're not the man your father was," Jerimiah taunts. "I can see why he was so disappointed in you. 'Piss weak' is what he would call you. He said you were just like your mother."

"Weak, is having blind faith in a soulless man who leeches life from others to stay youthful," I retaliate.

"Bruce was relieved to discover you were sterile," Jerimiah continues, unrattled by my comment. "He couldn't handle the thought of having another weak-minded family member inheriting his name."

His comment hits where it hurts, and I can't help but let it show.

"Go fuck yourself."

Sirens blare in the background, alerting me that help is on its way. I just hope they're not going to be too late.

Jerimiah and I both spot the glint of the gun where it's fallen and simultaneously pounce for it. Our bodies collide as we skid across the floor, scrambling to be the first one to reach it.

Jerimiah's hand closes over it first, and I wrap my fingers around his fist in a vice-like grip to stop him from turning it on me.

"Not so fast!" I've almost pried his fingers free when he grabs a handful of dirt with his free hand and flicks it in my eyes.

The grit stings like hell and blurs my vision, but I can't release my grip, or I'm a dead man. I blink like wildfire as we continue to roll and twist in a frenzied power struggle. Shots are fired willy-nilly as I bash our hands against the ground, trying desperately to get him to let go of the gun. Sparks fly from the metal sheet walls as the bullets make contact. We must've hit a jerrycan because the air fills with fuel fumes, and suddenly, bright orange flames burst into life around us. The scorching flames lick up the walls to the wooden shelves, and soon, we are engulfed in a raging inferno.

The heat is intense. It feels as though my body is being scorched by a hot iron. With the fast-burning wood comes thick plumes of smoke, polluting my airway and making it difficult to breathe.

I hear the click of an empty chamber, and now, knowing that the gun is no longer a threat, I release his hands and reach for the dagger that I'd put in my holster.

My fingers encircle the hilt, and I whip it out, plunging it deep into Jerimiah's side. He gasps and smashes me across the temple with the muzzle of the gun. I pay him back with a headbutt to the bridge of his nose and have the satisfaction of hearing the crunch.

I expect him to groan or curse, but instead, he laughs.

Blood spills from his nose down onto his teeth, making him look every bit the psycho he is. I stare down at this maniac of a man with a burning hatred. Not only did he have control over my father, corrupting him with his lies, but he drove away my mother and sisters so that I had no family.

My teeth grit. "You destroyed my family."

"Your yellow-bellied mother destroyed your family. She was weak-minded and bred weak-minded children like you. You are the reason Bruce is dead. If you'd had the strength to kill Monroe, Enzo wouldn't have been able to kill your father."

"If my father had killed you instead of Enzo, it would have saved a lot of suffering, but you tricked him into believing Enzo killed his niece, forcing him to do your dirty work for you." I stare him dead in the eyes. "I know it was you who killed my cousin."

"I've killed a lot of people." There is no remorse behind his statement; his voice is cold and matter-of-fact. "There was nothing special about her, but I kept her soul anyway, knowing it would destroy Enzo."

It sickens me to know that Indi had meant nothing to him. She was just another pawn in his heartless game of power and revenge.

"Well, your killing days are over," I growl. This time, I aim higher, plunging the dagger deeply with an upward thrust beneath his ribcage.

Jerimiah howls, his face contorting in pain. His breathing

becomes laboured, and his eyes flutter before rolling back into his head.

I stare down at Jerimiah's lifeless body, praying the madness has ended when suddenly, the air crackles with electricity. An explosion rocks the floor beneath me and my body is thrown with the blast. I smash headfirst against the back wall of the shed.

Thick smoke fills my lungs, and I cough uncontrollably. The flames are closing in, and it feels as though my skin is cooking.

I glance about, dazed, as the whole shed bursts into blinding white light, and that's when I see her—when I see all of them. The shed is filling with the spirits of the people Jerimiah had bound to him. Now free from his hold, they raise and disperse.

Indi crouches beside me and shakes my arm. "Owen, you need to get out of here."

I give a weak nod in agreement, but I can feel myself waning.

She takes hold of my hand and tries to pull me, but I'm so weak I don't have the strength to help her. A dark-skinned woman comes to our aid. She is elderly with a thin frame.

I recognise her, she is the spirit of Elias and Monroe's grandmother.

She grabs my other hand, and between the two women, they manage to drag me outside. They set me down, several metres away from the shed on a soft patch of grass, right before the entire structure explodes into pieces and a ferocious fireball lights up the sky.

CHAPTER 43

JULY 14TH, 1998

CORAKI, AUSTRALIA
∞ MONROE ∞

(15 MINUTES EARLIER)

There's a young man's body on the floor in front of me, lying in a pool of blood. His head is turned to the side, facing me, and I'm afraid I must be hallucinating because his profile is the spitting image of my own.

Shaina appears like an angel and slides down beside me, putting her arm around me.

A sharp pain shoots through my shoulder, sending me into a panic. "Shaina." My voice is shrill. "I don't know what's happening. I think I'm hal–"

"Shhh... Shhh... It's okay. Everything is going to be okay."

Her line of sight follows to where my eyes keep drifting, and her face turns ashen.

She glances up at Owen, who says, "It's Monroe's twin brother, Elias."

What? It can't be, I think. *Elias died before birth.*

Owen tells Shaina that my grandmother raised my twin brother and that she protected him from our father's spirit. Hearing this, triggers repressed memories of the nightmare I used to have as a child.

As though looking from a third-person perspective, I saw a flash of a pentacle surrounded by symbols and candles, and then my twin brother, Elias, being ripped away from me at birth. I saw a woman, who I now realise must've been my grandmother, but I couldn't see her face properly. It was dark and blurred.

"Come and find us, Child," she'd said in a thick Louisianan accent. "I'll take care of you both. Together, we will all be safe."

This was followed by flashes of—what I now recognise as—The East Coraki Bridge and Richmond Terrace.

She was guiding me to them.

As a child, I didn't understand the message. My mother led me to believe that my brother, Elias, had died in the womb, and it was my fault, so I thought the woman in my dream was asking me to jump off a bridge so I would die and join them in the afterlife.

"I need to find Jerimiah before it's too late," Owen tells Shaina, snapping me back to the present.

Jerimiah? As in Dirty Dick? I wonder. *Is he here? Have I been drugged again?* My mind spirals with questions.

Shaina and Owen have been conversing the whole time, but I've been too distracted to absorb anything else they've said. I'm about to ask Shaina to explain what's going on and why Owen's here when, to my astonishment, Elias rises from his body and shuffles over. He clasps my hands in his, and an ice-cold zap shoots through me, numbing my pain. I shiver, but I don't pull away as a sense of deep spiritual alignment and unity flows through me.

A voice, calm and gentle, echoes in the recesses of my mind like a telepathic message.

"It's not your time, Monroe. You need to hold on."

The words give me a sense of peace.

Owen leaves, but Shaina stays, pressing a cloth firmly against my injured shoulder.

"It's going to be okay," she murmurs, but I can hear the quiver in her voice. She's trying to convince herself as much as me. A tear slides down her cheek and drips onto my face.

"We need each other, remember, so stay with me. We will clear your name together."

Everything after this becomes a blur of sirens, cops, and paramedics. They poke and prod at me while asking questions. Thankfully, Shaina comes to the rescue and answers them for me. She and Elias stick by my side as I'm wheeled to the ambulance, keeping me calm and comforted the whole time.

CHAPTER 44
JULY 14TH - 17TH, 1998
LISMORE, AUSTRALIA
∞ MONROE ∞

My first two days in hospital are a blur, although I vaguely remember hearing the hum of Jackie's and Shaina's voices as I drift in and out.

It gives me comfort knowing they are close by, and that they're getting to know one another.

When I finally come to, it's only Shaina at my bedside. "You're awake," she says leaning in to caress my face. "Jackie's just gone back to the hotel to freshen up."

Shaina tells me that she and Isaac are staying in the same hotel temporarily, because her house has been taped off as a crime scene.

"Indi's and Enzo's bodies are being exhumed right now as we speak."

Goosebumps prickle my arms. "Are you seriously meaning to tell me that the two of them have been buried under your house this whole time?"

She nods. "According to Owen, Bruce buried them under the foundations nineteen years ago."

"So, Bruce killed them both?" It's a question, not a statement.

"No, Bruce killed Enzo, and Jerimiah killed Indi."

My teeth grind. "I knew it. That fuckin' bastard."

Shaina tilts her head, appearing baffled. "Do you really not remember anything that happened on Tuesday?"

"I remember Owen busting me in your bedroom and getting into a brawl with him." We share a look. "I also remember heading to my grandmother's place so I could hide out there for a while. I started feeling sick when we first arrived, and you cooled me with a cloth."

I wrack my memory bank.

"I must've blacked out after that because the next thing I remember is leaning against a church pew in agony. There was a body lying on the floor in front of me, and I could've sworn I was hallucinating because the person's face was the spitting image of my own. It wasn't until I heard you and Owen speaking that I discovered it was Elias. The thing is, Ma told me that my twin brother died in utero."

My gaze flicks to Shaina's and our eyes lock.

"When you slid down alongside me and wrapped your arm around me, I could've sworn you were an angel. You held me tight and kept telling me that everything was going to be okay. I could feel myself drifting, and then like magic, Elias' spirit rose from his body. He came over, grasped my hands, and took my pain away."

Shaina runs her hand over my arm, her expression sympathetic. "I'm glad you got to see your brother, even if it was only in spirit."

Instead of feeling glad, I feel sad.

"I never remember anything when I black out, but I've been told I say and do things that I wouldn't normally do," I admit. "It's almost as though I've fallen into a trance or gone sleepwalking or something. I still don't even know how or why I was shot. Is there any chance you can fill in the blanks for me?"

Shaina's gaze shifts and she bites her lower lip. "Are you sure you're ready for that?"

"I'm as ready as I'll ever be."

"Well, the good news is, you don't suffer from backouts, as such."

She forces a plastic smile. "But the bad news is, your father, Enzo, has been possessing your body periodically your entire life."

"What?"

My heart accelerates and my mind tries to reject what she is telling me. Nevertheless, it sure helps clear up why I've been suffering with memory lapses. I'd thought for certain I was losing my mind.

"I overheard Enzo telling Jerimiah that he wanted to cast a spell to bind his soul to your body," Shaina adds. "He didn't want to keep sharing. He was planning on taking over you completely."

While I'm still busy trying to process this bombshell that's been dropped on me, Shaina continues filling me in on the gritty details of who did what to who. As it turns out I'd been a busy man. A violent man. A monster. A murderer.

By the end of her recap, I'm left feeling sick and violated. Even though I know it wasn't me in control, it was Enzo, it still kills me to hear about all the heinous things I'd done.

For one horrifying moment, I begin to wonder whether *I truly am* responsible for the deaths of Lindsay and Christine.

"Jerimiah admitted to killing Indi, Lindsay, and Christine." Shaina pinkie swears when I express my self doubt. "Trust me, you have nothing to worry about."

I'm so grateful to Shaina. I find it hard to believe that she's still willing to stand by me after everything I've put her through. Not only has her faith in me been unwavering, but she put her life on the line to help clear my name, which is more than I could ever ask of anyone.

OWEN STOPS by on day three, telling me he's just been discharged. He'd suffered a bullet graze to his arm, wounds to his back, and mild first-degree burns.

Shaina and Jackie politely excuse themselves on the pretext of grabbing some coffee. I can't believe they're leaving me alone with the man who has threatened to kill me twice over, and then shot me.

I'm not exactly sure why Owen's here to visit, it's not like we're friends, however, I'm both surprised and relieved to discover he's come with a peace offering.

"I'm sorry for shooting you in the back of the shoulder, but it was the only way to take down Enzo without actually killing *you*."

"I heard I grazed your arm, as Enzo, which isn't quite as impressive." I chuckle, trying to make a joke of it. "Truce?"

A dry laugh escapes him. "Truce."

The room falls silent, and his expression grows serious.

"I met your brother, Elias. He talked about his life with your grandmother, and the physical and mental struggles he'd suffered because of the darkness Enzo bestowed on him. Your father was a selfish man, and you both paid the price."

"Enzo's not my father," I say dismissively. "As far as I'm concerned, he was just a sperm donor."

Owen nods in understanding. "Fair enough."

He digs into the bag, which hangs from his shoulder, and plucks out a wooden box.

"Elias asked me to give you this as his departing gift."

I open the lid to find a key and a scrolled document. Owen helps me to unravel the scroll, which turns out to be my grandmother's will. I scan the legal document with a heavy heart. I've been named as Dawn's sole beneficiary, set to inherit everything she owns, yet I barely even got the chance to know her.

Owen hands me a paper napkin with cursive handwriting scrawled across it. "Elias wrote you a departing letter, too. He quickly scribbled it down while we were in the paddy wagon on our way to Jerimiah's property."

Dear Monroe,

I'm not sure what you know about me, or if you
even do know about me, but I'm your twin brother,
Elias.
I've thought about reaching out to you so many
times, but I was afraid of what you might think of
me. Our father, Enzo, managed to bestow his
darkness upon me as an infant, which has had an
adverse effect on me throughout my whole life.
He did the wrong thing by separating us at birth
and by using our bodies as vessels for his own
selfish agenda. I've grown up hating him, but Gran
assures me he was a sweet boy once. She says dark
magic changed him. Apparently, it changed our Papa
as well. I've never touched dark magic, and I hope
you will steer clear of it, too. No good comes of it.
I'm sorry for the physical pain I'm about to put you
through, but the alternative would be to kill you,
and as Gran said, you don't deserve that. I don't
deserve to die either, but I have less to live for.
If your friend succeeds in killing Jerimiah, as I
hope, Gran will die with him, and we will be
together in the afterlife. Knowing that I can free
you from our father's clutches would be my dying
wish come true.
If you're reading this letter, I trust you have found
Gran's will and the key to the house. We don't own
much, but anything we have is now yours.
By the time you're reading this, I will be gone, but
my spirit will always be with you, a guardian from
beyond, watching over you until the day we meet
again.

Love Elias

Tears sting my eyes while my heart tears in two. "He sacrificed
himself to save me from our father's clutches."

Owen swallows, appearing moved. "Your brother did a brave
thing."

To discover that my twin brother Elias hadn't died in utero like I'd been made to believe is distressing enough, but to discover that he'd been living close by with my grandmother our whole lives, and I missed out on the chance of getting to know him, is absolutely gut-wrenching.

I wish I'd understood the cryptic message my grandmother had sent me as a child.

A part of me is frustrated that she didn't contact me in person. But then, an image of her frightful face flashes into my mind, and I realise, as a young child I would have been afraid of her. I would've taken one look at her and bolted away screaming. Dawn would've been aware of my reaction and that's why she would've sent me the dreams instead.

"You know, I never used to believe in spirits, witchcraft, and all that 'hocus pocus mumbo jumbo'" Owen says, cutting into my thoughts. "But it's impossible to deny the supernatural now after everything I've witnessed first-hand."

"That makes two of us," I admit.

"I haven't told anyone this because they'd pin me as crazy, but if it weren't for my cousin and your grandmother, I would be dead right now. Their spirits dragged me out onto the lawn just before the shed blew to smithereens."

CHAPTER 45

JULY 18TH, 1998

CORAKI, AUSTRALIA

∞ MONROE ∞

S haina places her hand on my knee and gives it an affectionate
squeeze as Jackie pulls to a stop by the curb at the cemetery.
"I'm here for you," she says.

Today is a big day. We have five consecutive services to attend,
which is five more funerals than I've been to in my whole lifetime.
Sadly, three of the people we're burying are my family members,
Elias, Enzo, and my grandmother, yet sadly, I know very little about
any of them.

Jackie shuts off the engine and turns to me with a sympathetic
glance. "Are you going to be okay?" she asks, using her motherly
tone. "It's going to be a long day. Don't forget I've got those extra
painkillers in my bag if you need them."

"Thank you, but I'm fine for now," I assure her.

Jackie and Raj aren't aware that my body had been possessed by
Enzo on and off over the years. Only Shaina and Owen know the
truth, and the three of us have sworn a pact of secrecy. Jackie and Raj
still believe I suffer from mental illness, and in time, they will come
to believe I've gotten better. All they've been told is what Shaina and
Owen told the authorities.

When questioned, Shaina and Owen said that Jerimiah had set it up to look like Enzo killed Indiana back in 1979. They explained how Owen's father, Bruce, was furious when he discovered Enzo was responsible for killing his niece and admitted to shooting him in a heated act of revenge. Bruce had panicked afterwards and buried both their bodies under his brother, Harold's, house so they wouldn't be found. He wanted to protect the name of their church.

Shaina and Owen colluded to get their stories straight before giving modified statements because, in this case, the truth really was harder to believe than fiction.

And so, the story went... Shaina caught a whiff that "Dr Jerry Richards" was in town, so we drove to his property to confront him about what happened with Lindsay. When we arrived, we found him inside the church, having just sacrificed my brother.

"Dr Jerry Richards" openly admitted to killing Lindsay and Christine, and meticulously framing me to take the fall because he was jealous of my close friendship with Lindsay.

Shaina also told the authorities what I'd told her about an employee from The Hoey Moey bumping into a man who'd been posing as my father. When the cops showed Sawyer the photo of "Dr Jerry Richards", he'd confirmed he was, in fact, the man he'd seen entering the tearoom. Shaina and Owen said "Jerry" admitted to keeping Elias and my grandmother hostage over the years and that he'd taken Elias to the church to kill him with a sacrificial dagger as a part of a cult ritual. They blamed "Jerry" for shooting both Bruce and Owen. And Owen admitted to accidentally shooting me while trying to shoot "Jerry", saying he later killed "Jerry" with one of his own sacrificial daggers.

The authorities hadn't been able to find any birth records for Elias Morgan, and when they'd contacted my mother, Leonie, she'd said that she'd lost Elias in utero, and he'd never been born. This had the cops scratching their heads. It wasn't exactly an open-and-shut case, and the cops were never going to get all the answers.

Shaina steps out of the car and offers her hand to lever me up.

She looks beautiful in a simple black dress that matches perfectly with her thick, raven-coloured hair.

We spend most of the afternoon at the cemetery, attending one service after the other. Two hours in, my shoulder is aching like fury, so I take my sister up on her offer of the extra pain medication.

Harold shows up for Bruce's and Indi's funerals, and I shoot him daggers throughout the services. I find it hard to accept that after the way he'd treated his wife and daughter, he's the one left alive and standing, facing no ramifications.

After learning that Harold was Indi's father, not Wyatt, I've been plagued by guilt. It seems I owe Wyatt and his wife, Ruth, an apology for the way I treated them. When I'm fully healed and feeling much better, I plan on paying them a special visit.

Owen speaks briefly to Harold, but it's obvious there's tension between them. Owen's new partner, Victoria, stays glued to his side, holding his arm possessively.

We are introduced to her between ceremonies. She's petite with a heart-shaped face, big hazel eyes, and curly auburn hair. She seems pleasant enough, although a little insecure.

The ceremony for Elias is held last. I stand there choked up with a heaviness in my heart, mourning for the brother I will never get to know.

Shaina slips her hand into mine on one side, and Jackie, racked in tears, links our arms on the other side.

Jackie was equally as devastated to hear the news about our hidden sibling.

When we've said the last of our goodbyes, Owen pulls Shaina aside for a quiet word. "Here, these are the keys to my father's place." He holds them out. "You and Isaac can stay there until I find you a rental."

Shaina groans. "I don't want to stay there, Owen. That place is disgusting, and there's too much land to take care of. I just want to go back to my own place."

"It's only temporary," he assures her. "I'll help you to get it cleaned up and I'll take care of the land until we come up with a permanent solution. Besides, you can't go back to your place. It's been half demolished with the investigations. You're going to have to do a knockdown and rebuild. I just hope the insurance will cover it."

He runs his hand through his hair, appearing agitated. "Plus, do you really want Isaac growing up there after all that's happened? The house has been all over the news. No kid in school is going to be allowed to come and visit 'the house where two dead bodies were buried'."

"But I like the area. It's close to the river and I have neighbours for security. I don't want to be out in the sticks."

"You and Isaac are welcome to move into my grandmother's place with me," I interrupt. "It's on the same street."

Both Shaina and Owen glance at me, one with surprise and the other with disdain.

I'd spoken to my sister about staying in Coraki earlier this morning and asked if she and Raj would write me a work reference.

"There are plenty of pubs around the Northern Rivers, and given I have my RSA now, I should easily get a job somewhere close by," I'd said.

Jackie wasn't keen on the idea of me living in Coraki on my own and had gently argued the matter, but having already met Shaina, she understood my reasoning.

I wonder if she'll be happy to learn I may not be living on my own after all.

"I don't know what condition the place is in," I continue. "I've never been inside, but—"

"I know what it's like," Shaina says, "I've been inside."

"Wait, wait, wait," Owen interjects. "I think it might be a bit soon for that."

Shaina side-eyes him. "I moved straight in with you after having Isaac. You literally picked me up from the hospital and took me back to your place."

He waves his pointer at her. "That was different."

"You've moved on." Shaina nods in the direction of Victoria, who's still standing by Elias's graveside, staring at us. "You need to let me move on too."

"What are you saying?" Owen's spine steels. "Are you genuinely considering this insanity? You barely know the guy."

Ignoring Owen's protests, Shaina's eyes met mine, soft, with a hint of vulnerability. "Are you sure about this?"

"Of course," I say, and then glance at Owen. "I'm not the person you think I am. I'll take good care of her and Isaac, I promise."

His jaw ticks, but in the end, he lets out a defeated sigh and says, "You'd better."

His gaze shifts to Shaina's, and he adds, "I'll be checking in. And I don't want to hear about Isaac touching *anything* to do with witch-craft, you hear me?"

Shaina rolls her eyes. "Yes, Owen."

As we turn to leave, I see a vision of my grandmother and Elias standing by one of the gravestones, and I gasp in wonder. They see I've noticed them and acknowledge me with a smile and a wave before fading in a haze of light.

CHAPTER 46

EPILOGUE

1 IVORY STREET, LEICHHARDT, NSW, AUSTRALIA 2040

∞ MATHEW HENDERSON ∞

(TWO MONTHS LATER)

Mathew opens the front door to the smell of fresh rosemary and garlic, and his mouth waters. His wife is in the kitchen, chopping carrots when he enters.

She smiles when she sees him. "How was your day?"

"Busy." He dumps his keys on the bench, next to a gift basket wrapped in cellophane, and greets her with a kiss.

"Where did that come from?" He points to the basket.

His wife shrugs, eyes glinting. "I don't know. It's not my name on the card."

Mathew plucks out the card to find "Mathew Henderson" scripted on the envelope. When opening the card, two greenbacks fall to the floor, and Mathew's brows dart to his hairline.

Dear Mathew,

Thank you for your kindness, you really helped me out during a time of need.

Cheers,

Monroe

MATHEW'S WIFE picks up the hundred-dollar bills, and peers over her husband's shoulder, glancing at the card.

"Who's Monroe?"

Mathew stares at the name in bewilderment. "I haven't the faintest idea."

ACKNOWLEDGEMENTS

I would like to give a special shout out to my partner Kieran, mother Carrie, daughter Lyla, and son RJ. Thanks for being my loyal beta readers. Together you really helped to improve, tighten and smooth out the wrinkles in my story. This book has truly been a family collaboration in the making.

Lyla, my darling daughter, you were a *brutal* editor, but I appreciated your honesty and took all of your comments aboard.

To my editors Alyssa Matesic and Sorchia Dubois, thank you kindly for your thoughtful feedback and expert services.

Many thanks to Indiana Maria Acosta Hernandez (@Indicreates), for once again delivering a glorious, eye catching cover.

To Shaina Anglum, Jacqueline Palicio, and Kerrie Anderson, thanks for being my NO:1 supporters. You have all gone well out of your way to help promote The Zadok Series on numerous occasions, which is incredible. Your unwavering support means the world to me.

Thanks to Two Birds Audio for producing my audiobook and bringing my story to life. Jodie Harris, James Fouhey, Karen Chilton, Ari Maza Long, and Tamblyn Lord, you are all outstanding narrators.

ABOUT THE AUTHOR

Born in Queensland, Australia, 1984, Nikki Minty rose into this world with a wild imagination. As a young girl, she would lay in bed with her family of a night, co-telling stories about the big bad wolf and his turbulent adventures.

Nikki Minty is the author of The Zadok Series.

WWW.NIKKIMINTY.COM

www.ingramcontent.com/pod-product-compliance
Ingram Content Group UK Ltd.
Pitfield, Milton Keynes, MK11 3LW, UK
UKHW020054270325
456776UK00001B/42

9 780645 314977